RAVES FOR THE NOVELS OF CHRISTINE DORSEY

Sea of Temptation

"In *Sea of Temptation*, the sensational conclusion to her outstanding Charleston Trilogy, Christine Dorsey demonstrates why she is one of the most talented authors of the genre today: strong, unforgetable characters, rousing adventures, and history combine to create 'keepers.'" —*Romantic Times*

Sea of Desire

"Christine Dorsey has written a tale of passion, adventure, and love that is impossible to put down. Her heroine is feisty and her hero will leave you breathless. *Sea of Desire* is a book you shouldn't miss and will need some space on your keeper shelf. It is marvelous!" —*Affaire de Coeur*

"Blazing passion, non-stop adventure, and a 'be-still-my-beating-heart' hero are just a few of the highlights of this captivating second novel in Ms. Dorsey's Charleston Trilogy. *Sea of Desire* is not to be missed!" —*Romantic Times*

Sea Fires

"From the instant Miranda and Jack meet, you know this is going to be a very special relationship and that *Sea Fires* is going to be a very special book. If this auspicious romance is any indication, the Charleston Trilogy is destined to be an excellent serie͟s ͟ ͟ ͟ ͟ Dorsey's sparkling pen. Be sure ͟ ͟ ͟ ͟ ͟ ͟ ͟ —*Romantic Times*

"*Sea Fires* is well plotted, sensual, and a pure delight!"
— *Affaire de Coeur*

"There is an undercurrent of dry wit and many humorous incidents that make this swashbuckling romance a most enjoyable reading adventure. Ms. Dorsey spins quite a tale."
— *Rendezvous*

Kansas Kiss

"*Kansas Kiss* is a tender, moving novel that touches the heart. Ms. Dorsey's star shines brighter than ever."
— *Romantic Times*

The Captain's Captive

"Make room on your 'keeper' shelf for *The Captain's Captive*. This mesmerizing novel has it all: rousing adventure, intriguing plot, and enchanting lovers sure to please lucky readers."
— *Romantic Times*

"From first page to last, the word for this book is captivating. It has all the ingredients for an excellent read. Adventure, verbal battles, sensuous love scenes, humor and above all, it's well written. This one is a keeper."
— *Rendezvous*

"Be sure to look for this one on the shelves of your favorite bookstore. It's great."
— *Affaire de Coeur*

Traitor's Embrace

"A bang-up story full of adventure, humor, wonderful characters and an interesting time period. This is one you shouldn't miss."
— *Rendezvous*

HIS SAVAGE TOUCH

Wolf stood in the open doorway. The sight of him there, watching her, his eyes dark and sensual, was paralyzing. It seemed an eternity till he reached behind him, leaned the rifle against the wall, and shut the door. An eternity punctuated by the rapid beating of Caroline's heart.

She knew he'd seen her, was still seeing more than propriety allowed. Yet she couldn't summon the energy to do more than turn to face him as he moved toward her.

The ribbons that held the neck line of her shift together draped across her breasts, untied. With each breath she could feel the soft linen spreading, revealing more of her flesh to him. Flesh that felt more fevered the nearer he came.

The cabin was small, his pace slow and deliberate. Each step he took accentuated his animal grace and -2power. Heightened the anticipation. His gaze stoked a blaze hotter than the one in the hearth.

When he was so close that Caroline had to tilt her head to see his face, he stopped. She knew she should turn away, to make some effort to cover herself. After all, her shift was old and threadbare. But he overwhelmed her . . . his towering height, the broad strength of his body, his musky scent. The dark intensity of his eyes.

He drew her to him with a force she couldn't begin to understand. And couldn't continue to fight.

With his first touch, a gentle cupping of her cheek, she was lost.

CHRISTINE DORSEY

MY SAVAGE HEART

ZEBRA BOOKS
KENSINGTON PUBLISHING CORP.

ZEBRA BOOKS are published by

Kensington Publishing Corp.
475 Park Avenue South
New York, NY 10016

Zebra, the Z logo Reg. U.S. Pat & TM Off. The Lovegram logo is a trademark of Kensington Publishing Corp.

First Printing: April, 1994

Printed in the United States of America

For the two new men in my life . . . Evan Marshall, agent extraordinaire, and my fantastic editor, John Scognamiglio.

And as always for Chip.

In memory of Domino, whose unconditional love enriched our lives for over fourteen years . . . and who never tired of sprawling by my computer to keep me company while I wrote.

Prologue

"You sent for me."

The figure slumped in the winged chair by the fireplace straightened, his head jerking around. Fear sparked to life in light green eyes as they scanned the room's shadows. When his gaze snagged on the man standing tall, filling the doorway, his frown deepened. His voice, rusty with sleep, nonetheless carried the sting of accusation. "Nearly a fortnight ago, aye. Where in the hell have you been?"

Wolf stepped into the small pool of light radiating from the single candle sputtering in its brass holder. Shifting the long rifle he held to the crook of his arm, he regarded the older man with narrowed jet black eyes. "I was on the summer hunt . . . with my people."

Robert MacQuaid's fingers clutched the checked cotton chair's arms, but his attempt to rise was thwarted by the leg, splinted and tightly wrapped, stretched out on the bench in front of him. "Hell

9

and damnation," he cursed, fisting his hand and striking at his thigh before settling back, red-faced, among the cushions.

Seeing such frustration might have moved Wa'ya, had it been any other who showed it. But Wolf's expression remained unreadable; the chiseled features of his handsome, bronzed face, unsympathetic. He knew of his father's leg. The injury was the only reason he'd come—that and the gnawing worry it was Mary who needed him. "You should be more careful," was all he said.

"A hell of a lot you care, coming here dressed like a savage!"

"My clothes suit me." Wa'ya watched as Robert's contemptuous gaze traveled downward from the long black hair that hung past his shoulders. The belted hunting shirt was homespun, the leggings doeskin. "Besides," Wolf continued before further disapproval could be voiced. "I never implied I cared."

"Why you ungrateful pup! I never should have—" Robert's face raged purple with anger as Wolf's large hand clamped over his shoulder, preventing him from standing more than the broken leg ever could.

"I did not come to renew old conflicts." Wolf turned, his moccasined feet silent on the rug as he headed for the door and the forest beyond.

"Wait. Raff. There is something you must do for me."

At the sound of his English name, Wolf glanced

over his shoulder. He raised a raven brow, and waited, annoyed with himself that he paused . . . even more annoyed that he'd even come to this place.

"You must go to Charles Town for me."

The words were no sooner out than Wolf lifted the latch.

"Hell and damnation Raff." Robert heaved himself forward on the chair, reaching for the crude crutch one of his servants had fashioned. "You owe me. Christ a'mighty you're my son."

"Your bastard son," Wolf amended as the door swung open. But Robert seemed to ignore Wolf's words as easily as he'd ignored Alkini, Wolf's mother.

"I can't go myself or I wouldn't ask."

Wolf's snort was derisive. "I've no doubt of that." No one ever accused Robert MacQuaid of not doing what needed done himself, whether it was working his plantation, cheating the Cherokee, or defiling innocent women. At the thought of his mother, Wolf took a deep breath of pine-scented air. He didn't look back when he heard the clomp, clomp of the crutch coming toward him. "Send someone else to fetch your supplies."

"I would, but there is no one else."

That, too, Wolf believed. Since the day Wolf left this house, Robert had ignored his son's presence in the Lower Towns of the Cherokee nation. If there was anyone else Robert could prevail upon, the message would never have reached Wolf that his father wanted him.

"Logan is north fighting the damn heathens, and I can't trust anyone else to bring her here."

"My brother should well consider his wife's safety before he searches for other battles."

"Mary's fine. And what in the hell are you talking about—her safety? The girl . . . hell, all of us are as safe here as we would be in Charles Town." Robert's light eyes narrowed. "I've dealt with those people for years. Not one of your so-called Cherokee brothers has the guts to cause any trouble in these parts."

It was a taunt, and in the past, Wolf might have responded. Trouble between the English settlers and the Cherokee was coming, faster and harder than Wolf seemed able to stop. But Robert was beyond enlightening, even if Wolf were inclined to try. And besides, Robert MacQuaid's words no longer had the power to wound him. He didn't care what the old man said . . . or did, either, as long as it didn't affect the Cherokee or Mary.

At least that's what he thought till he heard his father's next words.

"You're what?" Wolf turned on him so quickly that Robert, hunched over the crutch, flinched.

"I said I'm marrying again." Robert's voice was booming, defiant. "It isn't right that I should live without a woman. I've built this place." Robert's head jerked around to indicate what he considered

12

his domain. "I need someone to share it with me. Someone refined."

Wolf's burst of laughter woke the old dog sleeping on the porch. She lifted her head and sniffed the air before settling back on her paws. There had once been someone who loved Robert, though Wolf couldn't understand why she had. Perhaps she hadn't been refined by Robert's definition, but she had been sweet, with a pure, loving heart. But Wolf's mother was tossed aside by Robert with less thought than he'd give a weed he trod upon.

Robert puffed out his chest. "Lady Caroline Simmons is coming from England to marry me."

"Lady Caroline?" Wolf arched a dark brow. "What would a titled Lady want with you?" Wolf knew what they'd wanted with *him*. During the years he'd spent in England, he'd seen the inside of more ladies' boudoirs than he could recall. But *he'd* offered them youth, and a strong, powerful body. A body that would entice even without the added hint of savagery of which the English gentry seemed so in awe. He was amazed how many titled women wished to relieve the boredom of their lives with a half-blooded Cherokee. It was as if they sensed that no amount of silken waistcoats and lace cravats could ever tame him. As they peeled off each layer of civilization, they searched for some primitive passion to engulf them. Wolf had tried never to disappoint.

But it hadn't taken Wolf long to realize where he stood with the fine ladies of England. Whether maid or madam, the light of day sent them scurrying for the security of their stuffy convention. The tedium of which drove Wolf back to his native land.

"You find it difficult to believe that the daughter of an earl would marry me?" Robert said. He straightened as much as he could while forced to lean on the crutch for support.

Wolf didn't trust himself to speak. He'd been told by his uncle, Tsesani, how anxious his mother had been to wed Robert. But she'd died nine years ago, while Wolf was in England. He hadn't even known of her passing until he returned to his homeland the following year. But all the while he'd known this: Her only son, Robert's son, carried the title of bastard.

"Wealth!" Robert's shallow face lit up. "Wealth will buy you anything, boy. The sooner you learn that, the better. 'Tis the only thing that matters."

"And how you get it is immaterial, I suppose?" Wolf was annoyed with himself for getting embroiled in this discussion. He knew very well how this man thought. What he was willing to do.

"Do you think Lady Caroline cares how I obtained my wealth?" Robert's expression was smug.

"No." Wolf stared at him, not bothering to conceal his contempt. "I suppose not." Most of the women he met in England were vain and self-centered. If this Lady Caroline was willing to be bought, Robert was right. She probably wouldn't give a thought to the Cherokee people who'd been cheated or the woman who lived with Robert for years only to be cast aside.

"I'll pay you to fetch her for me." Robert's shoulder bunched beneath his ear as he balanced himself between the birch sapling and his good leg. "Lady Caroline Simmons should reach Charles Town within a sennight. Hell, she might be there now."

Wolf opened his mouth to tell him what he could do with his money and his fine English wife, but a vision of his mother swam before his eyes. That day when he was ten summers. The day her son was taken from her. Though she later died of the fever, it was Robert MacQuaid who had killed her. He'd stripped away her spirit. And her death had gone unpunished and unavenged . . . until now.

When Wolf looked up, his eyes, dark as the sky behind him, were hard. His father just handed him the perfect means of revenge and didn't even realize it . . . yet. But he would. Wolf would see to that. His wide, sensual mouth curved in a parody of a smile.

He would wreak his revenge, and no one could do anything about it. Lady Caroline Simmons didn't stand a chance against him.

"I shall fetch your woman," Wolf declared before leaving the porch and melting into the surrounding forest.

One

Late summer, 1759
Charles Town, South Carolina

She wasn't what he expected. But then women usually weren't.

Wolf leaned against the dingy whitewashed wall in the crowded taproom of Cooper's Inn studying the woman who had crossed the ocean to become his stepmother. If the notion didn't make him so angry, he'd laugh aloud at the thought. Robert wanted a refined lady, and this woman was willing to sell herself into the job. But it was all for naught. For this porcelain doll wouldn't last a fortnight on the frontier.

She lifted her face and glanced around the room, her eyes large, reminding him of a frightened doe, and Wolf felt a twinge of conscience. For what would happen to her. For what he would do to her. But he quickly suppressed any feelings of compassion.

He'd instigated none of this.

Lady Caroline Simmons, with her moonspun hair and cameo face, sealed her own fate when she allowed greed to lure her from her element. By coming to South Carolina, she offered Wolf the perfect chance to avenge his mother's disgrace. And Wolf wasn't one to ignore fate.

Schooling his features into a pleasant expression, Wolf pushed off from the wall and strode the length of the smoky room. Few patrons spoke as he passed, though more than one pair of eyes followed his progress.

"Lady Caroline?" Wolf stopped before the table in the corner. She didn't look up immediately, too busy pleating and unpleating the lace tipped handkerchief she held in her lap.

"Yes?" Caroline's voice cracked, and she cleared her throat nervously. Feigning courage was made more difficult when she glanced up at the man who addressed her. He was tall and imposing, lean, though larger than most men. At least he seemed that way to Caroline as he all but loomed over her. "I'm Caroline Simmons," she finally managed to say.

Caroline clutched the scrap of lace to keep from wringing her fingers. There was no denying this man made her nervous. Not that he didn't appear a gentleman. On the contrary, compared with most of the men in the taproom, he was well dressed, his suit of gray silk smartly cut, his linen fresh and snowy white. But Caroline thought his clothes suc-

18

ceeded naught in camouflaging his raw power nor an underlying streak of something not quite tame.

She blinked, forcing aside those fanciful thoughts when she heard his introduction. 'Twas only the last name she heard, *and* the fact that he'd come to take her home.

"MacQuaid," Caroline gasped, trying hard not to sound shocked. *"You* are Robert MacQuaid?" Though she had no inkling of her betrothed's appearance, she hadn't expected this . . . this overpowering man.

"No." Wolf's smile was brief but genuine. "I am Raff MacQuaid, his son."

"Oh." Caroline resisted the urge to press her palms to her hot cheeks. This man as her future stepson was nearly as disconcerting. She knew Robert had sons, two of them, but somehow she'd imagined them more like her brother, Edward, younger, more vulnerable . . . dependent upon her. She imagined this man depended upon no one but himself.

Caroline realized his dark, dark eyes were upon her, and she unconsciously wet her lips. "I'm very pleased to meet you, Mr. MacQuaid."

"Are you ready to leave?" Wolf asked without further preamble. He'd planned to make himself known to her then suggest she retire to her room, while he waited upon the governor. Even before hearing Robert's request, Wolf had his own reason for visiting Charles Town. But he found himself irritated by Lady Caroline's naive demeanor. He'd

19

known other women like her—women who used their innocence to beguile a man. A stint of sitting in the governor's anteroom would be a good . . . and humbling experience for her.

"Leave? Well, yes." Caroline stood, hoping her added height would make Raff MacQuaid appear less intimidating. It didn't. "I expected Robert . . . I mean, your father, to come for me." Caroline didn't add that she expected him two days ago when the *Sea Dove* sailed into Charles Town harbor. Her limited finances were sorely taxed by the cost of unexpected lodging.

"He's had an accident." Wolf took Caroline's elbow and felt her tense.

"An accident? I pray he's all right." Caroline wished her concerns were altogether selfless. But she couldn't help thinking of her position. What would become of her and of Edward if Robert MacQuaid couldn't marry her?

"It was nothing too serious. However my . . . father couldn't make the trip." Even pretending civility toward the man who sired him was difficult.

"I see." Caroline blinked against the bright sunlight as they stepped out onto Water Street. Except for the heat, she could be on the London street near the wharf that she left nearly two months earlier. Crowded and noisy. Wagons and people clogged the dusty roadway. Occasionally a chaise wended its way through the street that reeked of garbage and filth.

For just a moment Caroline allowed herself to

think of the peace and tranquility of Simmons Hall. Of the crisp, clean air and the woods full of song birds. Then she compelled reality to prevail. Simmons Hall no longer belonged to her. Nothing did.

But she wouldn't . . . couldn't dwell on that. The years had taught Caroline to accept what couldn't be changed. Accept and move forward. And this was definitely one of those times. She knew it from the moment her father's solicitor arrived at Simmons Hall the day after the Earl's funeral. Explaining the financial situation of the estate had embarrassed him. His large, bulbous nose was rubbed red by nervous fingers when he finished reviewing the sorry state of affairs.

"Then I'm to understand there is nothing left," she said, surprised by her own lack of emotion. But then she'd suspected the Earl had been spending more than the income provided by his estate.

"Nothing." Oliver Chipford scratched at his nose and cleared his throat. "The house and lands will be sold to pay off the debts." His features brightened. "Perhaps I can arrange for you to be wed. I'm certain—"

"That isn't enough." Caroline had turned from her contemplation of the garden through the mullioned panes. "There's Neddy to consider. He's not of an age to care for himself."

"He's at school, I believe."

"Yes." Caroline's voice quavered. Soon the powers-that-be at that lofty institution would know of

21

her circumstances. The tuition was past due as it was. For though she'd squeezed till it squealed the paltry sum her father allotted to maintain the household, she couldn't come up with the amount needed for Edward's schooling.

Considering her situation, she was exceedingly grateful when Mr. Chipford introduced her to a factor who arranged her impending marriage. She was relieved to receive Robert MacQuaid's proposal. Despite the fact it involved her leaving England . . . and her brother.

There was certainly no one else she knew willing to wed a penniless woman past her prime.

Raff MacQuaid's legs were long, and his stride matched. Though her hand, pale in comparison, rested on his, Caroline had to quicken her step to keep up as they wove through the people crowding the narrow wooden sidewalk of Broad Street. Soldiers in bright scarlet uniforms mingled with blackamoors. She even saw a man she thought must be one of the aborigines native to the New World. His head was shaved save for a long tuft sprouting from the top of his well-shaped head. He was tall, his body covered with a mismatched array of leather leggings and richly brocaded waist-coat.

Intrigued, Caroline considered asking her companion about the Indian. But one glance at Raff MacQuaid's profile told her he didn't wish to be bothered by idle questions. Caroline even hesitated to inquire how much farther they were to walk before reaching his father's house.

When he stopped, so abruptly that Caroline nearly bumped into him, in front of the structure at the corner of Broad and Meeting Streets, Caroline looked up questioningly. The building was brick and very imposing, with four large columns. She didn't think it was a private dwelling, but when Raff MacQuaid led her up the steps, she wondered.

"Does your father await me here?" she asked after hesitating to catch her breath.

His laugh was deep and low, and Caroline felt the heated blush that darkened her skin.

"My *father* awaits Your Ladyship at his home . . . west of here, at the base of the mountains."

Mountains? She'd seen no mountains. But before she could ask where there were mountains in this flat land, he opened the heavy paneled door and ushered her inside. "It is the governor whom we shall see here."

Rather *he* shall see, Caroline thought nearly two hours later as she sat straight-backed on the chair in the small anteroom. A cup of tea, cold and forgotten, sat on the small table at her elbow, fetched for her by the young man behind the mahogany desk. He wore a wig too large for his narrow face and sat hunched over a piece of parchment. He scrawled feverishly with a quill, and Caroline imagined he was pretending he didn't hear the shouting that came from behind the closed door. The door Robert's son had passed through.

Caroline shifted in her seat, meeting the gaze the young assistant darted her way, before quickly focusing on her folded hands. Whatever the dispute between Raff MacQuaid and the colony's governor, it was loud and heated. At least on Raff's part. Every now and then Caroline could hear the other voice—the governor, she assumed—take on a conciliatory tone. But her betrothed's son was having none of it.

"Does the treaty of 1730 mean nothing then?" she heard him ask in his deep, strong voice. "Is that what I am to tell my people when I return? That the English king in all his infinite wisdom has decided to break his word?"

Caroline sucked in her breath and bit her bottom lip, unabashedly listening for the governor's response to that question, which to her mind bordered on treason. She almost expected to see the governor burst through the door and call for guards to come haul away her companion.

But again his words were soft and soothing. . . . Caroline could almost imagine the governor wringing his hands. He mentioned something about raids on the colonists being punished.

"And what of the Cherokee warriors who were killed, their scalps sold to Virginia's governor. Was it not acceptable to avenge them?"

"English law states—"

"It is always English law. What of Cherokee law?"

In the silence that followed Caroline could feel

the tension through the walls with their elaborate carvings and pillars. Then the governor spoke. "I know relations between the Cherokee and English are strained. But it is nothing that can't be repaired." There was a pause. "Perhaps if trade resumed."

Raff's voice interrupted, low, barely audible in the anteroom. "Trade? You but remind me of how unscrupulous English traders can be."

Caroline strained, as, she noticed, did the assistant, but she couldn't understand the governor's reply. But Raff's next words were spoken loud enough to hear plainly through the closed door. "Yet you would have us leave our homes and fight your enemies for you."

"The French are your enemies, too."

"Only because we are your allies, drawn together by a treaty you English refuse to honor."

"Now look here, Raff. You can't possibly think the French would—"

Raff's voice cut off the governor's words. "I shall hold council with Little Carpenter when I return to the Lower Towns. Perhaps he shall view your betrayal in a better light than I."

Before Caroline could appreciate what he'd said, the door slammed open, and Raff strode into the anteroom. She was caught with her neck craned to the side in an obvious listening stance. Searching her mind for an explanation for her eavesdropping, she jumped to her feet.

But her companion didn't seem to notice her. He

stopped when the governor, looking exasperated and slightly dumbfounded called out. Caroline didn't know what he said for the word was foreign to her. But Raff seemed to recognize it. He turned to face the older man.

"I will see what I can do." The governor lifted his arms, the thick lace falling back over his wrists. "Perhaps if I could speak directly with the Headmen we could come to a compromise."

Raff's eyes narrowed as he studied Lyttleton's heavy jowled face. "I will take your words to the *Ani'-Yun'wiya*, my people. Much depends upon this."

Caroline shivered. She couldn't help herself. The air in the small stuffy room seemed suddenly charged, like the moments before a storm blows off the channel. Caroline wouldn't have been surprised to see the silk curtains that hung heavy and limp in the midmorning heat start trailing out like banners in the wind.

But there was no wind . . . no storm. Only the heightened emotion between the two men as they stared at each other. Then Raff turned abruptly, seemingly noticing Caroline for the first time since he entered the room. After a quick bow toward the governor, he grabbed Caroline's hand and practically pulled her from the room. The door slammed behind them.

They were halfway down the wide stairs before Caroline managed to catch hold of the railing and slow their pace. Her heart beat a rapid tattoo, and she looked down wide-eyed at her companion who came to a halt two steps below her. She watched as the expression on his face changed.

"I apologize," Wolf let loose her hand, noting the pale skin was red from his grip. He tried a smile, forcing himself to appear pleasant though his blood still boiled from the encounter with Governor Lyttleton. "We should leave while there are still hours of daylight." The touch of her fingers on his sleeve kept Wolf from continuing down the stairs.

"Wait." Caroline bit her bottom lip. Questioning what fate dealt her was rarely something she did. She should simply realize she was an unplanned spectator to the confrontation that just occurred and leave it at that. But somehow she couldn't. Whatever had transpired was important to Raff MacQuaid, vitally important. No amount of pretending on his part could hide that. "What did you mean by much depends upon it? Why are you so angry?"

He didn't answer, only continued to stare at her in a way that made her heart beat faster. Then he pivoted and continued down the stairs, his step less hurried. Surprised, Caroline lifted her skirts and rushed to catch up. She overtook him near the bottom, her quilted petticoat swirling out as she rounded on him. "Tell me," she insisted, wondering what possessed her to be so bold. "You said 'my people.' I don't understand."

She was in front of him, her arms spread slightly as if she were blocking his way till he answered her question. Wolf wondered if she knew how easily he could set her aside . . . break her in two if he wished. He considered telling her, watching as her chin, now set at a defiant angle, began to quiver. But then frightening his father's bride was not his objective.

Seducing her was.

Still, he could not resist a slight taunt, a verbal jab, to pierce the innocent veneer of this woman chosen by the man he despised. He leaned forward till she had to tilt her chin back to look at him. "My people are the *Ani'-Yun'wiya*, the Cherokee." His raven brow arched. "Your betrothed's son is of mixed blood."

Wolf watched the delicate line of her throat as she swallowed. She forced her blue eyes not to blink, and Wolf grudgingly admired her ability to mask her emotions. "Well, have you nothing to say to that, you who demanded to know why I was angry?"

"What do you wish me to say?" Caroline's eyes locked with his. It appeared her companion was daring her to take issue with his parentage. In truth the only emotion she felt was surprise. She told him so. "Actually, I was more astonished to find that Robert had a son nearly as old as I, than to discover he is part Indian."

"No one is ever *part Indian,*" he began. Then his voice turned soft, seductive. "And I would guess myself older than you by several years, Your Ladyship."

28

Caroline imagined he was right, but somehow it helped her peace of mind to think of him as she would Ned. In a motherly fashion. Or at least to try. But when he looked at her, as he was now, his dark eyes intense, it wasn't maternal thoughts that tightened her stomach. Caroline reached out for the carved banister and turned. " 'Tis unimportant which of us is the other's senior," she said, her voice firm, before lifting her chin and descending to the first floor.

She nearly added that she was to be his father's wife, but didn't. He knew that. She was the one who needed to remember it, and stop imagining intimate looks where none existed.

The rooms downstairs in the Meeting House were used as offices and courtrooms. There were people milling about the hallway. Caroline didn't pause until she was again outside.

The bright sunshine dispelled any lingering sensual draw she felt for Raff MacQuaid. At least Caroline thought it did until she turned toward him. Now that she knew of his mixed blood, she wondered why she hadn't guessed it before. His skin was dark, bronzed against the snow white of his linen. And his hair, tied back in a neat queue, shone so black and sleek that the sun seemed to pull blue highlights from its depths.

Caroline blinked and quickly glanced away. Raff MacQuaid was certainly a compelling man, but she had to stop thinking of him in that way. She took the arm he offered, deciding she needed to concentrate on Raff's father. But he seemed unwilling to offer much information when she asked about Robert.

"You shall have to form your own opinions," he said, his tone one that did not encourage further discussion.

They walked in silence down Water Street until Caroline recognized the Inn where she'd spent the last few nights.

"I've taken the liberty of having your things brought down." Wolf led her to the small courtyard to the right of the building. There a blackamoor was loading her small chest on the back of a pack horse. "Are the rest of your trunks stored elsewhere?"

"There is nothing else." Caroline said the words quickly. If he found it surprising that she traveled so lightly, at least his expression didn't change. But Caroline imagined it took quite a lot for him to reveal his true emotions. The thought caused a shiver to dance down her spine. His hand tightened on her elbow as he led her to another horse, this one a chestnut mare replete with sidesaddle.

Caroline swallowed. Her breathing was shallow, and she wiped her damp palms down the side of her flowered skirt. "Aren't we taking a coach?" She rarely rode. The once fine stables at Simmons Hall were empty by the time her father moved Ned and her to the country. And the large animals frightened her. But then, nearly everything seemed to.

Spoiled. He should have known. Well, Lady Caroline Simmons was going to have some difficult lessons in reality . . . starting here and now.

"We're heading for the frontier, Your Ladyship. The roads are mired with mud in the spring, choked with dust the rest of the year. At no time are they wide enough to accommodate a coach and four."

"I see." Caroline glanced back at the animal who pranced impatiently, and she sighed.

"You should go home."

"I . . . beg your pardon." The words were so unexpected, Caroline didn't know what to think.

The face she angled up toward him was pale. He could plainly see a light dusting of freckles across her nose. Which Wolf told himself was why he offered her an escape. Besides, sending his father's betrothed packing back to England was almost as effective as taking her to bed . . . at least that's what he tried to tell himself.

Wolf folded his arms. "I have no idea what you were told, but Seven Pines is not what you imagine. Life is hard. The frontier doesn't care that your lineage is pure or your skin soft as down. Return to England while you still can."

"No!" Caroline sucked in her breath. "I won't . . . I can't return." She felt childish blinking back tears that sprang to her eyes, but she couldn't seem to control her emotions. For months she had worried about what was to become of Ned and herself. The chance to come here had been a Godsend. She endured the long weeks alone crossing the stormy ocean, only to have Robert's son suggest she return . . . to give up the one chance she and her brother had to avoid debtors prison.

Grabbing the reins, Caroline put her fear into perspective. The ocean voyage had frightened her, but she managed it. She would manage this . . . and anything else that was necessary.

Wolf arched his brow, then merely shrugged. He'd given the woman her warning. His conscience was clear, he decided, as he cupped his hands to boost her up onto the saddle. But when he saw the expression of determination on her face, he wished she weren't so adamant about staying.

It didn't take Caroline long to understand why coach travel was impossible. They were barely out of the town before the roads deteriorated to mere trails. Most of them bordered dark, mysterious swamps. Large turtles sunning themselves on rotting logs glanced around as they passed. Later they traveled, often single file, through never ending forests of tall, stalwart pines.

Only once did they stop, and that was to rest the horses, and let them drink from a wide, slow-moving stream. But Caroline refused to utter one word of discontent. In the back of her mind lay the uneasy feeling that should she complain too much about the conditions, her companion would return her to Charles Town.

Besides, though her back ached and her legs grew stiff, she could bear this. And sooner or later

Raff had to grow tired. But as the sun tinged the sky ahead with a splash of mauve, their pace seemed to quicken. Caroline twisted in the saddle, causing the leather to creak beneath her skirts.

Wolf glanced over his shoulder. "We shall be at George Walker's soon. Then you can rest."

Relief washed over her, but Caroline refused to let it show. Somewhere on the arduous ride, she decided to prove to this arrogant man that he was wrong about her ability to last on the frontier. "I'm quite all right," she managed, only to see the ghost of a disbelieving smile tilt his lips as he righted himself in the saddle. With a slap of his reins, he prodded his stallion to a faster pace. Gritting her teeth, Caroline urged her horse to keep up with him.

Dusk was throwing eerie shadows across the trail when Raff led them onto an even narrower path that angled off to the south. Too tired to ask if this was leading toward the George Walker plantation he mentioned earlier, Caroline followed. Here she could see wide swathes of forest cut away to form plowed fields.

Civilization.

When a house came into view, Caroline sighed, obviously louder than she intended, for again Raff MacQuaid twisted to look her way. She kept her eyes focused on the house, refusing to acknowledge his stare.

Two storied, and whitewashed, age and the surrounding canopy of trees gave the whole a shadowed appearance. The dwelling had a wide front porch and shuttered windows. Beyond it and down a long sloping stretch of land, Caroline caught sight of a river. They reined in their horses, and a child of about ten came running from one of the outbuildings. He wore cutoff breeches and his dark bare feet were covered with sandy soil.

"Masta', he done just come back from de fields."

"He's in the house, then?" Wolf asked as he reached up to lift his father's bride off her horse. She sagged against him when her feet hit the ground, and his arms reached out to steady her. But she immediately righted herself and, with a murmured "thank you," stepped away.

"Yessah, he's in there. Gettin' on close to supper time." The boy took hold of the reins and led the horses toward the barn.

"That's what I'm counting on." Wolf turned and motioned Caroline forward with a wave of his hand.

She passed him, head held high, though her legs felt as if they would buckle beneath her at any moment. And worse, to Caroline's way of thinking, it wasn't just the long, unaccustomed ride that made her knees wobbly. Foolish as it was, the brief instant she'd stood in the cocoon of Raff's embrace had affected her equilibrium. She only hoped her future stepson hadn't noticed.

The door was partially open to allow the breeze off the river to come through. Wolf stepped inside just as a small dark-haired woman turned the land-

34

ing of the stairs. She gave an excited yelp and raced down the remaining steps, propelling herself into Wolf's arms. While Caroline watched, the tall, silent man lifted the woman and twirled her around till she begged for mercy.

"Papa said you might come," she said when he put her back on the floor. "But we didn't expect you this soon." The young woman flashed her dark eyes toward Caroline, before her gaze riveted once more on Raff. "How long are you staying?"

"Only overnight." Wolf brushed his finger across Rebecca Walker's pouting bottom lip before turning to Caroline and introducing the beauty that clung to his hand.

This time Rebecca Walker's attention to Caroline lasted a little longer, but it was as if an invisible string kept pulling her smiling face back toward Raff. "You promised to stay with us longer next time," she reminded him.

"I said *sometime*, Rebecca. And that sometime is not now. I need to deliver Lady Caroline to my father."

"Is that company I hear?" A big booming bear of a man with grey hair and a ruddy complexion came through a door near the back of the hallway. In half a dozen giant strides, he had Raff in a bear hug, repeating that the younger man wasn't expected this early.

"I was able to have an audience with Governor Lyttleton immediately and saw no reason to delay. Besides, as I just explained to your daughter, I'm escorting Lady Caroline to Seven Pines. She's to be Robert's wife."

Caroline didn't imagine the slight lift of her host's bushy white brows when Raff introduced her. But George Walker was extremely considerate and polite.

"You must be tired, my dear," he said as he took her hand. "Rebecca will show you to your room. As soon as you've freshened up, we'll eat."

After thanking him, Caroline began to follow an obviously reluctant Rebecca up the stairs. The girl fairly bounced when she walked, and Caroline thought she must look very drab and listless in comparison as she clutched the banister.

Below, in the hallway, George Walker clasped his friend's shoulder. " 'Tis glad I am, that you've come. And not just because Rebecca wonders constantly when you'll arrive."

"I do no such thing," Rebecca called back, stopping so abruptly that Caroline almost bumped into her. "Papa, don't you dare tell such tales on me."

Rebecca turned, hands akimbo, and glared down at the two men standing shoulder to shoulder below stairs. Her cheeks were flushed and her dark eyes sparkled, and in that instant, Caroline realized why. Rebecca Walker was in love with Raff Mac-Quaid.

Since she had little experience with romance of any type, Caroline wasn't certain how she knew. But know, she did. She glanced around, to see if she could discern if Mr. MacQuaid was privy to this tidbit of information, and her breath caught in her throat.

She'd thought of her future stepson as imposing and unmistakably masculine, in turn broodingly quiet and angry, but as she stared at him now, she appreciated how handsome he was. His hand rested on the rounded newel, as he grinned up at Rebecca. Then his piercing stare shifted, meeting Caroline's, and she felt as if all the air was sucked from her body.

Rebecca flounced about, continuing the climb up the stairs, and Caroline had no choice but to follow.

Dinner that night was delicious; Caroline hadn't realized how hungry she was. But afterward, when she would have preferred to climb into the soft down-filled bed and sleep, she adjourned to the drawing room with Rebecca while her father and Raff walked outside. Rebecca's vibrant mood vanished, and she sullenly stared out the window, answering only briefly Caroline's attempts at conversation.

Finally giving up, Caroline sat ignored and uncomfortable in one of the Queen Anne chairs, wondering when she could politely excuse herself. She'd just about decided she'd endured the woman's silence long enough when Rebecca turned, her dark head cocked to one side.

"He hates his father, you know."

"I beg your pardon?" Caroline wasn't sure if

she heard correctly. For the seemingly unsolicited statement made no sense.

"Raff. He can't tolerate Robert for the way he treated his mother . . . and the rest of the Cherokee."

Not knowing how to respond, Caroline studied the hands folded in her lap.

"He'll hate you, too. I know he will."

Caroline swallowed. "I don't think any of this is your concern."

"Oh, but everything about Raff is my concern." She smoothed the swaying skirts of her brocaded gown. "I thought you should know that he'll never care about you . . . because of his father."

" 'Tis very . . . kind of you to tell me." Caroline stood, not quite knowing what to say. She smiled, hoping to relieve some of the tension she felt emanating from the girl. "I'm very tired. If you'll excuse me, I think I shall retire."

"That's splendid. And don't worry, I'll make your excuses to Raff and my father."

With a nod of her head, Caroline left the room, closing the door behind her. The hallway was airy, the door leading from the back of the house open, and Caroline couldn't resist walking toward it. A breath of fresh air might clear her head and help her make some sense of Rebecca's remarks. It wasn't until she paused in the doorway that she realized Mr. Walker and Raff were nearby.

She couldn't see them in the darkness, but though they spoke in hushed tones, she could hear them. Caroline was about to turn back inside when something her host said caught her attention.

"You think there will be war then between the Cherokee and the English?"

But it was Raff's response that sent a shiver up her spine.

"Lyttleton sends talk of compromise. But I think it is too late."

Two

War.

Caroline took a deep breath and stepped back. She was assured by Mr. Chipford that the Carolinas would be spared the bloodshed that had plagued many of the other colonies. But that opinion obviously wasn't shared by Raff MacQuaid. He talked as if outbreaks of fighting would soon be common on the frontier. And that's where they were bound.

Caroline was so intent upon listening that the deep bong of the tall case clock in the hall was startling. Her small gasp was loud enough to interrupt the conversation on the porch.

Caroline stood frozen with indecision as footfalls headed her way. And then Mr. Walker came through the door, and it was too late for retreat.

Ah, Lady Simmons, were you seeking us?"

"Yes . . . yes, I was," Caroline lied, silently thanking her host for providing the chance to explain away her obvious eavesdropping. Her gaze shifted up to meet Raff's as he followed Mr. Walker into the pool of light from the brass sconces lining the hallway. It was obvious from his expression that he didn't believe her. Caroline cleared her throat. "I wished to . . . to . . ." Caroline forced her eyes from his dark stare and focused instead on Mr. Walker's jovial face. "To retire."

"Of course, you do, my dear. You must be exhausted. I know how Raff rides, never taking into consideration that the rest of us aren't his equal on a horse."

"Oh, Mr. MacQuaid was very kind during the journey." Caroline felt compelled to defend her future stepson, despite the fact that he still stared at her with enough intensity to make her uncomfortable. He made no comment, and all Mr. Walker did was laugh, a deep booming sound as he took her hand and accompanied her to the foot of the stairs.

"I hope you find everything to your comfort, Lady Caroline."

"I'm sure I shall. Thank you." Caroline rested her hand on the smooth banister, anxious to make good her escape upstairs. But she hesitated. Glancing around she smiled, first at her host. "Good night, Mr. Walker." Then at Raff who'd followed her to the stairs. "Good night, Mr. MacQuaid."

She didn't wait for any response, which from the older man was pleasant, from her future stepson nonexistent, before turning and hurrying up the staircase.

"Are you trying to frighten the girl to death?"

Wolf rested his hand on the newel, staring at the top of the stairs long after Caroline disappeared down the hallway. Then he turned to his friend. "What in the hell is that supposed to mean?"

"Simply that your expression when you look at her is so fierce I'm surprised the thought of you being in her household doesn't send her running home to England."

"You don't know what you're talking about. First of all, I *won't* be part of Her Ladyship's household, and second, this is the way I always look. Indian blood runs dark." Wolf pasted a smile on his face and clasped his friend's shoulder. But he couldn't help wondering if he was still trying to dissuade Caroline Simmons from going to his father.

He'd heard her in the hallway long before the clock struck nine. She was listening to his conversation with George and perhaps because of that he'd painted the prospect of war as grimly . . . as truthfully, as he could. He hadn't exaggerated. Unless something was done quickly to stop it, war between the Cherokee and the English of South Carolina appeared a reality. But was he trying to scare her off? To spare her the unpleasantness of wedding his father? The idea still puzzled him as he entered the parlor and Rebecca rushed across the floor to meet him.

* * *

How could she have been so stupid and ill-mannered?

Caroline leaned against the door, trying to calm her racing emotions. She'd been caught listening to a private conversation, and she'd been caught by Raff MacQuaid. Caroline shut her eyes. She could clearly visualize the expression on his dark, handsome face as she lied. It was not something she cared to see again. It was as if his eyes could bore straight through her . . . find her innermost secrets. And it was terribly disconcerting.

After taking a deep breath, Caroline walked to the window and stared out at the night. She should be concentrating on the things she'd heard, not Raff's reaction to her. But she couldn't quite separate one from the other.

Especially when everything about him . . . about everything was so disturbing.

"He hates his father. He'll hate you, too."

Caroline couldn't stop thinking of Rebecca's words. If Raff disliked his father so, then why had he come to fetch her?

With a sigh, Caroline sank onto the window seat and pressed her forehead against the cool pane. Her breath marbled the window. She'd never felt so alone, not even after her mother died. At least then she had Edward and her home. Now she was in a strange land, where war was a real threat and her only companion was a compelling man who

43

seemed not to like her at all. Was it because she was to wed his father?

Exhaustion overtook and while still trying to decide if she had any options at all, Caroline fell asleep.

In the middle of the night she woke with a start. Though the flame of the bedside candle sputtered in the hot tallow, it emitted enough light for her to see she wasn't alone. Her scream was muffled by a large hand held firmly over her mouth. Caroline's eyes widened in panic even though she now recognized Raff MacQuaid.

As disturbing as his presence in her room was, his touch still caused her light-headedness. Nothing in her twenty-two years prepared her for the depth of the emotions he caused her.

"There's no reason to be frightened. 'Tis only me."

Though the words were meant to be reassuring, it was his tone, soothing and smooth as silk that made her nod her head when he asked if he could remove his hand.

"What are you doing in here?" she whispered. A quick glance toward the door reaffirmed that it was shut. She may not have had much guidance in the ways of the world, but Caroline knew it wasn't acceptable for her to be alone with a man in her bedroom. Even if she was betrothed to the man's father.

"I came to tell you when we would be leaving in the morning." Not entirely a lie.

"Still . . ." Caroline shrank back against the window, wishing she didn't feel so drawn to him. His scent. The magnetism of his dark eyes. "You shouldn't be here."

Wolf shrugged and sat beside her, sensing the slight shiver that ran through her. The window seat was small and his hip pressed against her drawn-up knee. He could feel her warmth through the layers of petticoats. "I saw the light beneath your door, but when I knocked there was no answer."

"I heard no knock."

Fine white teeth showed against his dark skin when he smiled. "You were asleep." Wolf's fingers touched the collar of her gown. "Still dressed."

Caroline wondered if he noticed her racing pulse.

"And sitting by the window," Wolf continued, shaking his head. "Don't you know what's said about the night air? I wouldn't want you catching your death. What would my *father* say?"

"What would he say about your being in my room?" Caroline didn't know what made her so bold, but she was rewarded by another smile, this one somewhat wicked.

"Does it matter?"

Before Caroline could think of a proper response to him his hand moved up to her hair. "You didn't even take down your curls."

Goodness, she had to stop him from touching her, or soon she wouldn't want to. Caroline pulled away, but the hours of sleeping, her head awkwardly bent against the chilled windowpane had taken their toll. She sucked in her breath as her stiff neck rebelled.

"What is it?" His fingers curved around her throat.

"Nothing . . . really." There was no place to go to be away from him. She'd squeezed back in the corner as far as she could, and his large body blocked her escape into the room. "Don't. Please don't do that." His fingers massaged the sore tendons from her ear to the lace bordering her shoulder. Against all common sense, Caroline let her head drift to the side, giving him free access to her slender neck, belying her words of protest.

His hands were strong, the pads of his long fingers roughened, but his touch was gentle . . . soothing.

"Is that better?"

His voice, low and sensual, coaxed Caroline's eyes open. His touch relaxed her at the same time it excited. She cleared her throat, trying to regain control of a situation gotten too far out of hand. "Yes, that's much better, thank you." Abruptly she forced her feet to the floor, pushing past him, putting space between them. "You wanted to tell me what time to be ready in the morning." Caroline lifted her hand to her cheek. Somehow he'd removed the wooden pins from her hair, and it now hung free past her shoulders.

"I did." With her hair down and her color high, her blue eyes still languid from his touch, Wolf

46

found it difficult to look away from her. Perhaps he was under the spell of his own seduction. Who wouldn't be attracted to a woman so easily excited. "Plan to rise early. It's best if we leave by dawn."

"Because of the impending war?" The question was out before Caroline could stop herself. But there was no use pretending she hadn't overheard his discussion with Mr. Walker.

"No. Simply because I want to get as much traveling in by daylight as we can."

"Oh." Caroline twisted her fingers and began pacing the width of the room. He still sat on the window seat and though he made no comment about her question, she felt as though she should explain. "I didn't mean to listen to your conversation with Mr. Walker."

There was enough light in the room for her to notice the skeptical arch of his brow. Caroline rearranged the silver handled brush and mirror on the mahogany dresser. So much for her half-hearted attempt to apologize. She turned to face him. "Is there to be a war between the Cherokee and the English?"

"I think so. France and England seem unable to leave well enough alone."

"And what is 'well enough'?"

Wolf settled back against the window. "Excellent question. And one too complex to answer quickly. Perhaps we can discuss this issue in detail if you'd like me to stay."

He sounded almost as if he expected her to agree.

But with the distance between them, Caroline felt more confident. She shook her head slowly, aware of the soft, swishing sound of her hair against her silk bodice. "No. I thank you for rescuing me from my uncomfortable bed." She nodded her head toward the window seat. "But I think 'tis time you leave. If we are to be up before dawn."

Wolf shrugged and settled back against the window, ignoring her annoyed expression. "The Cherokee want fairness. Fair prices for our skins. Fair prices placed on the goods they must buy."

"From the English?" Caroline felt drawn in despite her contention that he leave.

"Or the French."

"But . . . but I thought the English and Cherokee were allies. How can they wish to trade with the enemy?"

"The English honor the treaties as long as it serves their purpose. They send traders to the Cherokee Towns as long as it remains profitable to do so. When they decide not to trade, our women are left with no pots, our warriors run out of bullets for their rifles." Wolf lifted his palms for emphasis.

Caroline left her position of safety beside the dresser. Like iron filings drawn to lodestone, she moved toward Raff. He shifted to the side so she could sit down. "Is that what has happened? Have the English stopped trading with the Cherokee?"

"That is one problem. The trade arrangement

always was one-sided. Now . . . the Cherokee have learned to rely on the goods from England."

"But surely if the traders understood . . ."

Wolf's laugh lacked humor. "The English understand what they're doing all too well. What they don't comprehend is the Cherokee. We will—" Shaking his head, Wolf pushed to his feet. "I was right before. This is a complex situation." He resisted the urge to touch her before striding to the door. "But chances of war are great."

Wolf opened the door, pausing to look back at her before shutting it behind him. She sat, picture perfect, framed by the rose damask drapes. "I will return you to Charles Town in the morning if that is your wish."

"Why don't you want me here?"

Wolf glanced up, surprised, as Caroline entered the dining room. He'd slept poorly, finally rising before the household and was now eating a breakfast of cold cornbread he found in the kitchen. The only light was a single taper burning in a silver candleholder on the table. He hadn't expected to see anyone, especially Lady Caroline Simmons, this early.

Yet there she was, dressed for traveling, and staring down the length of the polished mahogany table at him. Her fingers curled, white knuckled, around the back of a Queen Anne chair. Wolf took a moment to finish slathering butter on his bread.

With studied indifference he shrugged. "I don't know what you're talking about."

"Don't you?" Caroline sounded skeptical. "Since Charles Town you've been trying to scare me away." The realization hit Caroline sometime during the long sleepless night. "You've done everything you could to make marrying your father seem ill-advised. First in Charles Town. Now here with this talk of war. I wonder if any of it is true."

That he made no response both angered and emboldened her. Caroline let go of the chair and moved toward him. "I received a post from your father before I left England. In it he said nothing of danger. Nothing of Indian wars." Nothing about a half-blooded son. But Caroline didn't mention that. "I think you knew I was listening last night, and you exaggerated all this to persuade me to return to England."

"Why would I do that?" His voice was low, his dark face expressionless.

Compared to her own emotional state his apparent calm and reasonableness rankled. When she heard him walk past her room earlier this morning, Caroline decided a confrontation was needed. Not that she enjoyed them. Most of her life was spent trying to smooth out the ruffles of her existence. However, she'd known Raff MacQuaid only one day and already he shadowed her waking hours and invaded her dreams.

She expected him to vehemently deny that he wished her gone, or to confess all in a fit of anger.

50

But he did neither, only studied her with those dark, intense eyes. Caroline paced past him, then turned. "I don't know why," she confessed. She'd pondered the question most of the night. "Perhaps you . . . perhaps you dislike your father."

As she moved back to face him, his hand shot out, manacling her wrist so quickly Caroline barely had time to gasp. "How I do or do not feel about my father has naught to do with warning you about the dangers of the frontier."

His grip held her firmly, inched her closer. Fighting him was futile. Caroline concentrated instead on swallowing, trying to slow her breathing. "You aren't going to scare me away."

Wolf wasn't certain if she meant from the Carolinas or from the dining room, but looking at the determined expression on her face, he believed her. His fingers tightened as he stood.

He was overwhelming, large and powerful, looming over her. "I can't go back." Caroline looked up at him willing him to understand, nearly telling him of the necessity that drove her to the New World.

But she said nothing more, for it was then she realized he planned to kiss her. Slowly his face came closer till his breath wafted across her cheek. Somewhere in the back recesses of her mind Caroline knew she should resist. But the temptation not to was too great. Her eyes drifted shut. Her heart pounded. Anticipation made her light-headed.

"I know you're an early riser, Raff, but this is

ridiculous." Rebecca breezed into the room, stopping abruptly when she saw Caroline. Her gaze slipped to Raff, who had resettled in his chair.

Caroline leaned against the table, one hand flattened on her chest, her cheeks burning. Had she really almost kissed her future stepson? Or had she imagined the entire incident? Except for the warmth of her wrist where he'd held her, she might believe that her mind was playing fanciful tricks on her. Raff was busy chewing cornbread, seemingly oblivious to her.

He took a swig of milk, swallowed and flashed Rebecca a lazy grin. "What are you doing up and about so early? To hear your father tell it, you rarely grace your family with your presence till afternoon."

"Oh, pooh." Completely ignoring Caroline, Rebecca pulled a chair closer to Raff. "I wake up when I'm ready." She smiled. "And this morning I was ready." She took a piece of cornbread off Raff's plate and daintily nibbled a corner. Only then did she speak to Caroline. "Goodness, you look as if you barely slept. I hope the bed was to your liking."

Caroline met her gaze then looked toward Raff. He simply lifted his dark brow. "I slept very well, thank you." Caroline surprised herself with how steady her voice sounded.

"Well, you really must take care of yourself," Rebecca continued. "Life on the frontier isn't for everyone."

"How would you know?" Wolf chuckled. "This is hardly the frontier."

Rebecca's pink lips formed a pout. " 'Tis so. Why I have to travel an entire day to visit Charles Town."

"Poor Rebecca." Wolf tweaked her nose as he stood.

"What about poor Rebecca?" George Walker entered the dining room, buttoning a brightly colored silk coat. A matching cap rested askew on his head.

"She's bemoaning her life in the wilds of South Carolina."

"Oh Raff, I was not." Rebecca rose and took Raff's arm. "I simply pointed out that not everyone is suited for hardships." Her eyes slid toward Caroline, who could only imagine how true Rebecca must think her statement.

Caroline did appear ill-suited for life in any but the most civilized surroundings. But she would learn to survive in the frontier . . . because she must.

Less than an hour later they were on their way again. Raff rode ahead, followed by Caroline. The contents of her trunk—two gowns; several clean shifts; and hose—were transferred to saddlebags and now hung down the sides of both their horses. The packhorse and trunk were left behind at the Walkers. The new arrangement did seem to allow for a faster pace—which to Caroline's way of thinking, wasn't without drawbacks.

Her legs and back were still sore from the previous day, but she refused to make either an issue. Her resolve grew weaker as the day wore on.

Since the incident in the dining room, she and Raff had barely exchanged a score of words. The longer they went in this state of near quiet, the more uncomfortable Caroline became. They had never resolved the issue of Raff not wanting her here, but Caroline decided as they rode deeper and deeper into the Carolinas that it was a mute point. She *was* going to Seven Pines to marry his father.

"The land is very wild." Caroline spurred her mare forward, gritting her teeth against the added abuse to her bottom. "I don't believe I've ever seen so many trees." It was true, the path seemed to creep in on them from the sides, threatening to squeeze them toward the center.

Caroline watched as Raff turned in his saddle. Today he wore breeches of animal skin, buffed and molded to his powerful thighs. His shirt of the same material was loose and gathered at the waist by a belt that held his powderhorn. He looked as wild as the country.

He seemed to have left his manners behind with his silk clothes, for he only shrugged in a way that conveyed nothing.

Unexpectedly the path widened into a sandy lane dappled with sunshine. Caroline prodded her horse to ride abreast of his. "She's lovely."

"Who?"

She didn't know why he was being so obtuse. "Why Rebecca Walker. She's a beautiful young woman."

His stare was disconcerting. "I've known her for years. She's hardly more than a child."

"I don't think she considers herself one. And it didn't seem to me that—"

"That what?"

"Well, that you considered her a child, either."

"She initiated that kiss, Your Ladyship."

"I didn't mean . . ." Caroline couldn't quite meet his gaze, and she couldn't lie. The kiss *was* what she'd been thinking of. Just as Raff was getting ready to mount his horse, Rebecca Walker had stepped up to him. In front of Caroline and her father, she wove her arms around Raff's neck. The kiss was long and sensual, and the vision of them standing there was still seared in her memory. It reminded her of the kiss she almost received from him. Caroline squirmed in the saddle. "I simply thought that you and she were . . . were . . ."

"Sweethearts?"

"Well, yes." Caroline let out a breath she didn't realize she was holding and smiled.

His expression remained sober. "We aren't."

"Oh. I just thought—"

"Caroline."

"Yes." When he said her name like that it made her pulse race.

"I don't need a mother."

55

With that he urged his mount forward, ending the conversation . . . such as it was. Caroline looked down at her gloved hands, clutching the reins, not knowing what to think. Was she trying to act the part of a parent? To her mortification, her thoughts had been anything but maternal when Rebecca molded her body to his, or when she flirted unabashedly, or when her lips pressed to his.

Caroline shook her head, trying to dislodge those disturbing thoughts. She was making more of this than she should. He was rude. That was all. Or simply angry with her for deciding to ignore his advice and go to his father.

Or perhaps he knew what she was thinking when she saw the kiss between Rebecca and him. Caroline couldn't help touching her heated cheeks.

It was past time to rest the horses. Not to mention Lady Caroline Simmons. Wolf twisted in the saddle and cast a glance her way. He could tell she was tired. But she didn't complain. Damned if he didn't have to give her credit for that. It occurred to him that she wasn't as fragile as she looked, but he dismissed the thought. She was just angry with him and thus refusing to say anything.

And he could hardly blame her.

He wasn't known for his jovial nature, but neither was he a complete bore. Especially when he was planning a seduction. But the seduction was causing his ill-humor.

And the ill-humor caused him to be careless. The man stepped from the shadow of the trees before Wolf even sensed he was near. Both horses started, neighing and stamping the ground with their front hooves. Wolf had no trouble calming his mount, but Caroline wasn't so fortunate. He leaped from the saddle and grabbed for her reins, dodging the flailing legs of the mare.

Caroline felt herself slipping, and her fear of horses came jolting back. She'd tried to force those feelings from her mind but now they all but paralyzed her. By the time Raff quieted the horse and reached up for her, she slid willingly from the saddle into his arms. Her body trembled, and she did her best to fight the tears as she leaned into his broad chest. But it was as if a tiny dam broke, allowing emotions too long restrained to spew forth.

"I . . . can't . . . ride. Afraid of horses." Her words were punctuated by sniffles and hiccups. Some of them Wolf could make out, but not all. She looked up at him, her large eyes wet and prismed by tears, and Wolf felt an uncomfortable tightening in his chest.

These were not some dainty, feminine tears contrived to elicit a response from him. He doubted she thought of him at all as she ran through her litany of failures, continually mentioning someone named Ned. And he was damn certain she didn't remember that Dayunisi stood not five rods away, watching the scene with amusement.

"Hush now, Caroline. You're safe." Wolf pulled her more tightly into his arms. Her straw hat had fallen off and his one hand cupped her head, tangling with the soft, pale gold curls. The other caressed her narrow back while over her head he stared at Dayunisi, his eyes daring the Cherokee to laugh at his predicament.

Control is what she needed. Somewhere in the back of her mind Caroline knew that. But exhaustion and fear muddled her thinking. And it was such a relief to be cradled in strong arms . . . to have someone to lean upon. But it was the wrong someone. Caroline knew that.

Slowly she pulled away, wiping her damp face with her gloved hands. "I apologize," she whispered, unable to lift her eyes to look at him. "I don't usually act this way." He tried to pull her back closer to his body, and Caroline rebelled. "No, please, we shouldn't . . ."

"Caroline." Wolf lifted her chin with his finger. "We aren't alone."

"What? Oh, my goodness." Caroline wasn't sure whether it was embarrassment or fear that caused her to stay plastered to Raff's side after she spun around. Standing just out of the shadows of a tree was a tall, fierce-looking Indian. His head was shaved except for a topknot that hung down his back similar to the Indians she saw in Charles

Town. But unlike those men, who wore shirts and waistcoats, this one was nearly naked.

He said something Caroline didn't understand, and Raff answered in the same guttural language. Giving her shoulders a reassuring squeeze, he moved toward the Indian. They walked together down the path, leaving Caroline with the horses.

"Why in the hell did you jump out in front of me like that?"

Dayunisi's dark eyes narrowed. "I've followed you since the turn in the path. Didn't Wa'ya hear my signals?"

No, he hadn't heard them. He'd been too busy thinking about his father's betrothed. And he was lucky it had only been Dayunisi's presence he missed. Wolf stared off into the woods. "What word do you bring?"

"Creek are traveling the valley."

Wolf shrugged. "That is hardly news." The Creek from the south often traveled Cherokee land. They weren't allies, but most of the time there was an uneasy truce between the two nations.

"But this time, Wa'ya, they go north to fight the English. And they speak to our warriors about joining them."

"Do any of them listen?"

"Tal-tsuska."

Wolf would expect nothing else from his cousin, son of his mother's brother. Tal-tsuska's hatred of the white man ran deep. But Dayunisi's next words were more disturbing. Wolf listened, his expression grim.

"There have been raids upon settlers in Virginia . . . by Cherokee warriors."

Three

"What is it? What's wrong?" Caroline's skirt swished in the dusty road as she followed Raff around the horses. The red man had disappeared into the woods as quietly as he appeared.

"Step up." Wolf bent over, cupping his hands beside the mare's stirrup. He glanced up, annoyed when Caroline didn't comply.

"What did he say?" Standing her ground was not something Caroline did as a rule; and after studying Raff's dark countenance, she understood why.

"I'm taking you back to Charles Town."

He said the words so matter of factly that Caroline could only stare. It wasn't until he leaned over again to help her mount that she found her tongue. "I told you before, I'm going to Seven Pines."

He said nothing at first, only straightened to tower over her, his dark eyes intense. "Cherokee warriors have raided settlers in Virginia. Taken scalps."

Caroline's gasp was involuntary. "But why?" She looked away only to be drawn back by his gaze. "Mr. Chipford assured me there was peace between the Cherokee and the English. He's the factor who arranged the betrothal between your father and me," she answered his unspoken question.

"Well, Mr. Chipford obviously doesn't know the situation."

"But 'tis the same thing your father reported in his post."

"Listen Caroline." Raff took a deep breath. Dayunisi's news had disturbed him. It also made him all the more anxious to reach the Cherokee Lower Towns and report Lyttleton's request for a talk. He didn't have time for Lady Caroline Simmons, or her obstinance. "Believe whom you will, but I'm returning you to Charles Town. And I'm doing it now."

"Then you'll have to take me by force." The mare pranced nervously behind her, and Caroline stepped well out of the way. "I've come too far to turn back." She bit her bottom lip to keep it from quivering and stuck out her chin.

"Damnit, Caroline, there is more at stake here than your desire to marry my father."

"I'm not going back." Once, when she was a child, her father told her she was stubborn. The years had nearly erased that trait, but for some reason Raff MacQuaid revived it.

"You're not?" Wolf glowered down at her. "Well,

what if I do? What if I just leave you right here and return to Charles Town myself."

Caroline's gaze darted about quickly. To the thick, nearly impenetrable forest, dark and teeming with animal sounds. She swallowed. "Then I shall go on by myself."

If she thought his expression dark before, now it was positively thunderous. He took a step toward her, then another, until she was forced to back away or be overrun by him. Her back pressed against the mare's warm side, but she refused to look away even when his hands reached out to cup her shoulders.

"What is it about my father that draws you so?"

"I . . . I'm not drawn to him." To his son perhaps. Caroline ruthlessly shoved that thought aside. She had no right thinking of the man before her in any way other than a stepson. Then why did she notice the way he smelled, like musky leather and unbearable heat? And why did she tremble whenever he touched her, nay whenever he even looked at her?

"He will not make you a good husband."

His voice was low, and he left the meaning of his words unsaid. But a thousand vivid pictures came to Caroline's mind . . . and none of them centered upon her betrothed. It was the man before her, touching her, who dominated her thoughts. A husband whose hands were large and firm, whose lips were sensual. What that mouth could do to her, Caroline could only guess. But for one insane moment she wanted to know, wanted to know so badly she could almost feel him, taste him. . . .

"I'm going to Seven Pines!" Caroline twisted away from his grip on her shoulders and pressed her fist to her mouth. She sounded breathless and frightened, and she was both. But not of Indian raids, or even Raff MacQuaid's disapproval.

"Very well. But do not say you weren't warned." With that he quirked his brow and curved his hands around her waist. Hoisting her up, he settled her into the saddle. Then he lifted her knee over the pummel—it was only her imagination that his fingers lingered overlong—and handed her the reins. She watched as he mounted, then urged his horse along the path . . . westward bound.

Their pace was even faster than before. By the time they stopped for the night, Caroline was bone tired. Unlike the Walkers' sprawling house, their lodging this night was a cabin made of rough-hewn wood and a shake roof. But the food was good, and the bed in the loft that the mistress of the house showed her to was clean and welcome. Even exhaustion, however, couldn't keep away the troubling dreams that haunted Caroline's sleep . . . erotic dreams.

With the dawn they started down the path again, horses fresh, pace swift. By now Caroline knew the trip to Seven Pines would take a fortnight if all went well. That much she learned from Mistress Campbell who, along with her husband and five children, lived on the homestead where they spent the night.

A fortnight of such traveling loomed ahead as an eternity, but then compared to her sea voyage it didn't seem so long. At least now she had solid ground beneath her, even if a horse carried her plodding along on it. Actually, despite her near tumble, Caroline had lost her fear of the gentle chestnut mare. Or perhaps her mind was too pre-occupied to worry about the horse.

" 'Tis it your intention to hold your tongue until we reach Seven Pines?" Caroline prodded her mount forward till she was abreast of Raff. He had spoken no more than was necessary to her since her refusal to return to Charles Town. But he had plenty to say. Last night she'd heard the muffled rumble of voices, his and his host's, long after she'd climbed the ladder to the loft.

His stare made Caroline wish she'd kept silent. If he knew how he made her feel, like he could see through her clothing to the woman beneath, surely he would cease.

"I wasn't aware you wished conversation, Your Ladyship."

He was back to making her feel like unwanted royalty. Caroline ignored his sarcasm. "Oh, I should think anyone would appreciate a bit of company in this wilderness."

"Some find the forest companion enough."

"Do you?"

Today there was no ribbon or leather thong holding back his hair. It hung wild and free. A lock of his midnight black hair blew across his cheek as he turned back toward her. His eyes were no less intense, but the ghost of a smile altered the effect on her. Caroline felt as if her bones had turned to water.

"At times," he admitted, "I enjoy the solitude of the trees and mountains. The song of the wind and screech of the raven." He shrugged as if embarrassed by his own thoughts. "But then, there is much to be said for the company of a beautiful woman as well."

Caroline felt heated color blossom on her cheeks. She turned her head, pretending to assess the dense underbrush that lined the path, hoping he wouldn't notice her unsophisticated blush. He wasn't speaking of her, of course. No one ever implied she was beautiful. Nothing like her vibrant mother. Caroline was simply Caroline. Dutiful, dependable Caroline.

Several minutes passed before she glanced back at him. He didn't appear to have looked away, and Caroline nervously pulled her straw bonnet lower to shade her face. "You speak often of the mountains, but I profess, sir, to see none. The land is as smooth and flat as the water upon a lake."

"Here, perhaps. But to the west there are hills and valleys as far as the eye can see."

"It sounds breathtaking."

"Breathtaking, yes. But the frontier is an unforgiving place. Not for the likes of some."

Caroline straightened her shoulders. "You mean me. Not for the likes of me, don't you?"

"Had I meant you, I would have said it." With that he urged his horse forward, leading the way as the path narrowed. To the right the thick stand of trees gave way to the murky waters of a swamp.

There were alligators in the swamps they'd passed near Charles Town, hiding amid the cordgrass, and Caroline wondered if the same strange creatures inhabited this area. She was both repulsed and intrigued by the long, scaled animals Raff described to her. Though she'd yet to spot one, she'd heard its low bellow.

She saw movement and almost called out to her companion. His words about Indian raids were still fresh in her mind. But when she shaded her eyes and looked more carefully, she discovered only a large turtle sunning on an up-jutting tree trunk.

As the horses plodded along, Caroline was left to ponder her feelings. She was frightened, of course. But not as deeply as she would have thought given the talk of Indian savagery. She watched a redtailed hawk circle overhead. Could it be that she was equal to this strange but beautiful land?

They stopped that night in the small hamlet of Congreve. Mistress Flannery was a much friendlier sort than Mistress Campbell was the previous night. She immediately took Caroline, who Raff

67

introduced simply as Caroline Simmons, under her wing.

"The Flannerys are good people who come from Ireland by way of Pennsylvania," he'd explained. "They have an Irishman's inborn distrust of the gentry."

So Caroline dropped her title, which wasn't difficult. She rarely thought of herself as anything other than Caroline Simmons. It was only knowing that her title was what Robert MacQuaid was after, or when his son sarcastically called her "Your Ladyship" that she remembered it at all.

The eight families living in the settlement decided that the arrival of Raff and Caroline was reason enough for celebration. Mistress Flannery—Jane, as she insisted Caroline call her—spread the word among the women that tonight they would eat a communal meal beneath the large sycamore that served as the village green.

Caroline snapped beans with the other women as the men built a large fire. She turned her stool toward Jane to keep herself from watching Raff. They chatted mostly of the children that ran about the area, and of Mistress Dabney's impending confinement.

"Third babe in as many years," Jane chided gently. And from the smile and blush that colored Betsy Dabney's cheeks Caroline guessed this was a frequent refrain.

Betsy leaned forward awkwardly over her rounded stomach to pull a fussing baby onto her nearly nonexistent lap. She handed him a bean which he immediately began to gum. "Sam and I like children," she said in a soft Irish brogue.

"If you be asking me, both of you are too fond of what it takes to *make* babies," Jane retorted. This brought a deeper shade of pink to Betsy's apple-round cheeks. But she didn't deny the allegation even when the other women, laughing, took up the refrain.

"Aye, and you have to say no every now and again to that brawny husband of yours."

"And who says 'tis Sam doing the persuin'? I've seen the two 'a them when they thought no one was about," Mistress Andrews, the oldest of the women said. "Betsy here cannot keep her eyes nor her hands off him."

This brought a fresh burst of laughter from the group as Betsy sat her now-content child back on a small patch of grass at her feet. Caroline assumed the woman was embarrassed; but when she looked up, there was a smile on her pretty face. "I do believe 'tis jealous you are, Mistress Andrews."

"Jealous?" The older woman seemed genuinely amazed. "I'm through with rollin' about in the bedstead and glad of it. I wager the rest 'a you feel the same if truth be known."

"I wouldn't be sayin' that." This from a redheaded woman with more sunspots than fair skin on her face. "There be times when Jacob and I have a fair to decent time 'rolling about in the bedstead.' "

This statement brought such laughter that Sam, the tall, brawny husband of Betsy, called over, "What's so funny over there?"

None of the women answered, but his wife made a shooing motion with her hand, and he went back to carrying benches from their cabin.

"Now that's what you need, Mistress Andrews," the redhead whispered with a nod of her curls. "That one would make anyone eager for the sun to set."

The other women, except for Mistress Andrews, readily agreed, and Caroline didn't need to look up to know whom they were talking about. But she did anyway, and followed their collective gaze to where Raff chopped wood. The ax lifted and the muscles in his arms glistened. The buckskin shirt stretched taut across his powerful back as the blade bit into the log, cleaving it. Caroline's mouth went dry.

"Listen to us talking like a passle of randy men. And with a maiden among us."

Jane's words filtered through to Caroline, and she turned back toward the women realizing they all stared at her. She smiled tentatively and resumed snapping beans, even when Mistress Andrew's eyes narrowed.

"Where'd you say you was off to?"

"Seven Pines."

"She's to marry Robert MacQuaid," Jane said in a flat tone that seemed to end the discussion.

Caroline sensed rather than heard any disapproval from the women, except for Mistress Andrews. She definitely made a disparaging noise, though Jane tried to cover the sound by bustling to her feet and announcing they had enough beans.

It wasn't until after dinner when Sam returned from his cabin with a violin that anyone spoke to Caroline except to ask her to pass the cornbread. "You mustn't mind Mistress Andrews," Jane said as she draped her arm around Caroline's shoulders. "She hasn't been the same since the Indians massacred her children."

The sun had set, and except for the low-riding moon, the only light came from the bonfire. Caroline watched the shadows dance across Jane's broad, open face for a moment before she could speak. "They killed her children?"

"Scalped them." Jane shook her head. "Finding your young ones like that 'twould do strange things to a body."

"When . . ." Caroline swallowed. "When did this happen?"

Jane tapped her foot to the sound of the lively tune Sam urged from the violin. " 'Twas years ago, in Pennsylvania, where we come from. The Iroquois." She shuddered. "They're animals. Not like the Cherokee . . . at least not like they used to be."

"What do you mean?" The children except for the older ones were abed. The fiddle music faded and off in the night Caroline heard the lonely cry of a wolf.

71

"There have been some raids. My man is worried, but then you know how men are. I can't believe the Cherokee would hurt us. I mean 'tis often they stop here to trade on their way to Charles Town. Still." She took a deep breath, her thin breast rising and falling beneath the worn flowered stomacher. "I remember what it was like up north, the French always inciting those heathens."

"Is that what's happening here?"

"What?" Jane seemed to pull herself from deep thought. "Nay," she finally said. "If we have Indian trouble here it won't be the Frenchies that cause it. 'Twill be our own fault. At least that's what my man says."

Before Caroline could ask what she meant, Jane's husband, John, came over and grabbed her hands, pulling her up to join the other couples for a reel. To the tune of "Lord Alvemarle's Delight" Jane and her husband joined hands and danced down the line.

Their garments might be rough and faded and their dance floor, trodden earth, but as Caroline clapped her hands, she realized these dancers were enjoying themselves as much as any she'd ever seen at her parents' balls. Perhaps more. Their laughter seemed to push out the boundaries of the small civilized settlement. It made Caroline more comfortable with her journey into the wilderness.

Until she spotted him.

Raff sat, leaning against the Flannerys' cabin. His sprawl was loose-limbed and lazy with long legs spread, arms crossed. He appeared relaxed and at ease . . . until she noticed his eyes. Even with the space separating them, she felt their intensity, dark and fiery, directed at her. Swirling skirts, dancing legs and wisps of smoke from the bonfire intermittently blocked her view of him. But whenever the way cleared, it was obvious his gaze hadn't moved. Neither had hers. Despite the distance, Caroline felt closer to him than she ever had.

The pull was undeniable, and powerful. She wanted to turn away, but couldn't. In her mind's eye she saw him coming to her, reaching down, pulling her to her feet. Touching her.

But he didn't move. Nor did she. When the last strains of the fiddle drifted out over the sea of trees enclosing them, Caroline realized she'd forgotten to breathe. She did so now with a gasp as Jane flopped down on the bench beside her.

"I declare," she laughed, fanning herself. "Dancing sure can wind a person. But look at you, sitting there as calm as can be, and you just come from England. Teach us a new step."

"Oh, I really don't know any," Caroline insisted, but Jane was not to be denied.

"Nonsense. You have two working feet don't you? John, partner Caroline; and mind, follow her lead."

Pulled up by two work-roughened hands, Caroline had no choice but to join the dancers. They all turned to her expectantly, waiting to see the latest dance step from across the sea . . . and she had no idea what to show them.

Her mind raced back to the last time she attended a ball. Attended was the wrong word. She and Edward had sneaked down from the nursery to watch her parents' guests in the ballroom. But that was before her mother died and before Papa sent them off to the country.

Still, though many years had passed, Caroline remembered forcing Ned to dance with her the next day as she hummed the tune learned the previous night. Even then, her brother's world centered about his books, but he gamely tried to follow her lead.

Now as Caroline looked at the expectant faces, she tried to remember the steps. Her glance strayed outside the ring of people, but now that she was the center of everyone else's attention, Raff seemed unaware of her. He was involved in a serious conversation with one of the men.

" 'Tis not new." Caroline pulled her focus back. "But 'tis always been one of my favorite dances. Mr. Dabney," she said, turning toward Betsy's husband. "Are you familiar with the tune 'Goddesses?' "

"Now let me see." Sam tucked the polished wood under his chin, sliding the bow down to play the first few bars. "That what you're talking about?"

"Yes, that's it." She faced John Flannery. "Now for this dance, we stand in two lines men facing women." She hesitated. "Do any of you know this dance?" To a person they shook their heads, so

74

Caroline continued. When they were set and she'd talked them through the instructions, John called to his wife.

"Come on over Jane, you've got to be learning this, too."

"I'll just watch," she said, though Caroline could tell the woman was dying to join the set.

"Come along, Jane." Caroline took her hand, pulling her into the spot to partner her husband as Sam Dabney began playing.

"But what about you?" Jane held on to Caroline's arm as she called to Raff. "You know how to do this dance?"

"Oh, I really don't think we need to disturb Mr. MacQuaid." Caroline pulled gently, trying to extricate herself from Jane's grasp. It did no good. Neither did her words.

"Disturb him," Jane laughed. "Why he's not doing anything, are you Raff?"

"Nothing as important as partnering a beautiful lady."

Caroline turned around to see him standing before her. She curtsied to his deep bow and accompanied him to the head of the line. The fire crackled, and Caroline's heart seemed to beat in time to the lively music.

Any doubts she had about Raff knowing the steps were put to rest when he took her hand, dancing her down the row. When they separated, she to lead the women, he the men, Caroline couldn't stop watching him. He had a natural grace as obvious on the dance floor as when he rode a horse. Even in his deerskin leggings and shirt he seemed as masculinely elegant as any silk-garbed duke.

When they passed close, right shoulder to right shoulder, he returned her smile. "You've done this before," she said.

"Perhaps a time or two."

The music forced them apart again; but through all the steps, Caroline could feel his gaze on her. She watched him, too, at first surreptitiously, then as the pace quickened, openly. The other dancers seemed to disappear, and it was only the two of them, meeting, touching, and pulling away, in a parody of life.

Caroline wasn't ready for the dance to end, for the loss of sensuality. The music stopped and the fantasy ended abruptly. Jane's plump arm circled her shoulders, turning her away.

"Now wasn't that more fun than sitting on the side?"

Caroline nodded, unable to trust her own voice. After dancing with Raff, Caroline could no longer deny the attraction she felt for him. It was real and strong, frighteningly so. All she could do was hope he never found out.

It took them three days to reach the fort at Ninety-Six. Raff left her to rest at the home of a widow named Alexandra Trevor while he went to confer with the military commander of the fort. To Caroline's delight, Mistress Trevor had a tub, which she allowed her to use.

"You'll have to be filling it yourself. My joints don't take to me carrying too much water."

"I'll do it gladly." Fetching water from the creek and heating it at the fireplace seemed a small price to pay for ridding herself of all the dirt from the trail.

She bathed quickly, worried that Raff would return at any moment. Besides, the sensual slide of the heated water across her skin reminded her too much of thoughts she was trying to suppress. Scrubbed and dressed in a clean shift, bodice and petticoat, Caroline felt like a new woman.

But apparently she didn't look like one. She was sitting by the fire, brushing her damp hair, when Raff entered the cabin. Caroline tried not to feel a stab of pique when he ignored her. "Mistress Trevor went to visit a neighbor."

"Hmmm." He paid no more heed to her words than he did her appearance. "I'd planned to let you rest here a day or two before continuing but that's not—"

"I don't need a rest. I'm perfectly capable of traveling more . . . now if you like."

"That anxious to reach your bridegroom, are you?" He glanced up then.

Caroline's back stiffened at his words. "It has nothing to do with that." Then when her eyes met his, Caroline's blood ran hotter than the fire at her back. She wanted him to notice her, but she wasn't prepared for the power of his gaze when he did. Her clothing was perfectly respectable. Caroline had noticed that most of the women on the frontier forsook the cumbersome overgown and simply wore a long sleeved shift, boned bodice and petticoat. She chose to dress the same, saving her gowns for more formal occasions than riding horseback through the wilderness.

But he made her feel as if she'd failed to cover herself at all. Yet she knew better, for her stays seemed so tight she could scarcely breathe. Her hand trembling, Caroline once again tugged the brush through her tangle of curls.

"Allow me, Your Ladyship."

Caroline hesitated, maintaining her grip when he reached for the silver handle. Was he mocking her with that cool smile on his sensual lips? But then his long, brown fingers folded over hers, and she was lost.

"If . . . if I don't brush through it as it dries, my hair becomes . . ." Caroline finished the statement with a nervous shrug of her shoulders.

"It appears we've already wasted too much time." Raff inched his hand beneath the thick fall of sunshine blond hair. His knuckles brushed her warm neck.

"I . . ." Caroline tried to calm the quiver in her voice. He stood behind her, his muscular thighs pressed against her back. "I never have been able to control it."

"Perhaps it is time you stopped trying so hard." Raff began at her scalp and pulled the bristles through the rough silk of her hair. Her head fell back, and he allowed his gaze to drift down the front of her neck to where the stays pushed her breasts into his view. Her skin was creamy smooth and he forced himself to look away. But he couldn't ignore the clean fragrance of her hair, or the feel of her curls as they wrapped about his fingers.

With each sweep of the brush, Caroline felt her resistance slipping away. She knew she should stop him, but she couldn't summon the energy to do it. Her body seemed to lack a will of its own, falling back against his hard body.

He smelled musky, and the blend of that and her clean soapy scent was an erotic harmony to the senses. Her skin tingled and her nipples ached, thrusting forward against the fine linen of her shift. Every time the brush skimmed down, his roughened fingers touched her. And every time she longed for the contact to continue, to expand.

Her hair crackled with electricity and still he brushed. But his movements slowed. And then as if he read her mind, his touch lingered. He traced an imaginary line down her neck till his hand spread across her chest. Caroline thought her heart would stop beating when one finger dipped to the valley between her breasts. Her head fell back and to the side. And the touch of his lips, hot and moist, on the side of her neck was not unexpected.

"Would you like me to braid it?" The words, spoken against her skin, vibrated through her.

"Wh . . . what?"

"Your hair." His knuckle rose up the side of one breast then the other, feeling them tighten before trailing his hand up to her chin. With his thumb he shifted her face to look at him. Her eyes were nearly as black as his, the blue a mere ring around the center. "Do you wish me to braid your hair, Lady Caroline?"

Caroline swallowed. "Can you? I mean . . . do you know how?"

"I'm Cherokee, Your Ladyship. There are times I even braid my own."

She reached up then, the thick black hair too hard to resist. "When? When do you tame these wild locks?"

"When hunting." Wolf knelt beside her. His lips were inches from hers. "To keep from getting myself tangled in the underbrush."

"That's wise." Caroline's fingers fanned over his chiseled cheek. He shifted forward, and she felt the anticipation of his breath across her face.

"Lady Caroline."

"Yes." The word was breathless.

There was the briefest contact, his lips to hers before he pulled away and stood. "Mistress Trevor is on her way home."

"How . . . how do you know?"

"Her dog barks."

Caroline listened, trying to hear over the blood

that pounded in her ears. As he said, the elderly woman's dog was yelping in the yard.

By the time the good widow pulled the drawstring to open the door, Caroline's hair was braided, and Raff was seated at the hand-hewn table cleaning his rifle.

Four

By the time they started northwest toward Fort Prince George the next morning, a cold mist was falling. And Caroline had savagely brushed out the braid and wound her hair up beneath the straw hat. The weather might be foggy, but her mind had cleared. At least enough to realize she was falling under the spell of her betrothed's son. And that she allowed him . . . nay wanted him to take liberties with her.

She'd spent the night tossing and turning, thinking of him asleep on a pallet by the hearth, wondering what she was to do. By daybreak as she listened to the soft patter of rain on the roof, Caroline came to the conclusion that she must reach Seven Pines in all haste. That's why when Raff suggested she might wish to stay at Ninety-Six till the weather cleared, her answer was an emphatic "no."

Thus Caroline was not only tired and stiff, but cold and wet as her mare plodded along the path behind Raff. He seemed not to mind the inclement conditions. His hair, free of its queue, hung past his broad shoulders. It seemed to Caroline that as they made their way deeper into the frontier, he lost layer upon layer of his civilized trappings.

Now she had no trouble recognizing him as an Indian. But the thought didn't frighten her. Instead she found this metamorphosis from gentleman to savage fascinating. And compelling.

Realizing the direction of her thoughts, Caroline concentrated upon Edward, wondering how he was doing and if he missed her as much as she missed him. She'd written a letter to him, adding a bit every night, and left it with the widow Trevor at Ninety-Six. The elderly woman promised to send it to Charles Town the first time someone went that way. From there it would sail across the Atlantic. With a sigh, Caroline acknowledged that her brother might not hear from her for months.

"Do you wish to stop?"

"What? No." Caroline insisted, waving him forward. "I'm fine, really." Whether or not he believed her, Raff turned around in his saddle and kept going. Caroline pulled the blanket he'd given her more tightly around her shoulders, and head down, followed.

Late in the afternoon, he urged his horse off the trail. After dismounting, Raff came back to help her from the sidesaddle.

"Why are we stopping?" The rain fell in earnest now and cold water drizzled down her neck.

"Perhaps you don't mind the weather, but I do. And I imagine the horses would prefer to be out of it."

"But where are we going?" It seemed as if he was leading them into the depths of the forest. Beneath her feet, pine needles cushioned her step while wet branches slapped against her face.

"There's a cabin up ahead," was all he said.

But he was wrong. Caroline stood in the clearing under a rainy grey sky, holding the reins of both horses. Raff poked about the burned out shell that formed the perimeter of the cabin. All that remained intact was a stone chimney. "What happened?"

"I don't know."

"Was it Indians?" Caroline asked, cautiously inching forward.

"Could have been." Though Raff saw no sign of a struggle . . . and no bodies. "Or lightning, or their own carelessness." Raff moved back to Caroline. There was little to salvage from the cabin. What wasn't burned was soaked.

"What are we going to do now?" As much as she dreaded being alone with Raff in a cabin, she looked forward to being warm and dry. It didn't look as if she'd get either. Especially when Raff nodded toward a crude lean-to affair that had obviously been used as a barn.

It was crowded since Raff insisted the horses and not particularly clean horses, wanted out of the wet, too. But even though the shake roof leaked,

Caroline decided it was better than standing in the rain. The fire Raff managed to start gave off more smoke than heat, but she reached toward it eagerly.

It made sense that they sat close together in the back corner, the only spot that was relatively dry.

"When we were in Charles Town," Caroline began, after swallowing a bite of dried beef. "I heard Governor Lyttleton call you something."

"Wa'ya."

"Yes, that was it." Caroline slanted him a look. "What does it mean?"

"Wolf. It is my Cherokee name. My English name as well." Her puzzled expression made him smile. "Raff means wolf . . . actually wolf councilor."

'Wa'ya." Caroline said the word slowly, drawing out the syllables. "And is that how you are known? Wa'ya MacQuaid?"

"Wa'ya or Wolf is enough. It is the name given to me by my mother. It shows I am from her clan." He didn't add it was also how he thought of himself.

When a damp darkness closed in upon them, it seemed natural to lie down side by side. There was no touching today except where his body spooned hers. The ground was hard beneath her hip yet Caroline fell asleep almost immediately.

It took Raff longer to find his rest. His arm folded around her, and he nuzzled the damp, clean-smelling hair. But he didn't have seduction on his mind. It was not yet time.

* * *

It made little sense considering the circumstances, but Caroline woke more refreshed than since she left Charles Town. The day was bright, but cooler, the kind of crisp weather that reminded her of England.

Little was said between them as they ate a simple fare of fire-roasted fish Raff caught in the creek behind the burned-out homestead.

They made good time through the pine forests and spent the following night at another settler's cabin.

"Don't know what happened to cause the fire," Patrick MacLaughlin said. "But the Clancys was long gone before it happened."

"Then it wasn't Indians." Caroline turned from the fireplace where she was helping Patrick's wife, Anne, by stirring the venison stew.

"Now I didn't say that. 'Twas the Indians that drove them off. Leastwise that's the way Mistress Clancy told Anne."

"She couldn't live here worrying about them all the time." Anne looked up from nursing her youngest child.

"But I understood the Cherokee and the English settlers were allies." Caroline's gaze shifted to Raff.

"They are . . . for the most part." Anne shifted the babe to her other breast. "But you just never know."

"Besides," her husband added. "It's not just the

Cherokee that needs watching. Other Indians use this land as a roadway up north. The Creeks. Chickasaw."

"I suppose they figure it was their land before it belonged to the English."

"Now don't go taken on, Raff. You know I don't mean nothing by what I said." Patrick tamped tobacco into a pipe bowl. "I was just telling this here lady friend of yours how things are."

"And I appreciate it, Mr. MacLaughlin." Caroline ladled the savory stew into earthenware bowls.

"Course, I'm convinced things is gonna get worse before they get better."

"Patrick." Anne gave her husband a pointed look.

"Now Annie, I'm not sayin' a thing, Raff here don't already know. And I'm sure as we're sittin' here that he weren't in on any of them raids." He bent toward the fire and used a splinter of wood to light his pipe. He took a few puffs before continuing. "Word is that the Headmen are saying the whole thing is a mistake." After taking the chewed end from his mouth, he pointed the pipe toward Raff. "But I hear tell them Indians was allowed to dance around with them scalps."

Raff was angry, so angry Caroline noticed the way his hands clenched into fists. But he didn't say anything to repudiate Patrick MacLaughlin's words and the meal continued. But the next day as she and Raff stopped to water their mounts by the side of a fast running river, Caroline questioned him about it.

"What would you have me say?"

"I don't know." Caroline stripped leaves from a willow branch. *"Did* the Cherokee dance about with settlers' scalps?"

"It's possible." Wolf cupped his hands, drinking deeply of the crystal water. Then he glanced up, shaking his head at her expression. "Does that bother your sensibilities?"

"Of course." Caroline stepped closer. "Don't you find it repulsive?"

When he pushed to his feet to tower over her, Caroline wasn't sure what he would say. He looked at her a moment, then moved to gather the horses' reins. "Scalps are taken by the settlers as well as the Indians. It's not as one-sided as it seems."

"Then pray tell me of your side," Caroline said, for she truly wished to understand the new land that was to be her home. As usual she was unprepared for the intensity of the look he cast her way.

"My side," he said. *"I* have no side. Or perhaps I have two sides."

"I meant nothing by my choice of words." Caroline moved toward the river and looked out over the land on the far shore. No longer was the landscape flat. Now an occasional rolling hill pleased the eye.

"You wish neat, tidy answers, Your Ladyship, preferably showing the Indian as villain." Wolf glanced over his shoulder toward her. "I cannot give that to you."

"As I recall, I asked to know the source behind the trouble. 'Tis not vindication for the English I desire." She lifted her face to follow the gliding path of an eagle. "And I wish you wouldn't call me that."

His brow arched as he turned toward her. "But that's what you are. Lady Caroline Simmons, daughter of an earl, peer of the realm."

Caroline met his stare. Her nostrils flared as she breathed deeply of the cool air and ignored the angry set of his jaw. "I prefer in this place to think of myself as Caroline Simmons."

"Soon to be Caroline MacQuaid."

"Yes . . ." Her voice was low. "Soon to be Caroline MacQuaid."

Wolf took a deep breath, trying to quell the tempest that boiled within him. "You realize, of course, this *marriage* takes place only because you are the daughter of an earl." His mount pranced to the side, and Wolf sidestepped to avoid the hooves. But he never took his eyes from Caroline's face.

"I am aware of why your father offered for me," she said as calmly as she could. He was purposely trying to hurt her. And though she'd long since accepted the reality of her marriage, the knowledge that Raff disliked her enough to hurt her was painful. Especially when there were times he could be so . . . Caroline scooped a leaf off the ground, and slowly examined its toothed edges.

Wolf turned back to the horses, pulling them toward the road.

"You still haven't answered my question."

"Perhaps I have no wish to."

Caroline stepped in front of him when he would have brushed by her. "And perhaps I have a right to know. It was your father who brought me here."

He turned on her so quickly, cupping her shoulders in his large hands that Caroline gasped. "Never make the mistake of holding me responsible for my father's actions, or him for mine."

The horses, left untethered wandered toward a patch of grass. The river gurgled, its sound a sweet symphony of the wild. But Caroline noticed none of that. Her senses were overwhelmed by the man before her. By the power of his eyes. The secrets they held.

Her breathing was shallow, and she tried to control it before she spoke. "You really do hate him, don't you?" He said nothing, just continued to hold her prisoner with his dark eyes, and Caroline continued. "Rebecca told me you did, but I didn't want to believe her." Caroline didn't add that she didn't want to believe it because of what else the girl said. *He will hate you, too.*

"Believe what you will." Wolf released his grip on her and dropped his hands. "You say you want to understand the Cherokee." He laughed then, a deep, humorless sound that made Caroline shiver.

"You who are English and the daughter of an earl. Well understand this. Murder must be avenged . . . to restore the order of the universe. It is the Cherokee way. It is the English way," he added with a slight lift of his brow.

"Are you saying the Cherokee attacked settlers in Virginia to seek justice?" Caroline lifted her hands toward him. "For what? When did it start?"

"I did not realize Your Ladyship was a student of history."

Caroline's spine stiffened at the sarcasm in his tone. "I simply wish to understand."

"But Caroline, there is no 'simply' about it." He took a deep breath that expanded his chest. "Laws of the nations—the Cherokee, the English—run deep, nearly as deep as their rivalries. The Cherokee agreed to fight the Shawnee not so much because they were allies of the French, and thus England's enemies, but because of hatred of the tribe. But my people did not expect to be set upon by English colonists or to have their scalps exchanged for bounty by Virginia's governor."

Caroline stared up at him and swallowed. "Did that happen?"

"Yes." Wolf turned away.

"But why weren't those people punished, surely English law—"

"Applies to the English, Caroline." Wolf glanced over his shoulder as he gathered the horses. She stood as if rooted to the spot, her brow wrinkled as she tried to understand. Wolf shook his head.

"The warriors were on their way back from fighting the Shawnee when they lost all their supplies. They were starving. They killed some cattle they found on open range. Cattle that belonged to the settlers. The warriors were set upon and massacred. Governor Dinwiddie sent an apology to the Cherokee Headmen. But in it he emphasized the warriors' crimes against the Virginians."

He led the horses onto the trail and Caroline lifted her skirts and scurried after him. "But it seems to me," she said when she caught up, "that these are misunderstandings. Tragic, yes, but surely something that can be resolved if reasonable people on both sides—"

"Ah, but each side thinks theirs is the only reasonable position—"

Caroline's hand reached up to his cheek. She could not help herself. "And you are caught in the middle."

She thought he might kiss her then. And despite her earlier resolve to keep her distance, she wanted him to. Could almost taste him. But the passion that blazed in his eyes was soon shadowed. His sensual mouth curled at the edges. "Are you trying to mother me again, Lady Caroline?"

"No," she whispered and dropped her hand. But the feel of his skin, roughened by a day's growth of dark whiskers, stayed with her as they rode toward the fort.

* * *

Fort Prince George on the shores of the Savannah River, was nearly within shouting distance of the Cherokee Town of Keowee. Caroline's prodding elicited a history of the fort from Wolf.

"When the Cherokee agreed to send warriors to fight the Shawnee near the Ohio River, the stockade was built to protect their families." Wolf glanced over at Caroline as they sat on horseback looking down at the log fort. "They also constructed Fort Loudoun at the confluence of the Little Tennessee and Tellico Rivers and another in Virginia."

"Did the Cherokee want them built?" Caroline couldn't tell from his expression if he thought so or not.

"I suppose they did, though the cost was the service of Cherokee warriors to fight England's enemies. The treaty also called for many acres of land to be given to the English, and it strengthened trade agreements."

"This must have pleased your father." Caroline realized her mistake of bringing up her betrothed as soon as she saw Wolf's face. "I mean he is a trader."

"Yes." His succinct reply ended their conversation.

They stayed at the fort only long enough to rest their horses and for Raff to speak with the English commander, a man named Boyton. To the young officer's suggestion that they spend the evening, Wolf responded that he wished to ford the river before dark. "But I'm sure Lady Caroline would be better served by waiting till morning." Colonel Boyton smiled at Caroline appealingly.

"Lady Caroline is anxious to reach her new home . . . and her new husband."

The last was spoken so low and private that Caroline wasn't sure the fort commander heard it. But she did, and Caroline felt heated color rise to her cheeks. There was but one reason she wished this journey to end.

On their journey thus far they had forded waterways, but those paled in comparison to this one. Caroline looked down the slope to the swiftly rushing water and swallowed. Beneath her the mare pranced and pawed as if she shared Caroline's trepidation. But the trail to Seven Pines ended where the water gurgled onto the rocky shoreline and didn't pick up again till the other side.

Caroline wrapped the reins about her hands. "How deep is it?"

"Chances are you'll get your fancy boots wet, Your Ladyship."

Caroline ignored the sarcasm. The sound of rushing water filled her senses. "I've never done anything like this before," she called down to him. He'd dismounted and was leading her horse down the muddy path to the river.

"That doesn't surprise me. In England there'd be a bridge to cross."

Caroline leaned back to keep her balance. "Why don't they build one here?" She was almost willing to wait until one was completed.

"You're on the frontier now, Lady Caroline." Wolf swung back into his saddle and urged his horse across the potato-sized rocks that lined the shore. "Just keep behind me."

"But—"

Wolf twisted about to look at her, and Caroline realized how desperate her tone was. She tried to calm her breathing but the dark, swirling waters kept drawing her gaze. "There was a spring. I fell in." Caroline's fingers tightened about the leather. "If not for Edward . . ." She couldn't continue. The emotions, the fear she'd experienced swelled over her as quickly as that icy water of her childhood.

Caroline looked up, her eyes large and dry when she felt his hand enfolding hers. "Do you wish to go back?" He took a deep breath. "You can wait at the fort while I go to the Cherokee Towns. Then I shall see you safely to Charles Town."

She was tempted, almost beyond reason. To go back to the peace of Simmons Hall, with its well-manicured trees and gently flowing streams, nothing at all like this wild, virgin land. But as much as her fear threatened to overpower her, there was something about this place, maybe even the very untamed beauty that frightened her, that drew her under its spell. That, even more than the fact that she had nothing to return to, made Caroline shake her head.

"No," she said, her voice trembling slightly. "I can do it." She straightened her shoulders and gave him a weak smile.

"You are sure?"

"Yes."

"Very well then." Wolf sucked in a breath and sidled his mount along hers. With a fluid motion he slipped behind his saddle and straddled the stallion's broad rump. Then he reached for her.

"What are you doing?"

"I think, Lady Caroline, that it's time you learned to ride astride."

"But—"

"Hush now. Release your foot from the stirrup."

She did, and his hands clasped about her waist. Caroline was pulled across her saddle and onto his. He held her there a moment, her shoulder leaning into his chest before instructing her.

"Now lift your leg over." His hand wrapped about her thigh. "That's it." He settled her back into the saddle, pulling plain, white petticoats down over her exposed leg. "I know it feels a bit strange, but you'll get used to riding this way." His arms enveloped her from behind. "You may even learn to enjoy it." Without further ado, he tied the mare's reins to the saddle, shifted his rifle and powderhorn higher on his shoulders, and urged both mounts into the rushing water.

At first Caroline shut her eyes, too afraid to

look. But gradually as she felt the warmth of his body surrounding her, she opened them. His corded muscles were hard against her sides as he held the reins, keeping the horse on track when the stallion would have given into the force of the current.

The water that at first only covered her feet now splashed into her lap. But they kept going toward the wall of trees on the other side, and the immobilizing panic that Caroline expected didn't come.

Instead, when he whispered, "The worst is over," into her ear she felt herself relax. And begin to enjoy the adventure. She was shivering uncontrollably from the icy water, but laughing as their mount found his footing on the shore.

Wolf slipped from the stallion's back and reached up for her. With her hands resting on his shoulders, Caroline went willingly. She didn't resist when he pulled her to him. "We did it," she exclaimed, wrapping her arms around his neck. His hair was as wet as hers, and she tangled her fingers in the thick locks.

When he separated their bodies enough to see her face, his smile matched hers. "There's someplace near where we can rest for the night."

"But I thought we would reach Seven Pines by tonight." He had said as much when they were at the fort.

"Are you so anxious to end the journey?"

"No," Caroline admitted, though she added, "I

suppose 'twouldn't be proper to arrive with our clothes soaking wet."

His smile was all the more enchanting because it was brief. "We must do what is proper." The cocoon of his arms dropped away. "Come along, Lady Caroline," he said, leading her to her horse.

They rode for only a short time. The air carried a hint of autumn and Caroline was shivering. When Wolf slid from his horse, Caroline looked around her in surprise. She could see no reason why they stopped.

"We'll walk from here on," he said after helping her dismount. He led them onto a footpath she hadn't noticed from the road.

The way was not easy. Wolf took charge of the horses, leaving Caroline to lift up her skirts and follow behind. She was breathless when she stumbled into the large clearing. In the middle was a cabin, small and covered with bark. Between that and the neat garden curved a wide, shallow creek. Raff led the horses to the edge and began removing one of the saddles.

"Go inside," he told her. "I shall be in directly with wood for a fire."

The thought of warmth was wonderful, but Caroline hesitated. "Won't the people who live here mind us using the cabin?" It was obvious that no one was there. But she was just as certain that the homestead was not deserted. The garden looked recently weeded and ready to harvest.

"It is fine, Caroline." He looked up from his

work when she still hesitated. "You will find blankets to warm yourself."

The door opened easily. When Caroline closed it behind her she cut off the main source of light for the cabin's windows were small, no more than slits in the stick and wattle walls. Small ribbons of dust-laden sunlight streamed into the interior.

Few pieces of furniture cluttered the small room. The bed consisted of a neat pile of furs in the back corner. Clothing was hung from pegs, branches really, dried into the mud mortar. Use of the space was efficient, and Caroline wondered who lived here.

She walked across the brushed dirt floor to the only chair, a handmade affair, smooth and polished in the seat and arms, with the legs left barkcovered. Beside it was a table of similar design that held a candlestick and several books. Caroline picked one up and squinted to read the title.

"Voltaire," said the voice behind her and Caroline whirled around to see Wolf silhouetted in the doorway. "Do you enjoy him?"

"A . . . no, not really." Caroline replaced the book on the pile, embarrassed to be caught snooping.

He seemed to ignore her discomfort as he dropped the split logs near the simple stone fireplace and began building a fire. "The blankets are back there." His dark hair swayed around his shoulders when he motioned with his chin toward the back corner. "But I suggest you take off those wet clothes before wrapping yourself in one."

"Take . . . take off my clothes?" Caroline sounded as if she never heard of the concept.

Wolf paused in his labors and twisted around to look at her. "Stay as you are and you'll catch a chill."

He spoke in a no-nonsense way that reinforced the soundness of his message. Still . . . " 'Tis rather unseemly."

"So is dying of the fever." Wolf turned back to building the fire, coaxing the tiny flame by blowing on the dried leaves.

Caroline picked up a blanket of tightly woven wool. "I still don't know. What if the owners should return? What would they think?" It wasn't the owners she worried about, but that seemed as good an argument as any. His next words squelched it.

As the flames licked up about a chunk of wood, he stood. With barely a glance in her direction he headed for the door. "This is my home." He reached for a rope-handled bucket hanging from a peg beside the door before turning.

His eyes met hers and in the orange glow from the fire, Caroline imagined they saw through her excuses and found them childish and lacking.

"I am going for water. You do as you please, Your Ladyship." He grabbed up the long rifle he'd leaned against the wall and left the cabin.

It wasn't indecision but cold fingers and wet clothing that slowed Caroline's movements. Her first instinct was to keep on her shift, but it was cold and clammy next to her skin so she removed that as well. The blanket was large, covering her

100

completely from head to toe. That didn't stop the blush that seeped up her face when he reentered the cabin. But he seemed to pay little heed to her nakedness beneath the blanket.

She, on the other hand, could think of nothing else.

He made no comment as he poured some of the water into a large iron kettle that hung over the fire. Then he pulled a knife from his leggings and stripped off slices of a beef that hung from the rafter. He left again to return with potatoes and beans in a small woven basket.

"I can do that," Caroline said when he began snapping the beans.

His only response was an arched brow. But he allowed her to take the basket. It was difficult peeling the potatoes. The knife was heavy and very large, and Caroline had to be careful the blanket didn't slip open. She was relieved when he left the cabin again to return with the saddlebags stuffed with her belongings. However those clothes were damp, too.

"I'm surprised that you live here." Caroline hoped conversation would help alleviate her uneasiness. He was hanging her clothing from the pegs on the walls. "I assumed you lived with your father." She quartered a potato.

"No."

"Oh, well, I see that now." Caroline glanced around. "What are you doing?" Her voice rose, till the last word was nearly a shriek.

101

"Changing from my wet clothes."

"But I . . . I . . . ."

"If you do not wish to see, Caroline, don't look."

Embarrassed, because that was exactly what she'd been doing, staring at his broad, muscled chest, at the fascinating design of tattoos spanning him from shoulder to shoulder, Caroline spun around. She clutched at the blanket she'd let slip and felt foolish. Even more so when he touched her arm and she jumped.

"You needn't be afraid. I won't hurt you."

"I . . . I know that." She refused to turn toward him even when he held out a shirt of soft cotton.

"You might be more comfortable in this till your clothing dries. At least you won't have to hold it shut."

"Thank you." Caroline reached for the shirt. It matched the one he'd donned, white, and loose fitting. He wore his over leggings. But she supposed it would be long enough on her to forgo anything but the blanket, which she planned to keep wrapped about her till she left here for Seven Pines.

Wolf offered to finish cutting the vegetables and to keep his eyes forward as she changed. And she trusted him to do as he said. But that didn't really help. Because it was herself she didn't trust.

Five

"The stew is delicious." Caroline took another spoonful of the rich broth and glanced at Raff across the small table. He'd cleared away the books, and candle, and seated Caroline in the only chair. He sat on the lid of a wooden sea chest.

"Is something wrong?"

"No, what makes you think so?" Caroline responded quickly . . . too quickly she thought to herself.

"It is the third time in as many minutes you've commented upon the stew."

"Has it been that many?" Caroline's attention was focused on the folded hands in her lap.

"Yes it has."

She tried not to look up, but in the end she had no choice. His eyes were on her as she knew they would be, strong and intense. They held hers as if she had no will of her own. Caroline wet her lips, wondering why swallowing was suddenly so difficult. "Perhaps I am very fond of it . . . the stew," she clarified, feeling a rush of heat that had naught to do with the fire behind him. The fire that seemed to outline his body with a red glow.

"Perhaps you are."

His smile was impossible to resist. Caroline was fast learning that was true of so much about him. But that didn't mean she needn't try. She searched her mind for something to say . . . something other than a comment upon the stew.

She cleared her throat. "You must enjoy reading."

"Does that surprise you?"

"No. Why should it?" she added when he raised his raven brow. He shrugged and Caroline's eyes were drawn to the breadth of his shoulders, the open neck of his shirt. His skin looked dark and mysterious against the snow white cotton.

"It might seem incongruous to some—a savage who reads Voltaire."

"It might." Caroline took a sip of the tea he'd brewed. "But then, you forget, I saw you in Charles Town."

"The ability to wear a waistcoat and draw my hair back in a queue makes me no less an Indian."

"I never said it did." Looking at him now Caroline could no more deny the wild blood that coursed through his veins as fool herself into believing it didn't draw her to him. Dark and dangerous. Caroline's pulse raced.

Very dangerous.

She bent forward and plucked the top book off

the pile beside her feet. After examining the title she traced gold embossing with her fingertip. "Neddy admires David Hume. He used to read him then insist upon explaining his philosophies to me." Her smile faded. "I miss him very much." Caroline lifted her gaze to meet his. "But then you must understand. You have a brother."

"Ah, so Ned is your brother?"

"Of course. Edward. Who did you think he was?"

He leaned forward, his elbows on the table, amusement shining in his obsidian eyes. "A lover perhaps. Some young swain you deserted to come sailing to the New World."

"You're teasing."

"No, I'm not. When you mentioned Edward before . . ." Wolf sat back and folded his arms. "Well, that is what I thought."

Caroline shook her head. She could feel heated color in her cheeks. "I left no broken hearts behind." Rising from the chair, she gathered the empty pottery bowls and carried them to the bucket near the hearth.

"Do you need more water?" Wolf turned his head to follow her movements before standing and throwing more wood on the fire.

"No, 'tis fine." She angled her face toward him. "Tell me of your brother."

Wolf sank onto the floor beside her, reaching for the bowl she just washed. He dried it with a linen towel. "What do you wish to know?"

Lifting her shoulders, Caroline plunged her hands back into the warm water. Perhaps if she kept her mind occupied with conversation she wouldn't be so aware of him . . . of how near he was. "What is he like?"

"Are you asking if he is Cherokee?"

" 'Twasn't what I meant."

"Wasn't it?" Wolf leaned against the wall, one leg bent, his forearm resting on his knee, and watched her for a moment before continuing. "Logan's blood is pure. He was born of Robert's second wife. There was an older son also, born in Scotland, I believe. That is where Robert's first wife lived."

Caroline dried her hands. "I didn't realize I was to be . . . I mean that your father was married thrice before."

"He wasn't."

"But you just said—"

"There are men who marry their Cherokee mistresses, Your Ladyship. Robert MacQuaid is not one of them."

Realization of what he was saying came quickly. Caroline could feel the hurt and pain in his words and wanted to reach out to him. Wanted to so badly that she folded her hands to stop herself. She was beginning to understand why Wolf disliked his father. *She* was beginning to feel the same way.

"Logan is fighting to the north with the militia. I'm sure his wife will enjoy your company." When she said nothing, only stared at him with those large blue eyes, Wolf continued. "Logan's wife, Mary, lives at Seven Pines."

"I see." Caroline dried her hands. "You mentioned another brother."

"James. But I wouldn't mention his name if I were you."

"Why, pray tell?"

"From what I understand he was hanged for his part in supporting the Young Pretender."

"Oh, how awful. Your father must have been heartbroken."

"Actually, I believe Robert had declared the boy dead to him years before."

Caroline settled on the trunk lid facing Raff. "What of you?"

His dark brow arched. "What about me?"

She knew she was asking too many questions, but she couldn't seem to help herself. Everything about Raff MacQuaid fascinated her. "Tell me of your childhood."

"I lived with my mother's people. It is the Cherokee way." His fingers tightened into a fist. "Until my tenth year."

"What happened then?" Caroline moved onto the floor beside him.

"Then my father decided there was enough of his blood flowing through my body to warrant spending a few pounds on me. I was sent to England for schooling."

"It must have been difficult being torn away from all you knew . . . from those that loved you."

"It was hard for my mother," was all he said before changing the subject. It was not her pity he sought. Wolf leaned toward her. "You're shivering. Are you cold?"

"Not really." Before she could stop him, he'd reached across her and dragged another blanket over her lap. She already wore one wrapped around her waist. That and his shirt made up her apparel. "Perhaps my clothes are dry."

"I don't think so," he said as he tucked the blanket around her. His fingers brushed across her cheek. "Is that better?"

Caroline nodded, afraid to trust her voice. But it hadn't been the cold that made her tremble, and as he leaned over, staring at her, Caroline had the feeling he knew it.

When he picked up his rifle and left the cabin to look after the horses, Caroline rushed for the clothes hanging from the pegs. He was right. Her petticoats were still damp, but she didn't care. She whipped off the shirt, wishing the smell of it, so like him, didn't do strange things to her insides. The shift was just sliding over her body when the chill made her skin prickle.

Her pale-as-moonlight curls swung across her shoulders as she jerked her head around. Wolf stood in the open doorway.

The sight of him there, watching her, his eyes dark and sensual, was paralyzing. It seemed an

108

eternity till he reached behind him, leaned the rifle against the wall and shut the door. An eternity punctuated by the rapid beating of Caroline's heart.

She knew he'd seen her, was still seeing more than propriety allowed. Yet she couldn't summon the energy to do more than turn to face him as he moved toward her.

The ribbons that held the neck line of her shift together draped across her breasts, untied. With each breath, she could feel the soft linen spreading, revealing more of her flesh to him. Flesh that felt more fevered the nearer he came.

The cabin was small, his pace slow and deliberate. Each step he took accentuated his animal grace and power. Heightened the anticipation. His gaze stoked a blaze hotter than the one in the hearth.

When he was so close that Caroline had to tilt her head to see his face, he stopped. She knew she should turn away, to make some effort to cover herself. After all, her shift was old and threadbare. But he overwhelmed her . . . his towering height, the broad strength of his body, his musky scent. The dark intensity of his eyes.

He drew her to him with a force she couldn't begin to understand. And couldn't continue to fight. It was as if he sapped all reason, all notion of right and wrong from her body. With his first touch, a gentle cupping of her cheek, she was lost.

Caroline's eyelids fluttered shut, her lashes

forming a dusky shadow on her fair skin. His palms were weather-callused, but the contrast of soft and rough sparked a need in her to feel more.

On a moan her head turned into his hand. Her lips brushed his palm, tasted the saltiness of his skin. Wanted more.

Caroline's knees nearly buckled when he kissed the long exposed side of her neck. The feel of his firm lips and tongue in concert with the feathering of his hair across her skin sent tingles dancing down her spine. By the time he bit and caressed his way to her shoulder, Caroline writhed with the need to feel the imprint of his hard muscles against her.

But he held himself apart, touching her only with the palm of his hand and his mouth. Then his chin, whisker-roughened and firm nudged at the ruffled linen hanging precariously from her shoulder. Slowly the shift lost its hold, slipping sensually down to catch on the distended tip of her breast.

His fingers trailed down her neck to work the same magic on the other shoulder. Then he lifted his head, his eyes like smoldering coals, and looked at her as, with a flick of his thumbs, he released the shift. The linen drifted to the packed earth floor on a whisper of air, leaving Caroline completely naked and vulnerable to his hungry gaze.

She waited for the embarrassment to overwhelm her, after all, no one had ever seen her like this. But it didn't come, not even when he made no attempt to disguise his thorough scrutiny of her body. She could feel the heat as his gaze slowly traveled down her neck, resting briefly on her breasts, then down her stomach to the delta of tight curls at the apex of her legs.

When his eyes again met hers she let out a trembling breath.

"You're beautiful."

If Caroline heard a hint of surprise in his acknowledgement, it didn't make it sound any less flattering. But Caroline was beyond caring. For once in her life she was doing as she wished, not thinking of the effect it would have on others. She sucked in her breath as his fingers skimmed across her nipples, then moaned aloud when the moist heat of his mouth covered one swollen tip. His tongue tormented the fevered flesh till Caroline reached up, digging her fingers through his coarse hair.

When he dropped to his knees in front of her, leaving her breast wet and shimmering in the firelight, Caroline's legs gave way. If not for the strength of his large hands cupping her buttocks and the pressure of lips and chin against her stomach she would have fallen.

As it was she could barely stand the pleasure, so intense it bordered on pain. Below his chin an ache began. A knot that tightened.

She cried out when his long fingers inched between her legs from behind, urging her to open for him.

"Shhh." The sound whispered air across the pale hair guarding her womanhood. "I won't hurt you."

But she couldn't be quiet. Not when the tip of his tongue touched her. The knot tightened unbearably, then exploded, leaving her body wracked with wave upon wave of pulsating ecstasy.

Her fingers opened and closed, clutching first his hair, then the bunched fabric of his shirt. Her lips grew slack and her head lolled from side to side as the shivers skidded through her. She soared free like the winged hawks, circling high in the sky, then slowly, sensually slid back toward earth.

But before she landed Caroline found herself lifted again, this time by strong arms. Faintness overcame her and she clung to him, collapsing against his chest. When he lowered her to the bearskin, her arms lingered about his neck, pulling him down with her.

The kiss was deep and carnal, like nothing she ever imagined existed. And it fanned anew the spark of desire left tamped but smoldering beneath the surface.

Her hands tore at his shirt, pushing the cotton off his broad shoulders, reveling in the feel of his hot skin. And all the while he kissed her, feasting upon her lips, plunging his tongue to the deepest recesses of her mouth. His fingers dug through her hair, framing her face, holding her head still for his onslaught.

But her body would obey no civilized rules of

112

conduct. Beneath his weight she wriggled and writhed, rubbing against him. Uncontrollable.

A muscle-corded thigh straddled her waist. Pulling away, he savagely jerked the shirt over his head, tossing it across the room. His leggings were next. Firelight sent wild shadows dancing across his smooth skin as he bent back toward her. Then she felt his weight, the heat of his body, as he lay in the cradle of hers.

Raising onto his elbows Wolf studied her face for a moment before again attacking her mouth with his. "This may hurt." He whispered the words into her hair, but he doubted she heard him. He doubted she was aware of much but the consuming passion that shined in her light eyes.

His hips spread her thighs. He was hard and aching, had been since he walked in on her while she changed her clothes. Yet he hesitated. Was it conscience that kept him poised so near he could feel the heat radiating from her? Wolf didn't know. But he couldn't deny the doubts about doing this . . . to her.

"Please, oh, please," she begged, her voice barely more than a sob. Caroline didn't know what it was she wanted, but her body was as tense as before. She knew there had to be something he could do to relieve the savage hunger. Her body slid lower.

The control he'd worked hard to keep slipped as her moist heat skimmed the tip of his manhood. He thrust. Gently at first, then when he encoun-

113

tered the delicate barrier, more strongly. She made a low whimpering sound when he rent her maidenhood, and Wolf froze.

"Hush now, *Agehyaguga*. It is the way of men and women." He bent down and kissed her moist lips. "But only the first time, I swear it."

She looked up at him wide-eyed . . . trustingly. A hint of a smile was obviously to make him feel better for the pain he caused. It didn't. But Wolf soon forgot all but his desire to bury himself inside her. She lifted her hips in an instinctive move that made him surge forward.

Deeper and deeper he went, losing all thought, everything but the desire to mate with her. Each driving thrust was more powerful than the last. His pace quickened, and beneath the consuming passion was the knowledge that she met each sensual stroke, and reveled in them.

Instinct told him when she neared her release. Her body stiffened, and her breathing came in short, shallow gasps. He plunged again as she tensed, waiting till she jolted, her fingers digging into his back before allowing his own searing release.

When Caroline regained her senses enough to open her eyes, she found him staring down at her, his expression dark . . . unreadable. Her heart raced and she didn't know if she'd ever stop trembling. Still she smiled. He didn't return the gesture.

Instead his brows lowered in a frown. "I'm

114

sorry," was all he said, but it was his tone that made Caroline's skin prickle.

" 'Tis nothing to apologize for. There really wasn't much pain."

He levered himself off her, rolling to the side, his arm thrown across his eyes. "I'm glad," he finally said. Without looking at her, he drew a blanket up over them. "It is time we went to sleep."

But slumber came to him no easier than to her. Wolf lay on his back staring at the flickering shadows on the low rafters, knowing she did the same. God, he should say something else to her . . . something soothing and sweet. Something to take the sting from his actions.

But he could think of no words that would erase the deed. Nothing to soften the blow of taking her virginity. And he could not stop thinking of how good it felt to make love to her. He wasn't supposed to enjoy it so much. Nor was she, he thought ruthlessly. Revenge was not to be tainted by pleasure.

"Raff."

His name, though barely whispered in the half-light, made his body tense.

"Are you still awake?"

"Yes." Reluctantly he rolled his head to look at her. She stared at the ceiling, her profile clean and beautiful. Wolf took a deep breath. "Did you wish something?"

There was a slight hesitation then he heard the movement of her hair against the bear fur as she shook her head. " 'Tis nothing really."

115

He should leave it at that. Leave her to think what she may. In the long run that might be easier on her. But Wolf found it impossible to lie there, the distance between them farther than the span of an arm separating their bodies.

Telling himself he'd do as much for a whore who'd sold her body, Wolf reached out. His expression was grave as he gathered her into his arms.

She came without question, snuggling onto his shoulder, molding her small frame against his body . . . fitting perfectly. Wolf shut his eyes and silently cursed his father. If only the old man weren't such a bastard. If he hadn't cheated and lied to the Cherokee. If he hadn't lied to Wolf's mother, and hurt her. If he hadn't sent to England for Lady Caroline Simmons. God, if he just hadn't done any of those things.

"Is something amiss?"

"No." Wolf answered too quickly. He could feel her eyes on him, but didn't turn his head to face her. "What makes you ask?"

"I don't know. You seem . . ." Caroline couldn't imagine what made her so bold. But then nothing she'd done this night was like her.

"Tired is what I am," Wolf finished for her. "Now go to sleep, Caroline."

But despite his words, slumber was a long time coming to Wolf. He lay, her sleeping body in his arms, and he tried not to think.

He must have finally dozed for he awoke near dawn. Woke from an erotic dream to find it wasn't

116

entirely a product of his imagination. She'd shifted during the night and now one of her long, creamy smooth legs rested over his thigh, inches from his aching manhood. Her arm was flung across his waist, her cheek against his chest. And God he wanted her.

But revenge against his father was met.

If he took her again it would have naught to do with avenging his mother. And everything to do with desire.

The battle within him was short-lived and lost before it began.

His hand followed the curve of her hip, the gentle slope of her bottom. When his fingers skimmed down to her womanhood, he found her already hot and moist . . . perhaps she shared the dream that just woke him.

But she wasn't dreaming when she raised her leg higher giving him better access to her heat, or when she moaned, a deep, sensual sound that made him throb.

"Are you sore?" He had a firm enough grip on reality to ask that.

"Nay." There was a catch in her voice as his finger entered her. "What you do to me, it feels . . ."

"What?" Wolf rolled so he could look down at her, his hand still cupping her body. "How does it feel?"

"Wonderful," she breathed. "You make me feel wonderful."

She breathed the last word into his mouth as his lips crushed down on hers. She opened for him and his tongue found the sweet haven, its rhythm the same as his finger.

Her body tightened almost immediately. More responsive than any woman he'd ever known. He lifted his head, watching her in the soft pewtery light as she rode the waves of ecstasy. Satisfied for the moment to give her pleasure. To see the pearly skin flush, her small, ruched, rose-colored nipples, reach out to him. He tasted one, then the other as she drifted back to earth.

"Mmmm, wonderful," she whispered and Wolf chuckled, the sound vibrating against her stomach.

When she could summon the strength, Caroline lifted herself up on her elbows. The sight of his dark head resting on her body tightened her chest. "What of you?" she asked. His hair brushed across her skin as he turned his head to look up at her.

"What about me?"

"How does—" Caroline raised her hand, then let it tangle with his raven locks. "How does this make you feel?"

His smile, a flash of white teeth, brought color to her cheeks and Caroline was thankful for the dim light. He shifted his attention, moving slowly up her body till she had no choice but to lie flat again. Leaving a trail of nibbles and aroused skin.

"You take my breath away. I want you so badly, I—" Wolf stopped and rolled to his side. Taking her hand he guided it down his body. She didn't

118

resist as he wrapped her fingers nearly around his hard length. "I ache for you, Agehyaguga."

Her hand remained after his left to touch her. "What does that mean, Agehyaguga? You said it last night, too."

"Did I?" Wolf hadn't noticed saying it either time. "Moon woman." His fingers tangled in her curls. "Your hair is the color of moonbeams," he whispered. But he did not tell her that he had begun to think of her as Agehyaguga.

Caroline reached for him. His weight was welcome as was his first thrust, and his next, and all the others that surged faster and deeper. His powerful body plunged into her, sending her soul soaring, filling her completely. Making the word wonderful inadequate.

"What do these mean?" They were lying side by side, Wolf's elbow bent, his head propped in his palm. He tucked his chin to follow her finger as it traced a line of tattoos across his chest.

"I did not realize you were such an inquisitive little thing," Wolf teased, bending forward and nestling a kiss between her breasts. He straightened and took her hand. "Most of them do not really mean anything. They are just symbolic of my tribe or family."

"I like them." Caroline skimmed across one that traversed his ribs, surprised when he squirmed.

She tried it again and got the same reaction. "You're ticklish."

"No," he insisted, but he couldn't stop wriggling when she did it again. "If you do not stop, I will—"

"You will what? Oh!" His movements were so fast she barely had time to gasp. One moment he was lying beside her, the next he straddled her hips. His hands caught hers and stretched them high above her head. He looked fierce and wild looming over her, but Caroline wasn't afraid. When she started laughing, he threw back his head and joined her.

"You have a pretty smile."

His words surprised Wolf as much as they did her. They also made him realize he must stop this. No matter how much it pleasured him to continue. He agilely climbed off her and stood. "It is time we got up. I will build up the fire."

Caroline couldn't help watching as he laced up his leggings and donned a shirt. Then he was gone, closing the door behind him. Caroline scurried from the fur pallet. It was chilly this morning, and she quickly pulled on her shift. A boned bodice and quilted petticoat followed. The overgown was drifting down over her body when he tramped through the doorway. He dropped the split logs then set about stoking the embers to life.

"I told you I would start the fire up. You could have stayed in the bed until there was some heat."

" 'Tis not too cold for me." Caroline managed to keep her teeth from chattering while she lied.

He simply glanced over his shoulder and shrugged.

"I could make us something to eat." Caroline stepped forward cautiously. The way they were acting around each other it was hard to believe that she'd lain with this man. She longed to capture the comfortable feelings of before.

"Your Ladyship cooks?" His dark brows lifted skeptically.

"A little." There was no sense lying when he would discover the truth soon enough. "But I'm anxious to learn." She could imagine how it would be for the rest of their lives. He would hunt and fish, and she would cook for him. And every night they would share the bearskin bed.

"I'll take care of breakfast this morning," he said, motioning for her to sit in the chair.

She watched him, his animal grace, as he mixed cornmeal and water in a copper kettle and swung it over the fire. "How long have you lived here?"

"Since I returned from England."

"I see." He wasn't being very communicative but at least he answered her questions. Caroline hoped as they became more used to each other, they could talk more freely. "I thought you might live with your mother."

"You mean with the Cherokee?" He stirred the gruel.

Caroline nodded.

"I could, but my mother is dead, and I prefer it here."

So did she.

Caroline had come up with a plan during the wee hours of the morning while she lay in his arms. It was obvious she could not marry his father now. She and Raff loved each other. At least she loved him, and she was sure if he didn't feel the same, time would change that. She would live with him here in his cabin.

And she would send for Ned. She was sure Wolf didn't have the money to keep Edward in school. Her brother would be angry at first, forced to leave his familiar surroundings, but he would soon learn to love it in the New World. Besides Wolf could continue her brother's education with the books he had.

Best of all, they'd all be together.

Caroline was beginning to wonder if she'd done the right thing leaving Edward in England all alone. But it didn't matter now.

Telling Robert MacQuaid that she couldn't marry him would be difficult. But she was sure he'd understand eventually, especially after she and Wolf explained that . . . Caroline didn't know exactly what they would explain to Wolf's father, but she was certain together they would think of something.

The coming confrontation with his father obviously weighed heavily on Wolf's mind, too. He barely spoke as they ate, and later mounted for the final leg of their journey. An early morning mist curtained the path, making it difficult to observe too much of the landscape. But every now and again, the fog lifted enough for Caroline to make out a veiled vista of breathtaking valley.

They stopped midmorning to rest the horses. "Seven Pines is beyond that ridge," he offered after helping her dismount.

Caroline wanted to cling to him, to have him hold her as he had last night, but his manner invited no such intimacy. She followed as he led the horses toward a nearby brook that splashed over some rocks. When he ignored her presence, Caroline touched his arm. Just the feel of him, muscle hard and warm, brought back vivid, erotic memories. Caroline swallowed, ignoring the color flooding her cheeks. "I know this won't be easy for you," she said.

He turned and stared at her long and hard, and for a moment Caroline thought he was going to pull her to him. But he didn't. He only gathered the horses' reins and started back to the path. Before he bent forward to boost her into the saddle, his gaze met hers. "You are right, Caroline," he said. "This is not easy for me."

The house at Seven Pines was much grander in scale than the cabin where they'd spent the night. Caroline noted the comparison with little interest. Wolf's home was sufficient for her. She didn't need the two stories of planed wood to be happy. The house they approached appeared to be built in stages. The center section containing a door and two glass windows on the first floor and three on the second formed the base. What appeared to be a kitchen was on the left, and another room balanced the whole on the right. This area had its own door and several men, Cherokee by the looks of them, stood near the opening.

Wolf nodded their way, but said nothing as he lifted Caroline down from the horse. She could feel the tension in his hands and longed to make this easier for him . . . for both of them. She prayed the confrontation would be short, that his father would be understanding. Neither she nor Raff had planned for last night to happen.

But her heart was heavy and her step hesitant as she followed the man she loved into the house.

Inside heavy curtains draped the windows making it difficult at first for her to make out the man sitting in the straight-backed winged chair. His leg was wrapped and resting on a stool. But there was no missing his voice. It was loud and laced with a mixture of Scottish brogue and rum. "About time you got here, boy. Is this her?"

Wolf said nothing, though he stepped aside so that Caroline had a better view of the man she came to America to wed . . . and he had a better view of her. Caroline didn't know what to do except stand still and allow the thorough examination he gave her with his pale green eyes.

He didn't seem overly impressed with what he

saw. He ended his appraisal with a grudging, "I suppose she'll have to do," then yelled, "Mary!"

Caroline glanced toward Wolf, waiting for him to explain that it didn't really matter what his father thought of her because she wouldn't be staying with him. But as a young woman rushed into the room, a young woman heavy with child, Wolf turned on his moccasined heel and headed for the door.

"Mary will show you to your room," the older Mr. MacQuaid was saying, but Caroline paid him no heed.

She could only watch dumbfounded as Wolf opened the door and walked through it.

"Did you not hear me, girl? Where are ye going?"

Caroline ignored the questions hurled at her as she took one step, then another toward the entrance. She lifted her skirts and her pace quickened, but by the time she reached the porch, Wolf had remounted. His horse pranced nervously, and he turned the animal about in a tight circle when she called his name.

"I . . . I don't understand," was all Caroline seemed able to say as he looked down at her from atop the stallion. But he offered no words of explanation, simply met her stare, his handsome face grim, before twisting the reins.

As he galloped away, Caroline could only stand and watch in disbelief.

Behind her came the angry bellow of her name.

Six

"Lady Caroline. Lady Caroline."

Caroline responded more to the gentle touch on her arm than the sound of her name. She tore her eyes away from the empty trail leading into the tall pines and faced the young woman she'd seen in the parlor. She noticed calm grey eyes in a pretty face, but little else.

"He wants you, Lady Caroline." The woman seemed hesitant to reinforce the command, which Caroline now heard being bellowed from inside. Her smile was shy as she patted Caroline's hand. "Are you all right?"

Was she? Caroline didn't know. Physically she seemed fine, standing there on the wooden porch. But . . . Caroline glanced back toward the path, hoping . . . praying this was all a terrible mistake. Any moment now, Wolf would come riding back in a cloud of dust and explain why he left.

But there was no cloud of dust, only the endless

sea of pines and the sound of a mocking bird chattering away.

"He never stays here long."

Caroline twisted to stare at the woman when she spoke. "He comes by occasionally, and if his father was gone, he used to stay and chat with me a bit." She shook her head and wisps of brown hairs escaped her mob cap. "But he and the older Mr. MacQuaid don't get on. Come along now." The woman took Caroline's arm and turned her toward the house. "We might as well get this done with. Then I'll bring a nice pot of tea to your room. Doesn't that sound inviting?"

The woman—whose name Caroline now remembered as Mary—stood by her, arms locked as she faced Robert MacQuaid. He'd managed to get himself from the chair, though his fleshy face was red from the strain. He stood now, leaning heavily on a cane, glaring at her.

"What in the hell is the idea of running out like that?"

Caroline could think of no explanation so she said nothing, a response that seemed to anger him even more.

"Damnation girl! You might be used to all manner of bowing and scraping and the like back in England. But here I'm the king." He leaned toward her, his eyes narrowed. "And you do what I say."

When Caroline again said nothing, his expression darkened. "Are you deaf, girl? Did I send the whole way to England for a mite of a girl who can't even hear?"

"She hears fine, Robert. I think she's just tired from her journey. 'Tis a long way she's come."

Robert's eyes shot to the other woman, and his tone grew dangerously low. "I don't recall asking for your advice, Mary."

"But she's correct." Caroline felt the tension in the other woman's linked arm. She lifted her chin, trying to remember that, whatever the circumstances, she was still Lady Caroline Simmons. Despite the fact that she was penniless—and betrayed—she still had the heritage of her name to bolster her. "I am fatigued." She turned toward Mary, catching only a glimpse of the dumbfounded expression on Robert's face. "Would you please show me to my room."

But his apparent surprise at her dismissal of him was short-lived. By the time she and Mary entered the hallway behind the parlor, he was yelling that she best get herself rested. "I want you down here for dinner. Do you hear me?"

"One would have to be deaf indeed not to," Mary quipped as she led the way up narrow box steps. "But he isn't as bad as all that." She paused at the top to catch her breath. "He doesn't like being confined as he is."

Caroline made no comment. She felt as if what little strength she had was spent on defying him belowstairs. And she wouldn't have done that if

128

he'd kept to berating only her. For some reason she couldn't bear the awful man yelling at Mary.

"I hope you find this to your liking." Mary stepped back after she led the way into a small bright room. "There wasn't much but dress material to work with, but I thought you might like some fresh curtains."

"They're lovely." Caroline was surprised her voice sounded so calm. She felt shattered inside. "Everything is very nice." She touched the coverlet on the bed. It was made of the same pale yellow fabric as the curtains. "You needn't have gone to so much trouble."

Mary smiled and folded her hand over her rounded stomach. "It gave me something to occupy my time. With Logan away, I . . . Well, it can get lonely." She reached out toward Caroline. "I'm so glad you're here." Her smooth forehead wrinkled. "Are you certain you're all right? Your hands are like ice. And you're so pale." She wrapped Caroline's fingers in her own, then their eyes met. "It won't be so bad."

Turning away before Mary could see the tears that sprang to her eyes, Caroline made a show of examining the curtains. "You're very kind. But do you suppose I could be alone for a moment?"

"Oh, of course. I'll send one of the Cherokee women up with your things in a bit. Have a good rest."

When the click of the latch sounded, Caroline was tempted to call Mary back. Perhaps solitude was not what she desired after all. Alone in the room, she had nothing to do but think.

Caroline sank into the chair by the window. She tried to imagine a reason for Wolf's actions . . . a reason other than the obvious one. But try as she might, nothing came to mind. No one had forced him to abandon her.

But then no one had forced her to make love to him last night, either. He'd made no promises. She'd just assumed . . . closing her eyes Caroline leaned back against the chair.

Foolish. She'd been a foolish, foolish girl.

Hadn't she learned at her father's knee what she must always do? The lesson was plain. Rely on herself. Yet she'd been willing to toss aside that hard learned exercise, and for what? A handsome face and muscled body? Eyes that seemed to speak volumes but in truth said little.

Knowing that she wasn't the first nor unfortunately the last woman to succumb to her own passions didn't help Caroline feel any better. To her disgrace she still sat by the window, a part of her listening for the soft clop of horses' hooves to proclaim her mistaken about Wolf.

But the sound never came; and when Mary knocked timidly at Caroline's door, announcing the evening meal, it was a hardened, more cynical Caroline who bade her enter.

"I didn't want to disturb you, but Robert did say . . ." Mary left the rest of her sentence unsaid.

"I know." Caroline stood and shook the wrinkles from her skirt.

"Were you able to rest any? You still look pale."

"I'm fine. Really." Caroline smiled, for she had no wish to upset her. "Shall we go down then?" Caroline took Mary's arm . . . some small comfort as she left the room to face her future.

"I see no reason to delay. It's not often we get a visit from a man of the cloth."

Caroline kept her eyes focused on the tiny stitches she sewed into the shirt hem. "I suppose you're right."

"Speak up girl, I can barely hear you. Hell and damnation, you're as bad as Mary with your whining about."

Caroline tried to conceal the hatred in her stare as she looked up. Here hardly more than a fortnight and already she despised her betrothed . . . nay, almost husband, with an intensity that was difficult to hide. "Neither Mary nor I whine. You yourself have made it clear that we are to keep our voices low."

"You mean I don't want you harping at me like a pair of fishmongers."

"As you say." Caroline's tone was clipped as she resumed her stitching.

"You best watch it, girl." Robert slapped at the chair arm. "I could still change my mind about this marriage."

Do it! Do it! she wanted to scream the words at him, but they both knew she couldn't. It hadn't taken long for the lines to be drawn. Robert knew she was penniless. Knew of her brother and her desire to see him provided for. It was a convenient threat for Robert, and one he used often and well, to simply abandon her and her brother.

Caroline took a calming breath. "When will the clergyman arrive?"

"Any day now. Last I heard he was ministering to the Cherokee up near Estatoe. Though why he bothers with those heathens I don't know."

Caroline bit the thread to keep from telling him her opinion of his Christianity.

"Where are you off to?" Robert tapped his cane against the chair leg.

"I thought I'd help Mary oversee the candle making." Caroline folded the shirt into her sewing basket. "The day is too warm for her to work so hard."

He scowled at her, but did not call her back as she left the room. Another thing Caroline could count upon. Robert might summon her often to his side, but he never let on that he enjoyed her company. And though she knew his disability was irksome for him, and that he was often lonely, he couldn't bring himself to ask her to stay.

Caroline decided it was no credit to her kindness that she took every opportunity to leave him.

Mary was behind the wing that served as a kitchen. Several Indian women, whom Robert paid in goods to work for the family, stood with her beside a large kettle that hung over a fire. They each held a rod strung with wax covered wicks, and took turns dipping them into the hot tallow.

"You promised to only supervise." Caroline came into the kitchen yard carrying a windsor-style chair in front of her. "This is so you can sit in the shade."

Mary glanced around and smiled as Caroline placed the chair out of the sun. "I'll just be a minute more."

"Actually, you're finished." Caroline came up behind her and took the rod from her hand, motioning with a jerk of her head for the other woman to get away from the heat.

"We told her to take it easy," a woman named Sadayi said. "But you know Mary."

"Yes," Caroline said with a chuckle. "We all do. And if she doesn't start listening to us, we shall have to tie her to her bed until the babe comes."

"You make too much of this," Mary said as she settled heavily onto the chair. As she wiped perspiration from her brow with a linen handkerchief, Caroline simply rolled her eyes heavenward, causing Sadayi and her daughter Walini to laugh.

The work was hot; and by the time they'd finished, Caroline's back ached and droplets of moisture inched down the valley between her breasts. But it was a good feeling knowing there would be candles to light the house through the winter and that it was partially because of her.

Life at Seven Pines wasn't all bad. When she could escape—which unfortunately is how she felt about it—Robert's presence, there was much to see and do. The Indian women who worked in the house were interesting to talk with. At first, knowing she was to be Robert's wife, they offered little but civility. But as summer turned to autumn, they seemed to accept her more.

They came to Seven Pines trading their labor for goods their families needed. "It used to be the men who came," Sadayi told her one morning as they kneaded bread.

"Why has it changed?" Caroline gave the dough a forceful push with the heel of her hand, then another. Baking bread was becoming one of her favorite tasks, though Mary told her to refrain from pounding the dough so hard. "You act as if you're punishing it, and the poor lump of flour and water did nothing to you," she told Caroline the first time she helped with the chore. Caroline didn't care. And it wasn't simple dough she imagined when her hands hammered away.

Caroline forced her mind away from painful memories of Wolf to concentrate on Sadayi's answer. Sadayi was a handsome woman, taller and more strongly built than Caroline. She wore her long black hair pulled smoothly away from her brow and folded into a thick knot at the back of her head. She liked pretty things and wore an abundance of silver and bead bracelets that made a musical sound as she worked.

134

"Our men are no longer welcome. The Great Father Across the Water is punishing us," she said, her words fraught with sarcasm.

"Because Cherokee warriors attacked settlers?"

"I do not know. But they want our men to go fight their enemies, and then they refuse to trade."

"Our men are fighting the French, too," Mary said.

Caroline wiped her floury hands down the front of her apron and reached for her friend. "Logan will be all right. I just know he will."

Mary's smile was sad. "You're right, of course. I just wish he could be here when the baby comes." Mary touched her stomach lovingly.

"Perhaps he will."

"Humph." Sadayi covered a mound of dough with a clean cloth. "The English and French are not yet ready to exchange the peace belt." Though Caroline shot her a warning look, she continued. "I fear things will be worse before they are better."

"You can't know that, Sadayi."

"Caroline, you needn't try to protect me. My stomach may be large, but I still hear things."

"Wa'ya warns us to prepare for battle."

Caroline's jaw tightened. "What does he know?" Since her arrival at Seven Pines, Wolf's name had been mentioned several times. Despite her desire to accept what happened as a lesson, Caroline couldn't help the agitation that the sound of his name brought. If only he didn't invade her dreams every night . . .

135

"Raff is very knowledgeable about such matters. I realize Robert never listens to him, but Logan believes he should. And so do I."

"What is it that Robert should do?"

"The *inadu*, the snake, should not cheat."

Sadayi's words were so full of hatred that Caroline was speechless. It did not help to know that she was not alone in her dislike of Robert MacQuaid.

"There, bend forward so I can arrange this better." Mary backed up and tilted her head to admire her handiwork. " 'Tis lovely you look."

Caroline smiled her thanks. But she didn't care how she looked. She felt nauseated. The only reason she'd embraced the idea of dressing up for this day was to please Mary. The other woman insisted upon viewing this occasion as a celebration. Caroline certainly didn't share her assessment. "Are you sure the flowers in my hair aren't . . . well, a bit, too much?"

"Oh no. I wore roses entwined in my hair when I married Logan, and he complimented me on them."

Caroline made no comment, but it was painfully clear that one wedding had naught to do with the other. Mary obviously loved her husband. She spoke of him often, her tone soft and gentle. Caroline knew better than to hope for anything like that.

"Are you . . . frightened?"

"Of what?" Caroline glanced in the oval looking glass and tried not to scowl.

"Of . . . of you know. The marriage bed. Because I can assure you 'tis not as bad as some might tell you." Her thin cheeks turned a vivid red. "If truth be known, I find it quite enjoyable."

Mary busied herself arranging the folds of brocaded overskirt. Caroline imagined her friend's sudden industry was to hide her embarrassment, but she was glad Mary's preoccupation kept her eyes lowered. For she wouldn't have wanted Mary to see her distressed expression.

Caroline quickly masked her countenance, but she couldn't suppress the emotions that throbbed within her. She knew of the marriage bed—though before man nor God could she use the term with a clear conscience. But that didn't stop her from remembering. *Enjoyable* Mary called it. Caroline would go further.

Wondrous.

Celestial.

Heartbreaking.

Caroline's skirts swayed as she stepped away from Mary and faced the window. "Thank you for telling me." She took a deep breath. "But you needn't worry. I will get through it all right."

She had to. Caroline closed her eyes a moment, reminding herself she had no choice. When she looked around at Mary, her smile was in place. "I imagine it is time we go down."

137

Caroline's back was straight, her chin high as she entered the parlor. It was a quarter of an hour past the time set for the nuptials, but it appeared no one was especially interested in rushing the ceremony.

"Ah, there she is, my blue-blooded bride." Robert lifted a glass, spilling rum down the front of his silk waistcoat as he gave a mock salute to Caroline. "She's a pretty little sacrificial lamb, don't you think?"

His question was for the reverend, Mr. Appleby, who seemed to find nothing offensive about the remark. He laughed loudly and took another slurping swig from his own glass.

Reverend Appleby was nothing like Caroline remembered a clergyman as being. She didn't know exactly what denomination Reverend Appleby represented, and at this point didn't care. What did it matter if her bridegroom and the minister were deep in their cups?

Mary alone seemed anxious to make this wedding festive. She stepped into the room, a scowl darkening her face. "Shame on you, Robert, and you Reverend Appleby. This is no time for strong drink."

"And why not? 'Tis the only pleasure I'll derive from the day, thanks to this banged up leg." Robert gave his splinted thigh a slap, grimacing at the pain. He lifted bloodshot eyes to Caroline and his expression turned lecherous. "Unless Her Ladyship can be persuaded to ease my heated blood in other ways."

Mary's gasp interrupted the cool stare Caroline gave him. "She will await you in her bed like any other decent young woman," Mary said. Her hands were planted on her widened hips, and she reminded Caroline of a mother chicken protecting one of her brood. But then Caroline wasn't an innocent chick, nor a pure virginal girl. Still, thoughts of submitting to Robert MacQuaid's lust made her ill.

The ceremony was blessedly short, due in part to Robert's inability to stand for prolonged periods . . . and the minister's lack of sobriety.

When the final words were spoken, Caroline felt as if a trap had closed around her, but that was ridiculous. Now she and Edward were safe or at least secure financially.

Little was eaten of the wedding feast Mary had prepared. The ham tasted like dust in Caroline's mouth and Robert and Reverend Appleby quickly retired to the parlor to partake of more liquid refreshment.

"I don't think he meant it." Mary put down her fork, forgoing all pretense of eating. "He can't even make it up the stairs."

" 'Tis his right." Caroline sipped water to calm her stomach distress.

"Yes, but not tonight. Not till his leg heals. The grey eyes were filled with sympathy as she stared across the mahogany table.

"Whenever," Caroline answered, folding her napkin and placing it beside her plate. "If you'll excuse me, I need to lie down."

"Are you ill? Your cheeks are so pale."

"No. Just tired." Caroline pushed back her chair and rose, ashamed at her lack of bravery. But she couldn't seem to help herself as she nearly ran from the room.

Darkness added a new dimension to the worst day of her life. Caroline lay beneath the quilt, her limbs stiff, and listened to each creak of the floorboards. He'd said that he was coming to her tonight.

"Hell and damnation, you're my wife and I'll have you whenever and however I please." His words as he left the wedding meal echoed through her head. Caroline twisted to the side, grabbing the pillow and jamming it over her ears. She didn't want to hear him thump up the stairs. She didn't want him to come.

When she finally fell asleep amid tousled and tangled sheets her erotic dreams of Wolf were polluted with grotesque images of his father . . . her husband. She woke the next morning, thankfully alone, her head aching, her stomach rebelling. It was mere luck, but Robert had passed out in his own bed the night before. It was luck again that helped her make it to the chamber pot before sickness overwhelmed her.

* * *

"The bleeding is not that bad."

"Then stay abed to please me." Caroline gave Mary's shoulders a firm push onto the down pillow. "Besides, there is no need for you to rise today."

"The garden . . ."

"Is being picked. And as soon as I assure myself that you are going to do as Sadayi suggested, I shall go outside and help."

"But—"

"Mary." Caroline pulled the chair closer to the bed and sat down. "You don't want to do anything to hurt yourself or the baby. What would Logan do if . . . Well, you must simply take better care of yourself."

"I do love him so."

Caroline clasped her hand. "I know you do." She knew from the way Mary's eyes shone when she spoke of her husband, or the way she clutched the only letter she'd received since Caroline's arrival.

"If only he loved me as much."

"What are you talking about? I'm sure he adores you." Actually Caroline knew very little about Wolf's older brother. Mary, of course, spoke of him with great affection. Robert said next to nothing about any of his sons. But then he spent so much of his time a prisoner of rum that he seemed to care about little else.

"Oh, he cares for me." Mary turned her face away. "And I probably shouldn't even say this but, well, a woman can tell."

"Tell what?" Caroline fluffed the comforter. "I think worry has turned your mind to corn mush."

That statement brought the smile she wanted, but it didn't deflect the train of Mary's thoughts. "It was Robert's idea that we wed. He wished an heir for his name." She twisted her head to look at Caroline. "I heard them talking, yelling actually, about it one night. Logan wasn't happy here trading with the Indians. He and Robert fought constantly."

"About trading unfairly?" Caroline had learned much from Sadayi about the way the Cherokee felt about Robert.

"Yes. Logan despised some of his father's practices. He and Raff discussed it, and together they went to Charles Town to lay the truth before the governor." She brushed a lock of hair off her face.

"What happened?" Caroline remembered the meeting Raff had with the governor while she waited in the anteroom. By the looks of Mary as she raised her shoulders, Caroline imagined the brothers got as much satisfaction.

"Governor Lyttelton said he would look into it. He went so far as to appoint a commissioner, but nothing changed. Raff was furious."

"What of Logan?"

"Not long after that, Logan left me."

"It wasn't you he left. You said yourself he's fighting the French."

"A woman knows," was all she would say.

Caroline did her best to sway Mary's contention

142

that her husband didn't love her. Before she shut the door, leaving her friend to rest, Mary admitted that worry over her baby and fatigue were probably the main reasons for her melancholy. Still Caroline wished Logan MacQuaid would come riding down the path to reassure his young wife.

As usual when she approached the parlor, Caroline's step grew lighter. But this time it did no good. She cringed when she heard Robert's voice.

"Mrs. MacQuaid, I would see you a moment."

With reluctance she couldn't hide, Caroline paused in the open doorway. "I was on my way to the garden." The heavy curtains were drawn, but enough light filtered into the room for her to see his annoyance as he motioned her inside.

He'd become more fleshy since her arrival, and his skin had taken on a pasty hue. Yet his expression and tone remained the same, only modulated by the amount of rum he imbibed. This afternoon he appeared relatively sober, though a glass of amber liquid sat upon the table by his arm.

His stare was disconcerting as Caroline stood before him. But she'd decided not to be intimidated by him, and she did her best to school her features into a pleasant mask. "Mary is resting. I pray this problem won't harm the baby."

"Women have babies all the time. The savages simply drop the whelp and forget it. You coddle the girl too much."

"Is that what Raff's mother did, drop him and forget it?" Caroline couldn't imagine what possessed her to say such a thing. She'd never before mentioned his son's name, and certainly never to imply his mother was Cherokee. It hadn't taken her long to realize the contempt with which her husband viewed the Indians.

If she'd set out to raise his ire, which she tried very hard not to do, she couldn't have said anything more inflammatory. It didn't take the contortion of his face in rage to tell her that. But she resented his attitude, all the more because the Cherokee women were the first to suggest Mary needed to rest more. And she'd seen them with their own children. They were loving, attentive mothers.

Still, as she waited for the vile words to spew forth, Caroline knew she shouldn't have said it. She certainly owed neither Wolf nor his mother her allegiance.

"Damn you, girl!" Robert lunged to his feet so quickly he lost his balance and fell back heavily into the chair. "I've put up with your insolence too long. 'Tis time you learn your place."

Keeping quiet was her best defense, Caroline was smart enough to know that. But today it seemed a wayward imp had control of her tongue. "I have attempted to make a place for myself here." Caroline was proud of the work she did, the friends she'd made.

His laugh was evil. "Your *place* is in my bed, girl."

To this, Caroline managed to say nothing. It was

144

a common refrain . . . threat . . . she considered it. He seemed to enjoy watching her pale as he described in detail the vile things he would do to her when his leg healed.

"And if you think to escape me much longer . . ." He laughed again, wiping the spittle from his lips with the back of his hand. "My leg is getting better each day. Come, feel for yourself. The knot where the bones mend is smaller." He waved her forward.

Caroline knew it was cowardly, but she couldn't make herself move forward. Instead she made some quickly stated excuse about being needed in the garden and retreated through the door. But she wasn't fast enough to miss his raucous laughter, or his chortled, "Soon, girl. Soon."

Though she'd stopped outside the door to calm her agitated breathing, both Sadayi and Walini looked up, their expressions concerned, as she came down the path to the kitchen garden. "Mary is worse?" Sadayi asked after dropping a squash into the bag tied to her waist.

"No, no, she seems better actually." Caroline tied the ribbons of her bonnet as she walked toward them through the rows of corn. She retrieved her own bag from the hook near the kitchen door and began filling it, working side by side with the two women. They spoke of the weather . . . warm for this late in the season of corn. And the Cherokee women wondered aloud if the men would go to the winter hunt . . . or if war would keep them close to the villages.

Caroline listened to their talk and wished she could say something to ease their minds . . . to ease her own mind. When she could stand it no more, she changed the subject.

"Sadayi," Caroline asked as they finished picking a row. "Did you know Raff's mother."

"Wa'ya's mother, Alkini, came from another town, but I knew of her."

"She was very beautiful," Walini said.

"Phew." Sadayi made a face toward Walini. "You never saw her. You are too young."

"I know what I've heard," Walini countered.

Sadayi lifted her shoulders. "What Walini says is true. She was beautiful."

"Did she live at Seven Pines long?"

"I do not know. It is said she came here to marry the snake who cheats."

"Oh." Had Robert promised to marry her, then turned her away? "What happened then?"

"Nothing happened. She lived. She grew old."

"But Robert . . . Mr. MacQuaid never married her?"

"Not in the way of the white man. But the Cherokee way is simpler." Sadayi said it as if she thought their way was also far superior. "We exchange gifts, and that is it. If either decides it's not to be, they leave."

"Did Alkini decide to leave?" Caroline couldn't imagine anyone staying with the man willingly.

Sadayi shook her head. "She was sent away. Then many years later, he came and took the boy."

146

She made a tsking sound with her mouth. "Wa'ya should have stayed with her. Learned from his uncles. It is our way."

Later as she sat by the creek that ran behind the house, Caroline thought of what the women had said. It had become her habit to sit here for a few moments before going into the house. She enjoyed the quiet time to herself as the day gave way to twilight.

The magnitude of the surrounding forest fortified her, helping her face the evening. A time she was forced to spend with her husband. Today, dreading the certain confrontation, she lingered awhile longer, sitting on a moss-covered rock and watching as the crystal water chuckled over the polished stones.

No one ever bothered her when she came here, which was one reason the sound of her name, spoken softly, startled her so. The other reason was that even before she turned, she knew who was behind her. It was almost as if her mind had conjured him up.

Caroline slowly looked over her shoulder, assuring herself she was prepared for the sight of him. Realizing immediately she wasn't. "What are you doing here?" Her tone was as haughty as months of built-up hurt and anger could make it.

"I've come to take you away," was all Wolf said.

Seven

"Are you mad!" Caroline took an involuntary step backward. In her haste her foot tangled with an exposed root. Raff's hand shot out, catching her by the upper arm before she could fall. Caroline should have been grateful for the assistance, but she wasn't. As soon as she regained her balance, she pulled away from his touch.

There was no denying, despite all that had happened, he affected her as strongly as before.

Caroline took a deep breath. "I think you should leave."

"Not without you."

Her gasp was audible. His words sounded so familiar. Caroline heard them in her dreams nightly. It was always the same. He came for her, begging her forgiveness. Insisting she go with him. Swearing undying love . . .

But this was not a dream. Even though the nebulous light of dusk gave the whole a surreal quality, Caroline knew the flesh and blood man standing before her was no fantasy. And his words were not something she wished to hear.

Not now. It was too late.

Yet after her first request that he leave, she seemed incapable of doing more than staring at him. Regardless how strong and compelling her memories of him were, they paled compared to reality. He was taller, broader of shoulder and more darkly handsome. And though his garb was more civilized than when last she saw him—hair tied in queue, linen hunting shirt and leggings— the real Wolf exuded more savage strength than her dreams allowed. Even the most erotic ones.

The sound of his voice, low and deep, served to break the sensual spell he'd cast over her. "Caroline—"

" 'Tis Mrs. MacQuaid." she didn't imagine the tightening of his jaw. "I'm Mrs. Robert MacQuaid now."

Caroline thought she saw regret and something else in his eyes before he lowered his gaze. For a moment his long dark lashes shadowed his skin. But when he looked at her again his expression was unreadable.

"Listen to me, Caroline—"

"No!" Caroline twisted away when he tried to touch her again. "I won't!" She felt tears building behind her eyes, hot, bitter tears, and she did her best to keep them at bay. "I've listened to you all I intend to. Just go away and leave me in peace."

She turned back then, her mask of angry indignation crumbling. "Haven't you done enough?"

He knew it would not be easy, seeing her again. A part of him, the coward that tempts all men, urged him to go directly to his father with the news. But she deserved more than that . . . much more. Wolf took a step toward her and another when she didn't move away. "This place is not safe."

Her chin notched higher, and he saw anger flare like lightning in the depths of her blue eyes. "You brought me here."

"At your insistence. Or am I wrong that you traveled from England to come here?" The heat of his words faded. "To make this marriage."

She said nothing, only stared at him hard before turning away. Then, her voice strong she said, "Go away."

"I cannot." He resisted the urge to cup her soft shoulders, to feel again the warmth of her nape beneath his lips. "I am sorry for—"

"Don't." Her skirts billowed out as she whirled around to face him. "Don't apologize for what you did. I can't bear that."

"I regret only the hurt I caused you."

"That is good." Caroline pushed by him to start back toward the house. "I hope your regrets last you a lifetime."

He did touch her then, grabbing her arm and swinging her back to him. His face was inches from hers. "I don't recall forcing you to do anything."

150

His words were cruel, forged by anger . . . and guilt. Guilt that had plagued him since he left her to the mercies of his father. A man with no mercy.

"You're right, of course." Caroline didn't want to be so close to him she could smell his scent. To have that sense awaken so many memories.

"Nay." Wolf's forehead dropped till it touched the crown of her head. "It was not your doing, but mine."

Caroline took a shattered breath. "Leave me . . . please."

Instead of doing as she asked, he drew her closer. She could feel the imprint of his strong body and wanted to collapse against him. When he lifted her chin so he could look at her, she wanted his lips to come crushing down on hers. Hard and hungry. She wanted to feel the sweet oblivion of his kiss, his touch. She wanted to forget that he left her. That she was wed to another. That the other was his father.

But she couldn't. Her hands came up between their bodies. Fingers fisted, she pushed at him. "Let go of me."

"You will listen first." Wolf held her tightly. The fog clouding his reasoning lifted. "You are in danger."

"From you perhaps." Curls escaped their pins as she struggled. But fighting him was useless, and when he gripped her shoulders and gave her a shake, she stopped.

"Hear me. There is talk among the Cherokee of righting past wrongs."

"What is that supposed to mean?" Despite her anger, and the sexual pull that to her shame blunted it, Caroline sensed he was sincere and very troubled by what he said.

"Revenge, Caroline. Against those who have wronged them. There is much talk of it among some of the warriors. They feel if the British want them to fight then they shall. But they will choose the enemy."

"You're talking in riddles." Caroline twisted her head away, forcing herself to remember how she felt when she last saw him . . . riding away without a backward glance.

"This is not a word game . . . or a game of any kind. Most of the Headmen preach patience and compromise, but the young warriors are out for blood."

Caroline stood, a prisoner of his gaze while her mind registered what he said. She broke his hold with a slight shiver. "You are wrong. You warned me of this before and things couldn't be more peaceful. Why Sadayi and Walini come here everyday. We are friends."

"There are few the Cherokee dislike more than him." Wolf motioned in the direction of the house.

"Robert?" She had heard as much from the women, but that did not mean she thought the Cherokee would do anything about it. Caroline took a deep breath. "I realize my . . . husband is not always easy to . . ." She wanted to say with" but didn't want to bring this discussion to personal level. "He may have done things to the Cherokee that he shouldn't have, but—"

"You think that is it? That I came to lay my people's grievances at your feet?"

"I don't know why you came." Caroline bit her bottom lip to keep it from quivering.

"I told you why, Caroline." His strong hands gripped her elbows above the ruffle of her shift.

"Don't call me that." Her attempts to pull away were futile.

"If the Headmen lose control over the warriors, they will strike out. I have seen it happen before." His eyes caught hers again. "And when they do, it will be to destroy those they feel have hurt them. I want you out of here, safe, when that happens." The force of this last admission surprised Wolf. He told himself he came to Seven Pines as he would any place, to warn the inhabitants. He certainly felt no special duty toward his father, though he cared about his brother's wife.

But now he had to admit, to himself anyway, it was Caroline who concerned him most.

Caroline's mind reeled. What she told him was true. Since her arrival here, there had been little to indicate any trouble existed between the Cherokee and white settlers. Still, no Indian she'd met held her husband in anything other than contempt. But then neither did she.

But if Wolf was right . . . if there was fight-

ould happen to him? she had to

will you stand?"

s war?" He turned his head to stare

s the creek. "I do not know." He looked

his eyes catching hers. "There may still be

hope," he said. "I understand the ways of both nations. I am on my way to the Middle Towns to talk with the Headmen. To persuade them to travel to Charles Town and meet with Governor Lyttelton. In the meantime, I want you and Mary to go to Fort Prince George."

"And what of your father?"

Wolf's dark brows lowered. "If it is his wish."

"He's my husband." Caroline's gaze met his and held.

"I am aware of that." Sadayi told him of the wedding. And though Wolf knew it would happen, the news was more difficult to accept than he'd expected.

"Has it been . . . ?" Wolf faltered, at a loss for words. "Are you all right?"

"Yes." She turned out of his grasp, refusing to let him see her unhappiness. Her fingers fisted at her side, and she took a deep breath. "I think you should tell your . . . Robert and Mary what you told me."

"The hell you say!" Robert spit the words toward his son as he sat in the parlor.

Wolf paced the length of the room and back, as

154

he'd done since following Caroline into the old man's presence. At her suggestion, he laid the facts, as he knew them, on the line. He wasn't surprised when Robert scoffed at the notion of bloodshed.

"There will be no trouble with the Cherokee, and do you want to know why?" Robert didn't wait for an answer. "Because they're all a bunch of spineless women."

Caroline standing near the curtained windows watched as Wolf's back stiffened. He took a step toward Robert, but stopped.

"Oh, they talk big," Robert continued. "Taltsuska and those who trail along behind him. But not one of them has the nerve to stand and fight. They'd rather complain about not getting enough beads for their hides."

"Few men of honor stand by quietly when they are cheated."

The air between the two men seemed to crackle with animosity. Caroline watched a heated flush sweep up over her husband's usually pallid features. He gripped the chair arms but made no attempt to rise. Perhaps he knew, even standing, he was dwarfed by his tall, powerful son. "What are you saying, boy? Or are you like the rest of your kind, afraid to say what you really think?"

The only light in the room was a taper burning on the table beside Robert's chair. Wolf moved forward till he stood near enough to the old man to see him clearly . . . and to be sure he was seen. "I am talking about using short weights. About trading inferior goods and knowing it." Wolf's eyes narrowed. "I am talking about the way you ran your business."

His words were delivered in a low, emotionless tone, but to Caroline's way of thinking that made them all the more damning. She never doubted what he said was true. But she did wonder what Robert would do now that the accusation was out in the open. When he threw back his head, his jowls shaking and laughed, she let out her pent-up breath.

"You're always full of brass . . . not like the rest of those cowardly heathens." Robert wiped at his eyes with the back of his hand. "But then I always thought that was because you had my blood running through your veins."

"It is not something of which I am proud."

The mirth left Robert's face. "Well, you should be, boy. How many of your kind have what I gave you? Hell, I sent you to school in England. I spent money trying to make a gentleman of you, willing to overlook the Indian blood that taints you, and look at what you do. You could be wearing silk waistcoats, helping me run Seven Pines, but instead you live in that shack and dress like a savage."

"I don't think—" Caroline began.

"You stay out of this, girl."

The words were Robert's, but it was the look Wolf sent her that made Caroline step back into the shadows and give up any notion of interceding

156

in their controversy. Besides, she told herself, it was not her problem. Neither man meant anything to her. Still it was Wolf she watched as he resumed pacing the room.

The younger man strode to the window and back, trying to regain control of his anger. Confrontations with Robert were useless. He learned that long ago. The man who'd sired him felt no remorse for the things he did, whether it be cheating people who relied on him, using then discarding a woman who loved him, or degrading a son. Caroline drew his attention and for a heartbeat their gazes met.

Dear God, what had he done, bringing her here?

Wolf turned to face his father. "I have told you what is happening . . . what is likely to happen. Within the hour I shall be leaving for Fort Prince George. Are you coming with me?"

"Hell boy." Robert slapped at his leg. "I can't go anyplace."

"Then at least send the women to safety."

"Well now. I just might—"

Caroline stepped forward to explain that Mary was in no condition to travel, but a sharp look from her husband made her pause.

"But I can't be deciding that before morning." His pale green eyes shifted back to Caroline. "Hadn't you best see about those lazy women getting us something to eat?"

"I will stay the night, but I am not interested in eating with you."

The insult seemed to fall short of its mark for again Robert laughed. A very evil laugh in Caroline's opinion. "Nonsense," he finally said. "You wouldn't wish to deprive my beautiful wife of your charming company, would you?"

Damn the old man to hell. Wolf sat across the polished mahogany table from Caroline wishing he hadn't given in to Robert's taunt. He knew at the time it was a mistake to prolong the meeting, but he couldn't make himself sacrifice seeing Caroline. And he had the uncomfortable notion the old man knew it.

"Tell me Caroline," Robert questioned now. "You've never said. How did you get on with Raff on your journey here?"

Caroline forced herself to continue slicing a piece of beef, not allowing her eyes to stray toward Wolf. She swallowed. "He was . . . we got along fine."

"You didn't have a problem with him being a savage?"

"No!" Caroline choked out the word, and this time her gaze did flash toward Wolf. He sat, tall and straight, his handsome face a study in contempt. "He was a gentleman," Caroline said, feeling compelled to defend the man who betrayed her.

"That's good." Robert took a hefty swig of Madeira. "I wouldn't want to think he didn't treat you with all respect due the daughter of an earl."

He said the last with his usual contempt. But that wasn't what bothered Caroline. She'd become immune to his degrading sarcasm. No, it was the way her husband looked at her, then at Wolf . . . as if he knew.

Caroline took a quick drink, choking on the amber liquid.

"What's wrong with you, girl?"

"Nothing." Caroline coughed into her napkin. Robert was watching her, that same grim satisfied expression on his face, and Caroline couldn't bear it anymore. She wondered briefly if Wolf told him about the night they spent together. Was that the real reason he'd come? But she didn't believe that. Wolf's animosity toward his father ran too deep for shared confidences.

No, Robert's apparent suspicions must be something she'd done. The tone of her voice when she spoke to Wolf . . . or the way she couldn't seem to stop looking at him. For as much as she should hate him . . . did hate him, Caroline found it difficult to fight her attraction to him. And she was worried it was obvious to everyone.

"Would you please excuse me?" Caroline had to get out of his presence. She pushed her chair out and rose before Wolf could help her.

"Where do you think you're going, girl?" Robert twisted in his seat. His broken leg was propped on the chair beside him.

"I . . ." The magnetism of Wolf's eyes drew hers, but she pulled her gaze away quickly, then concentrated on her husband. "I should check on Mary." Before either man could say a word, she turned and rushed from the room.

"She's a beauty." Robert turned his head from the door to meet Wolf's eye. "Don't you agree?"

Wolf kept his expression blank. "I suppose so."

"You suppose so? Are you blind boy? Or are you so used to those dark-skinned savages you can't appreciate a fine looking white woman?"

Wolf ignored the question, asking one of his own to hopefully change the subject. He didn't wish to discuss Caroline with her husband. But he also knew better than to rush off after Caroline's hasty exit. "How is Mary? I was surprised she didn't join us for dinner."

Robert brushed the concern aside. "She's fine. Gets tired easy because of the baby." He took another drink of wine. "I guess I should thank you for what you did for Caroline."

Wolf said nothing.

"I appreciate your bringing her to me." Robert's smile was lascivious. He made a crude sound with his tongue. "She sure can make me forget about this broken leg."

Wolf laid his fork across the plate.

"How she learned some of the things she does, I'll never know. Guess their nursemaids must teach these *ladies* how to please a man."

Wolf's jaw tightened, but he said nothing. What

had he expected? He brought her here. Hell, he'd taken Caroline's virginity just so the old man would suspect that his wife was Wolf's leavings. But the way he was talking, the lack of a maidenhead hadn't meant a thing to him.

"You ever had yourself one of them *ladies*, boy? Don't be shy now. You aren't a bad looking boy when you aren't dressed like a savage. I'll bet you had your pick of blue-blooded women when you were in England."

Robert seemed not to notice Wolf's lack of response.

"Well, I can't swear that they're all like that one." Robert motioned toward the door Caroline passed through minutes ago. "But she's a real animal. Tires me out, she does. Wants it every night. Sometimes more." He groped at the flap of his stained breeches. "She's keeping this thing busy." Robert licked his lips as he fondled himself. "Where you going, boy?"

Wolf strode across the dining room, pausing at the door. He almost said nothing, fearing if he opened his mouth, he'd say something he'd regret. Something that Robert might take as proof that he cared about Caroline. And if he knew that . . . Wolf knew the old man pretty well. Too well. Anything or anybody Wolf cared about was fair game for Robert. He knew what to say or do to cause the most pain. Wolf had seen it with talk about his mother, and about the people he called his own.

These comments about Caroline must be the result of some real or imagined attraction Robert noticed between his wife and son. And if somehow Robert failed to note that his wife had come to him less than an innocent, Wolf wasn't going to do anything now to bring Robert's wrath upon Caroline.

And who knew for certain. Perhaps for once, Robert spoke only the truth. Wolf couldn't argue that Caroline was an extremely beautiful and sensual woman. The texture of her pale skin, the silkiness of her hair were things he could not forget. And her taste, no amount of wine could purge it from his mouth. He dreamed of her nightly and woke hard and aching.

But that agony was nothing compared to thoughts of her doing with Robert the things they'd done together. It made him sick. It made him want to plow his fist into something.

But as he left the room, Wolf couldn't deny that he deserved to feel as he did. After all, he had used her, then left her here. And he'd known what would happen when he did.

It was a reality he could not change. One he must learn to accept no matter how difficult. Except . . . one question still lingered.

"What? What did you ask me?" Caroline shrank back, clutching a shawl tightly about her shoulders as he pushed into her room. She wore only the simple linen shift that served as her night rail, and the lack of proper dress seemed to add to her vulnerability.

It was late, well past midnight she imagined, and she would never have opened the bedroom door had she realized who was on the other side. Her first thought, when she heard the knock was that Mary was worse. Seeing Wolf standing before her should not have been such a shock since she thought of little else since he arrived, but she didn't think even *he* had the nerve to come to her alone, in the middle of the night.

Yet her initial outrage at his appearance paled in comparison to the question he asked her before she could say anything.

"I believe you heard me, Caroline. And it is a simple enough query. Are you with child?" Wolf reached behind him to close the door. The key turned in the lock with a soft metallic click.

The sound galvanized Caroline to action. She stepped forward, anger replacing her initial surprise. "If you do not leave this room immediately, I shall scream."

The light was dim—a wash of silvery moonlight, tinged with an orange glow from the banked fire— but she could still read the amused expression on his face. He arched a dark brow.

"And what good would that do, Your Ladyship? Who would come to your rescue? Your husband?" His tone held scorn. "I doubt he could maneuver the stairs if his life depended on it."

"No, Lady Caroline, you should have gone to him this night, if you wished to protect yourself from visitors. But you needn't worry. I won't stay long. And," he said more gently, "I won't hurt you."

She believed him.

But that did nothing to relieve her anxiety. He sent her senses soaring, and all reason seemed to scatter whenever she was near him. His presence made thinking difficult. Then why was she understanding something clearly for the first time?

"Please go." She turned away, moving toward the window so he couldn't see how her hands shook as they clutched the woolen fabric.

"Caroline, I—" Wolf followed her, but though he wanted to, he didn't touch her narrow back. "I need to know if you are carrying my baby." Much about what he'd done to her caused him regret. But nothing more than the thought that she might be pregnant. With his child. Though that might be the perfect revenge against his father, it would prove a living hell for the child . . . for Caroline.

She almost turned back to him when she heard the pleading in his voice. Did he have the right to know? But she gripped the sill and forced herself to think rationally.

First of all, though his question brought many things into focus: her uneasy stomach when she rose in the morning, the tiredness, her bouts of crying, she still wasn't completely certain she was with child.

There were explanations, explanations that did not include a child, explanations she'd accepted readily, for all her symptoms. Thoughts of submitting to Robert made her ill whenever they occurred. She was working long and hard, especially since Mary needed more rest. And then there were the tears. She was trying her best to control them.

But even if she was with child . . . especially if she was . . . she could never let on to Wolf. She was married to his father. Any child she brought into the world must be a result of that union. Or at least must seem to be.

Bastard was such an ugly word. Surely Wolf understood that.

Caroline schooled her features, then slowly turned to face him. He was closer than she assumed, and his nearness was almost her undoing. Oh Wolf, she wanted to cry, throwing herself into his arms. Why did you do this to me? Why did you leave me? She would have gone with him anywhere. Even now, wedded to another in the eyes of man and God, she was tempted to beg him to take her away.

But there was more to think of than herself.

"There is no child," she heard herself say, and she could barely believe the soft, calm voice was her own.

"You are certain?"

"Yes." She couldn't tell if she read relief upon his features. "Now will you please go?"

He should be pleased. Wolf wondered why he

wasn't. Hands clenched, he turned and started for the door. But he paused and turned back. She stood in a puddle of moonlight, looking beautiful . . . and vulnerable. He tried to ignore the desire that burned within him.

"There is one more thing."

Caroline lifted her chin, hoping she could maintain her composed facade until he left. "What is it?"

"The threat of war is real. No matter what your . . . husband says, I want you to leave here with me tomorrow."

"I don't think that's wise." She gave no explanation, but then he needed none.

"You have my word that I'll see you safely to Fort Prince George."

Again she believed him.

"I can't."

Anger flared in the depths of his obsidian eyes. "Are you willing to risk your life to stay here with him?"

Him? Lord help her, she hadn't even thought about Robert. Her husband. She shook her head, her unbound hair brushing softly across her back. " 'Tis Mary I cannot leave."

"She will come, too." It had never been his intent to leave his brother's wife behind.

"She can't travel. She can barely leave her bed."

For what seemed an eternity, he stood there, staring at her. Then slowly he reached down and drew a knife from his legging. The long polished

166

blade caught what light there was, reflecting it. Moving toward the chest, Wolf placed the knife beside the silver-handled brush. The contrast between the two made the knife appear even more deadly.

"What are you doing? I don't want that."

When he turned to face her, there was very little of the civilized white man in his expression. "You may need it." Again he headed for the door, but this time it was Caroline who stopped him.

Rushing forward, her bare feet padded on the wide boards. She reached out, but didn't touch him. "Do you think the Headmen and the Cherokee can work out a compromise?"

"I don't know," Wolf answered before facing her. When he did, his hand, of its own volition, cupped her cheek. Dark against pale. Weather-hardened against soft. The contrasts nearly unmanned him. "I must try to bring them together at least."

"And if you can't? She was playing with fire, but as Caroline turned into his palm, she seemed helpless to stop herself.

"I don't know." Her sweet breath fanned across his flesh, and he lost control. His fingers dug into her hair. His mouth attacked hers.

The kiss was deep and desperate. Tongues searched and mated, probed. Caroline clutched at his shirt, wishing it were his smooth skin beneath her hand, needing to hold onto him.

By the time he tore his lips away, Caroline

could feel the hard ridge of his manhood pressing against her stomach. Her own body was molten fire.

"Please," she whispered and neither knew if it was a plea to stop or to assuage the awful ache they caused each other.

Wolf bracketed her head and stared, studying her face, naked with desire for him, and he could do nothing but twist away.

Caroline watched him leave, then slowly shut the door and turned the key, though she knew he would not return. Her lips were bruised, her skin was so sensitive she could barely stand the slide of the sheets as she climbed back into bed.

She lay awake till the rooster crowed and the sky paled to pewter. Then she rose and dressed. When she went belowstairs, she wasn't surprised to learn that he was gone.

Eight

A fortnight passed since Wolf's sudden appearance at Seven Pines. Then another. On the surface life continued much as it had before.

The Indian women either came from the nearby town of Kawuyi to help, or they didn't. Robert scoffed at their lack of work ethic, but Caroline understood their need to take care of their own homes first.

Mary grew larger and larger as the days passed. She tired easily and complained less about spending her time abed. "If anything should happen to me," she began one day as Caroline sat in the light of her window sewing.

"Nothing bad will happen," Caroline interrupted, almost angrily.

"Yes, but if something should . . . it's not as if women never die of childbirth," Mary added gently.

And Caroline felt guilty for constantly dwelling upon her own concerns. Not that she hadn't gone through the motions of caring for Mary, but her mind had been elsewhere. Now she set the partially completed shirt for the baby on the chair and went to the bed where Mary sat propped against pillows. She clutched the other woman's hand, and Mary smiled.

"Just promise me you'll look after my baby."

"I shall." Caroline squeezed her fingers. "You needn't worry about that."

Caroline's pledge appeared to relieve Mary, for her spirits seemed lighter even as her body continued to grow heavier.

And even as Caroline grew more and more worried.

There was little doubt in her mind now that she was with child. Her seemingly innocent queries of Mary concerning the early stages of pregnancy, and the other woman's answers only confirmed the idea that Wolf planted in her head.

She carried Wolf's child.

No, Caroline admonished herself. It could never be his child. For the baby's sake it must be Robert's.

Thus Caroline viewed her husband's recovery as a mixed blessing. She knew she must submit to him . . . and soon. Yet she could scarcely stand the thought.

"Get in here, girl."

Caroline couldn't keep herself from cringing when she heard him summon her. Sadayi and Walini were here today, and Caroline had decided to wash the bed linens. They built a fire outside since there was no laundry room, and

170

filled a large kettle with water from the creek. While Walini stirred the sheets about in the soapy water, Caroline decided to check on Mary. But she never got past the parlor.

"You wished to see me?" The words died on Caroline's lips as she stared at her husband.

"I got rid of it," he said, glancing down at his leg, now free of the cumbersome splints.

"Are you certain that's wise?" He stood balanced on his crutch, obviously putting little pressure on his one leg.

"Hell girl, I'm tired of being laid up."

"Yes but if—"

"If nothing. It's gone and it's going to stay gone." As he spoke, his head drooped. He stared first at the swollen leg, visible beneath his ripped breeches, then lifting only his eyes, at Caroline. "You know what this means, don't you, girl?"

He reminded her of the bull out in the pasture, hunched shoulders and hard stare. Caroline swallowed and said nothing.

"You're finally going to be my wife in more than name." His eyes narrowed. "That's what you want, isn't it, girl?"

Caroline's throat tightened, but she managed to croak out a strangled, "Yes." It was what she wanted . . . what she needed. For her child's sake, Robert must believe . . . must accept this baby as his.

His laugh sent ribbons of revulsion streaming across her flesh, but she tried to ignore them when he summoned her closer. "I need your help getting into the chair."

Caroline allowed him to throw his arm about her shoulder, accepting much of his weight as she guided him back to the large armchair. He was heavy. It seemed to Caroline that he'd gained a good deal of weight in the months since she'd arrived at Seven Pines.

He fell back into the chair with a grunt of relief, and Caroline tried to move away. He smelled of sour whiskey and unwashed skin. But his hand shot out, capturing her wrist.

Her first response was to struggle, but his fingers tightened as if to remind her that he had the right to touch her if he chose.

"You're hurting me."

"Then come closer, girl."

"My name is Caroline."

"I'm well aware of who you are, Lady Caroline," he grunted as his fingers bit into her skin, forcing her down to her knees beside his chair. "The high and mighty Lady Caroline. Thinks she's too good for the likes of me."

"No." Tears burned Caroline's eyes, but she blinked them back.

"Too good to spend time with me. But you're not too good for the filthy savages, are you?" When she said nothing, his fingers twisted. "Are you?"

"I . . . I don't know what you're talking about. I help Sadayi and Walini. I thought that's what you wished."

172

"Such a dutiful little wife." His color darkened with anger. "And did you think it was my pleasure for you to be nice to my half-blood son?"

"I don't—"

"Don't what?"

The tears did come now as he pushed her lower. Caroline struggled, but he was too strong for her. She considered screaming, but the only person she was sure could hear was Mary, and she didn't want her jumping up and running downstairs. Besides, he was her husband and she had to learn to deal with him.

"As you say," she said with as much dignity as she could, considering she was on her knees, her skirts billowed around her. "He *is* your son."

"So were those 'motherly' looks you were passing him across the table?"

Caroline said nothing, but she felt the blood drain from her face. She had tried so hard not to look at Wolf at all. To do nothing that might give away her feelings for him. But apparently she failed for there was no denying Robert's anger, or the reason he felt justified in his actions.

"What you planning girl, to go running off with him? Is that the reason he came here wanting to take you away?"

"No." Caroline shook her head, relieved there was something she could deny with a clear conscience. "I'm not going anyplace. I'm here aren't I?" She hoped he didn't notice how desperate and unhappy her voice sounded.

Apparently he only concentrated on her words, for the pressure on her wrist lessened. "Because *I've* got the money," he said angrily.

"There never was any secret about our marriage agreement."

"You're penniless. Your father gambled and driveled away all your wealth and you want to keep some holier than thou brother in silk breeches."

"That's right. And you wished a titled bride," Caroline said, reminded him of his side of the bargain. She jerked her arm and though he didn't let her go, he did loosen his fingers.

"You're damn right I did." He jerked her hand up pushing it into his lap, rubbing her palm over himself, laughing at her struggles to pull away. "And tonight I shall have one."

He was still laughing when Caroline gathered up her skirts and ran from the parlor.

"What's wrong with you? That water is hot," Sadayi warned as Caroline stuck her hand into the laundry kettle. It scalded, and she pulled her hand out quickly, though she almost welcomed the pain.

"I suppose I should use a stick to remove the linens," she said with a shake of her head.

The rest of the day passed too quickly. Tea was an abomination. Robert refused her request to take her refreshment upstairs with Mary.

"You're up there all the time. Today, you stay with me."

So she did. Doing her best to ignore his lewd expressions and suggestive remarks. But she couldn't overlook his statement when she excused herself from the table. "Tonight, girl," was all he said.

"You seem upset."

"What? No, I'm fine. Perhaps a bit tired." Caroline forced a smile and laid down her sewing. She'd spent the evening in Mary's room, but it was getting late. And if Robert did manage to make it up the stairs, she didn't want him coming here looking for her.

She would be ready for him.

"I'll see you in the morning." Caroline leaned down to kiss Mary's wan cheek, but before she could straighten up, the other woman caught hold of her arm.

"What happened to your hand? It looks burned."

"I wasn't thinking and stuck it in the wash water." Caroline shook her head. "It was foolish of me."

But then not the only foolish thing she'd done since her arrival in the New World, Caroline thought as she entered her room. Mary had admonished her to rub butter on her palm, but Caroline couldn't bring herself to go downstairs.

She stripped from her gown, trying not to feel like a sacrificial virgin. For one thing, she reminded herself, she wasn't one, sacrificed or not. For another, as much as she loathed the thought of Robert touching her, it was necessary that he did. She kept on her shift, wrapped a shawl around her shoulders and blew out the candle. Once in bed, she lay stiff and still. Her eyes shut, she listened. Through the closed window came the distant sound of a solitary wolf crying into the darkness. She ignored it, concentrating instead on any noise from inside the house.

When she heard him, Caroline couldn't stop the tears from coming, but she scrubbed at her face. "For the baby," she whispered to herself over and over . . . like a litany. "For the baby."

His progress was slow; and when he shoved open the door, Caroline realized it was more than the crutch that made it so. The smell of whiskey preceeded him into the room.

"Light a candle, girl. I can't see a damn thing."

He was difficult to understand because the drink slurred his words, but Caroline grasped his meaning easily enough. Having deliberately doused the candle earlier, she now relit the wick. But she couldn't make herself look at him. Not until he'd stood for long minutes looming over the bed.

As soon as she glanced up, he laughed, a sound that sent gooseflesh crawling over her skin. Then he dropped the crutch. It crashed onto the bare floor as he threw himself across the bed.

His weight was oppressive, his smell overpowering. Caroline turned her head away only to have his fingers dig into her cheek and twist her back. She nearly gagged when his open mouth descended on her. He pried open her jaw and his thick, foul-tasting tongue filled her.

For the baby. For the baby.

When he lifted his head he was breathing heavily . . . and Caroline bit her bottom lip to keep from screaming. But the sound echoed in her head as he grabbed hold of her shift's neckline and yanked.

He groped and he squeezed, and all the while he talked. Slurred, silly words about how he would please her, and what a virile man he was. There was more, but Caroline blocked it out. She no longer thought of her child and the sacrifice she was making for its legitimacy.

She no longer thought at all.

Caroline registered what he was doing as if it happened to another. His fumbling attempts to open the flap on his breeches. The way he jerked up her shift. And still the overwhelming weight of his body.

"Damn it, girl, do something!"

The angered intensity of his words brought Caroline back to reality with a thud. She suddenly realized that the pain she'd expected . . . the pain of his entry . . . had yet to occur.

With an animal-like growl he rolled off her. His movements jerky, he grabbed his shriveled manhood, pulling and squeezing the flaccid flesh. The sounds he made disgusted her, as did the spittle drooling from his mouth. But it wasn't until he glanced up, his eyes meeting hers that she understood the significance of his dysfuntion.

The blow came so quickly, Caroline had no time to prepare herself. Pain exploded along the side of her face, and she tasted her own blood. Before she could move, he hit her again.

"Damn your uppity ways," he yelled. "See what you've done!"

But Caroline could see nothing through the red haze of suffering. She raised her arms, deflecting his next blow, which only enraged him. He couldn't seem to coordinate the stream of obscenities he spewed her way with striking her. And right now he appeared more prone to vent his anger with words.

Caroline rolled away from him as hard as she could. She fell from the bed, landing on the wood floor with a thud. But she ignored the agony in her hip as she scrambled to her feet. She sensed more than saw him lunge after her. He managed to catch a ragged edge of her shift, and Caroline heard the fabric rend. But it didn't change her focus.

The top drawer.

The pulls were slippery, and Caroline realized dispassionately that it was her own blood that made them so. She yanked, pulling the drawer open as he hobbled toward her. Her hands were frantic now, digging through the cotton shifts and stockings. She almost gave up to run from the room when her fingers folded around the carved bone handle.

The expression on his face when she whipped around, the blade of Wolf's knife pointed toward his bloated midsection was almost comedic. He managed to retrieve his crutch and stood braced against it now, his anger tempered with caution.

"Give me that knife, girl."

"Get away from me." It was heavy and her arm trembled with the effort to hold it steady.

"You're going to go getting someone hurt with that thing." His eyes narrowed.

"Get back." Caroline gave a quick jab, and he did move, though not as fast and far as she wished. "Out of my room."

"Now aren't you forgetting this is my house, girl? And you're my wife."

"That doesn't mean I shall take this . . . this . . ." Caroline blinked back the tears.

"Now I admit I might have been a little hard on you." The knife seemed to have sobered him some.

"If you ever strike me again, I'll kill you. I swear I will."

"Now you're going and talking like one of those savages. Is that where you got the knife? Did my boy give that thing to you?"

Yes, she wanted to scream at him. He gave me this and he gave me much more. But she didn't. Because his next words left her nearly speechless.

"I guess that fancy English lawyer didn't tell you

everything. His eyes narrowed. "There's only one way Seven Pines or anything else will ever be yours." He hobbled closer. "You must bear me a son."

Blood pounded in Caroline's head. "You . . . you already have sons."

"Phew," he snorted. "My first didn't have sense enough to stay clear of a losing cause. The second hasn't the stomach to run a business. And we both know what Wolf is."

"Get out of here now."

At first she thought he wasn't going to comply. He stood still a moment looking at her, his hateful light eyes expressionless. Then he maneuvered himself around. Caroline stood her ground, watching until he disappeared through the doorway. Cautiously she crept forward, waiting till she heard his crutch on the stairs before shutting and locking the door.

She forced herself not to think as she placed the knife on the commode beside the candle. Then with unsteady hands she splashed water into the porcelain bowl. After stripping off the torn shift, she used it to clean her face. The water stung; and in the washbowl, it became a coppery red. Moving slowly to the dresser, she removed a clean shift and pulled it over her head, then collapsed onto the bed.

The sheets smelled of her husband. With her remaining strength, Caroline rose and stripped them. Afterward she lay on the bare mattress. The tears came then, hot and heavy, burning their way across her torn skin.

Pounding at the door woke her with a start. She moaned aloud as she reached for the knife only to let her hand fall when she heard Sadayi's voice.

"Caroline. Caroline, are you all right?"

"Yes." Her voice sounded strained. "Please stop all the noise." It was morning. She could see light through the one eye she could slit open. "Don't wake Mary."

"She's already awake," Sadayi began when Caroline finally opened the door. When she saw Caroline, her eyes widened. "She sent me to find out why you didn't come this morning," she continued calmly. It wasn't until she pushed through the door, closing and locking it that she put her arm around Caroline's shoulders. "What happened to you?"

Caroline just shook her head and tried to move from the awkward embrace.

"It was the *inadu*?" When Caroline looked up questioningly Sadayi continued. "It means snake. It is the Cherokee name for Robert MacQuaid."

Despite her discomfort, Caroline took some degree of pleasure in hearing her husband referred to that way. But she shook her head again and moved toward the chair. "I don't want Mary to know. She has enough to—"

"She's stronger than you think." Sadayi pulled

clean sheets from the wardrobe. "At the moment she's a lot stronger than you." She snapped the sheet across the bed.

"Just tell her I'm not feeling well," Caroline whispered as Sadayi led her back to bed. Certainly no lie. She felt awful.

Caroline didn't even realize the Cherokee woman had gone till she returned to the room. She carried a bucket of water and after emptying the bowl into the chamber pot, filled it again. From around her neck she took a leather pouch. Opening it, she produced a pinch of brown powder.

"What are you doing?"

"This will make the swelling go down," Sadayi said as she stirred the herbs into the water.

The cool liquid soothed as she blotted it onto Caroline's skin.

"Do you hurt anyplace else?"

"My hip." Caroline didn't protest as Sadayi lifted her shift. When she heard the older woman's tsking sound, she closed her eyes. "I . . . I may be with child," she said, and felt Sadayi's stare on her. "Is there . . . ? Do you think the baby is hurt?"

The Cherokee woman's examination was brief. When she finished, she pulled the shift down and the blanket up.

"There is no blood. But I can help you purge the child from your body."

"No." Caroline's arms folded protectively across her stomach. "Don't hurt my child."

Sadayi said nothing as she stirred something into a tin cup. "Drink," she commanded, lifting Caroline's shoulders.

"This won't—"

She shook her head. "It will only make you stronger."

Caroline stayed in her room for a sennight with only Sadayi to care for her. The Cherokee tonic did seem to make her stronger and the mixture she put on Caroline's face helped heal the cuts. But she still looked as if she'd been beaten.

"Which is exactly what happened to you," Sadayi said in disgust, as Caroline turned away from the mirror.

Caroline ignored her words. "But I suppose I shall have to face Mary sometime."

"She's planning to get up and come to you."

"Even though you told her she might catch my fever?"

"She is concerned."

Caroline took a deep breath and nodded. Sadayi and Walini had concocted the story that Caroline was suffering from a fever to explain her keeping to her bed. Robert had neither questioned the excuse nor inquired about her health. His lack of concern meant nothing to Caroline. She still slept with the knife beside her bed in case he returned.

The time alone had given her the opportunity to think. Her first reaction was to flee, as far and as fast as she could. Anything to rid herself of Robert MacQuaid. And if there were only herself to consider she would. But there was Edward . . . Mary . . . her baby.

Caroline smoothed her skirts and glanced toward Sadayi. "I suppose I'm ready."

"My heavens, what happened to you?" Mary sat in bed leaning against pillows when Caroline entered her room.

"I've been ill." Caroline lingered by the door, staying in its shadows as much as possible. "It isn't a good idea for me to get too close."

Mary brushed away that explanation with a wave of her hand. "Your face? It's bruised and—"

"Oh that." Caroline managed to laugh as she absently touched her still tender cheek and lip. " 'Tis the silliest thing. I fell from my bed while trying to get up. 'Twas when the fever was at its worst."

Whether or not Mary believed her, she said nothing to dispute it. That was not the case with Wolf.

He appeared as before, when she least expected him. Caroline had been out of her room for days, working alongside Sadayi and Walini preparing Seven Pines for the coming winter. During those pleasantly chilly days, Caroline began to feel better. She was healing. She rarely saw Robert. He stayed to the parlor and his room, never venturing outside. Sadayi reported that his leg was worse, but Caroline felt no pity. Her main concern was that one day he would denounce her child as a bastard. But for the moment she didn't know what she could do about that.

So it was that, early one morning in October, Wolf found her walking along the creek. The sun was barely risen and an ethereal mist hung close to the ground, swirling about her skirts with each step. Overhead a hawk circled, and Caroline glanced up to follow his progress.

"Don't you realize how easily you could be captured out here by yourself?"

Caroline whirled around at the sound of his voice. She'd been thinking of him and wondered if her mind had conjured him up. But he was flesh and blood . . . and wet. The pewtery light reflected off beads of water that clung to his unbound hair, his naked chest.

Caroline's breath caught at the sight of him. He was dressed only in a breechcloth and leggings; and though she shivered beneath her brocaded gown and shawl, he seemed unaffected by the early morning chill. She'd seen him like this before, on their trip to the frontier. It was his custom to rise early and bathe in the nearest water. Apparently it didn't matter how cold that water might be. "What . . . what are you doing here?" He tilted his head and Caroline watched a drop of water from his hair slide down the smooth bronzed skin of his chest to disappear into the leather thong at his waist.

He opened his mouth to answer, and Caroline

was drawn to step closer . . . out of the willow shadows that shielded her. Wolf's expression darkened, and he closed the space between them in three long strides. "When did he do this to you?"

"I . . . I don't know what you mean?" Caroline had come to think of her face as presentable. The cuts were nearly healed, and the bruises no more than a slight yellow tinge.

"Don't lie to me, Caroline." Wolf cupped her shoulders, turning her face into the sun now exploding over the treetops.

"I fell. The fever made me disoriented," she began, but her words of denial died when he gave her a shake.

"You sound like Alkini, my mother, protecting him. Lying." He dropped his hands and turned away abruptly. "I should kill the bastard."

"No!" Caroline grabbed his arm. It was hard; and despite the sheen of water, she felt the heat of his skin radiate through her body. "Don't you see, you can't do that."

His head whipped around, dark eyes burning into her with their intensity, but he said nothing.

Caroline swallowed and tried to speak rationally. "If you . . . hurt him, it will be you who suffers."

"And you?"

Ashamed by what she must admit, Caroline's lashes fluttered shut. "Yes. I shall suffer, too."

He grunted and twisted away, but Caroline did not let him retreat. Gathering her skirts, she ran ahead, blocking his way. "It is not what you think.

I care nothing for him, but he is still my husband. We are joined by God."

"My people believe that a man and woman stay together because it is their choice. If the woman no longer wishes to stay, she returns to her family."

If only it were that simple. Caroline took a deep breath and allowed her eyes to meet his. "I have no family in England, but a brother who cannot provide for me," she told him honestly. "My family is now here. Mary and you . . . even Robert."

He stared at her so long, Caroline thought he would say nothing. She yearned to wrap her arms around his strong body and make him understand. Tell him everything, all her reasons, but she knew better than that.

"When I was older, after she died, I heard that he had beaten my mother. But I thought it was because she was Cherokee." He shook his head and looked out across the creek. "I never thought he would do this to you." *But you should have,* a small voice within him said. *What did you imagine he would do when he discovered she was not a virgin?*

" 'Tisn't your fault. And you needn't worry. It shan't happen again."

"You are right about that." With those words, Wolf turned and strode toward the house.

It took Caroline a moment to realize what he was about, but when she did, she hurried after him. "What are you going to do?" There was a knife handle, carved like the one he'd given her, sticking out of his leggings, and a tomahawk stuck

187

in the thong about his waist. "No, no. You can't kill him." She lunged for his arm, but he stepped out of her reach and quickened his pace.

"I have no intention of making you a widow," he said, his tone full of contempt. "You may keep your precious husband."

"But . . ." Caroline hesitated only a moment before following Wolf into the house. He burst into the first floor bedroom without knocking, crossed the room and grabbed an obviously startled Robert.

"What the hell?" Robert struggled, but Wolf held him firmly by his bunched-up nightshirt.

"Hell is where you'll be if you take a hand to her again. Do you understand me, old man?"

Robert's grizzled head swung around, and his gaze caught Caroline. "What's she been telling you?"

"Nothing." Caroline moved into the room. "I didn't tell him anything." She didn't want Wolf to know why Robert beat her. It was best he not think she and her husband had never consummated their marriage. It was best if no one knew that.

"She didn't have to say a word." Wolf shook the whiskey-bloated body, trying hard to control his desire to wrap his hands around the flabby neck. "I recognized your handiwork."

Robert groaned and reached for his leg when Wolf lifted him higher.

"Stop it!" Caroline rushed into the room. It smelled of sour whiskey and an even sourer body.

188

"It won't happen again," she insisted, but neither man paid her any heed.

Wolf smoothly transferred his burden to one hand. With the other he whipped out the tomahawk, holding it threateningly above Robert's head. "I have no doubts it will not happen again." His voice grew lower. "And do you know why?"

Robert's response was little more than a squeak.

"Because if you do, I shall return and sever the top of your head with this." The honed blade glistened in the first rays of sun shining through the window as he twisted it meaningfully in his palm.

Robert's pale eyes bulged, but Wolf took little pleasure in his fear, except where it emphasized his point. With no care for his leg, Wolf dropped the old man back on his mattress. He fell with a flop.

Turning, Wolf replaced the tomahawk, then strode by a startled Caroline. He was out the door and nearly into the surrounding pine forest when he heard her call his name. Wishing he could continue as if the trees had absorbed her words, Wolf stopped. She came running to his side.

Caroline's first impulse was to scream at him for confronting Robert. But when she reached him, she couldn't waste time on that. He'd done what he thought he must, and she was grateful for his concern.

"Where are you going?" It suddenly seemed more important to know that than to chastise him.

"To the Overhill Towns. It is what I came to tell

you. Most of the Middle and Lower Town Head-men have agreed to speak with the governor. I carry their message to the mountains."

"That's good, isn't it?"

A ghost of a smile flirted with his sensual lips as he raised his hand to cup her cheek. "Yes, Caroline, that is good. Perhaps we can lessen the chances of war between my people and the English."

Then as if he remembered who he was . . . and who she was, he let his hand fall to his side. "It is still no reason to take foolish chances. Stay close to the house, Caroline."

She took a deep breath and nodded. Though she knew there was no choice, she didn't want him to leave. But he seemed to know reality better than she.

"Go in to your husband now," he said, before turning and jogging toward the woods.

Caroline watched him till he disappeared among the trees, and then she reentered the house. But she didn't go to Robert. Instead, she slowly climbed the stairs to her room. Once inside she locked the door and allowed the impassioned tears to fall.

Nine

The screams woke her with a start. No, not screams. Shrieks. Wild savage shrieks that had Caroline's heart pounding and skin crawling before her body jackknifed up.

Her first instinct was to grab for the knife on the commode. The knife Wolf had given her. The handle felt solid cradled in her hand, anchoring her when all her other senses were scattered. Who or what was making that terrible noise? She jumped from bed, running to the window. Outside, the night glowed a red-orange, grotesque reflections dancing on the walls.

Fire! Flames shot from the outbuildings and barn, illuminating the yard as if it were midday, and forming a backdrop for the fiercely-painted warriors running toward the house.

Now a new sound, shrill and terrifying, rent the smoke-filled air. It rang in her ears and held her prisoner with its heart-stopping intensity. It took Caroline a moment to realize it was her own terrified voice that reverberated in her head. Clamping a hand over her mouth, she tried to gain control of herself. But panic still held her in its grip as she watched, wide-eyed the scene below.

The Indians were almost to the house now, yelling and screaming as they came. There were too many to count, and they were like no Cherokee she'd seen before. They carried tomahawks and muskets, and they would be upon her in a matter of minutes.

Mary. Caroline turned, running wildly for the door when that rational thought broke through her terror. The hallway was dark and smoke-filled. Her eyes watered and her throat felt raw.

Mary's door was locked and Caroline pounded on the wood with her fist. "Mary! Let me in!"

"I'm going to shoot." Mary's voice sounded strange, tight, with the same fear Caroline felt. But she tried to sound reassuring as her fingers clawed at the wood.

"No, Mary it's me, Caroline."

"Caroline?"

Leaning her forehead against the solid panel, Caroline could hear the soft click of the lock. Then the door swung open, and she threw herself into Mary's arms. But their reunion was over quickly. "Come on," Caroline yelled, grabbing her friend's arm. Mary did indeed have a pistol. It hung limply from her hand as Caroline bustled her through the doorway. "We have to get out of here!"

Mary's swollen belly made maneuvering through

the hallway difficult. Caroline rushed down the narrow steps, pulling the other woman behind her. When they reached the ground floor, Caroline raced down the hall toward the door off the kitchen garden.

She was nearly there when it burst open. Indians, their faces painted black and ochre poured into the house blocking her escape. Turning, Caroline saw more savages screaming in through the front door. Without thinking she shoved Mary behind her, against the wall, and lifted the knife.

Caroline lunged at the first Indian that ran toward them. He stopped abruptly, naked legs spread, glaring at her as she held the knife out in front of her. He was tall and intimidating with a face pitted by pock scars and a streak of red paint across his nose. Strange, how she saw that more clearly than the tomahawk he held poised over his head.

With all her energy she fought him. He feinted from her next swipe and her next. She held the handle tightly in her fist and poked and jabbed, cutting through the air with the silvery blade. Missing him every time. But Caroline was beyond knowing what she was doing.

The high-pitched scream was loud, even amidst the riotous confusion as the Indians ran through the house. Caroline glanced around to see Robert being dragged from his room. His wails echoed in her head until she thought it would burst. Behind her she could hear Mary's broken sobs and in front of her the fierce Indian seemed not to move as she stabbed at him over and over.

But of course he did move, for no matter how many times she tried to wound him, he was still unscathed. Then after what seemed an eternity, he appeared to grow weary of the game.

His hand came down on Caroline's arm, and the knife clattered to the floor. Caroline dove for it, but a steel-like arm snaked around her waist, lifting her off her feet.

"Mary!" Caroline kicked and scratched, trying to free herself from the Indian's hold. Then from the corner of her eye she saw Mary's pale face as she lifted the pistol. The gun was aimed at her captor . . . and her. Above the clamor of yelling Indians, Caroline heard the metallic click. But there was nothing else. No loud boom.

Another Indian came from the side and grabbed the pistol, knocking Mary to the floor as he did. The pregnant woman fell hard.

"Mary! Mary!" Caroline yelled her name over and over as she attempted to free herself. She had to see if her friend was all right. But the Indian held firm, hefting her up against his hip. He carried her, screaming and kicking, into the yard. And everywhere there were more Indians shouting and running about.

Her captor tossed her to the ground and Caroline's shift rose up about her knees, but she didn't even notice. He pulled her hands forward and wound a thong around her wrists. She tried

194

not to whimper as he pulled the cords tight. Caroline couldn't believe what was happening, but she knew it was no nightmare. The smells, the sounds were too real, too awful.

Then from the midst of savages by the sycamore tree came a cry that seemed inhuman. It was blood-curdling, more pitiful and horrible than any she'd ever heard. And it screeched on and on through the night.

Caroline tried to look away, but something compelled her to watch. Then the Indians shifted, and she caught a glimpse of what they'd done to Robert. She sucked in her breath and swallowed. He was bound hand and foot and tied to the tree's trunk. His broken leg was twisted at an unnatural angle and his other leg was bare beneath his nightshirt.

While she watched, the Indians jabbed and prodded him with pointed sticks. Each time they cut into his swollen flesh, Robert screamed. "Stop it!" Caroline yelled at the Indian standing beside her. She twisted onto her knees and dove forward in the dirt, grabbing at his leg when he paid her no heed.

Her captor stamped his foot, knocking away her hands, and growled something undecipherable at her.

"Make them stop," she cried again, but he only shrugged and looked away, back to where his fellow -2raiders tortured Robert. Sobbing, Caroline hunched over on the lawn, wondering if she'd be sick . . . but unable to look away.

Robert's screams were weaker now and the savages seemed less willing to simply taunt. Their cries of *"Inadu!"* grew louder. One of the Indians took out his tomahawk and with a loud scream held it high above his head. Before Caroline could look away, he brought it down across Robert's head. Blood sprayed everywhere as the Indian held up his trophy—Robert's scalp.

She couldn't believe what she'd just seen . . . didn't want to believe it. Black dots danced in front of Caroline's eyes; and, with a thud, she fell forward onto the dirt.

She woke with someone pulling on her arms. "Get up," a guttural voice demanded.

Caroline spit dirt from her mouth and scrambled to her feet. She must have fainted; and, by the looks of her surroundings, she hadn't been unconscious long. Not nearly long enough. Averting her eyes, Caroline tried not to look toward the tree. Toward the grotesque body that hung limply from its binding.

She wished she could mourn for Robert, but the truth remained that it was too late for him. Caroline twisted to look back toward the house, as her captor pulled her along the path into the woods. There was no sign of Mary.

"Mary?" Caroline stumbled forward until she

196

was even with her captor. He didn't slow his pace. "What have you done with her?"

Whether he understood her or not, and Caroline couldn't tell, he ignored her pleas and pushed her forward, to march in front of him. The path was well worn; but beneath her bare feet, the rocks and brambles were bruising. As she walked along, mile after mile, Caroline found herself wishing she'd pulled on her clothes before rushing out to brave the Indians. The result would have been the same, but at least she wouldn't be so cold and her feet would feel better.

When she found herself thinking of her discomforts, she was ridden with guilt. At least she was alive—cold, hungry, and tired—but alive. That was more than could be said for Robert. And probably Mary.

Caroline could tell the other woman wasn't with her group. When they stopped for a drink from the creek, she was able to see that. But the Indians must have split up before leaving Seven Pines, for there were only nine traveling together now. Was Mary a hostage of other Indians? Was she, like Robert, dead?

Caroline tried not to believe the latter. But it was hard to keep her hopes up when she was surrounded by savages that told her nothing and forced her to keep going when she was ready to drop from exhaustion.

When they finally did rest, it was with only the shelter of the trees above them. Caroline leaned

197

against the rough bark determined that she would not sleep. Not surrounded by the heathens. But the toll of the day was too much for her; and though she shivered beneath the light linen, it wasn't long till her head nodded to the side.

Almost immediately she saw it all again as if a series of paintings were stretched before her eyes. The frightening faces painted red and black, the fire, the blood. Always the blood.

And then the screams came, echoing in her mind.

But it wasn't the noise that woke her. It was the firm pressure held over her mouth. She could barely breathe. Caroline's eyes popped open, and she bucked, struggling against the hand covering her lower face. But her strength was nearly gone. She fell back onto the hard, leaf-covered ground.

It was very dark, but even through her panic she knew it was the Indian with the scarred face who held her. Her body stiffened as he moved closer to her. "Quiet." The word was a low threat growled in her ear. With his hand covering her mouth she had no choice but to comply.

Then slowly he released the biting weight of his fingers. When he lifted his hand, Caroline sucked in the cold night air, grateful for the chance. Her breath came in low, painful gasps, but even as starved as her lungs were, she tried not to make noise. Wordlessly her captor had reminded her how vulnerable she was. How dependent upon him for even her next breath.

Still she could not help the whimper that escaped when he let his hand drift down her body. Between her breasts. Past her tied hands to curve at her waist. Oh God no! Fear seized her, and she tried to roll away. But her hair was pinned beneath him, and though pain tore at her scalp she could not escape.

Her heart pounded. She had tried not to dwell on this possibility through the long day. Be thankful you are alive, she kept telling herself. Stay alive for the sake of your child. But always in the darkest recesses of her mind she'd worried about what the Indians might do to her when they stopped for the night.

He jerked her back against his body, his motions rough. Panic built up like water dammed against its flow. Before she would submit to this heathen she would—What? What could she do?

But for now at least, she did not have to find an answer. He simply wrapped his arm about her middle. Hardly daring to breath, she waited for him to touch her again. But he didn't. When she heard snores vibrating in her ear she knew he was asleep.

Slowly, muscle by muscle, Caroline let herself relax. Her body was pressed to his, a fact she couldn't overlook. But there was warmth now. If she was to survive she must accept even the smallest advantage.

Caroline closed her eyes. She inched closer to her large captor. His breathing never changed, and she sighed her relief. When she was as comfortable and warm as she could get, Caroline willed herself to sleep. Rest. She needed it. Her baby needed it.

As she drifted toward slumber Caroline imagined she saw Wolf. His sensual lips smiled their approval. He took her hand and led her deeper into oblivion.

It seemed no more than minutes later that she was dragged to her feet, barely awake. Caroline blinked, trying to remember where she was and why. Comprehension swept over her painfully. The Indian she'd come to think of as hers gave her a shove toward a small thicket of trees. She stumbled, but kept her footing. When she glanced back at him, he jerked his head, motioning for her to continue.

He'd done the same last night, giving her a bit of privacy to take care of her bodily functions. Caroline hurried toward a twisting of vines that formed a natural shield.

As she had before, Caroline considered bolting and running away. The urge was so strong she could almost taste it, now that she was out of her kidnapper's reach. But the inevitability of recapture weighed heavily on her. She was tied and tired, weak from hunger. And though she tried to pay attention yesterday when they left the trail to forge through the woods, Caroline had no idea where she was.

Coupled with the certain knowledge that she couldn't escape was the taunting fear of what the

Indian would do when she was in his grasp again. In the end she walked resolutely back to him.

This morning she was given a few bites of dried meat before they set out again. The sun, when it finally rose, offered some warmth, though Caroline still shivered constantly.

One step in front of the other. Survival seemed reduced to that. Caroline tried to keep her mind blank but thoughts of Wolf kept surfacing. At first she fought them, but they soon overwhelmed her. She glanced ahead, only to imagine she saw him standing there, musket raised. "I've come to rescue you," he said. "Save you from these savages."

Her joy was boundless until reason won out. He would never say that. These were his people. He'd told her so often enough. Of course, Caroline couldn't be sure it was Cherokee who captured her.

Beneath their paint, they looked like the other Cherokee she'd seen, tall, muscular bodies, heads shaved except for the topknot they decorated with feathers. But perhaps all Indians looked like this. To her knowledge Caroline had never seen any others.

Besides, what did it matter? She was their prisoner and there was no one to rescue her. Even if Wolf did learn of the massacre at Seven Pines, he was in The Middle Towns—too far away to help her.

They paused midmorning to drink from a small stream. Caroline fell to her knees on·a flat rock by the shore. She had reached the end of her endurance. Even when her Indian nudged her, then kicked at her bloodied feet, she couldn't move.

"Get up," he said, grabbing her elbows and pulling her to standing. He bent toward her. "Not far now."

The words offered her just enough hope to push forward.

But his idea of far wasn't the same as hers. She could barely move by the time they stopped at the head of a valley. Clustered near the river were over a score of cabins, built much like Wolf's. They were squat, appearing to be single rooms covered with bark. Near the center, on a slight rise was a larger building, circular in shape and covered with dried mud.

It was toward this they walked. The dogs were the first to notice them. They set up a howl that attracted some small boys playing by the river. They ran along beside the warriors, asking questions that Caroline couldn't understand and staring at her.

By the time they reached the larger building, other Indians had joined the procession. The women she saw reminded her of Sadayi and Walini. Though no one did anything to her, Caroline felt their curiosity, their animosity. She lifted her chin and forced her knees to hold firm.

She was left outside, under guard, as her Indian and several others entered the large cabin. It didn't take long for them to come out again. They were accompanied by an older man. His skin was leathery and wrinkled, but his dark eyes remained clear. He looked her up and down then said something in the low guttural language. Her captor answered, and the older man nodded, seemingly in agreement. Then another Indian stepped forward and held something out for the older man's inspection.

Caroline didn't recognize it at first. But when she did, her stomach recoiled and she thought she'd be sick. She looked away quickly from Robert MacQuaid's scalp. But the proof of his death seemed to spark excitement in the village. Everyone from the youngest child to an old woman with hair the color of steel, gathered closer.

"Inadu! Inadu!" Again and again Caroline heard the word the Indians had shouted during the attack. Snake. The name Sadayi said the Cherokee called her husband.

After a short conversation with her captor, one of the women grabbed Caroline's arm and shoved her toward a cabin. The woman was obviously not pleased to be given this task. But after pushing her inside she did return in a few minutes with a bowl of something hot that made Caroline salivate. She set the food on the floor then pulled a small knife from her pocket.

Caroline cried out and backed toward the wall, but the woman ignored her obvious fear. With a flick of her wrist she severed the leather strap that bound Caroline's wrists. Her tone was agitated as she spoke. She turned abruptly and left the cabin.

This encounter set the tone for the following

days. Caroline was confined to the cabin, but she was given food and water. The woman built a fire for warmth and provided enough sticks and twigs for Caroline to keep it going.

Several times others would walk into the cabin unannounced. Once it was the old man. He simply stared at her, then nodded and left. Her captor also came. He spoke some English and asked her several questions concerning her comfort. He seemed anxious that she should be warm and well fed and was almost congenial.

But when Caroline asked about Mary, his manner turned gruff. And even though she was sure he understood at least part of what she said, he only shook his head. "Tell me if she's alive," Caroline insisted, but he only turned on his heel and left.

Caroline was used to commotion and excitement in the camp. The first night there, a festive atmosphere prevailed, with drums and dancing long into the night. After that whenever someone came or left the town, the people would call out. So when there was a definite rumbling of activity on the third day since her arrival, Caroline thought little of it.

She was huddled by the center fire, trying to stay warm when a shadow blocked the light from the door. She sensed who it was before she turned.

Tears sprang to her eyes when she saw Wolf, and she scrambled to her feet. But when she would have flown to his arms, he held his hand out, and she noticed the sharp warning in his stare. The motion of his head was barely perceivable, but Caroline expanded her focus and noticed the women bunched into the doorway.

Wolf turned and said something to them, and they left, but not without grumbling their protest. Then he carefully shut the door. When he turned back, Caroline stood her ground, no longer sure of her welcome.

"Are you all right?"

His tone was not that of a lover wrought with concern. And that bothered her. "If you mean am I alive, the answer as you can plainly see is yes."

He arched a dark brow but made no comment. Instead he shrugged a leather pack from around his bare shoulders. He held it out to her. "This is for you . . . from Mary."

"Mary?" Caroline stepped toward him. "You saw Mary? Is she . . . ?"

"Mary is well."

"Oh thank God." Tears of relief sprang to her eyes and ran unchecked down Caroline's cheeks. "I thought they'd killed her. I thought—" Her words caught on a sob, and she turned away, suddenly too spent to go on. But after a moment, she glanced over her shoulder. He still stood by the closed door. He still held the pack out toward her as if he didn't know what to do with it.

"Robert is dead."

"I know." He dropped the bundle to the dirt floor and moved toward her when he saw her shoulders tremble. She'd turned away from him again, and he hesitated. When Wolf had seen Caroline for the first time, he'd thought that she looked fragile, like a rare China doll. Though he knew now how strong she was, that image still remained. It seemed to him as if she'd shatter under his touch.

As gently as he could, Wolf reached out. Her beautiful hair was matted and tangled. He felt her stiffen, and he nearly pulled away, but the next instant she whirled around, burying herself in his arms. Letting out a deep breath, Wolf tightened his embrace.

"They scalped him."

"I know." Wolf repeated. He could think of nothing else to say that might soothe her. Her tears were hot against his chest, and her fingers dug into the skin of his back.

"There was blood everywhere, and he screamed and screamed."

"Hush now, don't think of it."

"But I can't stop." She pushed away enough to lift a wet face to him. "Can't you understand? I keep seeing it again and again . . ."

His hand cupped the back of her head, and he touched his lips to her forehead. He did understand. The scene played itself out in his imagination. But he wouldn't allow her to become a slave to her memories. He pressed her cheek back against his shoulder. "You must put this behind you."

"But—"

"Behind you, Caroline, do you hear me?" She glanced up at his sharp tone, and he softened it. "It is over." He knew what she'd been through—as much as he could piece together from talking with Mary—but her ordeal wasn't over yet.

"I was afraid you wouldn't come." Caroline breathed in the male scent of his bare skin. "How did you know? You were on your way to the mountains."

"I stopped at Fort Loudoun. Word reached me there. I returned as soon as I heard." He didn't tell her of the terror that had sliced through him when the messenger related the news of the raid. When he reached Seven Pines, riding non-stop, and found her gone, he'd been half crazed. Mary had calmed him.

"If they were going to kill her, Raff, they would have done it here," Mary had said logically.

He held onto that notion as he made his way to Estatoe. Once here, he'd been so relieved to find out she was safe that it took him a moment to understand what the Headman of the village was saying to him.

Wolf held her a moment longer. "Come," he said when he finally, reluctantly, let her go. "Let me take care of you."

After leading her to a mat and motioning for her to sit, Wolf went to the door and called to the woman standing near the entrance. She entered the cabin carrying several pottery dishes and laid them on the floor. With a nod, Wolf dismissed her.

"What are you doing?" Caroline propped herself onto her elbows to watch him.

"I'm going to use an ointment on your cuts and bruises. Just lie back."

"I want to know about Mary. Are you certain she's all right?"

"Yes."

"But I saw them strike her. She fell." Caroline sucked in her breath when he squeezed water from a rag onto her soles.

The bottom of her feet were blistered. He felt her pain as he dipped his fingers in the foul smelling medicine and applied it to her bruised skin. But he kept his expression blank and his tone unemotional. "She was not injured. Sadayi is with her."

"And the baby?"

"She still carries the child."

"I'm so glad." Caroline lay back as he wrapped her feet in clean bandages he took from the pack Mary sent. She had worried constantly about her own child at first. But days passed, and she saw no sign that she would lose the baby.

"I have your shoes," he said, "but there is no need to put them on yet."

"Why not?" Caroline sat up and stared at him. "I want to leave here."

"I know." If only it were that simple. Wolf moved around to her head. "Lean back," he ordered.

"What are you doing now?"

"Washing your hair."

"But I—" Caroline put a hand to her head. "I can do that." But he was already pouring water from a gourd over her curls. It dripped down her shoulders, absorbing into her dirty shift.

"Put your head back," Wolf urged. "Pretend you're in England, and I'm your lady's maid."

"I never had one." But she bent her neck and allowed him to continue his ministrations—in part, because it felt so wonderful. His strong fingers worked through the tangles then massaged her scalp. And every place he touched her, she burned with sensual awareness.

She didn't resist when after he rinsed her hair and wrung out the excess water, he skimmed the shift from her shoulders. He washed her face, and then her neck. And all the while, his eyes held hers.

Caroline knew she should protest when he nudged the shift over the tips of her breasts, but she could only suck in her breath. Her nipples were beaded; and when he drew the wet linen across them, Caroline closed her eyes. But she could still see him. His vision was etched in her mind, his eyes dark and intense, his nostrils flaring.

He reached behind her, and the cool cloth slid around her rib and across her back. With every breath she took, her breasts skimmed his chest.

"Stand." Wolf's voice was husky. He helped her up and the torn shift floated to the floor. He forced himself to concentrate upon washing her. The swell of her hip, the plain of her stomach. Wolf dipped the cloth in the pail of water then wiped it across her pale skin. But each stroke was torture. He ached for her, and it was only the memory of what she'd been through, of what was yet to come, that kept him from succumbing to his desires.

Her legs were long and firm, and Wolf dropped to his knees in front of her. His movements grew slower, more caressing. But he didn't realize how intimate his touch was until he felt her fingers in his hair.

"Raff."

The imploring way she whispered his name forced him to face reality. He leaned into her, his face pressed to her flesh. "Not here," he said, his breath fanning the tight curls between her legs. "Not now."

Wolf stood. Forcing himself to look away, he searched through the clothing Mary packed and found a clean shift. Her hair was still wet; and as the soft linen drifted over her body, it left patches of damp cloth. He handed her a corset, unable to meet the questioning expression in her eyes.

"What 'tis it you aren't telling me?" She took the garment. " 'Tisn't Mary . . . ?"

"No." Wolf took a deep breath. "I am not sure I can simply take you away from here."

"I don't understand."

"Tal-tsuska has claimed you for himself."

Ten

"What does that mean?" Caroline tried to comprehend what he told her, but it seemed as if he spoke a different language. Earlier when she turned her head to see him standing in the small cabin that had become her prison, she assumed he was there to rescue her. Perhaps she'd forgotten how rarely he did what she expected.

Now she stalked away, back and forth between the fire and opposite wall. "Why did you come here if not to rescue me? 'Twas it to gloat? I wouldn't listen to you when I had the chance, and now look where I am! 'Tis that it? Or did you think I would accept my fate better if you washed me first? Touched me . . . ?"

During her tirade, Wolf stood by dispassionately, as if carved from marble. Nothing moved but his dark eyes as he followed her pacing. When she stopped, her bottom lip quivering, Wolf strode quickly to her side. His hands cupped her shoulders, forcing her to look at him. "Have you finished?" he demanded, shaking her when she tried to turn her head from his hard stare. "Have you?"

Caroline swallowed the tears clogging her throat and nodded. She had nothing else to say. She'd already said too much.

"You have been through a difficult time, so I will ignore most of your words. But hear me, Caroline, and hear me well, if we are to leave here, you must be more circumspect."

We. He'd said we. Caroline wet her suddenly dry lips.

"Tal-tsuska is the man who captured you," he said. "He is a relative, but that will mean nothing. He desires you, and his claim is valid."

"Well, I don't want him." She sounded like a petulant child, but at the moment didn't care. The memory of her captor was vivid from that night, the painted face and fierce expression.

"That is of little consequence."

Caroline wanted to scream at him. His voice was so flat, as if he spoke of the trees in the forest, or the weather. But she did listen as he continued.

"You are a captive and though the Headman is denouncing the attack on Seven Pines, in his heart he applauds the warriors' courage."

"Courage? We were an old man with a broken leg and two women."

"They defied the British," he said simply. "But that is not for us to debate. I merely tell you how the Headman . . . how many here, view the act. How it effects you."

"There seems to be little doubt how it effects me."

"Except that I have also claimed you."

"What?" Caroline's stomach dropped as she stared up at him.

"A member of my family was slain. It is my right to be compensated."

"With me?"

"That is what I choose." Wolf let his hands drop and turned toward the door. "The Headmen await me, and I shouldn't tarry." He didn't tell her that he'd stayed too long as it was. His only goal when he entered the cabin was to assure himself that she was alive. There had been no plan to bind her feet, or wash her hair . . . or touch her.

"Wait." Caroline grabbed for his arm before he could leave. "What are you going to do?"

"Tal-tsuska and I will each speak. Then the Headmen will decide."

"But what if they . . . ?" Caroline blinked back the tears. "I don't want to stay here."

His hand tightened over hers, and Caroline forced herself not to collapse against him. "You will not."

But she knew he couldn't be sure.

And Wolf was not without his doubts as he crossed the foot-packed ground toward the Council House. Tal-tsuska stood by the doorway of the circular building, his arms folded across his chest. He had not approved of Wolf's visit to Caroline's cabin. His protest was loud and vocal to the Headman, but he had agreed with Wolf that he needed to see for himself the wife of his dead father.

"They will not allow you to take her," Tal-tsuska said now. "She was wife to the hated *inadu*."

"Who is now dead." Wolf pushed past him, not wishing to argue the point. His blood ties with Tal-tsuska were strong—he was son of his mother's brother. Stronger still were the ties of youth that bound them. But Wolf had told Caroline the truth when he said it would make no difference.

It didn't matter that Wolf had been forced to leave the village and his mother's people when Robert sent him to England—it didn't matter to Tal-tsuska. Nor did it matter that Wolf came back. In Tal-tsuska's eyes, he was now English. And Tal-tsuska had only hatred for the English, the white man. Which made his claim of Caroline all the more sinister.

First Wolf slipped the leather musket strap from around his shoulders. He laid the gun along with his powderhorn, tomahawk, and knife on the ground beside the weapons of Tal-tsuska. He ducked his head to remove the beaded belt of his grandfather. Beneath his fingers the tiny shells that told of his family gave comfort as he entered the council building.

Inside it was dark and smoky, the only light coming from a small fire that smoldered in the center of the room. The Headman, Astugataga, sat watching solemnly as the two young men entered. The hair protruding from his topknot was white with

214

age, and his face was mapped by many lines, but his vision was clear and his judgment strong.

With quiet ceremony Wolf offered the belt of his ancestors to Astugataga as proof of his sincerity. *"Asiya,"* he said in greeting. "I have come to ask for your wisdom."

"What is it you desire, Wa'ya, son of Alkini?"

Wolf kept his eyes on Astugataga, but he knew Tal-tsuska had followed him into the building and stood behind him to the right. "My father has been killed." He did not like laying claim to Robert, but had no choice.

"I know of this deed. And I have already re-proved the men responsible." His gaze shot briefly toward Tal-tsuska then back to Wolf.

"Then you also know it is an act that cannot go uncompensated, by the English or myself."

"I have reprimanded those who took part," Astugataga repeated. "But the attack at Seven Pines was not without provocation."

No one knew that better than Wolf; but, at the moment, he chose to ignore it. "I have heard the warriors were permitted to hold scalp dances."

Astugataga said nothing, only nodded his agreement.

"The British will hear of this also. Not from me, but they have their ways. Even now their tongues wag of this deed."

"Perhaps that is good." Tal-tsuska stepped forward, not waiting his turn to speak. "We have shown the English that we are not a band of old women who will fall before them in the dirt. We are great warriors."

"Who attack a crippled old man and two women." Wolf's use of Caroline's argument turned Tal-tsuska's scarred face red with anger. Though fighting within the Council House was forbidden, he took a menacing step toward Wolf. But with his dark eyes leveled on his adversary, Wolf held his ground.

"Tal-tsuska. Wa'ya." The Headman's voice was firm. "We have agreed to the exchange of words. Nothing else."

Wolf turned his attention back to Astugataga. "The attack at Seven Pines was an act of war, where none exists. The English will view it as such."

"Let them come, we will show them the *Ani'-Yun'wiya*, the Cherokee avenge their slain."

"And the valleys will run red with blood. Is that what you want for our people?" Wolf asked Astugataga, though it was the young warrior who'd spoken.

"He speaks of 'our people' but he is not *Ani'-Yun'wiya*. He is the son of *inadu*, the snake. He is English."

Wolf said nothing. The Headman knew of his history. He would allow his deeds to speak for him.

"Unlike his father, Wa'ya has always been a friend to us. His mother was Alkini of Wolf Clan." Astugataga lifted the belt given him by Wolf. "And his grandfather was a great warrior."

"But he talks of surrender."

"I speak of compromise," Wolf corrected. "Even now our Headmen ponder Governor Lyttelton's invitation to come to Charles Town for a talk." Wolf paused, his eyes meeting those of the old, wise man. "I have been across the sea to their land. It is vast and the people are as many as the mosquitoes in the summer. They will not let this act go unpunished." Wolf took a calming breath. His argument was sound, but it wasn't what he should be debating. He knew it and so did Astugataga.

"You speak of the English, how the death of the *inadu* affects them. But it is you who come to me claiming the woman."

When he spoke again, Wolf's voice was less impassioned though his resolve was as strong. "I have lost a relative. The tribal laws are clear. I wish to be compensated for my loss by claiming your hostage, the white woman, Caroline MacQuaid."

"She is mine!"

Tal-tsuska stepped forward angrily, but Wolf ignored him as did the Headman. Astugataga held up his hand; then, with a wave, he dismissed them both. "I have heard you both and know of your concerns. I shall think on what you have told me."

Caroline slept poorly, and when she did, she was plagued by dreams. Screams echoed through her head, and blood covered everything. She jerked

217

awake only to remember that though the attack was over, her nightmare was just beginning.

Wolf had not returned. In his place the Cherokee called Tal-tsuska, her captor, had come. He informed her in his broken English that she was his. Caroline had only been able to stand in silent terror as he explained that he would move her into his cabin tomorrow after she was prepared by the women.

He was lying. Caroline had been so sure of that. Wolf told her she wouldn't have to stay here. She'd paced and waited for him the rest of the day and long into the night, before accepting that he was gone.

He had left her . . . again.

Caroline lay awake on the mat, staring into the dark, wondering how she could have been so foolish a second time. She tried not to think of her fate, there would be time enough for that. But Wolf . . . she had trusted him.

Near dawn she again drifted into a fitful sleep, so troubled that the hand on her arm brought a terrified cry to her lips. A cry that was stifled as her mouth was covered.

"We must hurry. And you must be quiet."

She twisted, staring wide-eyed over his hand. When Wolf asked if she understood him, Caroline nodded. "I thought you were gone," she whispered when he took his hand away.

"What made you think that?" He handed her a shoe and Caroline sat up, pulling it on as she spoke, trying not to grimace as the hard leather rubbed her feet.

"Tal-tsuska came to me last evening and said I was to move into his cabin today." In the dim light she saw his expression grow dark.

"He only spoke the truth as he wished it to be. Not as it is. Now, no more questions."

Her other shoe on, Wolf pulled her to her feet and led her to the door. They stepped out into the pearly grey of dawn. Few Cherokee were up and about, and those that were, paid little heed to Wolf and Caroline as they made their way out of the village.

Caroline had only seen the Indian town when she was brought here. And then she'd been too numb with fright and fatigue for her mind to register more than a blur of small cabins. In the pewter wash of dawn she noticed the neat, sturdy cabins, covered with bark like Wolf's. There were gardens and large loom-like structures that held animal hides. She wanted to ask Wolf about everything she saw, but he was leading the way and his pace was fast. It was all Caroline could do to keep up. It seemed almost as if they were stealing away.

They left the clearing and entered the path leading through the forest. His hand, firmly gripping hers became a lifeline. The trees didn't seem so dark, the call of wild animals so ominous when she concentrated on the warmth of his fingers.

How long or far they traveled, Caroline couldn't say, but gradually the angle of the sun penetrated the thick canopy of pine and oak shading the trail. And Caroline knew she needed to rest. Wolf must have sensed it too for he sank down against a tree, pulling her after him.

Though he seemed barely winded, it took Caroline a moment to catch her breath once she sat in a bed of pine needles facing him.

"I don't understand." Even though they were alone, Caroline found herself whispering. "What happened?"

Wolf shrugged. He didn't like taking her as he had, as if he were running away, but he'd agreed with Astugataga it was for the best. Especially after hearing of Tal-tsuska's visit to Caroline. Both of them had been told to stay away from the white captive. And though he feared Caroline would worry, Wolf complied. Apparently Tal-tsuska had not.

"The Headman summoned me early this morning," Wolf finally began. "I am not sure he felt my claim to you was the strongest, but he said I was to take you."

Caroline closed her eyes and sighed deeply. "But why did we leave as we did? If the Headman gave his permission . . ."

"He also had not yet told Tal-tsuska of his decision. And he thought we should be gone when he did."

"He shall be very angry."

Wolf couldn't tell if her words were a statement or question, but he nodded. "Yes, very angry."

Caroline swallowed. "What do you think he will do?"

"It is my hope, nothing."

For several minutes, they sat in silence. Though Caroline noticed Wolf's one hand curve about the stock of his rifle, he seemed relaxed as he rested. She took the opportunity to study him.

He wore a gathered hunting shirt over doeskin leggings. The tattoos that graced so many Cherokee warriors were only visible now around his strong wrists. His chin was darkened by a day's growth of whiskers, and his dark hair was tied back in a queue. He was a paradox, a strange mixture of the Cherokee she just left and the English to which she returned. If the two cultures were difficult for her to accept, what must they be for him?

"Why did they let me go?"

He glanced around, and his gaze locked with hers. "I have told you."

"No," Caroline shook her head and curls spilled forward across her breast. "You only said they made the decision to let you have me. But you also said your claim was not the strongest. Tal-tsuska must have felt the same when he came to me yesterday."

"He was not to do that. Neither of us were." His dark brows lowered. "You were not hurt, were you?"

"No. Only frightened."

"I am sorry for that."

"But then you warned me, didn't you?" Caroline buried her face in her hands for a moment,

221

then looked back at him. He dropped the hand he reached toward her. "Please, tell me why I was released."

"Astugataga fears the English," Wolf said simply.

"And Tal-tsuska doesn't?"

"Not as much as he hates them."

"And Robert," Caroline said softly. "He hated Robert." She could close her eyes and see the fiendish delight Tal-tsuska took in watching the torture.

"Yes, he hated him."

" 'Twas more than because Robert cheated the Cherokee, wasn't it?" Sadayi and Walini disliked Robert because of that, but she couldn't see them taking pleasure in his screams.

"My mother was Tal-tsuska's aunt. As a male of her family, he feels the need to avenge her treatment at Robert's hands."

"Have you ever felt that need?"

The air surrounding them seemed to grow deathly still as Caroline waited for his answer. His eyes never left hers as he spoke. "Yes," he said simply.

He was still a moment longer, giving her the opportunity to ask the next logical question. But Caroline couldn't make herself ask it. And she wasn't sure why.

At any rate, the opportunity passed, for he pushed to his feet and leaned over to help her up.

"We should go."

"Back to Seven Pines?" Caroline shook out her skirts. " 'Tis that where we are going?"

"We will stop at Seven Pines to pick up Mary," he explained. "Then I will take you both to Fort Prince George. You should be safe there for the time being."

"But what about you?" Caroline trudged after him. They seemed to be following no path that she could discern. "Will you stay at the fort with us?"

Wolf paused long enough to glance back at her. Caroline's pale hair curled wildly about her shoulders. There were brambles and scatters of pine needles caught in the tangles. He resisted the urge to comb them out with his fingers. Turning back he stepped over a log and heard her follow. "No," he said, but he couldn't erase the expression in her mauve crescented eyes as he made his way through the forest.

By the time they reached the curve of the river, Caroline was exhausted. She rued her inability to sleep while she had the chance. Doggedly she kept moving, trying her best to ignore the pain of her unhealed cuts and bruises. But she couldn't help noticing that her companion seemed even more alert than usual.

He halted their tiny procession with a lift of his hand before they stepped from the shelter of the forest to the open shore of the waterway.

"What is it?" Caroline whispered, because his manner seemed to dictate such precautions. "Do you hear something?" Now Caroline turned her head carefully, searching through the bramble of holly and vines. But with the exception of a white-tailed deer nosing its way as carefully as they through the brush, she could see nothing.

"I suppose not," Wolf said, but he felt a strange prickle at the back of his neck that wouldn't go away. He took Caroline's hand and pulled her toward the water. "We can cross here."

There were flat rocks, oval in shape and smoothed by the splash of uncountable water droplets sliding over them. From one to the other there was space filled with swirling eddies, but these gaps were easily crossed. At least for Wolf they were. Caroline needed assistance to leap the gaps. The distance from the last one to the steep shoreline was particularly long.

The bloodcurdling scream sounded across the valley just as Wolf bent forward, grasping her hand to pull Caroline toward the shore. Both their heads whipped about in time to see Tal-tsuska hurl himself at them.

Wolf only had time to deflect the blow with his forearm as he shoved Caroline out of harm's way. She slipped, then fell backward, fighting to keep her footing as water swirled about her thighs.

To her right the river boiled as the two men fell as one into the rushing current.

Caroline opened her mouth to scream, but some new instinct kept her quiet. Instead she struggled with her sodden skirts, trying to reach Wolf. Amid the thrashing of arms and legs and white foam, it

MORE PASSION AND ADVENTURE AWAIT... YOUR TRIP TO A BIG ADVENTUROUS WORLD BEGINS WHEN YOU ACCEPT YOUR FIRST 4 NOVELS ABSOLUTELY *FREE*
(AN $18.00 VALUE)

Accept your Free gift and start to experience more of the passion and adventure you like in a historical romance novel. Each Zebra novel is filled with proud men, spirited women and tempestuous love that you'll remember long after you turn the last page.

Zebra Historical Romances are the finest novels of their kind. They are written by authors who really know how to weave tales of romance and adventure in the historical settings you love. You'll feel like you've actually gone back in time with the thrilling stories that each Zebra novel offers.

GET YOUR FREE GIFT WITH THE START OF YOUR HOME SUBSCRIPTION

Our readers tell us that these books sell out very fast in book stores and often they miss the newest titles. So Zebra has made arrangements for you to receive the four newest novels published each month.

You'll be guaranteed that you'll never miss a book, and home delivery is so convenient. And to show you just how easy it is to get Zebra Historical Romances, we'll send you your first 4 books absolutely FREE! Our gift to you just for trying our home subscription service.

BIG SAVINGS AND FREE HOME DELIVERY

Each month, you'll receive the four newest titles as soon as they are published. You'll probably receive them even before the bookstores do. What's more, you may preview these exciting novels free for 10 days. If you like them as much as we think you will, just pay the low preferred subscriber's price of just $3.75 each. *You'll save $3.00 each month off the publisher's price.* AND, your savings are even greater because there are never any shipping, handling or other hidden charges—FREE Home Delivery. Of course you can return any shipment within 10 days for full credit, no questions asked. There is no minimum number of books you must buy.

4 FREE BOOKS

TO GET YOUR 4 FREE BOOKS WORTH $18.00 — MAIL IN THE FREE BOOK CERTIFICATE T O D A Y

Fill in the Free Book Certificate below, and we'll send your FREE BOOKS to you as soon as we receive it.

If the certificate is missing below, write to: Zebra Home Subscription Service, Inc., P.O. Box 5214, 120 Brighton Road, Clifton, New Jersey 07015-5214.

FREE BOOK CERTIFICATE
4 FREE BOOKS

ZEBRA HOME SUBSCRIPTION SERVICE, INC.

YES! Please start my subscription to Zebra Historical Romances and send me my first 4 books absolutely FREE. I understand that each month I may preview four new Zebra Historical Romances free for 10 days. If I'm not satisfied with them, I may return the four books within 10 days and owe nothing. Otherwise, I will pay the low preferred subscriber's price of just $3.75 each; a total of $15.00, *a savings off the publisher's price of $3.00.* I may return any shipment and I may cancel this subscription at any time. There is no obligation to buy any shipment and there are no shipping, handling or other hidden charges. Regardless of what I decide, the four free books are mine to keep.

NAME

ADDRESS _____ APT

CITY _____ STATE ____ ZIP

(   )
TELEPHONE

SIGNATURE _____ (if under 18, parent or guardian must sign)

Terms, offer and prices subject to change without notice. Subscription subject to acceptance by Zebra Books. Zebra Books reserves the right to reject any order or cancel any subscription.

ZB0494

GET
FOUR
FREE
BOOKS
(AN $18.00 VALUE)

was impossible to tell who was winning the conflict. They tumbled about, their bodies soaked and sleek, each striving to outmaneuver the other.

Swiping wet hair from her face, Caroline frantically searched for something she could use to tip the battle Wolf's way. That's when she saw Wolf's rifle on the shore. He must have dropped it when he pushed her. Her heart pounding, she lunged toward the weapon. But she lost her balance, and fell into the rush of water. Pain shot up from her knee as it cracked against a sharp rock, but she did her best to ignore it as she pushed to her feet.

White water foamed about her as she threw herself again toward the shore. The gun's barrel gleamed in the slanting rays of afternoon sun . . . beckoning. She was almost to it, fighting the slippery bottom and swirling flow with every step, when she glanced behind her again.

Water stung her eyes, and she quickly scrubbed her hand across the clumping hair, her breath catching when she made out Tal-tsuska standing, ready to leap upon Wolf. She did scream then, a strangled, "No!"

Tal-tsuska's head jerked up, and his eyes met hers before Caroline whirled away. Frantic to keep her composure, feeling its fragile hold slipping away, Caroline splashed toward the side.

The bank was steep, the soil washed away by the lively current, and Caroline scrambled to get a toehold. She grabbed for a sapling and pulled, trying not to think about what she would do when she reached the weapon.

All she knew was that she must save Wolf. She could not allow him to die because of her.

Caroline lurched forward, falling almost on top of the rifle. She'd never fired one before, but had watched Wolf once when they were coming from Charles Town. It was heavier than she thought, and she nearly staggered under the weight of her sodden clothing and the gun.

But she managed to bring the carved stock to her shoulder just as something rushed past her. She turned in time to see Tal-tsuska running along the shore. Without thinking she aimed the gun at his fleeing back, and would have pulled the trigger if not for the hand that closed over hers.

Her breath catching, she looked up, into Wolf's dark eyes.

"Let him go, Caroline," Wolf said as he gently pried the weapon from her locked fingers.

"But he . . ." Caroline couldn't finish. When she'd realized it was her captor running past her, she assumed he'd killed Wolf. And her mind and body had exploded with the need for revenge. That gone, she could barely stand.

"Tal-tsuska only wished to let me know of his displeasure."

"Displeasure!" Caroline nearly screamed the word. "He tried to kill you."

"No, Caroline." Wolf touched her shoulder and she collapsed against him, throwing her arms about his neck. Wolf held her as tightly as he could. "If killing me was his desire, he could have done it from the shore. With one shot." What he said was true, but Wolf doubted when they met again, his cousin would be so generous.

"Come," he finally said. "We must find a place to camp."

"I can keep going." Caroline pulled away enough to look up at him. She wanted to return to Seven Pines and Mary as quickly as possible.

"Well, I cannot." Wolf gave her a fleeting grin and brushed wet hair from her face. Then with his arm around her shoulder, he began walking along a path that followed the river downstream.

They stopped on high ground above falls that thundered down to a gorge below. They were both soaked, and Raff emptied his wet pack, hanging a blanket from the low branches of an elm. Then he gathered twigs and started a fire.

Caroline moved close to it, gratefully reaching toward the flames. Since the episode by the river she hadn't stopped shivering, and the setting sun made her even colder. Still, she shook her head when Raff suggested she remove her wet clothing. He had already shrugged out of his shirt and leggings leaving his strong body covered only by his breechcloth.

"Here." He squatted beside her and held out a clean shirt. "It is a bit damp around the edges, but the blanket kept it from getting a soaking."

When Caroline still hesitated, he cocked a dark brow. "It is not as if I haven't seen you before."

Which wasn't the problem at all, Caroline admitted to herself as she took the shirt and stood. She didn't trust herself. No matter all that had transpired since they last made love, she wanted him. Every time she looked at him, Caroline feared he could see the longing in her eyes.

Which was all the more reason she should go off into the woods to change, or at least step behind the blanket. But she did neither. Instead Caroline turned her back on him.

She'd already removed her shoes and stockings, and now stood barefooted on the carpet of pine needles. Her fingers wouldn't stop shaking as she unlaced her corset. Then came her petticoats. Her shift was last, drifting down around her body on a whisper of air.

Caroline stood perfectly still. The night air tingled her skin, teased her nipples. She wanted to turn to him, to offer herself, but at the last moment her courage deserted her. Taking a deep breath, Caroline reached for the shirt she'd hung from a nearby branch.

His hand stopped her. She hadn't heard him move, but knew from experience how silent his steps could be. Caroline's eyes shut as he slid his rough-tipped fingers up her arm. His touch brought heat to her flesh. Her blood pounded through her veins, and thrummed in her ears, louder even than the waterfall's roar.

When he skimmed around to her breastbone, her head fell back against his chest, and she began to tremble. His lips touched her exposed neck, the rounded curve of her shoulder, and Caroline moaned.

It was she who brought his hand down to cover her breast, he that rubbed his thumb across the distended tip. His lips were hungry now as they feasted on the underside of her jaw. Caroline could feel the hard throbbing length of him against her back and her legs spread.

His left hand pushed lower, past the slight swell of her stomach. His fingers tangled with the tight curls guarding her womanhood, and Caroline squirmed against him.

But before she could turn to face him, his teeth nipped at her earlobe. His tongue was hot as it followed the curve, his voice husky as he whispered, "You realize, of course, that you shall regret this by the light of a new day."

Eleven

Regrets. Caroline closed her eyes and tried to concentrate on what he said. But it was the feel of his tongue, the vibrations of his words through her head that held her attention. She turned in his arms, the sensual slide of her skin over his heightening her desire to a fever pitch.

He held her loosely, and Caroline leaned back against the hands clasped at the small of her back. Her breasts filled, missing the contact of his body. Slowly she lifted her arms till her palms flattened against his chest.

She heard his quick intake of breath; but, other than that, he didn't move. In the firelight his face seemed cast of bronze, the flesh pulled taut, the handsome bones standing out in bold relief.

Caroline could see in his stark expression the price he paid for holding himself still. Especially when she began a careful exploration of his muscled chest. Her finger spread, following the hard ridges, trailing the line of tattoos.

When her nail skimmed over the hard nub of his male nipple, she felt him tremble. "Caroline." Her name was filled with raw emotion.

Her hands stilled and her eyes lifted till they met his. The burning passion she saw in the dark depths made her bolder still. "I don't want to think about tomorrow," she murmured, her voice breathless. "I don't want to think about anything but the way you make me feel."

Her lashes lowered. "The way I feel when I look at you." Silently her gaze caressed his body, the wide breadth of shoulders, the strong rack of his ribs. "Touch you." Her fingertip traced a crescent-shaped scar that only seemed to make his body more perfect. Then followed the elongated V of a tattoo down his muscled stomach.

"Please," she whispered, her eyes locking again with his. "Let me forget everything but you . . . at least for this night."

She didn't wait for his answer, but pressed her lips to the hot skin of his chest. The pounding of his heart thundering in her ear, the salty taste of his skin urged her on. His hands flexed spasmodically, but he allowed her the freedom to explore.

She wet a trail of discovery down his flat stomach with her tongue, while her fingers tested the lattice of bone and sinew across his back. He still wore a leather breechcloth though it did little to hide the size and power of his manhood.

Her hands moved lower, as did her open mouth. "Let me . . ." she felt his stomach muscles quiver against her lips. Anticipation coursed through her making the simple job of untying a knot seem endless. But again he allowed her the time she needed. Then he stood before her, tall and straight, legs apart, and gloriously naked. And now Caroline was the one quivering.

She couldn't stop shaking as she let her hands follow the natural curves of his body. Lightly, lovingly, she touched him, and he seemed to thrust forward, filling her hand with his hard, hard length. Satin over steel, she longed to know more.

At the first touch of her mouth to him, he yelled a shattered word. It was Cherokee, and Caroline couldn't understand what he roared to the heavens. But she was beyond caring. His hands which had dropped to his side as she moved lower now dug into her hair. With each fresh foray of her tongue, his fingers tightened around her skull.

Caroline's own fingers clasped the tight curve of his buttocks as she clung to him, savoring his feel . . . his taste. Savoring, too, the spring of desire that wound tighter and tighter within her own body.

"Stop!" Wolf realized the force with which he shoved her away and dropped to his knees in front of her. His hands still tangled in her curls as he tilted her face up to his. The kiss he gave her was openmouthed and carnal. When he tore his lips away, it was to scrape his teeth along the tense cord of her neck. He bit her earlobe. "Any more of your sweet torture," he breathed, "and I would have spilled my seed. Besides," he moved to the underside of her chin. "Now it is my turn."

He stood, and pulled Caroline gently to her feet. Unable to resist Wolf touched the tip of her breast and watched it tighten. She was so responsive, so giving, and he wanted to give to her in return. Trying to rein in his passions he led her to where he'd hung up the blanket. It was still damp, but he yanked it off the branch and spread it on the ground. Then he lifted Caroline, and lowered her onto the woolen surface.

For a moment Wolf only stood, staring down at her, wondering at her perfection. When she raised her arms to him, he lay down beside her, returning her smile. Wolf tried to ignore the tightening around his heart as he traced the fragile lines of her face with his thumbs.

He had once thought she would never survive the harsh life of the frontier, but she had proven him wrong. The cameo was stronger than she looked.

"What does that mean?"

Until she spoke, Raff didn't realize he had. Now he whispered his fingertip across her bottom lip and translated the words, "You are beautiful," to her. Even by the flickering light of the fire, he could see her blush.

"My words embarrass you?" Wolf bent forward to kiss her nose, the tip of her round chin.

"You make me feel beautiful," Caroline whispered, barely able to catch her breath as he skimmed his mouth toward her ear.

"It is because of the power you hold over me." Wolf spread her pale curls onto the blanket, fanning them around her face. Then, unable to control himself any longer, he angled her toward him for a kiss. Deeper and deeper he drove his tongue until they were forced to separate to breathe.

"God, Caroline." Wolf's heart pounded, and he ached. He wasn't sure he could take this slowly; give her all the pleasure she'd given him. When his mouth went to her neck, he could feel the gooseflesh prickle across her skin.

"Are you cold?" She tasted of honeysuckle and sweetness and he couldn't stop feasting on her skin. He'd worked his way down the valley between her rounded breasts before he realized she hadn't answered. He lifted his head and stared down at her questioningly.

Slowly her eyes focused on him, and she shook her head. "I'm hot," she finally managed to say, and Raff smiled. He burned with desire.

Her nipples seemed to reach out to him, and Wolf took one then the other into his mouth. She moaned when his tongue flicked across the crest.

But now his patience was at an end. Savagely he tore his mouth away to forge a path down her stomach. At the juncture of her thighs, he paused and buried his face in the tight curls, breathing in her musky scent. He lifted her legs, feeling her sudden jolt as his hand skimmed across her moist heat.

Then he touched her with his tongue. The convulsions began almost immediately. Deeper and deeper, Wolf savored her release, stoking the fires until she collapsed on the blanket. Then he reluctantly moved his mouth to her thigh.

But the flames still burned brightly in him; and when he moved up her body, he found it easy to rekindle the spark in her.

Caroline tingled all over. Every place his mouth touched vibrated, sending out rays of heat. The small of her waist, the underside of her arm. He seemed intent upon covering every part of her, making her want him again. By the time he skimmed up across her collarbone she was gasping for breath and near begging him. Her hands clutched at his back.

His first thrust was deep, the second shattering. Caroline threw her head back and cried out her joy as waves of ecstasy swept through her. The sound mingled with the rushing water, the night sounds of the forest. And the pleasure purged her memory of the blood and pain . . . at least for the present.

When Raff joined her in release, Caroline held on to him as tightly as she could. His head dropped beside hers, his face buried in the hair he'd washed. He stayed that way so long Caroline thought he'd fallen asleep. But then his raspy whisper fluttered the short curls around her ear.

"I must be heavy."

"No, you're not," Caroline lied. She didn't want the spell to be broken yet.

Raff seemed to understand, or perhaps he felt the same, for he rolled them to their sides without breaking the seal of their lovemaking. Her head rested on his arm, and he brushed a stray lock of hair from her face.

"Isn't this better?"

His smile was infectious. All the more so because she rarely saw it. Now she traced the sensual line of his lips with her fingertip. When she stopped near the corner, he slowly drew the digit into his mouth. Caroline's insides turned to liquid.

She closed her eyes lest he see in their depths the smoldering of her desire. But as he caressed her with his tongue and teeth, she realized his passion was as volitile as hers. She moaned when, fanning her remaining fingers across his strong jaw, he hardened inside her.

"I cannot seem to get enough of you," he said as she trailed a damp line down the underside of his chin. She skimmed her nail across his breast and his lower body jerked. She raised her leg, wrapping it over his hip.

But neither of them felt the need to rush.

"What do these lines mean?" Caroline traced the dark lines across his chest, feeling powerful and alive when his stomach muscles contracted.

"They are proof of my manhood," he said and

236

again the smile showed his teeth white against the sun-darkened skin.

"I don't think you need to prove it," Caroline quipped and a giggle bubbled up. In the next instant they were both laughing.

The mirth ceased when Wolf thrust deeper into Caroline's body. His hand closed over her breast. Caroline sucked in her breath as his thumb slowly drew circles around her sensitive flesh. With each turn he grew bolder, closer to her nipple. The torture was exquisite.

"You are beautiful," he said, and this time Caroline recognized the words spoken in Cherokee. She wrapped them around her like a down comforter. For tonight she felt beautiful . . . was beautiful.

But then he said something that threatened to break the spell. Still touching her, still carefully working his way toward her nipple, he leaned forward and kissed her chin. "My memory is a poor substitute for reality, for I recall your breasts as smaller." He flashed her a grin before taking the distended tip in his mouth.

Caroline tried to think of a response, one that didn't involve her pregnancy. She had noticed herself the subtle changes in her body, and knew that soon they would not be so subtle. Then she would have to tell him . . . what?

The truth?

You are the father of my bastard child. She closed her eyes and tried to keep her mind clear as he drew her deeper and deeper into a web of passion. Caroline imagined telling him right now, pushing him away and telling him the truth. What would he do? She didn't know; and as he moved his hand down toward the juncture of their bodies, she hadn't the nerve to open her mouth.

He touched her, and she cried out, but it was the alternative to telling him the truth as much as the pleasure that made her do so. If her child was to be born without stigma, she must claim Robert as his father. There was no one to deny her. But could she tell that lie to people . . . to Wolf?

"Caroline?"

She opened her eyes and stared into his. Heavy-lidded and black as night, they held a trace of concern. "Did I hurt you?"

"No!" Caroline wrapped her arms around his neck and pulled him closer. "No," she whispered again as his thrusts grew faster and harder, wiping her decisions from her mind.

When they both could breathe evenly again, Wolf pulled the edge of the blanket over them, and they both slept. Later he woke and added wood to the fire, then cuddled her closer when he lay beside her. She opened her eyes and reached for him, and they made love again.

Sometime later, she was awakened by the smell of something mouth-watering. Caroline stretched, realizing for the first night since the attack she hadn't been troubled with the dreams of blood

238

and violence. She colored when she remembered why.

Sitting up she brushed tangled curls from her face and looked around. She was alone. Spitted over the fire on a double Y of branches was a rabbit. The skin crackled and sputtered hot fat into the smoldering flames. And the aroma. Caroline took a deep breath, and her stomach growled. How long had it been since she'd eaten? Not a complete meal since the attack surely. All Caroline knew was that she'd never been so hungry.

Gathering the blanket around her, she stood and inched toward the fire.

"You will burn yourself," came a voice behind her.

Caroline whirled around to see Wolf, soaking wet and dressed only in his loincloth. Streams of water ran from his slicked-back hair, down the broad chest and lower. Just looking at him made Caroline long to be held in his arms. She wet her dry lips and decided perhaps breakfast could wait.

But Wolf didn't seem so inclined. Though his manner was friendly, there was none of the passion from the previous night, flaring in his dark eyes. He nodded behind him toward the pool of water above the falls. "I'll take it off the fire while you clean up. Your clothes are dry."

When he shrugged into his shirt and hunched by the fire, Caroline turned away. He was right, of course. There was no time for anything this morning. She wanted to return to Seven Pines as quickly

239

as possible. To assure herself that Mary was all right. Still, Caroline thought as she dipped her hand into the cold water, a kiss would not have taken too long.

By the time Caroline returned to the camp, her attitude had changed. As she stepped, shivering and covered with gooseflesh from the water, she remembered that what happened last night was not reality. She had asked him to help her forget. And he had.

It was not his fault but hers that she wished to pretend past the dawn. But she couldn't. She was his father's widow. And carrying a child who must be acknowledged as her late husband's. Love played no part in this. Especially a one-sided love like hers. For Wolf might desire her, but that was all. He proved that when he left her at his father's house. She had been foolish enough then to expect more from him. Now she knew better.

They traveled the better part of the day, resting only occasionally, and by late afternoon, they entered the clearing at Seven Pines.

Caroline had tried to brace herself for the scene she'd find. The view she saw when the Cherokee led her away. But there was no grotesque body draped from the sycamore tree. The smokehouse was gone, a mass of burned rubble on the ground, and so was the storage barn where trade goods had been kept, but the house stood, apparently unscathed.

When Wolf touched the small of her back, Caroline realized how long she was standing . . . staring. When she looked up at him, he glanced toward a grassy knoll toward the right of the main building. It took her a moment to realize that he was pointing out her husband's grave. She felt ashamed by her lack of remorse.

The chickens scattered, protesting, as Wolf and Caroline started toward the house. Before they reached the porch, the front door opened, and Mary rushed out. She carried a musket.

"What are you doing out of bed?" Caroline asked as she hurried forward and wrapped her arms around her friend. It seemed a foolish question considering all that had happened, but it was all she managed to say before tears sprang to her eyes.

Mary returned her hug, and Caroline noticed through blurry eyes that Wolf had removed the gun from her grip. He stood to the side for a moment before entering the house. When he came back onto the porch, both women were wiping their damp faces.

"Where are Sadayi and Walini?" he asked.

"They stop in occasionally to see how I'm doing, but they have their own families. Besides, I have nothing to trade them for being here."

Caroline caught a glimpse of Wolf's dark expression before he turned away.

241

"I know they agreed to stay," Mary said, moving toward her brother-in-law, "but I really have been all right. Worry over Caroline was my main· problem, and now that is relieved." She gave Caroline's hand a squeeze.

Her words didn't seem to brighten Wolf's countenance. He scanned the area around the house. Except for the burned buildings, all seemed serene and peaceful. A bluejay chattered in the birch, and in the background, was the gurgling sound of the creek as it tumbled over rocks.

But Wolf knew how deceptive such a scene could be. He ushered the women inside. "Pack a few things, necessities," he emphasized, "Then we will be on our way."

When Mary looked to Caroline for an explanation she said, "Raff is taking us to Fort Prince George."

"But why? Sadayi indicated the trouble was over. She said the Headmen denounced the raid." She grabbed Caroline's hand again. "I don't want to leave Seven Pines."

There was something in her eyes that made Caroline draw her to the nearest chair. After she'd settled her into it, Caroline sank to the rug in front of her. "Raff thinks it best if we go to Fort Prince George . . . and so do I." She glanced up to him for support, but he seemed willing to let her do the talking. He disappeared toward the back of the house.

"I realize the Cherokee Headmen are going to

242

Charles Town to work out a treaty with the English, but we can't forget what happened here."

"Raff buried Robert on the hill." Mary shut her eyes. Tears leaked from the corners. "There was no minister to say any words over his grave." She lifted her wet lashes. "No one deserves to die like that, Caroline."

"I know." Caroline rested her head on Mary's knees which was about all the lap she had left.

"I didn't like him," Mary said, simply. "I know it wasn't very Christian of me to feel as I did, but—"

"I didn't like him, either," Caroline said. "He wasn't a very nice man."

"Still . . ." said Mary, "if you could have seen what they did to him."

The fingers braided with Mary's tightened. "I saw." Caroline lifted her head. "We must get ready to leave, Mary," she said gently.

"Logan doesn't know about his father."

Caroline took a deep breath. "He will find out when he returns."

"He won't know where to find me." Mary's brows drew together. "Logan will come home and see that grave . . ." Her voice trailed off. "And I won't be here to tell him what happened."

"Raff will tell him." Caroline wanted to scream for Wolf now. Wanted him to come talk to Mary. Instead she drew the pregnant woman to her feet. "Don't worry about Logan. He'll know where to find you."

"What if he doesn't come?" Mary stopped her

progress toward the stairs and turned toward Caroline. "What if he never comes home?"

"He will," Caroline assured her. Glancing back into the parlor, Caroline guided Mary back into the room. "I have an idea. Why don't you lie on the settee, and I will bring you a cup of tea? Would you like that?" Caroline smiled when Mary nodded. "And something to eat? I'll bet you're hungry, aren't you?"

Mary didn't answer, but she seemed to relax as Caroline continued to speak to her in quiet tones. After she was seated, and as comfortable as Caroline could make her, she rushed toward the kitchen. Caroline had hoped to find Wolf, but he was nowhere in sight.

The fire was almost out so Caroline built it up and poured water from the bucket into the kettle. Then she went about finding something to eat. There were no muffins, or fresh bread, either. But Caroline managed to find some apples and day-old cornbread. While the tea steeped, she cut the apples, then carried it all into the parlor on a pewter tray.

Mary appeared to be sleeping, but she opened her eyes when Caroline entered. She smiled, and Caroline sighed with relief. Though she looked very pregnant and tired, the panic was gone from her expression.

"Thank you." Mary accepted the tea and leaned back against the cushion. "You are so good to me,

Caroline." Their gazes met. "And I was so frightened they would kill you."

"They didn't hurt me at all," Caroline assured
her. "And then Raff came and brought me back."

"I'm glad." Mary smiled. "Aren't you having
any tea?"

Caroline glanced down at the hands folded in
her lap. "No actually, I'm not thirsty. What I do
think I'll do is run upstairs and pack a few things.
Don't trouble yourself, I can take care of your necessities, too." She was to the door before Mary's
voice stopped her.

"I don't want to leave. Logan . . ." She left the
rest of her thought unspoken.

"Raff will take care of it, of him," Caroline insisted before she ran out the door.

Up in Mary's room, Caroline rolled clean shifts
and the tiny baby clothes she and Mary had made
over the fall into a blanket. Then she went to her
room and did the same thing with her shifts and
stockings. Knowing they would have to carry anything she packed, Caroline tried to take as few
things as possible. But she had no idea how long
they would be staying, and Mary's baby would assuredly be born at the fort.

She was dragging clean sheets from the wardrobe when she heard his voice. "Damnation
Caroline, I said a few things."

"Don't you curse at me! Just don't do it," she
added almost in a whisper as she threw the sheets
onto the bed.

Wolf stepped into the room and shut the door. "What is it?"

"I told you. I don't wish for you to—"

"Yes, I know what you said." He stepped closer.

"Well then—" Caroline snapped the sheet out. "Your father yelled at me all the time and cursed, and I hated it. I won't have his son doing the same."

"I don't wish to think of myself as his son."

"Well you are," she said. "Rafferty MacQuaid, son of Robert MacQuaid."

Wolf grabbed her shoulders, twirling her around to face him. "What is wrong with you?"

"Not a thing. What could possibly be the matter?" Her tone was petulant and childish, and she didn't care. "I've seen my husband tortured and slain, been kidnapped by Indians, my feet are sore—"

"You are telling me nothing I do not already know." His eyes narrowed. "Why now are you acting this way?"

Caroline tried to wrench from his grasp, but he held her firm. "How am I supposed to act, Raff?" She sucked in a breath. "Perhaps you are used to this but I—"

"I know it has not been easy for you. If you recall, I warned you not to come."

"Yes, you did." Caroline turned her face away. "Perhaps I should have listened to you then."

"Perhaps you should have." His fingers tightened, and Wolf forced himself to hold her at arm's length. "But you didn't, and now you are here. And we should leave while we still have some light."

"Mary is acting strange." Caroline's eyes caught his, hoping he would understand.

"She has also been through a great deal."

Caroline sighed. "I don't know what to do. She's worried about Logan."

"My brother can take care of himself."

"He should be here, with her," Caroline argued.

"But he is not. And we are." Wolf gave in to his desire and pulled her close to his body. She resisted at first, but then came against him. Wolf savored the feel of her.

"I'm worried about her," Caroline said against his chest. He smelled of fresh air and pine, and security. Her arms wrapped about his lean waist. "It will be hard on her to travel."

"I understand, but the best thing we can do for her is take her to safety." It was also the best he could do for Caroline. He felt her nod and closed his hand over her curls. "You go down and get Mary, I'll finish wrapping these sheets into a roll."

"They're for Mary when the baby comes."

"I know. I should not have yelled at you."

"And I'm sorry for what I said earlier. I understand why you don't wish to be reminded of your blood link with Robert."

"But you are right. He was my father."

Their eyes held a moment longer then Caroline left the room. She was still thinking of Wolf when she entered the parlor.

Her heart skipped a beat.

"Mary! My God, Mary!" Caroline rushed across the room and fell to her knees beside Mary where she lay on the floor. She cradled her head, and wiped tendrils of hair from her face.

The carpet was stained as were Mary's skirts, and Caroline had a sick feeling in the pit of her stomach even before Mary opened her eyes.

They were glazed with pain, but she attempted a smile when she recognized Caroline. "My baby," she whispered. "My baby is coming." Then her face contorted in agony.

Twelve

"What the hell is going on?"

Caroline jerked her head around when she heard Wolf's voice. She caught a glimpse of him frozen in surprise, looking much as she must have moments earlier. " 'Tis the baby. Help me get her to a bed."

Before she even finished her request, Wolf was across the room. He scooped Mary into his arms as Caroline pushed to her feet. She led the way into the room Robert MacQuaid used.

"Did I hurt you?" Wolf asked Mary, repeating the query to Caroline when Mary didn't answer and only cried out in pain.

" 'Tis not you." Caroline clasped Mary's hand. " 'Tis the baby." Glancing around, Caroline was surprised to see the bewildered expression on the usually stoic man. He swallowed, and she almost smiled at the way his Adam's apple bobbed. She might have if not for the bite of Mary's fingers around her own as another wave of tightness consumed her.

Caroline's mind snapped back to the situation at hand. There'd be time enough later to wonder at Wolf's transformation . . . she hoped. "Water," she said twice before he tore his attention from Mary and looked at her. "Bring me some hot water." She hesitated a moment to make certain he understood, then turned back to Mary. In the next instant she heard him leave.

"It hurts. Oh, Caroline."

"I know it does, dear." Patting Mary's arm with one hand, Caroline used the other to unhook her gown. "Here, can you shift up a moment? You'll be more comfortable with this bodice off." At least Caroline hoped she would be. She couldn't help wondering if anything would help, but she had to do something besides offer hollow words of reassurance.

By the time she'd removed Mary's wet garments, tossing them into a pile in the corner, Caroline was exhausted. And she could barely imagine the discomfort Mary was in. But she did *seem* to rest better at those times when the pain loosened its grip on her. Caroline draped a fresh sheet over her distended body and brushed back the damp, brown hair. Then she could do nothing but stand by the bed, her hand in Mary's and wait.

The minutes ticked off on the clock on the mantel. Time divided into moments of intense pain, when Mary cried out and Caroline soothed her, and movements when the pale woman collapsed onto the mattress, spent.

"She's not . . . ?"

Wolf's voice startled Caroline. She'd been thinking not of Mary, but selfishly of herself, months from now in the same position, delivering her baby . . . Wolf's baby. Hoping he couldn't read her thought, she turned to him and shook her head.

After gently extracting her hand, she met him by the door. He carried an overflowing bucket of steaming water in each hand.

"She's sleeping."

"Then she isn't going to have the baby now?"

His tone was hopeful, and Caroline hated to dash that hope, but she did. "Mary just rests between pains."

"But it is too soon, is it not? I thought her child was due in December."

"It was." Mary started to fidget in her sleep and Caroline turned toward the bed, stopping when a wet hand clamped about her upper arm.

Wolf leaned forward till he nearly touched her hair with his chin. "Have you ever done this before?"

Slowly she shook her head. Then as if struck with inspiration, she twisted her head around. Their faces were very close, and she stared into his dark eyes. "Have you?"

"No." He shrugged. "I've seen animals give birth."

" 'Tis not the same thing," Caroline insisted, though she had no idea if it was or not. But the

251

idea of him comparing her friend to a cow or horse, didn't sit well.

"Sadayi knows what to do, I am certain."

"But she's not here," Caroline pointed out more reasonably than she thought his words deserved.

"I could run and get her."

"There isn't time," Caroline said as she twisted away. Mary was awake now, her body stiffening as another wave of agony hit her.

"But what should I do with all this water?" Wolf glanced down at the buckets that were spreading wet rings on the carpet.

Back at Mary's bedside, Caroline wanted to tell him to pour both buckets over his head, but she knew her annoyance wasn't so much with Wolf as with the situation, so she merely shrugged her shoulders and hoped he wouldn't leave her.

He didn't. Though he approached the bed with less ease than he would face a barrage of arrows, Wolf moved to Caroline's side. She was bent over Mary, who was now awake and breathing hard as the pain subsided.

"Mary." Caroline waited until her expression was calm.

Mary's smile was weak. "You're here."

"Of course, I am. We are." She stepped aside so her friend could see Wolf.

"Drink. May I have some water?"

Before Caroline could form the words to ask him, Wolf thrust a glass into her hands. Together they lifted Mary's shoulders so she could take a sip.

"Is that better?" Caroline fluffed the pillow before they settled her back down. "Mary. You're going to have to tell me what to do. Do you think you can do that?"

Mary's voice was raspy but firm as she gave instructions. And to Caroline's chagrin, it did sound much like birthing a foal. Mary stopped talking and her breathing quickened. Caroline's gaze locked with Wolf's. At least for now they were allies.

Three hours later everything was much the same. Wolf had built a fire in the hearth, and was hunched beside it poking at the blazing embers. It was a needless task but it gave him something to do. He glanced back at Caroline sitting by the bed, her head bent forward and pushed to his feet.

"Come, rest here a moment." His arms around her shoulders, Wolf urged Caroline to stand, then guided her to the rocking chair by the fireplace.

"I should stay by her." Caroline twisted her head to look back at her friend.

"She's sleeping now, and I'll sit with her awhile."

By late afternoon when Caroline jerked awake, Mary was still sleeping. "My goodness." Brushing aside the quilt he'd spread over her lap, Caroline stood and rushed to the bedside. "How could you let me nap like that?" she scolded, more angry with herself than him.

But he ignored the bite in her voice, leveling

her with his dark stare as he turned from the bedside. "You needed your rest as much as Mary did."

His words made her pause as she reached for Mary's hand. Did he suspect she was with child . . . his child? It was true that she grew weary more easily and slept at unlikely times. But he appeared to know little about the birthing process . . . even less than herself.

Besides, it wasn't as if she hadn't missed most of her sleep the previous night. Caroline leaned toward Mary to hide the color flooding her cheeks as vivid memories of lying in Wolf's arms, their naked bodies entwined, filled her head.

Caroline reached for Mary's hand. It looked pale in hers. She traced the network of spidery blue veins with her thumb before looking up at Wolf. "How long has she been like this?"

"An hour, maybe a bit more." He motioned Caroline toward the door to the hall. There was no fire burning in the parlor, and Caroline felt the chill as soon as she stepped from the bedroom. She wrapped her arms about her waist. The shiver that ran down her spine when she noticed Wolf carrying the long rifle had naught to do with the lack of heat. She'd almost forgotten that the birth of Mary's baby wasn't their only problem. Apparently Wolf hadn't. His next words proved it.

"I hesitate to go."

"You're leaving us?" Caroline's voice rose with each word.

"Only to get help." Wolf leaned the rifle against

the chair railing. With his hands free, he cupped Caroline's shoulders, forcing her to look at him. "Mary grows weaker, and I don't know what to do."

Caroline swallowed the tears in her throat, ashamed of the selfishness that made her wish to beg him to stay. She lowered her lashes. "I don't, either."

"I can run to Kawuyi in less than an hour."

"Do you think Sadayi will come?" Caroline's gaze met his.

"She will come," he said, and Caroline believed from his tone that he would throw the older lady over his shoulder and carry her back if need be. "I do not like leaving you here alone."

"I can take care of Mary," Caroline told him with more assurance than she felt. But when he pulled the pistol from the leather belt around his waist, she knew that wasn't his only concern. She followed as he led the way to the window where the slanting rays of late afternoon streamed through the mullioned panes.

Slowly, carefully, he showed her how to load the pistol. When he retrieved his rifle, he'd scooped up a powderhorn as well. Now he pulled the plug with his teeth and poured a small amount down the barrel.

Caroline wiped her damp hands down the panels of her flower sprigged overskirt and watched. "You don't believe they will attack us again, do you?" Anxiety made her voice tense.

"No." He tapped the powder and wadding down, then handed the pistol to Caroline. "The Headman has given his word."

"Then what?" True the forest was filled with wild animals, mountain lions and bears, but they rarely roamed close to the house. His concern as he focused her attention on the gun seemed to go beyond protecting herself from four-legged predators. "Tal-tsuska," she said on a surge of comprehension. "You think Tal-tsuska will return."

He didn't glance up, but the skin across his cheekbones tightened enough for Caroline to realize that was exactly what he feared. "But I thought he meant only to show you his displeasure before. You said be could have killed you if that was his choice."

"It is true he could have shot me as we crossed the river."

"But then you wouldn't have known." His dark eyes raised to meet hers. "That's it, isn't it? He wanted you to know how angry he was . . . and to be wary."

"I'm always wary," Wolf said with a slight shrug.

"Do not play word games with me." Caroline forced her attention to the pistol when he pulled the hammer back.

"You aim the barrel at the chest and hold yourself steady as you pull the trigger. I do not play games, Caroline."

He handed the gun to her, and Caroline wrapped her hand around the butt. The pistol was

eavier than she thought, and she steadied her
hand to keep her arm from drooping. But she
didn't allow him to distract her from discovering
the truth behind his insistence that she learn how
to load a gun. "Why are you so worried about Tal-
tsuska? 'Tis Tal-tsuska who concerns you, isn't it?"

"Yes."

His ready reply surprised Caroline.

"But if he . . . ?"

"It is not me he wants, Caroline."

"But who?" Her lips were still forming the question when she realized the answer. She tried to
swallow, but her mouth was suddenly too dry.
"Why?" The word was little more than a croak.

Wolf shrugged, but it was more to ease the tension in his shoulders than for any other reason.
"Perhaps he is fond of your hair the color of
moonlight. Perhaps your eyes appeal to him. Or
your mouth." Wolf realized he was listing some of
the things he found attractive about the woman
before him and stopped. As lovely as she was, Wolf
didn't think his cousin's intention toward Caroline
had anything to do with her appearance.

"Tal-tsuska's wife and son died of smallpox. He
survived, but bears the scars of his illness."

"I'm sorry." Caroline shook her head in confusion. "But I don't understand what that has to do
with me."

"He blames the English for bringing the disease." He hesitated, his eyes growing darker as he

stared at her. "Smallpox is but one pestilence the white man has introduced to the land."

"They also brought civilization." Caroline had seen the towns, Charles Town, and the plantations. Certainly they hadn't been there before. But his deepened scowl spoke volumes.

"We haven't the time to debate the merits of the English *civilization*," he said as he handed her the pistol. " 'Tis primed and ready. I shall leave you a powder horn and shot."

When Caroline hesitated to take the pistol, he pressed it firmly into her hand. His fingers lingered on hers. Slowly Caroline lifted her face to return his stare. He stood tall and straight, the one strong pillar in the chaos surrounding her. Caroline could barely resist leaning into him. Especially when his expression softened.

He was close enough for her to smell the outdoors and manly scent of him, to feel the heat that radiated from his large body. And she could not help the memories his assault on her senses evoked.

She wanted to throw herself in his strong arms and beg him to stay. To stay with her always. To tell him of their child.

Before she did something she would regret, Caroline turned away. His hands gripped her shoulders forcing her back to him. And his words showed he misinterpreted her actions as fear, which Caroline admitted to herself, should be her prime consideration.

"I shall return as quickly as possible."

"I know you will." His fingers tightened and her heart beat faster.

"You will be fine."

Caroline detected the hint of a question in his words. She nodded because she didn't trust her voice to answer. Subtly, surely, he drew her closer. Her hands hung by her sides, the pistol dangling from one. But each time she breathed, her breasts flirted with the homespun weave of his shirt. The touch, barely there, should have been imperceptible, but Caroline felt it down to her curled toes.

He wasted time. Wolf knew he should leave, for the sooner he did, the sooner he could return. But he seemed unable to release her. The alternative was to draw her closer. He meant to do it gently, but his arms didn't follow his mind's directive. She gasped as he pressed her against his body.

Her lips were warm and tasted of surrender. He couldn't help drinking his fill. When he pulled away she moaned and swayed toward him. It was all he could do to step back.

Wolf slung his musket over his shoulder and glanced back toward Caroline. Her mouth was red and damp. Her golden hair mussed. She was his father's widow, and he ached to take her there on the floor. Nearly groaning, he headed for the door. His hand gripped the latch, but was stilled when the cry sounded from the bedroom.

Caroline was down the hall ahead of him. She was leaning over Mary when he rushed through the doorway. Logan's wife was pale as the sheet she lay on. When they left the room moments ago she was sleeping soundly and Wolf had thought there was time to seek help. Now he knew that hope was unfounded. Her eyes were still shut, but her breathing was heavy, rasping from her dry lips. Between gasps, she called for her husband in a weak strangled voice.

He'd always understood his brother's reasons for leaving . . . neither of them could stand the man who sired them. But now Wolf wondered if Logan should have thought more about the wife he left behind.

"I think the babe is coming." Caroline's tone, surprisingly calm despite the pounding of her heart, gave her a little confidence. "Perhaps you should wait in the other room." She guided Mary's hands to the knotted rags she tied earlier around the bedposts. With a surge of energy, Mary grabbed hold.

Caroline flipped up the sheet, pausing only a moment as she caught sight of Wolf still standing in the doorway. He hadn't moved; and if the situation wouldn't have been as it was, she might have laughed at the expression on his face as he stared at Mary. He was nearly as pale as the woman about to deliver her child. Paler, for exertion now colored Mary's features bright red. As she gritted her teeth and pushed, her skin grew damp with perspiration.

"Raff!" Caroline had to say it twice before his eyes met hers. "The water needs to be warmed."

was all she could think of to get him moving, but it worked. Not seeming to care how much he spilled, Wolf scooped up the hemp-handled buckets and rushed from the room.

Shaking her head, Caroline focused her attention back to Mary. Earlier when Mary explained what needed to be done, Caroline was certain she'd never remember, let alone be able to handle any of it. Now she found herself working more on instinct than anything else.

"Keep pushing, Mary. I can see the baby." Caroline leaned forward to give her friend's arm a reassuring pat. "You're doing a wonderful job." Though she doubted Mary could hear her murmured words over the sounds she made as she pushed with all her strength, Caroline found them comforting. Besides, maybe Mary did realize what she said, and maybe it would keep her trying a little longer.

Because her strength was ebbing. "Come Mary. You can't stop now. You've a baby to birth." The cry that tore through Mary's slight body raised the hair on Caroline's nape. It also exposed the baby's head. "Just a little bit more. There," Caroline gasped as the slippery baby slid into her hands. Tears sprang to her eyes, but it was with a laugh that she turned to Wolf when he came bursting through the door.

"It's a girl." Caroline carried the tiny crying child around to the side of the bed. "Mary, you have a daughter." But there was no glad adulation.

As if she'd done all she possibly could, Mary lay quiet, her head resting listlessly upon the pillow. Her breathing was shallow, and no amount of calling her name would awaken her.

"Raff, come here." He was by her side before she'd finished her sentence, and Caroline turned, handing the squirming infant toward him.

"You want *me* to hold her?" His tone indicated he thought she'd lost her mind.

But Caroline just nodded toward the swaddling of linen laid out on the chest. "Fetch that and hurry," she said and he seemed to understand that there was no choice. The baby fit comfortably in his out-stretched hands.

While he stood beside the bed, Caroline worked quickly on Mary, pressing the afterbirth from her body and tying off the cord. Occasionally she glanced at Mary, hoping to see some improvement in her color and breathing. There was none. Wolf did look better though, less like he would swoon onto the floor.

"Is she supposed to be this small?" he asked when Caroline wrapped the tiny body snugly in the toweling.

"I don't think so. But she was born too early." Even with her small size, the baby seemed better off than her mother. Caroline handed the wrapped bundle back to the tall man and dipped a scrap of cloth in the bucket by the bed. The water was barely tepid, but that was better than hot she decided as she wiped it gently across Mary's face.

Not knowing exactly what to do, Wolf started pacing, holding the baby out in front of him as if he were made of glass. He was aware of Caroline leaning over the bed, crooning to his sister-in-law, and wished there was something he could do to help, but was almost afraid to take his eyes off the tiny blood-smeared baby cradled in his hands. He wanted to ask if she was cut or something but figured Caroline would know if something needed to be done . . . at least he hoped she would.

He was wondering where he'd left his musket when Caroline called him to the bed. The baby wasn't wimpering anymore, and Wolf was glad he didn't have to hand a crying baby over to her mother when he noticed Mary was awake.

"Let me hold her." Mary's voice was weak. Caroline took the infant, laying her carefully on Mary's chest. The wisp of a smile that lifted Mary's lips was gone almost before Wolf saw it, but he couldn't help responding in kind. It wasn't till he noted the serious expression wrinkling Caroline's brows that he sobered.

But Caroline went on talking in that soft, low way she had, telling Mary how beautiful her daughter was and how proud she should be.

It wasn't till he left the room to look for his musket, thinking he must have left it in the parlor, that he guessed anything was wrong.

Caroline was bent over the bed, cleaning Mary . . . finally using the water he'd heated and reheated . . .

so he was surprised when she followed him into th
hallway, shutting the door behind her.

The only light came from the single candle he'
lit in the parlor, but it showed him enough o
Caroline's expression to see her distress. "What i
it?"

"I'm concerned about Mary." Caroline wrappe
her arms tightly about her waist and walked to th
window. Outside the moonlight silvered the oa
leaves that clung stubbornly to the limbs despit
the cold air. She watched a raccoon scurry acros
the clearing before turning back to Wolf. He stoo
silently by the fireplace. "She's so weak."

"Perhaps she's tired," he responded with a lift o
his brow. "You're exhausted yourself, aren't you?"

Caroline's laugh was self-deprecating. "She cer
tainly has a right to be worse off than me." Her gaz
sought again the peace and beauty of the outside
"I just wish I knew more about caring for her."

"You did fine."

The words were spoken low and close. Carolin
hadn't heard him move, but now when she looke
around he was right behind her, looming over her
His nearness was disconcerting enough to mak
her twist back toward the window. Her hea
dropped forward till what was left of her topkno
brushed against the chilled pane.

"Mary was lucky to have you here." Wolf re
sisted the urge to taste the delicate curve of he
exposed neck.

"I didn't know what to do. If she wouldn't hav

told me . . ." Caroline let the rest of that thought go unsaid.

"But she did tell you."

With that she looked around at him, her blue eyes serious. "I think you were right when you saw me in Charles Town. I don't belong here."

"What made you come to that conclusion?"

He hadn't actually taken a step away from her, it only seemed as if he had. "Oddly enough it wasn't the attack, or even being kept prisoner."

"What then?"

Caroline took a deep breath. "Knowing that Mary might die . . . and I wasn't able to save her."

"Don't you think you're taking a lot on yourself?"

" 'Tis an odd thing for you to say." When he raised his brow quizzically, she continued. "You seem to think you're responsible for keeping peace between the Cherokee and the English."

His grin was brief. "We are not discussing me. It is you who seem to have some mistaken notion that you are not suited for this place."

"I'm only accepting what you've known from the first."

"I was wrong."

"What?" Caroline's face tilted up toward his.

"I mistook your fragile appearance as an indication you had little inner strength. It was an error on my part."

"Why do I feel this apology does not come easy for you."

The smile lasted longer this time. It transformed his face. Still breathtakingly handsome, he didn't appear so fierce. "I have made many mistakes, Caroline."

Was one of them making love with her? Caroline turned toward the window before she was tempted to ask. Her eyes drifted shut when she felt his hand cup her shoulder.

"I will take a look outside. When I return, I shall sit with Mary awhile so you can rest."

Caroline could still feel the warmth of his touch after she watched him skirt the clearing and disappear into the shadowy forest. Only then did she return to the downstairs bedroom.

Mary's fever came on the third day.

The night before as Caroline walked the fretting baby back and forth across the parlor, Wolf had asked when she thought Mary and the baby could be moved. He was anxious to see them safely behind the log walls of Fort Prince George.

"I don't know," Caroline had snapped, then stopped in the middle of the rug and turned to him. It wasn't his fault Mary showed no improvement. Or that the baby seemed to wimper all the time. But he knew as well as she that Mary couldn't travel. She could barely make it out of bed to attend to her private needs.

Without saying a word, he'd stepped forward and took the tiny bundle from her arms. The infant didn't stop fussing but at least Caroline could sit down. She was so tired of late, and knowing the reason didn't help.

She had apologized for her tone. He had accepted with a nod of his head. And they'd decided to discuss the possibility in the morning.

Caroline had set up a pallet in the room Mary used. She slept lightly, listening as a mother would for any sounds the baby made. Mary had named the child Colleen for Logan's mother. When Colleen fussed, Caroline rose, and after changing her diaper, carried her to Mary to nurse.

Those were the only times Mary seemed to have any energy. She'd bring her hand up to rub the baby's fuzzy head and croon to her softly.

"She really is beautiful," Mary would whisper to Caroline. "She's like her father."

Caroline always agreed, telling Mary how wonderful the small child was, and how happy Logan would be when he came home. And all the while she worried that Mary didn't seem to improve, and the baby only suckled halfheartedly.

But this morning, Mary didn't say anything. Dawn was just beginning to lighten the sky outside, though she'd heard Wolf leave the house for his morning swim before Colleen started whimpering.

"Mary," Caroline said as she rocked the fussing baby in her arms. "Your daughter is hungry."

Mary's moan sent shivers down Caroline's spine. Quickly she put the baby back in the hickory cradle that had been her father's. This brought a louder wail from the child, but Caroline paid no mind as she leaned over the bed. Mary's skin was hot and dry to the touch. Burning.

Not knowing what else to do, Caroline rushed to the pitcher on the commode, but it was empty. The pail was gone, but she couldn't wait for Wolf to finish bathing and come back with more water.

"I have to go to the river," she announced though neither of the room's other occupants seemed to understand or care. "I'll be right back."

With that, she picked up her skirts and ran for the back door. The trees stood out in bold relief against the paler sky and the ground was covered with a light frost that made her slippered feet slide. But she kept running toward the river.

A sound caught her attention to the right, and she ran toward it thinking it was Wolf returning from his swim. "It's Mary," she called. "She has the fever. I need—"

The word water was drowned out by her gasp as she ran into the arms of a dark-skinned savage.

Thirteen

An involuntary scream tore from her body as naked arms clasped around her. Instinctively, Caroline knew it was hopeless to fight. Her assailant towered over her; and though his body didn't feel as hard as Wolf's, he was easily stronger than she.

But Caroline wasn't the same woman who might have swooned at such an onslaught months ago. She struggled with all her might, scratching and slapping, biting, till she'd worked her right hand free of his grasp. Wriggling, she managed to turn herself slightly. Then she clawed at her skirts, her heart pounding in her ears.

When her fingers found the slit in her overskirt a bubble of excitement forced aside some of her panic. The pistol butt felt smooth as her hand clasped around it. With all her strength she tried to angle the weapon toward the man who continued to hold her up against him. She couldn't manage to pull the gun from her pocket, but that didn't matter. She would blow a hole through her skirts to kill her attacker. If she could only point the pistol toward him.

"What the hell . . . ?"

Caroline was too caught up in her struggle to notice anything until she was unceremoniously dropped to the hard ground. Pain shot through her shoulder, and she could feel the air whoosh from her body, but her arm was free. Free to aim the pistol.

A hand clasped around hers, skirts and all, an instant before she pulled the trigger.

Sobbing, she tried to free her hand, but it was useless. The grip on her was unyielding.

"Caroline!"

Her head jerked up. She saw Wolf leaning over her, his black hair wet and slicked back from his face, and she cried out with relief . . . then fear. Couldn't he see the danger?

But he seemed unconcerned as he knelt beside her. His wet arm snaked around her shoulder though he didn't loosen his grip on her hand. "It's all right, Caroline," he said.

"But—" Her explanation to him that there was an Indian, bent on harming them was interrupted by a string of low, guttural words that she didn't understand. She whipped her head around to see the Indian who attacked her looming above Wolf and her. Fear shot through her again, but to her dismay, Wolf laughed. She could feel the vibrations through her body as he pulled her to her feet.

"Are you hurt?" he asked as he carefully extracted the pistol from her grasp, then pulling it from its hiding place in the folds of her skirt. She thought he might aim it at the tall imposing Indian, but he merely let it hang by his side while his finger combed pine needles from her tangled hair.

More guttural words came from the stranger, and this time he held his hand out toward Wolf who examined it with a shake of his head.

"What is he saying?" Caroline demanded. Perhaps Wolf acted as if there was nothing to fear, but he hadn't been accosted by this fearsome-looking Indian. "And why are you just standing there?"

"He says you are a wildcat." Wolf's eyes held hers for a moment.

"Me?" Caroline's chin jutted up with indignation. "Ask him why he attacked me!"

More words from the Indian.

"He seems to feel it was you who attacked him." Wolf leaned forward giving the Indian's finger a cursory examination, making a tsking sound with his mouth as he did. "Gulegi wonders why the white woman found it necessary to bite him."

The amusement in Wolf's dark eyes annoyed her. If this Indian was a friend, she had no way of knowing it. Besides he didn't exactly step from the path and introduce himself. And she didn't appreciate Wolf making light of her fear. Her heart still pounded like the drums she'd heard in the Indian town. Caroline stepped from Wolf's loose embrace, flinging curls back from her face as she did. "He attacked me," she stated calmly, staring straight at her assailant. "I was running to find you—" Oh my God! How could she have forgotten?

Caroline clutched Wolf's arm. "Mary has a fever. She's burning up. I need water," she yelled as she turned on her heel. Not waiting for his reply, Caroline picked up her skirts and hurried back toward the house.

Wolf said a few words to the man who was still examining his finger and followed. By the time he reached the bedroom, Caroline had scooped up the baby and held the crying infant to her shoulder. They approached the bed together.

Wolf didn't need to touch his brother's wife to know she was feverish. Her skin looked parchment-thin and dry.

Caroline shook her head slowly. "I need water," she reminded. Caroline knew of no other way to bring her temperature down.

"Gulegi is bringing it."

Moments later, true to his words, the burly Indian stomped into the room, carrying a pail of water. Caroline handed Colleen to Wolf and set about wiping Mary's face with the cooling liquid. Mary moaned but still didn't open her eyes.

Wolf paced the room from the hearth to the opposite wall, trying to quiet the child. "She's hungry," Caroline said as she looked up. "But I don't think Mary can feed her."

"Do you know what is wrong with her?"

Tears of frustration sprang to Caroline's eyes, but she blinked them back. "I don't know."

Turning away from her Wolf spoke in a low tone to the Indian. Caroline watched as the strange Indian nodded, then left the room.

"What did you say to him?" A movement outside the window caught her eye, and she saw the Indian lope across the clearing. He passed the tree where Robert was killed and faded into the forest.

"I sent him to the village to fetch Sadayi."

"He is a friend of yours, isn't he?" When Wolf nodded, Caroline looked away. "I nearly shot him."

"I am sorry he frightened you, but not every Cherokee is an enemy to you." He patted the baby's back with his large hand, and she whimpered in response.

Now that she thought about it, Caroline admitted to herself that she probably did run into the stranger. And though he'd held onto her, he hadn't hurt her. Still, after what she'd been through, and the vigilance kept by Wolf, she had a right to be wary. " 'Tis impossible for me to know the difference upon first glance," she said before turning back to Mary.

"I realize this has been difficult for you."

"More so for Mary, I would say." Caroline didn't turn when she spoke, but kept her hands busy blotting her friend's face with the damp cloth. She could tell he was close to her. His scent surrounded her. Caroline tried not to allow that to affect her. But it did. Why could she not resist even the most subtle thing about him? Even when her concern for Mary was so great?

At least she wasn't the only female who couldn't resist him. Baby Colleen, soothed into momentarily forgetting her hunger by his gentle touch, slept soundly against his shoulder.

His naked shoulder.

He'd come running from his swim in the river, dressed only in his loincloth, his bronzed skin shimmering with water. Would she ever be able to look at him and not be affected by his powerful body? Caroline forced such thoughts from her mind, but she didn't glance around toward him. "I shall hold Colleen if you wish to put something else on. You must be chilled," she added, hoping he'd think that was the reason she wanted him dressed.

He made no comment, but she could hear him moving about the room, depositing the baby in her cradle, then returning to glance over her shoulder at Mary before leaving the room.

She didn't hear him return. Convinced that Mary felt a bit cooler, Caroline arched her back to relieve her aching muscles. She stiffened when she felt his hand upon her shoulder.

"I will do that for a while."

When she glanced around, he nodded toward the pail by Caroline's feet. He had pulled on a linen hunting shirt and tied back his hair, though it was still wet enough to dampen a V on his shirt. "I suppose I could use a rest."

"Only a change of tasks. I brought some watered-down gruel to feed Colleen."

"Can she eat that?" When Raff only shrugged, Caroline moved to the cradle. The baby was crying again, a weak, low keening that tore at Caroline's heart. She thought of her own child nestled safely inside her body, and she held Colleen closer.

The infant didn't take to the gruel at first, puckering her little face and crying louder. But Caroline cuddled her, rocking back and forth in the chair by the window and patiently putting her gruel dipped finger to the child's rosebud mouth.

Caroline looked toward Wolf and smiled the first time Colleen stopped crying to suck. His answering grin made her feel wonderful.

They spent the rest of the morning and part of the afternoon taking turns between feeding Colleen and sponge-bathing her mother. They were pleased when Colleen slept; and when Mary woke enough to utter a few words, Logan and her child were what she asked about. Caroline assured her both were safe, hoping she spoke the truth.

Wolf heard the small group approaching even before they hailed the house. He hurried from the room and opened the front door. Caroline, expecting only to see Sadayi and the Indian who frightened her earlier, was surprised when a half dozen Cherokee entered the room.

Sadayi came to her and reached down for Colleen, grinning her nearly toothless grin as she did. "Pretty baby, but too small," she said then handed her to another woman that Caroline didn't recognize. This woman motioned for Caroline to rise from the chair. When she did, the young Cherokee settled herself in Caroline's place, untied her blouse and offered Colleen her breast. The hungry baby latched on immediately. All three women laughed at the loud sucking noise made by the tiny infant.

"Cahtahlata lost her baby," Sadayi explained, "but she still has milk."

"I'm sorry—about your child, I mean."

The young woman nodded, apparently needing no interpreter to understand Caroline's words of sympathy.

When Caroline turned her attention to Mary, she found her friend's bed surrounded by three people she didn't know. Wolf was no longer in the room. "The Sachem has come to help Mary," Sadayi said. "She will be fine."

"But what's wrong with her?" Caroline glanced back over her shoulder as Sadayi led her from the room.

"Milk fever. Many get it. But she will be fine. You are the one who must rest." Sadayi nudged her along toward the stairs.

Caroline caught a glimpse of Raff and another Cherokee in the parlor, but Sadayi was not in a mood to tarry. At the top of the stairs she made pushing movements with her broad hands until Caroline entered her room.

"How long has it been since you slept?" Sadayi asked as she pulled down the quilt.

"I'm not tired, really. 'Tis Mary that concerns me."

"She's being taken care of. And it will do neither you nor your baby any good to get no rest."

Caroline turned, ignoring Sadayi's clucked protest as she tried to unhook Caroline's bodice. "How can you know for sure that I am with child?" She had mentioned the possibility of a baby once, the day after Robert beat her. But since then, she and Sadayi had not discussed it.

The Indian woman simply made a face as if to say she wasn't stupid.

"I want to know," Caroline persisted. She'd studied herself in the mirror before the Indian attack and was convinced no one could tell. That had been no more than a sennight ago. True, she had not paid much heed to her appearance since then, but surely nothing had changed that much. Now she glanced down quickly as the lacings of her stays loosened.

"I can see you are *taluli*, pregnant, here." Sadayi touched her cheek. "And," she added tilting her head to the side and examining Caroline with her sloe eyes. "You are not as skinny as you were." She removed the stays, leaving her dressed in her shift and petticoats. "But do not concern yourself, I do not believe Wa'ya has noticed."

"Why should I care about that?" Caroline forced her voice to remain calm.

"The baby will be his *tsunkinisi*, his younger brother. Wa'ya will take care of you."

"Oh . . . yes. 'Tis true, I suppose." Caroline allowed the older woman to settle her on the bed. Her baby would be considered Wolf's half brother. *Unless you tell him the truth*, a small voice reminded her.

"Sadayi."

The Indian woman stopped her progress toward the door and glanced over her ample shoulder.

Caroline bit her lip. "Please don't tell Raff . . . about the baby, I mean."

The Cherokee woman only shrugged. "It is not my place to tell."

As tired as she was, it still took a long time for Caroline to fall asleep. When she did, her dreams were as troubled as her mind. A child stared up at her with eyes as dark as night, questioning. She tried to tell him the truth, but he turned away from her and disappeared in the haze that swirled up around his chubby legs. In her nightmare Caroline chased after him, calling his name over and over, begging him to come back to her.

Her child.

But he wouldn't stop, and finally she grew so weary she had to stop. When she dropped to her knees, she felt warmth, and Wolf rolled over to greet her. His hands were hard as they grabbed her elbows pulling her down to his mouth. The erotic pleasure he gave her made Caroline moan in her sleep.

She gave herself to him completely, holding nothing back. Together they soared so that it was almost as if they were watching yet participating in the pleasure they gave each other.

And then it was over and he was studying her, his eyes dark, questioning. "Why have you done this to me?" he asked. "To my son?" She tried to explain, but he wouldn't listen and then he too was leaving her, taking away the warmth of his body and his soul.

"No. No, please. I had to do it. Don't you understand?"

"Caroline. Caroline wake up."

She jerked awake so abruptly that she couldn't tell if the man before her was a dream or real. Reaching out, she touched the hard line of his jaw, the roughness of his whiskers, and a sob escaped her.

His eyes narrowed as he brushed a stray curl from her forehead. "What troubles you, Caroline?"

She wanted to tell him. Her mouth opened, but no sound came out. In her dream he was hurt because she kept his son from him. But real life was different. What would he do if he knew she was pregnant with his child? The man she knew seemed unlikely to embrace the news with joy. The best she could hope for was a reluctant proposal of marriage for the child's sake.

Then, like Mary's husband, he would be off, leaving her alone. She didn't need a marriage with him for that. She was alone now.

And what if he rejected her completely? Her child would be branded a bastard. She could end up with nothing. And with Edward and her child to consider, that was not a chance she could take.

What troubles you, he had asked. She almost smiled thinking how many different ways she could answer that, and not even brush the real truth. "It has been a difficult year," she finally said.

"Since you left England?"

"It began before that." He settled into the bedside chair, dwarfing the furniture with his size, and Caroline wondered why he was here. Since he first brought her to Seven Pines, he rarely seemed eager to merely converse. The loss of his friendship was only one of the things she missed when he left her. Now his concern sent chills down her spine. "What is it?" Caroline dragged his attention away from the window he stared through. "Is Mary worse?"

"No." His eyes met hers, unblinking, and Caroline let out her breath. "Sadayi gave her some herbs for her fever. Colleen is sleeping, her belly full."

Caroline wriggled higher against the headboard, pulling the quilt up as she did. "But something is wrong."

"Not wrong." He leaned forward resting his forearms on his leather-covered legs. He was perhaps three feet from the bed, and the urge to bound across the space and slide into the bed beside her was overwhelming. Wolf clenched his hands together. "The Headmen are leaving for Charles Town."

"That's wonderful." Caroline loosened her grip on the blanket. " 'Tis what you wished would happen, isn't it?" His expression did not reflect the news he'd given her. "I'm sure the problems between the Cherokee and English can be resolved."

"To whose satisfaction?" Wolf stood, pushing the chair against the wall as he did. "You are right, I should not doubt these negotiations before they begin." He paced to the far corner of the room. Unfortunately, it was not a large room. He could still smell the sweet flowery scent that was hers alone. He shouldn't have come in here. Actually he made that decision as he stood outside her door earlier. It was only her cries that made him open the door.

"Then why do you?"

He arched a brow. She seemed to know him well. "Perhaps a basic distrust of the English," he said.

"Some would consider you English," she quipped, lifting her chin a notch.

"They might, but I think you know better."

"What I *know* is that you are torn between the two cultures, and you don't have an inkling of where you belong." The words were out of her mouth before she thought them through . . . before she considered how he might take them. But Caroline felt sure she was right—even though being right was unlikely to keep his anger in check. She steeled herself for his raging denial.

But it never came. Instead he threw back his head and laughed. It was such a rare sound coming from him that Caroline couldn't help staring in amazement. At the moment he looked very wild indeed. His dark hair was loose, and his open-throated hunting shirt showed a broad expanse of bronzed chest—more savage than cultured Englishman.

Yet she'd seen him in silk waistcoat and silver-buckled shoes. A gentleman, she thought then. Now she didn't know.

When he finished laughing, Wolf strode back to the window. He could sense her behind him, still wrapped in the bedclothes. She had spoken boldly and probably regretted it. He heard the rope springs moan, and he twisted around to look at her. Her face was alive with color, but she met his stare without flinching.

She obviously considered her assessment of him correct, and Wolf couldn't argue with her. But he had no intention of agreeing with her, either. Or even discussing the matter further. "I'm going with them," he said as his eyes sought again the forested vista through the panes.

"With them?" Caroline was momentarily baffled at this sudden switch in the conversation. "Ah, the

Headmen," she said, and watched as he nodded. He didn't turn around.

"I feel I can be of help."

"Of course you can. 'Tis obvious." Oh, she didn't want him to leave.

"I don't want to leave you here."

His voice was low, and Caroline leaned forward to make certain she heard him correctly. "It should be safe enough as long as both sides talk of peace," she said.

"I'd still feel better if you went to Fort Prince George for a while."

He did look at her now, and Caroline sucked in her breath at the intensity of his eyes. "I won't leave Mary," she insisted.

"I intended to see her and the baby safely to the fort also."

"Even if she didn't have the fever it would be a sennight till she was strong enough to travel. You will be long gone by then."

"Sadayi will stay with her and Gulegi will take her to the fort in my stead when she is strong enough."

"I won't leave."

"Damnit, Caroline." Wolf advanced toward the bed. "You are being stubborn."

"It is you who persist. Seven Pines is my home, Mary is my friend, and I shall not go." She swung her legs over the side of the bed, no longer content to lie passively while he loomed over her. "Besides," she continued as her bare feet hit the floor.

"If it is safe enough for her to stay, then I see no reason—"

"Have you forgotten Tal-tsuska?"

The shawl she was about to swing over her shoulders dropped from her fingers. "No," she whispered, but as he bent to retrieve the woven garment, she knew he didn't believe her. But what did it matter what he thought? "With the Headmen working for peace, he wouldn't dare do anything," she insisted. "You said yourself he could have killed you and didn't."

Wolf stood slowly, his eyes traveling up past her fragile ankles and legs to the shift that skimmed over her curves. She said nothing, but he could tell his survey was not without its effect. He meant to intimidate, to remind her that he was in control. But by the time his gaze leveled on her distended nipples, Wolf admitted to himself he failed.

She was no more intimidated than he. It was desire that ruled them both. Wolf thrust the shawl into her hands and turned quickly lest she notice the hard bulge that tented his loincloth.

"Might I remind you that you stay at Seven Pines due to my hospitality." It didn't please him to discuss this, but nothing else had worked. He shot her a look over his shoulder and seeing her bewildered expression raised his brow. "Perhaps you've forgotten the codicil to your marriage agreement. The one stating that you inherit Seven Pines and Robert's wealth only if you bring forth issue."

"How did you know about that?" Caroline

stepped toward him. As far as she knew, that had been arranged between her lawyer and Robert. She hadn't even been told until that fateful night that Robert came to her.

"You thought to keep it a secret, Lady Caroline?"

"No, of course not." Caroline swiped her hair behind a shoulder. "I just didn't realize you were privy to your father's personal affairs."

"Only when he wished to flaunt them before me."

"I don't under—"

"Personal matters, Lady Caroline. My father took great pleasure in telling me about bedding you." His eyes narrowed. "In great detail."

"But that's a . . ." Caroline bit her tongue to keep from telling him his father had lied to him.

"A what, Your Ladyship?"

"Nothing. And please stop calling me that."

"What should I call you then?" He stepped closer.

Caroline's jaw tightened, but her eyes never wavered. "What about lover?" She was angry. At Robert. At his son. "You were quick enough to take me as that, if I recall."

"And as *I* recall, you didn't fight the idea over much. Then or later."

"To my shame, you remember it quite well."

Wolf's lashes closed, and he took a deep breath. When he opened his eyes, she had turned away from him. He reached for her shoulder, not surprised when she shrugged away his hand. "I apologize for my remarks. It was not very—"

"Gentlemanly of you." Her expression was full of contempt when she shot a look back at him. "Is that what you intended to say? But then you aren't a gentleman, are you? Not really. I think, Wolf MacQuaid, you are every bit the savage you purport to be."

Wolf opened his mouth to counter her statement, but before he could, she said something else that left him speechless.

"And I think you have a lot of nerve chastising your father for his indiscretions in telling you of our *personal* life. Wasn't it your intention from the beginning to show to your father that you had me first. Never mind." Caroline lifted her hand. "You needn't say a thing. I see the answer in your eyes."

"Caroline." Wolf stepped forward, but though she didn't retreat, the expression on her face told him touching her would do no good. Nor could he explain. Or even ask her forgiveness. What he'd done was unforgivable. And they both knew it.

It seemed so perfect at the beginning, a way to settle things with his father, to avenge his mother. But he hadn't counted on Caroline being the person she was, a person he now cared about more deeply than he wished to.

But if she ever felt anything for him, it was gone, snuffed as surely as the light that usually shone in her blue eyes.

"Please go." Caroline managed to keep her voice steady and her bearing straight, all the while praying that he would do as she asked. She saw him lift his hand toward her and just as quickly let it drop to his side. If he touched her, would she be able to keep from throwing herself into his arms and demanding to know why he'd done this to her? But she wished to make a fool of herself no more. And when he finally turned and left the room, she sighed with relief.

Crossing to the rocking chair by the window, she sat. The shock of what just happened was beginning to wear off, and the blessed numbness was replaced by anger and hurt. She hadn't meant to say what she did. Until that moment, the idea that he would do such a thing had only been a niggling doubt that teased at the back of her mind. By sheer will, she'd forced herself never to think on it. It was too awful to comprehend. But now she knew the truth. And it nearly broke her heart.

It took Wolf three days to leave, and Caroline couldn't imagine how she managed to endure with him there. But Mary was improving, as was her child, and Caroline tried to keep her mind on that. But every time she glanced across the room to see him watching her with his probing dark eyes, she wanted to cry.

She wished for nothing more than that he would go. And when he did, she was as unhappy as before. But there was much to do. Several Cherokee men stayed at Seven Pines, and according to the directions Wolf gave them, they rebuilt the burned-out barn.

The weather grew colder. Winter was upon them. Any lingering doubts Caroline had about being with child were dispelled. Even though her waistline had yet to expand, she could almost feel the new life within her.

One evening as they sat in the parlor, huddled around the hearth, Caroline told Mary. The grey-eyed woman dropped her sewing onto the floor and rushed to Caroline's side. Leaning over, she hugged her to her bosom, crying with joy.

"I'm so happy," she said as she straightened and glanced toward the cradle where Colleen slept peacefully. "Our children will grow up together and become great friends, just like we are."

Caroline joined in her happiness, answering the myriad questions. "Had she thought of any names yet? Was she hoping for a boy or a little girl like her Colleen? When did she expect the child would be born?" Then a cloud seemed to pass over her kind, open face. "It is just too bad Robert didn't live to know he was to be a father again."

Mary never questioned that the baby was Robert's. And for that Caroline was grateful.

As the weeks passed, Caroline herself almost forgot that there was a decision to be made about the child. Until she glanced up one day as she carried milk in from the barn and found Wolf standing in the clearing.

Fourteen

"I didn't expect you back so soon." Caroline tried to slow her pounding heart. She even wondered if he could hear it as he stood tall and powerful across the clearing.

Wolf slung the musket across his shoulder by its strap and strode toward her, his eyes never leaving her face. "Did you not?" he asked while taking the pails of milk even though she protested.

She hated him, Caroline reminded herself, annoyed because the reminder was needed. He had used her and left her and done it with a ruthless premeditation that still left her weak with anger. Yet when she saw him like this, weary from the trail, his features forced into calmness she knew was thin as veneer, her heart went out to him.

He should be jubilant. He had accompanied the Cherokee Headmen to Charles Town. Surely with both sides desiring it, a plan for peace had been agreed upon. But then he'd barely been gone a fortnight, hardly time to reach the capital and return, let alone devise a scheme to put an end to the hostilities plaguing the frontier. "What is it?" she asked. " 'Tis something amiss?"

He answered her question with one of his own. "What of Mary and her baby? Are they well enough to travel?" Wolf's long strides continued eating up ground toward the house across the chicken-pecked yard, till he realized Caroline no longer followed. Turning, he waited.

"What happened?"

"Can they travel?"

Their eyes locked, each expecting an answer. Caroline took a deep breath, deciding she would never find out what disturbed him so unless she responded. "I suppose they can if they must. Mary isn't strong, though she tries her best to hide it. And Colleen . . ." She lifted her hands, letting them fall again in defeat. "She's so fussy and irritable all the time, even though she gets most of her nourishment from the wet nurse Sadayi brought."

"Is Sadayi here?"

"No," Caroline admitted with a shake of her head. "She went back to Kawuyi two days ago, I expected her to return last night, but she didn't. Neither did Cahtahlata, the woman who's been feeding Colleen."

"Word must have reached there by now," he said more to himself than Caroline. But she heard and rushed forward. Reaching out she grabbed his arm, spilling some of the frothy milk in the process. Steam rose when it hit the frosted ground.

"Word of what? Tell me."

His eyes focused again on her, and Caroline felt a chill that had naught to do with the northerly wind swooping down through the valley.

"The governor is holding the Headmen as prisoners."

"What?" A lock of curling hair swirled out of Caroline's cap, and she impatiently swiped it off her cheek. "But how can he do that? They went in peace at Governor Lyttelton's suggestion." He said nothing, and she continued. "They were going to work out all the problems between the two nations." Caroline realized her voice grew higher and stopped. She took a calming breath. "Tell me what happened."

"We should go inside." The air seemed to grow colder as they stood there. The wind crackled through the dried-up oak leaves that clung stubbornly to the branches and bent the tall pines. Wolf couldn't tell if Caroline shivered from the cold or the news he imparted . . . or because of her anger with him. But as she shook her head, it didn't seem as if she even remembered the words they'd had before he left for Charles Town.

"Mary's still in bed. I don't wish to disturb her."

Wolf shrugged. He might as well allow her to rest while she could. And Caroline didn't seem willing to do anything until he told her what he knew. He set the milk on the ground then took Caroline's arm, touching her just below the elbow where the ruffle of her shift gave way to smooth

291

skin. She stiffened but allowed him to lead her back toward the barn.

The log walls offered protection from the biting wind, and the body heat from the two cows and one horse—which had survived the Indian attack—took the worst of the chill from the air. The early winter sun crept through the chinks between the logs, throwing a striped pattern of light and shadows across the straw-strewn floor.

"Well?"

Wolf almost smiled at her impatient tone. But then what he had to say wasn't at all amusing. "It was a trap. At least it appears that it was," Wolf added, for he couldn't be certain what was in other men's hearts. "Oconostota and the others went to Charles Town at Lyttelton's request, assured of their safety."

"Yes, 'tis as you told me before you left."

"Except that when we arrived, Governor Lyttleton did not act as if he wished to negotiate. A deerskin, the symbol of the bond between the Cherokee and the English was laid at Lyttleton's feet." Wolf's eyes narrowed. "He refused to pick it up."

"But what does that mean?"

"At the time, I wasn't sure. Oconostota had given his talk, stating he wished no war with the English. He spoke of the warriors, both the English of Virginia and the Cherokee acting like boys. He said he desired to bury the hatchet of his young people."

"And what of Lyttleton? He must have appreciated that sentiment." Caroline wrapped the shawl more tightly about her, but in truth she'd all but forgotten the cold.

"Lyttleton repeated his demand that the murderers of the King's subjects must be turned over to English justice. He also said he would hold the Cherokee Headmen *as his guests* until all the guilty warriors surrendered."

Caroline took a moment to absorb all that Wolf told her. "But they were promised safe passage," she said again.

"It is not the only time the *Ani'-Yun'wiya,* the Cherokee, have listened to the false tongue of the English."

Wolf turned away so quickly Caroline wondered if he spoke of what happened in Charles Town or his own experience with his father. But she couldn't let empathy for his past cloud her judgment. Especially when her experience with lies and deceit were mostly at his hand. Caroline opened her mouth to tell him as much, but closed it again with a click of her teeth. What purpose would it serve? Besides, at the moment, she cared more about what he was saying. Her own naïveté was a thing of the past.

"Where are they now, Oconostota and the rest?"

"On their way to Fort Prince George."

"But you said—"

"They are in the company of Lyttleton, the provincial regiment and the regulars from Charles

Town. The Cherokee are kept under constant guard, as was I at first."

"Do you mean the Governor held you hostage as well?"

"You needn't sound so shocked. It is no secret that Indian blood runs in my veins."

"As well as English."

He ignored that remark as he strode to the doorway. He'd told her what she wished to know. "Pack as few things as you can manage with and be ready to leave within the hour."

"Leave for where?" Caroline whirled around and caught the loose fabric of his sleeve. Her hand slid down his arm, touching the strong bones of his wrist. She hadn't meant to touch him, only keep him from leaving the barn, but the contact affected him as much as it did her. He twisted around, his eyes a dark fire that seared her defenses before he lowered his lids and looked away.

"Fort Prince George," Wolf said when he could trust his voice to be steady. He had not been prepared for the sensual spark that shot through him.

"But you said that is where Governor Lyttleton is taking the Headmen."

"It is also the largest garrison in the area. Since we do not have time to return you to Charles Town, let alone England, I think you and Mary will be safest there." With those words, he left the barn.

By the time Caroline reached the house, he had awakened Mary and was explaining the situation to her, though in less detail and without the need on Mary's part to drag information from him. What did she expect? He cared for Mary, he'd told her so from the first. Whereas she had never been anything to him save a tool for vengence. The thought sent renewed anger surging through her body. Her fists clenched, relaxing only when Mary glanced toward the doorway and saw her.

"Oh Caroline, did you hear? Wolf says we must make all haste to arrive at Fort Prince George."

Her voice was agitated but weak. Caroline moved toward her, smiling as reassuringly as she could. It seemed to her that Mary's eyes had sunk deeper since the night before.

"I'm not sure leaving 'tis what we should do," Caroline said as she plumped the pillows under Mary's head and shoulders. From the corner of her eye, she noticed Wolf pause as he leaned over the cradle. His hunting shirt was stretched taut over his back, and she watched as the corded muscles tightened.

Then her attention was drawn back to Mary who looked up at her, grey eyes showing bewilderment. "But Raff said—"

"I'm sure he meant our traveling only as a suggestion, Mary." Caroline helped her scoot up against the bolstered pillows. She didn't glance around when Wolf handed the young mother her fussy baby, but she couldn't help noting how small the child looked in Wolf's large hands.

Then those hands were upon her, not gentle as when he handed Colleen to Mary, but strong and commanding. With no more than a mumbled excuse to Mary, he propelled Caroline toward the open doorway. Any thoughts she had of protesting evaporated when he nudged the door shut with his shoulder.

He nearly dragged her into the parlor, shutting that door also before letting her go with enough force to make her stumble.

"Are you so enamored of Indian attacks that you wish for another?"

"Don't be ridiculous." Caroline tried to regain some measure of dignity. She brushed out her brocaded skirts and refused to meet his stare . . . until doing so became impossible. God, why was she drawn to him so?

"It would seem so to me, with that foolish talk of staying here."

"Just because I don't agree with you that we are at danger does not mean I am foolish." Caroline lifted her chin and tried not to cower as he stalked closer to her. "You said yourself revenge against Robert spurred the other attack."

"I said it may have helped spur the attack." The look he gave her was hard, lacking any sign of the passion she'd thought she saw earlier when they touched. Or had she only imagined it? "But even if that was the only reason before, I think you will agree that circumstances have changed."

"Mary and I have lived here for nearly a fortnight with nothing but friendship from the village." He stepped closer but still she refused to retreat. "I don't think—"

"Your Ladyship," he began his voice all the more ominous for its low tone. "Do not allow your dislike of me to cloud your judgment."

"I do not dislike you," Caroline countered, nearly choking on the falsehood. "You mean nothing at all to me."

He was so close now she could smell the woodsy, outdoor scent that enveloped him. Leather and horses, wood smoke and the cool crisp fragrance of winter blended with his own scent. Her senses were inundated, and her body responded to the memories his smell evoked. Her nipples tightened; and between her legs, where he'd touched and caressed, she felt the moisture of wanting him.

Aghast, embarrassed by her traitorous body, Caroline turned away, but his hands were quick and before she could stop him, he cupped her shoulders, forcing her to look up at him.

It was there again, the flare of passion shining from the depths of his obsidian eyes. Desire flared hotter in her, warring with the memory of his betrayal. She thought she might melt from the battle till he began speaking. Then her attention became riveted on his words.

"I came to you first. First, do you understand me?" His fingers tightened. "My people will soon be pressed into a war they neither want nor can win. But they will fight, because they are proud and have no choice. And I should be there in my village, at least trying to talk some sense into the young men who see only the glory of battle. But I am not there. I am here, because you are here, and I cannot stand the thought of you suffering as you did before."

"My *suffering* has been primarily at your hand. Caroline lashed out with those words and immediately wished them back. She didn't want him to know how very deeply he'd hurt her.

"You may think so now," he said, his voice gentler but just as intense. "But I did not rape you, nor force you to do naught that you did not wish."

"You used me. You brought me here . . . to him. And abandoned me." Caroline turned her face away, embarrassed by the tears that threatened to spill from her lower lashes.

Wolf took a deep breath, forcing himself not to pull her into his arms and assuage her tears . . . assuage his own guilt for the way he'd treated her. Instead he offered what he could. Safety . . . at least as much as there was on the frontier. "Please ready yourself for the trip," he said, releasing her arms. "I shall pack some provisions."

She missed the warmth of his hands. Caroline rubbed her own up and down her arms and wished it weren't so. But wishing did no good, as he'd taught her only too well. So Caroline sniffed, scrubbing her hands across her face before heading back toward Mary's bedroom.

Caroline avoided Mary's eyes as long as she could, busying herself with rolling petticoats and stuffing them into a saddlebag she dragged from the top shelf of the wardrobe. But not meeting her eye wasn't enough.

"What was that all about?" Mary asked as she closed her bodice and shifted the sleeping baby to her shoulder.

"Nothing."

"It didn't sound like nothing to me. What happened between the two of you?"

"We had a simple disagreement about whether or not we should go to Fort Prince George." Caroline yanked open a drawer and began stuffing Mary's stockings into the leather pouch. "I've decided he's right, that we should leave."

"I imagine he is." Mary crawled out of bed and carefully lifted Colleen. "Wolf knows a great deal about the politics between the English and Cherokee." With a smile she settled the infant into her cradle then slowly straightened to face Caroline. "But that's not what I mean and I think you know it."

"I know nothing of the kind." Caroline dropped the saddlebag on top of the dresser. "Since you're finished nursing Colleen, perhaps you can finish packing your things. I'll see about the—"

"Why won't you ever talk to me about this?" Mary, dressed in a shift and bodice that seemed made for someone larger, came forward. She grasped Caroline's hands. "You've been wonderful to me. You've taken care of us. Done all the work and listened when I poured out my heart to you about Logan. Even telling you the secrets I can barely admit to myself. Yet you won't let me help you at all."

"Mary." Caroline grasped her cold hands, trying to press some of her warmth into them. "There is nothing you can do."

"I can listen, Caroline. 'Tis what friends do for one another."

" 'Tis nothing to tell." Caroline forced the lie through her lips, then reached out when Mary turned away. "Please don't be angry."

"I'm not." Mary moved haltingly toward the hook where her skirts hung. " 'Tis just that there is something when he looks at you. And when you look at him . . ."

She shook her head, leaving the rest unsaid, and for that Caroline was grateful. For she didn't want to deny the undeniable. And lying was becoming too easy.

Yet she thought of the child nestled deep inside her and knew the untruths would continue. And escalate.

"Mary." Caroline stood clutching the saddle-bag's leather straps until her friend looked around. Her excited expression dimmed with Caroline's next words. "I don't want you to mention to Wolf that I'm in the family way."

"Why? I should think he would be pleased to know."

Though she doubted Mary's assessment, even if the question of the baby's conception didn't spring immediately to his mind, Caroline nodded. "You are right. But I'm still not completely sure I am with child, you know. And I'd just rather wait a bit to tell anyone else."

"Of course, I shall respect your wishes, Caroline." Mary tied the tabs of her skirts. "I am your friend . . . always."

By late morning, the four of them were on their way. Mary rode sidesaddle on the only horse that survived the Indian raid, her child wrapped to the front of her body Cherokee style with a long shawl. She looked tired with shadows beneath her grey eyes, but her spirits seemed high. Caroline chose to walk behind, leading the horse Wolf brought. Wolf, himself on foot, was at the head of their unlikely procession, his long rifle cradled in his arms, his posture alert.

The trail they took was the one on which Wolf and she had traveled on her way to Seven Pines . . . was it only months before? So much about her life had changed since then. But Caroline tried not to dwell on that as she plodded along listening for anything that might mean . . . What? An Indian attack? Wolf hadn't said so, but she imagined that's why he scouted a bit ahead, peering into the woods on either side of the trail.

But she heard nothing, save the call of a hawk and the occasional rustling of a fox or rabbit in the underbrush. When they stopped by the bend of a stream to rest, Caroline stood back as Wolf helped mother and child from the saddle. Mary smiled at him wanly when he settled her on a carpet of moss, leaning her back against the burly bark of an oak tree. Colleen fussed irritably until Mary managed to bring her to her breast.

Caroline watched her friend a moment then followed Wolf downstream where he'd taken the horses to water them. "Are you certain this trip is necessary? Mary doesn't look well, at all."

Wolf glanced over his shoulder at Caroline, then through the web of leafless saplings that separated them from Mary. His dark brows lowered. "We will be at the fort by this time tomorrow. Then she can rest."

"You didn't answer my question." Caroline wished she could deal with him in a reasonable way, but anger seemed to seep into her words whenever they spoke. She wondered if the anger wasn't her way of dealing with the hurt she felt. Or the desire that still strummed through her whenever he looked at her. She was a foolish woman to want him after what he'd done. Foolish. Foolish, she told herself, as he settled his obsidian gaze on her.

"I would not risk any of you, if I did not think it necessary."

She should accept his word and return to Mary, Caroline knew that. Yet she didn't, continuing to sting him with her doubts. "Wouldn't you?"

His eyes narrowed. "What is that supposed to mean?"

"Only that I find it difficult to trust you," Caroline said before turning her back on him so he couldn't see she lied. For as ridiculous as it was, she did trust him. Not with her heart of course, but to keep her safe from bodily harm.

She didn't expect his hand on her shoulder, so she wasn't prepared for the flame of desire that shot through her.

"What do you wish from me, Caroline? An apology?"

"For what?" She glanced back over her shoulder and realized her mistake immediately. She had no resistance where he was concerned.

He studied her with his dark eyes a moment before shaking his head. "You surprise me. I'd thought you more honest than that."

"I wonder what you know or care about honesty."

"Because I used you."

Now that he'd said it . . . admitted it . . . Caroline wished he hadn't. She turned away only to be caught by his strong hands and twisted back to face him.

"Is that why you don't trust me, Caroline?"

"Yes! Isn't that a good enough reason to distrust you . . . even to hate you?" Caroline said the last in as quiet a tone as she could, hoping Mary couldn't hear her. But she was so agitated, her breasts rose and fell with each breath.

His gaze slipped down to where her bosom curved above the ruffle of her shift, then slowly resought her face. Her cheeks were crimson, and her blue eyes sparked with anger, but still he held her shoulders, refusing to let her loose when she would have pulled away.

Though she knew it was useless, Caroline jerked again. "How dare you look at me like that!"

"I think we both know I dare that and more." Without thinking of the consequences, only knowing he had to kiss her, Wolf's face bent to capture her lips. She fought him, squirming in his grip, and doing her best to keep her mouth shut. But Wolf could be patient when there was something he wanted. And he wanted Caroline. Her smell, her taste had haunted him since he last held her.

His tongue teased, his teeth nibbled, and he pulled her closer into his embrace. She must have realized that all her wriggling only heightened his desire for she stopped suddenly, holding herself stiff as a planed board. But even that did not deter him, and slowly but surely he felt the thawing of her body.

His hands curled around her back and followed the lines of boning down to her rounded hips, then back up. And all the while, he grew harder and harder. When her mouth opened on a sigh, he filled it quickly, completely, with his tongue. Her hands, that had hung limply by her side, grabbed hold of his arms then snaked around his neck, holding on as he deepened the kiss. As he ignited them both with wild, untamed passion.

When they separated, it took them both a moment to calm their breathing. Their eyes met and hers skittered down. With his thumb Wolf lifted her rounded chin, forcing her to confront him as surely as he'd forced her to kiss him.

She didn't seem pleased by either.

"Are you happy now?" she asked, her voice husky with the passion that still bound them from chest to hip.

Not knowing how to answer such a question, Wolf said nothing, only rested his chin upon the crown of her head. Soft tendrils of clean-smelling hair teased at his jaw. But her next words had him pulling back and studying her upturned face.

"You've proven to both of us, yet again, how difficult it is for me to resist you. Even knowing what I do about you—how you used me to punish your father—I still can't turn away. 'Tis a shame I shall live with forever."

His hands tightened on her shoulders, and he held her at arm's length. "There is no shame in feeling desire."

"Then why do I spend so much time regretting what I've done?"

His hands dropped from her shoulders.

"Please, leave me alone. 'Tis all I ask of you."

Before he could answer, she turned and slipped through the underbrush. Wolf watched as she knelt beside Mary who had fallen asleep along with her child. Caroline reached out her hand and brushed her fingers across the sleeping woman's cheek, gently awakening her. And Wolf's loins tightened. Just watching her made him want her.

And Caroline was right, he'd proven to her . . . to both of them . . . that she wanted him, too. But what good did it do? She hated him. And with good reason. Wolf shook his head wondering what in the hell he was trying to prove by that kiss.

He seemed to take her at her word, and for that Caroline was grateful. By the time they reached Fort Prince George, she and Wolf barely spoke, and only then when necessity required it.

If Mary noticed the hostility between them, she said nothing. But then she seemed to grow weaker by the hour. When they finally stood on the hillside looking down on the fort, Caroline felt a surge of relief.

Inside the log walls the fort seemed ready to burst. Word of the governor's actions had spread through the frontier and many of the settlers had come to the same conclusion as Wolf. The Cherokee would not sit peacefully by and allow their Headmen to be held against their will.

Families camped within the shadow of the fort, their children ran about playing tag and chasing dogs. Across the river in Keowee, Cherokee children did the same, as everyone awaited some word as to what would happen.

Caroline was thankful that Wolf secured them lodging in the fort at the cabin of a Mistress Quinn.

"He pounded on my door near dawn two days ago," Mistress Quinn said, "Beggin' me to save a place for you. Then he left without so much as a bite to eat."

"I'm grateful for a place to stay. And so is Mary." Caroline walked the floor, holding Colleen to her chest and rocking her softly as she moved. She didn't like to think that she had Wolf to thank for it.

"Wolf said you had a hard time of it," the elderly woman said as she leaned back in her rocking chair.

Pausing, Caroline met the woman's eyes, wondering exactly what Wolf told her. Mistress Quinn didn't leave her in suspense for long.

"Nasty business," she said with a click of her tongue. "I'd hoped the Cherokee were different from the other heathens. I come down from Pennsylvania, don't you know, with my husband Edgar. The Shawnee, now they was an untrustworthy lot. But I thought the Cherokee was different," she repeated.

"How do you mean, different?" Colleen had quieted, her dark blue eyes closed in sleep and Caroline lowered her into a basket she and Mistress Quinn had lined with batting.

"You know." The women ran a hand down across her sagging jaw. "Like us."

"Honest and trustworthy?" Apparently Mistress Quinn didn't notice the sarcasm in Caroline's tone for a snaggletoothed grin split her wrinkled face.

"Exactly." She leaned forward in her chair, peering toward the basket. "Is the little one asleep then?"

"Yes, like her mother." Caroline couldn't dislike the woman, regardless of her narrow-minded views on the Cherokee. Caroline would probably feel the same if she hadn't lived so closely with Sadayi and Walini . . . if Wolf hadn't explained the intricacies of the Cherokee's treaty with the English.

There she was, thinking of him again. Caroline decided to peel potatoes for the evening meal. Anything to keep busy. She glanced back when Mistress Quinn spoke again.

"I'm thinkin' she has the setbacks."

"The what?" Caroline joined the older woman where she now stood looking down at the baby, who seemed even smaller lying in the basket.

"She ain't gainin' like she should. Looks to me like she's losin' weight."

Caroline touched the baby's fuzzy head with the tip of her finger and wished she could argue with Mistress Quinn's opinion.

A sennight passed. Anticipation grew. Caroline could feel it in the air like the chill that blew down from the mountain passes. Word came that the governor and the militia were on their way, along with the Cherokee Headmen. It was also an ill-kept secret that the English would be attacked when they forded the creek below Keowee.

Wolf was gone. He'd done no more than see Mary and her to safety before taking his leave. Caroline assumed he went to the Cherokee towns . . . the ones he would have visited when he came to Seven Pines for Mary and her instead. She thought often of how he looked when he'd told her that. How a savage fire seemed to burn in his eyes.

And she wondered what he said to the elders and to the young men who longed to prove their bravery as warriors. Did he convince anyone that peace was the only answer?

But as great as the magnitude of the troubles that surrounded her, Caroline still worried about Mary and her baby the most. Neither were strong, and the sojourn at the fort with its crowded conditions seemed to make them worse.

She thought about taking them home. Commandeering the horse that they brought and somehow getting Mary and Colleen back to Seven Pines. But the rumors that filled the fort, drifting in the air like the smoke from countless campfires frightened her and kept her from doing anything rash.

The days grew shorter, colder. Then one morning when Caroline dressed, hurrying to keep the gooseflesh at bay, she noted a slight swelling where before she'd been flat. She doubted anyone else would notice, especially under the flare of her skirts, but it eliminated the last vestiges of doubt about her condition. Oddly enough, she felt stronger knowing for certain.

She was so engrossed in her thoughts that she nearly missed hearing the commotion outside. It wasn't till Mistress Quinn called up to the loft where Caroline slept that she paid the noise any heed.

"They've come at last," she called.

Caroline finished dressing quickly then scrambled down the ladder to see Mary had bundled up the baby and along with Mistress Quinn stood waiting for her.

"We thought it might be interesting to go watch them arrive," Mary said, as she transferred the baby from one shoulder to another.

All three women jolted when the first cannon fired. "It ain't nothing but a salute," the older woman assured them as they walked through the open gates. Across the Keowee River, Caroline could see Cherokee, apparently as curious as she, watching the long line of red-clad soldiers snake their way along the flats surrounding the fort.

"There's the governor," Mary called, pointing toward a group of mounted men off to the side of the column.

Caroline followed her friend's gaze, and her breath caught in her throat. For beside the governor, tall and erect upon his chestnut stallion sat Raff MacQuaid.

Fifteen

"You're looking as lovely as ever, Lady Caroline."

Caroline doubted the governor remembered her from their brief encounter in Charles Town. At the time Wolf's anger over the broken treaty had prevented even an introduction. Nevertheless, Caroline curtsied and gave him a demure smile for his compliment.

"I'm so glad to see this infernal frontier hasn't sapped your beauty." He took her hand, seeming not to notice the calluses that toughened her skin, then placed it on his scarlet sleeve and led her into the room that served as his parlor. There she was introduced to several of his officers. One of them a Major Mulhanny from somewhere near Lands End, she thought. He seemed an eager fellow who complimented her lavishly and often.

Captain Godfrey also stepped forward as if she were a duchess rather than an impoverished daughter of an earl and widow of a slain trader. He regaled her with some witticism when he was presented to her, and Caroline imagined she answered in kind, for he smiled, revealing straight white teeth that seemed a trifle large for his face.

The next three men were equally attentive, though Caroline failed to listen closely enough to catch their names. Her attention kept wandering to the man standing off by himself, lounging indulgently against the back wall. He watched her, too, an amused expression on his handsome face as she was led from one officer to the next, from one admiring man to the next.

"And, of course, you remember your—" The governor sucked in his breath as if he realized the absurdity of calling this man her stepson. As smoothly as he could, and being a politician, that was with practiced aplomb, Governor Lyttelton changed the course of his introduction. "Rafferty MacQuaid," he finished.

"Yes, how are you Mr. MacQuaid?" It amazed Caroline how manners drilled into her head so many years ago could surface to help her through a difficult moment. For her heart was pounding and she wanted nothing more than to turn and run from this place.

"I'm very well, Lady Caroline." He pushed off from the wall and took her hand, swallowing it up in his. "May I add my compliments to the multitude you've recently garnered?" His gaze took its time roaming from her face, down her body, clad simply in the bodice and quilted overskirts he'd seen many times, then back up to arrogantly meet her eyes.

He smiled at her briefly, as if they shared a secret that would shock the other occupants of the room—which was exactly the case—and handed her back to the governor. Lyttelton led her to a chair by the hearth where a fire took the chill from the evening.

"I can't tell you how pleased I was that you could accept my invitation," the governor was saying to her as he drew his chair closer to hers. "We've been too long in the wilds without benefit of hearing a soft, feminine voice."

The other men agreed, except for Wolf who had resumed his position against the far wall. The ornate silver branch of candles, which to Caroline's mind was as out of place in these primitive surroundings as the scarlet-clad men, failed to light all the corners of the log-walled room. Certainly Wolf remained in shadows.

But Caroline didn't need to see him to feel his eyes upon her or to remember how he looked. Unlike the governor and his officers, who were all impeccably garbed from their powdered wigs to the polish on their gleaming boots, Wolf wore leggings and a loose homespun shirt. The one concession he'd made to civilized attire was tying back his dark hair with a leather thong. Nor was he carrying his long rifle, although Caroline noticed it leaning in the corner, no more than an arm's length away.

And he was far from unarmed. Caroline couldn't help but wonder how the fancy swords the British sported would compare in battle to the broad-bladed knife sheathed by Wolf's narrow hip.

"Oh, I'm sorry, did you ask me something?" Caroline smiled into the hazel eyes of one of the men whose name she'd missed. He was young, his skin smooth as Colleen's bottom, and he was telling her some tale about their trip from Charles Town.

"I asked Your Ladyship if you'd ever encountered a bear," he repeated good-naturedly.

She managed to make some inane response to the lieutenant who didn't seem to notice or mind her inattentiveness.

Caroline was thankful when dinner was announced. The governor escorted her into another room of the barracks and seated her to his right. Wolf sat to his left, directly across the lavishly set table.

It appeared the governor refused to sacrifice his comforts even when he visited the frontier. More silver graced the table, holding the candles that lit the room, and lined up beside the fine bone china. The tablecloth was Irish linen and the food more fancifully prepared than she'd had in a long time.

Caroline wondered how Wolf would handle the table setting, but as they dined on a clear broth of unique flavor, Caroline noted his long fingers seemed as much at home lightly gripping a silver

314

spoon, as steadying his rifle . . . or caressing a woman.

Caroline nearly choked on her wine when that vision popped unbidden to her mind. Delicately wiping her lips with the lace-trimmed napkin, Caroline turned to the governor. After complimenting him for the fine cuisine, she broached a subject no one had yet to mention.

"What do you feel are your chances of avoiding a devastating war with the Cherokee?"

Caroline thought a hush trickled down the length of the table, and the officers seemed to glance toward the governor in unison. He lifted his goblet as if offering a toast. "Look before you, Lady Caroline." With the sweep of his hand, he indicated those sitting at the table. "Here we have representatives of his Highness's army. How can we fail to resolve this. . problem to our satisfaction?"

"The heathens just need to be shown what they are up against on occasion." This came from the officer to her right, Captain Godfrey.

Caroline's eyes shot to Wolf. She expected he might be getting ready to vault the table and grab the officer by his gorget for his reference to "heathens." But to the contrary, his expression was bland, his posture almost lazy. And his eyes were locked with hers. Almost as if he dared her to pursue the subject she opened. And since her life might depend upon the results of the governor's plans, she cared far more about this than the tenderness of the beef . . . which was currently being discussed.

"I understand the Little Carpenter is expected to arrive at the fort soon." Caroline had heard he was the most important Cherokee Headman . . . and also their best negotiator.

The governor paused, his fork held motionless inches from his mouth. "How did you know that?"

"Governor Lyttelton," Caroline laughed. "Rumors are the mainstay of our conversations here at Fort Prince George. I'd hoped this one was true."

"It is. The Second Man of Conasatchee brought a talk today. We should have those warriors who are guilty of slaying the Virginia settlers delivered to us soon."

"And then the Headmen you're holding hostage will be set free?" This time there was no mistaking the gasp in the room.

"I'm afraid someone has misled you, my dear Lady Caroline." The governor stared pointedly at Wolf. "We hold no *prisoners* . . . there are only guests here."

"I'd thought perhaps several of your Cherokee *guests* might have joined us for dinner tonight?" Caroline wasn't sure why she was being so bold. But she could tell her questions weren't endearing her to the governor. However, when she slipped a look across the table, Wolf seemed amused.

But this time when the governor changed the subject, Caroline let him. He obviously wasn't going to tell her anything of import about the Cherokee problem.

"Do you plan to return to England?" Governor Lyttelton asked. "Raff has told me something of your circumstances. Allow me to offer you my sincerest condolences on the loss of your husband."

"Thank you." Caroline lowered her lashes. "He died rather tragically." She looked up, meeting first Wolf's dark eyes, then the rummy ones of the governor. "But I intend to stay in the Americas . . . at Seven Pines."

"Really?" The governor sounded surprised, and Caroline imagined Wolf had given him to believe otherwise.

"Yes. As it happens, I intend to write my brother as soon as it's safe and have him come also."

"Your brother?" Wolf's voice was deep and low. "That would be the next Earl?"

"That would be Edward . . . Ned, actually, and I think he would like it very much here." Actually she wasn't certain how her brother would view the colony. But she wished to let Wolf know that she was serious about staying.

The rest of the meal—the best Caroline had had in some time—passed with little consequence. By the time dessert was served, the conversation centered upon plays the young officers had seen in London, and how primitive they thought the frontier.

Caroline said little. She'd seen no plays, and she was becoming very fond of the land that was now her home. But she concluded that more than anything else, the officers were homesick. It mattered naught what she said, as long as she offered an English ear . . . a feminine English ear.

When the governor's personal servant brought a bottle of cognac on a silver platter, Caroline decided to take her leave. She was tired, and she'd been spelling Mary when Colleen woke in the night. Since it was but a short walk across the parade grounds to Mistress Quinn's cabin, Caroline saw no need for an escort and courteously declined when Governor Lyttelton offered one.

It was more difficult to say no to Wolf.

For one thing, he didn't politely request. He told her he'd be accompanying her to the cabin. And though her impulse was to resist, Caroline decided it best to simply let him have his way rather than to argue the point in front of the governor and officers. Wolf was, after all, the son of her dead husband. Though the family connection was no more than a thin veneer as far as society was concerned, it was there.

"You seemed quite at ease in the governor's presence, Lady Caroline."

He waited only till the door was shut behind them and they were barely out of earshot before his low, sardonic voice broke the silence. Caroline glanced at him through her lashes, though the occasional smoky brand that lit the fort's interior was not enough to see him clearly. But she could imagine the expression on his dark, handsome face.

She'd seen the sarcastic turn of his lips, the intense fire of his obsidian eyes often enough.

Partly because she didn't think any comment by her was needed, and partly because she didn't wish to prolong this encounter, Caroline said nothing, and kept her pace brisk.

"Of course, it was nothing more than I expected," he continued. "However, I was a bit surprised by your referring to the Headmen as prisoners. Governor Lyttelton did not seem pleased."

Caroline paused then, forgetting her vow to take her leave of his onerous company as soon as possible. "If I recall, hostages was the term I used. And shocking you was not my goal."

He'd stopped, too. They stood in the lee of a storage shed, partially hidden from the view of anyone who might pass their way. Raff loomed over her, and Caroline wished she'd kept walking. But she refused to retreat, even when he took a step forward.

"I never thought it was," he responded. "But it surprised me all the same. You sounded almost as if you cared about the Cherokee."

She did. Because of Sadayi and Walini and most of the others she'd met and learned to like. And because of Raff, a small voice whispered in her ear, but she tried to ignore it. And him. He smelled faintly of the brandy he drank before he insisted upon accompanying her. For the briefest moment, Caroline allowed herself to wonder what the smooth liquor would taste like on his tongue.

Then reason and the stupidity of her thoughts whisked her back to reality. "I care about returning to my home," Caroline said, her tone as firm as she could make it.

"Ah, the motherland. Where exactly in England are you from?"

"Gloucester, but I wasn't referring to England as you well know. 'Tis Seven Pines that I call home."

Even in the dim light that flickered from a nearby torch, she noticed the narrowing of his eyes. "I don't suppose now is the time to discuss which of us owns Seven Pines, especially with Logan off in the wilds of Pennsylvania?"

Again Caroline said nothing. Regardless of her anger with him, she couldn't bring herself to profess to carrying his father's child. There would be time enough for that later, she assured herself.

"What's the matter, Your Ladyship, have you nothing to say to your *stepson?*"

Apparently he'd drunk more than she thought, or he just felt like being a boor. He normally didn't push her this way. No, he was usually more taciturn. Seduce and leave. He seemed to have the sequence down to an art. But tonight he was more interested in taunting her, and Caroline was quickly tiring of it.

But escaping him would not be easy. Somehow he'd backed her into a corner, with his large body blocking her into the V of log walls. She could scream, but then that would appear melodramatic considering he'd done nothing but talk. So she decided she would simply make known her wishes to leave.

She lifted her hand to push him aside and immediately realized her mistake. His large hand covered hers, pressing it firmly against his chest. She could feel the steady pounding of his heart, the warmth of his skin through the homespun shirt. Did he notice how her breathing quickened?

"I wish to return to Mistress Quinn's cabin." Caroline kept her voice level with difficulty.

"Do you?"

She could almost hear the disbelief in his tone and wondered how much of it came from his ability to read her thoughts. "I should think you would want to return to the governor anyway," Caroline said, deciding that to attack was her best weapon. "Now that you've chosen to side with the English, it wouldn't do to let them make decisions without you."

Caroline felt the sudden stiffening of his body and almost smiled. But he didn't release her hand. If anything, his fingers tightened.

"I believe Your Ladyship has a mistaken notion of where my loyalties lie."

"Do I?" Caroline decided the ability to sound aristocratic must be inborn. She certainly had no practice with it until she met Raff MacQuaid. Now she used it so often and so convincingly, she almost fooled herself. "It didn't appear that way when you rode into the fort by the governor's side. Nor tonight when you were included as a guest for his intimate dinner."

She'd thought to make him angry which was why his reaction—throwing back his head and laughing—was all the more disturbing.

"Are you trying to bait me, Caroline?"

"No. I simply wonder why all other members of the peace delegation that went to Charles Town are held hostage and you walk about free."

"First of all, I am not the only one given their freedom. Two of the Headmen have already left for the Middle Towns. Secondly, I presume no one considers me important enough to keep. I am not one of the Headmen."

"But you're listened to by the Cherokee . . . trusted."

"Listened to, perhaps. Though I fear my link to the Little Carpenter's ear has been sorely strained by the governor's acts. But I have never been truly trusted, Caroline. My father saw to that."

Caroline didn't know what to say so she kept quiet, which is the only reason she heard his next softly murmured words. "My legacy from the man who sired me."

She was doing it again. Seeing him as a person. Caring about him even though that caring wasn't reciprocated. Caroline did her best to harden her heart. She concentrated on the seduction. But when that began to stir longings best left buried, she forced herself to remember the morning he left her . . . left her to his father's bullying.

322

And all the time he held her hand against his chest, and the frosty winter evening surrounded them.

"Perhaps I should return you to Mistress Quinn's."

His words interrupted her musings, and Caroline tugged at her hand. He let it go without a struggle, and she wondered if she might have done the same as soon as he captured her hand. He stepped aside, and Caroline proceeded him across the parade grounds.

When they reached the rough-hewn door with the drawstring left out for her, he asked about Mary and the baby.

Regardless of her feelings for him, Caroline knew he cared for his brother's wife and wished she could tell him something more positive. "She isn't getting any worse. Some days she seems almost well. Then . . ." Caroline sighed. "She should be regaining her strength by now," Caroline said of Mary. "And the baby is so small. Is there any way to get word to Logan?"

Wolf took a deep breath. She could see the expansion of his chest in the moonlight. "I've sent a letter. But the war has made communication between the colonies slow, so . . ." He let the rest of his words trail off. "I don't know if Logan would be able to come even if he knew."

"Wouldn't be able to . . . or wouldn't bother to?"

"What do you mean by that? Mary is his wife."

A soldier ambled by with his arm around the daughter of one of Mistress Quinn's friends. The girl giggled up at her companion, obviously smitten by him. Caroline wanted to call after her to beware of a handsome face. Instead she turned her attention back to the man who taught her the hard-earned lesson.

"I don't mean anything I suppose. It just seems odd to me that Logan would leave his wife and go off to fight when she was in danger herself."

"Has Mary been talking to you about this?"

Caroline turned her face away, not wishing to lie, yet unwilling to betray a confidence from her friend.

"She was not in danger when he left for one thing." Wolf apparently decided she considered his question rhetorical. "And our father made it impossible for him to stay any longer."

"Because of their disagreement over trading with the Cherokee?"

"I see she has been talking." Wolf leaned against the wall. "Logan planned to save his money and come back for her, I believe. In the meanwhile, Robert treated her fairly well."

"It's difficult not to like her."

He agreed with a nod of his head before continuing. "Logan did not know she was with child when he left . . . at least he did not mention it to me."

"And would he?"

"If you mean did we confide in one another,

324

the answer is, yes, at times. Still, there was plenty to separate us."

"Your Cherokee blood?" Caroline was beginning to wonder if Wolf didn't make more of that than he should. Mary had indicated her husband was very fond of his brother.

"For one thing. Circumstances of birth for another. Logan and his brother were born on the right side of the sheet. A difference hard to ignore."

Caroline turned toward the door. "I think I should go in." She'd tarried much longer than she planned as it was. But before she could reach for the drawstring, Wolf's hand circled her arm. She slowly twisted her head to stare at him, hoping her expression revealed nothing of the desire his touch sparked.

"Are you all right, Caroline?"

"Yes. Why do you ask?"

"I am not sure." His dark eyes narrowed. "You seem . . ." He shook his head. "Stay away from the soldiers. Actually it would be better if you and Mary kept to yourselves. Measles have broken out, and Lyttelton fears the smallpox might spread from Keowee."

"I've seen the fires as they burn their houses."

"It is Lyttelton's idea. He thinks it may curb the epidemic."

"And what do you think?"

His eyes met hers. "I think I was a fool to bring you to the frontier in the first place."

Caroline's chin notched higher. "But then it wasn't your decision, was it?" His fingers still gripped her arm, and Caroline felt them tighten, felt herself being drawn toward him.

"Very few things have been under my control since I met you, Lady Caroline. And those that have . . ."

Caroline never discovered what he planned to say. Leaving his words unspoken, Wolf lowered his mouth until it touched hers. The kiss did not last long, as he used his tongue to but briefly wet the closed seam of Caroline's lips, yet the contact still left her breathless. She managed to pull away and enter the cabin before her knees gave out, but long into the sleepless night she thought about him and what he'd left unsaid.

December seemed endless.

A cold spell froze the ground and brought the first swirling snowstorm. The fort was abuzz with gossip each time a new delegation of Cherokee met with Governor Lyttelton. And that seemed to be an ongoing occurrence.

December tenth brought word that the Little Carpenter would arrive soon with word from the Overhill Towns. Rumor had it that they desired peace with the British, and everyone breathed a sigh of relief.

Everyone except Wolf, who seemed as skeptical as ever. He sat in front of the fire holding Colleen in the crook of his arm while Mary stitched a tear in one of his shirts. He hadn't asked Caroline to do it, and she tried to convince herself she was just as glad. Why should she wish to perform wifely duties for him?

But she couldn't help watching him out of the corner of her eye as she sliced bread for the evening meal. And she couldn't help thinking of him holding the baby that now rested beneath her heart.

"The English have named him emperor of the Cherokee," Wolf said of Little Carpenter. "Though he is powerful among my people, it is a title that means nothing."

"Do you mean he doesn't speak for them?" Anticipation over his arrival at Fort Prince George was discussed with such enthusiasm, Caroline hated to think it was for naught.

"Some of them, yes." Wolf's gaze met Caroline's, and she quickly glanced away. "He is mighty among the Middle Settlements. But he does not carry the talk stick for the council."

That seemed to make no difference to the governor, who greeted the Little Carpenter on the nineteenth with all the pomp he could muster. A warm breeze freshened the air, and Caroline and Mary decided to walk outside to hear the band play and watch the Cherokee arrive. Mistress Quinn, who declared she'd seen enough Indians to last a lifetime agreed to stay with Colleen who slept in her basket.

The weather and the possibility of a break in the boredom of fort life caused most of the inhabitants to think as Caroline and Mary had. It was difficult to find a spot from which to view the welcome. When they finally managed to wriggle their way through the crowd, Caroline wasn't surprised to see Wolf standing between Governor Lyttelton and the Little Carpenter, and the other Headmen who just arrived, Ocayula of Choata, and Ucanokeach.

"Is that what I think it is?" Mary asked, and Caroline nodded as the British-proclaimed head of the Cherokee people handed the governor eight scalps. He also held out a string of beads, and the women watched as the governor removed the three black beads which stood out on the otherwise white belt.

"That's to symbolize that the governor is no longer displeased with the Cherokee." When Caroline glanced over at her, Mary continued. "Raff told me."

"I didn't realize you talked to him so much." Caroline stretched onto her tiptoes to see over the head of a tall matron in front of her.

"Yes, you do. You just always have some excuse to be out of the cabin when he comes by. Why is that, I wonder?"

Caroline shot her friend a scowl, then inched to her right. "I don't know what you're talking about."

"Don't you? I'm not the only one to notice how you avoid him. Raff commented upon it."

"Did he now? Since when am I the subject of your conversation with him?"

"Since he asks about you all the time, and since you leave the moment he arrives." Mary wrapped her shawl more tightly about her shoulders. "Do you know what I think?"

"I haven't a clue."

"I think you two care about each other."

Caroline said nothing for a moment, just stared at Mary. Then she closed her mouth and shook her head. "That's ridiculous. I think we should be getting back to the cabin." She suddenly lost her desire to see the ceremony.

"You love him, don't you?"

Caroline stopped short, then grabbed her friend's hand and pulled her to the side of the parade ground. "Where did you ever get such a preposterous notion?"

Mary just stared at her in a way that made Caroline know all the denying in the world wouldn't convince her. "Mary, there are things you don't know about. Things I can't tell even you. Please never bring this up again."

And she didn't. Caroline was grateful for that. That wasn't the only thing that made Caroline thankful during the following weeks. Negotiations seemed to be progressing. Wolf was still pessimistic, but Caroline was beginning to convince herself that was his nature. Not that she didn't agree with most everything he said when he stopped by the cabin—she'd decided it looked less like she cared

329

for him if she stayed when he visited. But it was so much easier to believe the feelings of optimism that permeated the fort.

The governor released two of the "guests" that he held. When Tistoe of Keowee and Sheroweh of Estatoe crossed the river to the Indian town, an English flag rose above the town house. The following day two warriors, Young Twin and Slave Catcher, were delivered to the fort. They had taken part in the Cherokee raid on Virginia settlers. Caroline watched their arrival with sadness in her heart despite the fact that their surrender was a vital step toward peace.

"They are a sacrifice," Wolf said that night as he and Caroline sat by the fitful fire. The wind howled outside, dipping down the chimney at intervals and driving smoke into the small room. Mary was asleep as were Colleen and Mistress Quinn. Given the events of the day, Caroline wasn't surprised when Wolf stood at her door. She'd even been able to convince herself she hadn't waited for him. But now she couldn't mistake the pain in his eyes or the corresponding ache in her heart. Still, she tried to be the voice of reason.

"They did kill the settlers in Virginia."

He made a crude comment in Cherokee that Caroline was grateful she couldn't translate. "They acted as Cherokee warriors, avenging the deaths of their family members. And now they will be put to death." He turned from her and stared into the

330

flames. "And the worst part is, their sacrifice will be for naught."

"Raff, how can you say that?" Caroline hadn't remembered moving, yet now she was on her knees in front of him, grasping his hands. "Talk of a treaty between the English and Cherokee grows stronger everyday. Why Governor Lyttelton said—"

"He is a fool on a fool's mission." Wolf's deep breath expanded his chest. "The Cherokee will not abide this forced peace."

"You sound almost as if you don't want them to. As if you favor a war between the white man and *Ani'-Yun'wiya*." She'd slipped into his use of the word for his people without realizing it.

"No, Caroline." He seemed to notice their positions, he leaning forward on a handmade chair, she kneeling on the floor, her skirts swirled out about her. His voice gentled. "No one desires a fair peace more than I. But there is the rub. With the English it will never be fair. And there is nothing the Cherokee can do. I have lived among the English, seen their might." He shook his head, and the thick black hair swung loose about his shoulders.

Caroline couldn't help herself. When he was dark and arrogant, her desire for him nearly overwhelmed her, but she resisted. She could not resist his vulnerability. Her hand touched his cheek; and like a parched man seeking water, he turned into her caress.

He pulled her from the floor onto his lap, and she cradled his head, running her fingers through

331

the rough silk of his hair as he buried his face against her breast.

Comfort. 'Twas all she offered, Caroline tried to tell herself. No less than she'd give Mary or baby Colleen or even Mistress Quinn if they needed it. But she felt the warmth of his breath against her skin, through the layers of cotton fabric and the sensations that raced through her body told her she lied.

When his mouth inched up to wet the skin above her shift ruffle, Caroline knew the pretense was over. Passion flared between them as it always did, like a dry twig igniting. His open mouth moved up her neck, and Caroline leaned back in his strong arms, arching her body toward him. When his lips reached hers, his tongue hot and demanding, Caroline lost all touch with reality.

Sixteen

"Nakwisi' usidi', I can not stop thinking of you. Wanting you."

Those words murmured against her neck in Wolf's whiskey-roughened voice sent shivers of excitement across Caroline's flesh. Could he possibly be afflicted with the same malady as she? Except right now it didn't feel like a malady. His whiskered jaw abraded her tender skin, his mouth followed to wet and soothe.

She wanted to push him away, to prove to him . . . to herself that he alone was beset by desire. But it wasn't possible. Her hands could only clutch at his strong shoulders, feel the heat of his skin beneath the homespun.

His lips covered hers again, hot and hungry, opening her lips to the invasion of his tongue. Caroline's moan sounded loud in her ears, and she jerked, suddenly, embarrassingly aware of their surroundings. She thought of the women, her friends, who'd be shocked if they came investigating the sound and found her sprawled across Wolf's lap, his large, long-fingered hand covering her breast.

"No . . . please." Her initial plea didn't begin to carve through the savage passion that engulfed him. "Raff." Her strangled cry along with the twisting of her face away gave him pause. Caroline's hand's stilled as well, and she twisted back staring into his dark, dark eyes. "We can't do this here," she whispered, her voice fraught with barely suppressed frustration. "Mary . . . Mistress -2Quinn," she managed to say between taking ragged breaths that wouldn't calm.

If she thought to refrain him, for him to release her, the strong hand that curved about her hip, drawing her firmly against his loincloth quelled that supposition. He was hard and throbbing, and her body ground against him instinctively.

"There is nowhere else," he sighed, his mouth again covering her. Yet when the kiss ended, he lifted her, standing himself and took the few strides necessary to blanket them in shadows.

They stood in the corner of the cabin set aside for storage: Caroline, her back flush against the rough wall; Wolf, his body hard and protecting against hers. It was foolish, she knew, partially surrounded by barrels of bacon and bags of cornmeal to want him. More foolish still to want him period. But there was no denying it.

And no stopping her body from reacting to his touch.

They were both fully clothed, and if anyone should awake, which Wolf thought doubtful, they would see only a kiss. The fact that it was this man and this woman exchanging the caress might surprise some, though he had a feeling not Mary. But still it was only a kiss.

Except that Wolf wondered if he could stop with that. Even now his hands itched to touch her in all the places he'd touched her before. He spoke the truth when he told her of his inability to forget her. What he hadn't mentioned was how damnably hard he tried.

But it did no good. Neither did his visit to a doxy in Charles Town that left him disgusted with himself, nor the difficulties between the Cherokee and English. Good Lord the act of trying to help the two sides work out a fair peace plan should take all his energies. Yet here he stood, pressed against this slip of a woman, fingers curved around her ribs, thumbs tucked beneath the swell of her breasts. His body aching.

She wore no stays, and Wolf deepened the kiss while his hands moved settling over her distended nipples. Whether she sensed that no one was coming from the other rooms, or whether she was too drugged by passion to care, Wolf didn't know. But she sighed into his mouth and her arms wrapped tightly about his neck as he pressed closer.

Her skirts were few. She'd long ago given up the English desire to wear as many petticoats as humanly possible. Still, Wolf had a difficult time working his hand beneath the layers of linen. The feel of her skin, smooth and silky, made him wish savagely for an hour of privacy. Her thighs opened instinctively and he sought her moist heat.

"Raff." The word escaped her on a breath of air as he slid his fingers into her body.

"Shhh. No one can see," he assured, hoping his back proved a wide enough barrier should anyone come into the room . . . barely caring. She was tight and hot . . . wet. Wolf relished the feel of her, the way her hands tightened in his hair, the expression in her shadowed eyes when the tremors started through her body.

"Touch me." Wolf wasn't sure that he'd spoken his request aloud till he felt her fingers fumbling beneath his shirt and loincloth. Her hand circled his swollen flesh.

He lifted her then, impaling her upon his length, wrapping her skirt-covered legs around his hips. She climaxed instantly, milking his body with her own, causing him to spill his seed into her.

Their breathing was still raspy when he leaned his forehead on hers and shut his eyes. "I did not plan this."

"I know you didn't." Reason was clawing its way through the sensual haze of Caroline's existence. And its message wasn't pretty. She made love with him before when she fancied herself in love, and then even after he'd left her. Before she'd been foolish, thinking he cared for her. But now she knew the folly of that. He'd used her as a means of revenge. She knew the truth from his own lips and still she couldn't seem to stop herself from making love to him. And worse, from loving him.

He lifted her from him, and Caroline did her best to straighten her petticoats, turning away when he tried to help. "Don't, please."

"I will not apologize."

His tone made Caroline stop brushing at her skirts and glance up at him. His expression, what she could see of it, was hard. His black hair hung around his face and at the moment he looked very much the savage. Caroline wondered that she wasn't the least frightened by his scowl. "I don't recall asking you to."

"I did not force you."

"You never have," Caroline conceded with a lift of her head. "All you need do is wait for me to act like the foolish woman I am." She tried to move past him but his hand caught her upper arm. Even when she yanked, he held tight.

"You are not foolish."

"Really?" Caroline shot him a look over her left shoulder. "What would you call a woman who allows herself to be used, not once but over and over again?"

"I did not use you, Caroline."

"Oh please, don't lie." She faced him, hands on hips. "We both know the truth of it."

"Is it the truth you desire?"

" 'Twould be a pleasant change. And we both know I can handle it. After all, look what has happened even after I knew what you did to me had naught to do with caring and everything to do with revenge against your father."

He said nothing then, only staring at her, his eyes dark in his dark face.

"Well, what were you planning to tell me this time?" Caroline waited a moment, glaring at him, then whirled around, giving him her back. "I think you should leave."

"Not before I have had my say."

The hands that clasped her shoulders gave her no choice but to be still even when the door to the bedroom opened and a sleepy, disheveled Mary stepped into the room. " 'Tis everything all right?" she asked as she dragged a shawl around her shoulders.

"Yes." Wolf was annoyed by the interruption.

"I'm sorry if we woke you." Caroline tried to take a step forward, but the pressure on her shoulders stopped her.

"Oh, you didn't wake me. Colleen did. I just was surprised to hear voices coming from this room." As she spoke, Mary backed into the doorway. Caroline could hear Colleen whining in the basket by Mary's bed.

"Caroline and I were just talking." Wolf's tone was more friendly this time. "I will be leaving soon."

"Actually he's leaving now. Aren't you Raff?" Caroline twisted enough to stare at him.

"I said soon—"

"I'm going back into the bedroom now."

Caroline and Wolf looked around in time to see Mary shut the door behind her.

"Now see what you've done." Caroline took an indignant breath.

"What I have done is assured us a moment of privacy."

"Well, I don't want to be alone with you," Caroline hissed.

"That is not the way it appeared earlier."

With a sudden movement, Caroline managed to yank herself free from his hold. She stood in the middle of the room, her back to him, her pride in shatters. "Please go."

"Caroline." He stepped closer, his arms wrapping around her slender form. But this time there was no force, only a gentle caress as his hands linked about her waist. "Please," he murmured, his mouth so close to her ear that his breath fluttered the tendrils that curled about her face. He felt a shiver race through her.

"It was never my intent to hurt you. I admit that before we made love the first time my motive was revenge. But when I held you, that was not what was in my mind." When she said nothing, he began moving his hands, caressing her . . . letting her know how much he desired her. She relaxed against him and he lowered his face to breathe in the sweet, clean scent of her hair. Wolf gave himself a moment to savor her essence.

He was a man of words yet he never before felt

so clumsy. He wished she understood Cherokee for he felt he could tell her more of his feelings in that language. But though she'd learned much he doubted Sadayi had taught her what was in his heart.

Wolf pulled her more firmly against him, his hands on her hips. "You must know that I care for you, that—"

His words stopped so abruptly that Caroline opened her eyes and tried to turn around. That's when she realized where his hands were.

She'd known he would find out . . . this was hardly the sort of thing one could hide forever. Yet as often as she'd thought about this moment, she hadn't prepared herself for the silence that followed his discovery. Outside the wind howled, a chilling counterpart to the pounding of Caroline's heart. She wanted to say something . . . to explain. But what? Her lips were dry, and she wet them, swallowing as he slowly turned her to face him.

Caroline wished she could see him better, then nearly laughed at her foolishness. She had no desire to read the disappointment in his dark eyes.

If she were to waste her time on wishes, it should be that she'd made a decision about what to tell him. Should she opt for the truth no matter who was hurt by it . . . or the lie that would assure her baby his birthright? Truth or deception? Her mind vacillated between two sides of the same coin.

He waited for her to say something . . . anything. Wolf hadn't imagined the swell of her stom-

340

ach beneath the camouflaging skirts. The pronounced curve was in sharp contrast to the rest of her body that appeared to have lost weight since her arrival on the frontier.

Seconds passed, punctuated by the beating of his heart and still she said nothing. When Wolf finally broke the silence, it was with a question more circumspect than his typical abrupt manner. But he found himself unable to ask who had fathered her child. His weakness where she was concerned disturbed him.

"When?"

Caroline took a calming breath and purposely misread him. "In the spring."

His hands dropped from her shoulders, and Caroline missed his warmth. "Ah, the spring," he said, pacing to the hearth and back. "Such a perfect time to give birth. The trees are in bud, the air is warm, a time for renewal." As he spoke, keeping his voice low, he moved back toward her. When he stopped, she was close enough to touch. His thumb caught beneath her chin, lifting it, forcing her to look at him.

"When in the spring is your baby due to arrive?" It was difficult not to take her in his arms and demand to know the truth. He slowly, purposely, dropped his hands to his side.

"I'm not certain." Caroline wanted to look away from him, but couldn't. She wanted to tell him he had no rights to her. He'd given them up that day he left her at Seven Pines. Left her to his father.

To marry. Wolf must have known then that she would have stayed with him forever. That she loved him. But he abandoned her, forcing this decision on her. This decision she didn't want to make.

How could she choose between what was best for the man she loved and what was best for her child? How could any woman?

And she wasn't even certain that Wolf wanted to know the truth. After all, he'd made no declarations of love. No vows of undying devotion. She was a recent widow, true. But on the frontier, women did not stay unmarried long, especially young women. Had he come to her with a proposal of marriage? No. He wanted her body to be sure. That he would admit to.

But nothing he ever said led her to believe he wished the responsibilities of a family. He was like his brother. A wanderer, who'd soon be off, leaving her alone. Leaving their child.

She had shown herself to be foolish where he was concerned since she first set eyes upon him. Time and again. She'd risked her future, her brother's future for the touch of his hands on her body. This time had to be different.

"All right, Caroline. You seem vague about the timing. Are you implying you do not know who fathered your child?"

"Must we discuss this now?" Her voice bore the unmistakable tone of pleading, and she didn't care. "Mary can no doubt hear us, and she—"

"Yes, Caroline, we must." Wolf gave in then and

reached for her arms. "I imagine Mary knows more of this than I."

She couldn't deny that . . . didn't even try.

"Now I believe my inquiry was simple enough. Do you know who fathered your child?"

"Does it matter so much to you?"

"Hell yes it matters." Wolf realized he had raised his voice above the whispers they were using and shook his head. His voice was low when he spoke again. "It matters a great deal. Now, do you know?"

"Yes."

He seemed not to have expected that response. Or at least if she acknowledged that much, he expected her to continue . . . to tell him what he wanted to know. But she didn't. Caroline simply stood, his hands cupping her shoulders and waited.

"Is the child mine?" His fingers tightened. "Is it my father's? Damnation, Caroline, tell me!"

But in the end, when the decision rested squarely upon her, she could say nothing. It was as if her mouth wouldn't even open. Silence was the only protection she could offer her unborn child.

And it was that silence that drove the man she loved away.

"Since you refuse to enlighten me, I am forced to assume the worst," he said before turning away. This time he didn't stop.

A bitter wind swept through the room as he opened the door. And then he was gone.

If Mistress Quinn noticed that Wolf no longer

stopped by in the evening, she didn't mention it. Mary was not so obliging.

"I don't know what you wish me to say." Caroline was sorry for her annoyed tone before she finished her words. But she was not in the best of humors, and Mary would not let the subject of Raff Mac-Quaid rest.

Dropping to her knees in front of Mary who was busy nursing her fretful child, Caroline took her free hand. "Please, Mary, I don't want to talk about him." It was a simple enough request, but Caroline found she had to look away from the hurt in those trusting grey eyes.

"I know something is wrong, Caroline. You can deny it all you like. But it isn't my curiosity that needs appeased. 'Tis your happiness that worries me."

"I am happy. You are getting stronger and talk of a treaty with the Cherokee is everywhere—"

"Yes, yes. And you adore being cooped in this cabin with an irritable old woman and a sickly child whose mother is barely able to care for herself. Tell me how you enjoy doing more than your share of the chores even though you awaken each morning to divest your stomach of its nourishment."

She stopped suddenly, and Caroline couldn't help but laugh. It was so unlike the optimistic Mary to talk so. "Goodness," Caroline said with a shake of her head. "I didn't realize my morning bouts of nausea awakened you. Perhaps I should learn to gag a bit more quietly."

"Don't make light of it."

"Believe me, Mary, I don't consider my morning ritual of leaning over the slop jaw amusing. Still, I don't quite understand your outburst."

"Are we friends, Caroline?" Mary turned over her hand and grasped Caroline's, holding it tight.

"Of course we are."

"Yet you won't let me help you."

"Don't be ridiculous. 'Tis obvious Colleen takes much of your time, and that is as it should be, but—"

"I'm not referring to physical labor, and I think you know it." Mary took her sleeping daughter from her breast and handed her to Caroline. With a quick kiss to her smooth forehead, she placed the child in her basket. When she would have stood, Mary again clasped her hands. "You listened to me, when I told you of my love for Logan . . . my fear that he didn't feel the same." Mary took a deep breath that shook her thin breast. "It helped me to speak of it . . . with a friend."

"And that's what you wish me to do?" Caroline felt annoyance building in her and tried to suppress it. "Bare my soul. All right, Mary. Where shall I begin? I didn't love my husband. Nay, let me be honest. I loathed my husband. Does that honesty on my part make you feel better?"

"Robert wasn't a very likable man."

"No he wasn't." Caroline felt a layer of anxiety melt away. "But I wed him and owe him some

345

measure of loyalty." She didn't like to think about the way she deceived him.

"At the sake of your own happiness?"

"There are more important things to consider."

"Your child is Raff's, isn't it? Oh, please don't look so stricken." Mary leaned forward and threw her arms around her friend. "Mistress Quinn is out for her constitutional, and you know I would never breathe a word of this to anyone."

"How did you know?" There was no sense in denying it, Caroline could see that by the expression on Mary's sweet face. She was convinced and lying about it wouldn't help.

"I'd like to say 'twas my intuition." She hung her head and a few soft curls escaped from her cap. "But I fear in part, I know because I heard you and Raff talking last week."

"Mary, I'm shocked." Caroline tilted her head. "You were eavesdropping?"

"Perhaps a bit. But you and Raff weren't exactly keeping your voices down. Oh Caroline, why didn't you tell him the truth?"

"What if I don't know the truth?"

"Stop that right now!" Mary stood, pulling Caroline up with her. "We both know Robert never touched you. Do you think I wasn't aware of what went on in that house? He threatened often enough; and if he could have, you'd have been bedded often. But the truth is, he spent his days drinking and his nights alone."

"Goodness." Caroline found the heated flush

that crept up her face embarrassing. "I never knew you to be so forthright."

"I just want what's best for you." Mary threw her arms about Caroline's waist. "You are my dearest friend."

"Then trust me to do what I must."

"You mean you aren't going to tell him?" Mary leaned back to study Caroline's face.

"Mary." Caroline let the word drag out.

"All right. I shall leave it up to you."

"And you won't tell Raff?"

"Nay, I shan't say a word."

Caroline decided later that week that she should have demanded another promise—that she and Mary would discuss the matter no more. Mary apparently decided that if she couldn't inform Wolf of his impending fatherhood, she must convince Caroline to do it.

"He really can be very civilized, you know. Logan told me once he was an excellent student while at Oxford. And he was considered quite the thing in society."

Caroline paused, the spoon she used to stir the Indian corn bread poised in mid-stroke. She swiped at an errant strand of curly hair with her free hand. "Dare I guess that the 'he' you refer to is Rafferty MacQuaid?"

Mary had the decency to look contrite. "He is a remarkable man," she said. "I just didn't want you to overlook that fact because he has Cherokee blood."

This time she dropped the spoon into the corn-meal mix and turned to face her friend. "Is that what you think, that I'm rejecting him because of his race?" Caroline didn't wait for an answer. "Nothing could be further from the truth."

"But you love him, I know you do."

"Perhaps I do." Caroline's voice was as impassioned as her friend's. "But the problem is, he doesn't love me."

There was nothing Mary could say to counter that. Certainly Raff hadn't disproved Caroline's words by returning to the cabin after the night he found out about her pregnancy. His absence had even been noted by the unobservant Mistress Quinn. She commented the night before that there was a lack of fresh meat in their stew. Since Wolf was the one who had brought a rabbit or squirrel whenever he stopped by and since she'd accompanied her remarks with a pointed look at Caroline, it seemed obvious she connected the two.

"I believe Mr. MacQuaid is absent from the fort," Caroline said, using her best *Your Ladyship* voice. She should have known better than to put on airs with Mistress Quinn.

" 'Mr. MacQuaid' is it?' the old woman said with a throaty laugh that sent her into a coughing spasm. "Thought you two were beyond such formalities," she continued when she'd caught her breath.

Beyond such formalities indeed. The woman was incorrigible. But even though there were many times Caroline would have preferred to be alone, away from Mistress Quinn's raucous comments and even Mary's bittersweet romanticism, Caroline stayed near the cabin.

Smallpox was more a threat than ever. Its presence hung in the air, a constant reminder to Caroline that she needed to take Mary and the baby and return to Seven Pines.

With the treaty negotiations progressing as they were, leaving the fort seemed more and more a possibility. Governor Lyttelton, at the Little Carpenter's insistence, had released more of his hostages. It was a sign of good faith, and it precipitated the drawing up of a new treaty between the English and Cherokee.

Mistress Quinn returned from her daily walk to inform Caroline and Mary that there was nothing more to fear from the Indians. "They done put their mark to the agreement," she called out as she entered the cabin. "No more worrying about being scalped in our sleep," she said with a whoop of joy.

"What has you so excited?" Mary leaned back in the rocker and laughed as the older lady grabbed Caroline's hands and danced her about the room.

"Didn't you hear what I said?"

"We heard," Caroline said, pressing her hand to her heart when Mistress Quinn let her go. "Tell us about the treaty. What did they agree upon?"

"There's to be a ceremony tomorrow, but they already signed it." Mistress Quinn sank heavily into her chair by the fireplace and spent a few moments catching her breath. "Lyttelton's agreed to release the Headmen when the guilty Indians are brought to the fort."

Caroline couldn't see anything new there, but she said nothing.

"There's to be friendship between the two nations," Mistress Quinn was saying. "And they're to set up the licensed traders again."

It all sounded well and good, and a treaty was certainly what Caroline had hoped for. She toasted the peace with a mug of apple cider, sharing in the good spirits that prevailed in the cabin. But secretly she wondered what Raff thought of this agreement. Was she missing something, or did the treaty change very little?

Peace and friendship were noble words, but the governor still held innocent Cherokee Headmen against their will. And he still demanded the surrender of twenty-four Indians who killed white settlers in Virginia . . . who, according to Wolf, were only avenging the deaths of their slaughtered brethren.

Caroline lay on her bed that night, her hands folded over her slightly mounded stomach and watched the fire make shadows and light dance across the ceiling. It was so hard to understand the relationship between the Cherokee and the British . . . her people. It 'twas no wonder she and Wolf couldn't seem to be of a like mind about anything. But she still couldn't stop thinking of him. He wasn't in the fort. Mistress Quinn had mentioned that—again staring pointedly at Caroline.

So he was gone. Presumably somewhere among the Cherokee. Caroline couldn't help the sadness that settled over her spirit. But it was probably for the best. Her fingers splayed over her womb. Now there would be no one to stop her from leaving Fort Prince George and returning to Seven Pines.

The English planned to start up trade again with the Cherokee, and she was determined to be one of the traders. And unlike her late husband, Caroline would be fair and aboveboard with the Cherokee.

The next day was full of pomp and elaborate costumes. The Cherokee, among them Little Carpenter, Attakullaculla, Round O, and Killianca, wore their finery. The December sun shone on their silver armbands and breastplates. Their shirts were of English-made material, colorful and covered by long capes that fluttered in the wind. Like Wolf, their bodies were tattooed, but where he wore his hair long and sleek, the Headmen's scalps were shaved except for the topknot they decorated with wampum and feathers.

Not to be outdone, Governor Lyttelton and his officers appeared in full military dress. Their scarlet tunics and white powdered wigs offered a colorful counterpoint to their Indian allies.

Speeches were given and presents were displayed . . . though not exchanged. In a move that Caroline considered less than friendly, the governor decided to withhold the gifts of peace—muskets, powder, and such—until all the Cherokee guilty of raiding the Virginia colonists were turned over to him.

But as Caroline watched the ceremonies, the Headmen gave no indication that they were offended. To the contrary, all seemed pleased with the agreement.

Certainly Governor Lyttleton did. Within days he made plans to quit the fort. Of course, he really hadn't much choice. Nearly half his men were gone, having left for Charles Town when he hinted that those who wished could decamp. The fear of smallpox was a strong motivator.

Not that Caroline begrudged any of the soldiers that fled the dreaded disease. She was preparing to do the same. As weak as Mary and the baby were, she could only thank God they hadn't succumbed yet. And she was taking no more chances. The treaty was signed. The soldiers, except for a token force, were gone, and the Cherokee from all she could tell would be ready for a new trader. It was time to leave Fort Prince George.

"Are you certain you won't come with us?"

Caroline glanced over her shoulder toward Mistress Quinn, who sat in her chair puffing on her clay pipe. Caroline resumed rolling her petticoats and stuffing them into the saddlebag when the woman shook her grizzled head.

"I'm planning to go to Charles Town as soon as I've the chance." She blinked through the smoke curling up from her mouth. "But I ain't sure you should be going further out on the frontier yet."

"I explained to you about the smallpox," Caroline said, lowering her voice so she wouldn't disturb Mary. She'd gone to bed early in anticipation of the morrow's journey, and Caroline knew Mary would need all the rest she could get.

"I done had smallpox back in '35. Almost died, I did." She puffed again. "But I pulled through." She twisted her head toward the door. "Now who do you suppose that is at this time of night?"

Caroline hadn't heard anything before Mistress Quinn spoke, but sure enough there came a pounding on the door. With a nod, the older woman indicated Caroline should answer it.

It was dark outside, but she recognized Wolf's large frame instantly. He stood in the doorway, his face in shadows, his musket cradled in his arms, and Caroline felt a bittersweet longing that all but carried her forward. If not for the memory of their last encounter and his stance, so tall and rigid, she might have thrown herself into his arms.

How long they stood there staring at each other, Caroline didn't know. It was Mistress Quinn who broke the silence, with a bellowed shout. "Who in the hell is at the door? It's cold enough to freeze a witch's tit."

"It's Raff, Mistress Quinn," he called in. "I have someone here who wants to see Caroline."

"Well bring 'em in for goodness sakes."

Stepping back Caroline let Wolf in, only then noticing that there was someone else with him. She smiled tentatively at the young man who was wrapped from head to toe in a greatcoat and muffler. He reached up and unwrapped a layer, laughing at Caroline's shocked expression.

"So, Caro, is this all the welcome I receive after traveling so far to see you?"

"Ned?" Caroline flew toward the stranger. "Ned, it *is* you."

Seventeen

"And that is where Mr. MacQuaid found me." Edward Simmons, Eighth Earl of Shewbridge finished his story with a flourish. With his elbows planted on the hand-hewn table, he glanced first across the room toward Wolf and then back to his sister. She sat beside him, her hand on his arm. For a moment the only sound was a shifting log in the hearth that took most of one wall in the log cabin.

Then Caroline shook her head. "But I don't understand. 'Tis not that I don't love seeing you." Her fingers tightened on his sleeve. "But what possessed you to come?" She may have thought about sending for him . . . at first, when she thought she and Raff . . . that wasn't even worth remembering. She even considered that some day he might choose to come to the New World. But not now—certainly not now.

"I just thought it would be an adventure," he said, unaware that Caroline caught the nervous blink of his right eye.

He may have grown a foot since she last saw him, now standing taller than she, but Caroline could still tell when he was lying. And he was doing it now.

"An adventure, you say," she said, cocking her head to one side. He only nodded before digging into the bread pudding he'd pushed aside moments ago, pleading he would burst if he ate another bite.

"What of school?"

"I quit," he said around another mouthful of the cinnamon-laced sweet.

"Quit? Ned . . ." Caroline pushed away from the table and stood. " 'Tis impossible to believe you would do such a thing. Especially when I—" Caroline caught herself before mentioning all she'd gone through to provide for him. Folding her arms, she turned her back, trying to regain her calm. And missing the furtive look her brother shot toward Wolf, and the supportive nod he received in return.

"I was asked to leave."

"What?" Caroline's skirts swished on the packed-earth floor as she whirled around

"It wasn't as bad as that," Edward said with a forced grin. "They were very nice about it really, considering . . ."

Caroline was almost afraid to ask. "Considering what?"

"That they'd received no coin for over a year."

Blood drained from Caroline's face and she had

the uncomfortable feeling she might swoon. She clutched the chair back and closed her mouth. "There must be a mistake. Paying your school was part of the—" Her eyes darted to Wolf lounging in the corner, leaning on his long rifle. "There must be a mistake," she repeated.

"I thought as much also, being as you told me it was a condition of your marrying that colonial. But then Mr. Chipford came around and assured me 'twas true."

"There was no money transferred?" Caroline didn't like discussing private affairs in front of Wolf, but he didn't seem inclined to take his leave, and he'd already heard enough to guess the rest.

"Not a farthing," Edward said and stood, moving over beside his sister. The arm he put around her was tentative at first. He was used to her comforting him, her taking care of him. "I thought it best I come find you," he said when she rested her head against his shoulder. "I'm sorry if things didn't work out as you'd planned."

Caroline reached up to touch his cheek, surprised that the hint of whiskers deprived it of being baby-soft. But he'd grown more than physically. "I'm glad you came," she said. "As it was, I'd thought to send for you."

"Really?"

There was a glimpse of the same old Ned as his blue eyes opened wide.

"Yes, really. Now off to bed with you. I'm sure you're tired after your *adventure*."

"I am a bit buggered out. But where do I sleep?" He glanced around the room as if he half expected there to be a secret hallway that led to a separate wing of bedrooms. Caroline almost laughed at the thought and for the adjustment he would have to make.

" 'Tis up yon ladder," she said with a sweeping motion of her hand. "You'll find a reasonably comfortable mattress and a modicum of privacy."

To Edward's credit, he simply nodded and swung onto the bottom rung. But halfway up the ladder he paused and looked down at his sister. "I'm glad I came, Caro. It never did please me having an entire ocean separating us."

"I didn't like it, either, Ned."

Caroline stared at the crude ladder as long as she could before turning toward the only other person in the room. She would have thought he'd see her brother's departure as the perfect opportunity to take his own leave. But he seemed rooted to the spot, watching her from beneath hooded eyelids, his expression unreadable.

Caroline swallowed and began clearing the dishes from in front of Ned's place. Her brother had eaten two bowls of stew, cornbread and dessert so quickly, Caroline had to wonder when he had his last meal. Raff on the other hand had accepted only hot mulled cider. Caroline decided she wasn't going to go close to him to retrieve the pewter mug.

"Thank you for delivering Ned," she said when

the silence became unbearable. "Exactly where did you find him?"

"Not far off the trail, near Estatoe. He had built himself quite a campfire. He wasn't hard to spot."

Caroline poured steaming water into the dishpan, adding a scoop of soft lye soap and set the pottery dishes to soak. "Well, thank you again. I'm sure Ned was pleased to have your guidance getting to Fort Prince George."

"I do not know." Wolf left his gun standing in the corner and came toward the table. Pulling out a chair he turned it, straddling the seat. "He seemed more excited to learn that I knew you."

After acknowledging his remark with a slight nod of her head, Caroline started scrubbing the few dishes Ned used. She didn't like the cozy feel of having Wolf so near, nor the way she could feel his stare burn between her shoulder blades. Despite the chill in the air, beads of perspiration dotted her forehead.

The splash of water. The crackle of burning wood. Those sounds seemed to echo through the night-silent cabin. When Caroline could stand it no more, she whirled around, soapy hands akimbo and faced him. He didn't appear surprised by the sudden movement.

"So now you know."

He only arched a brow, which caused Caroline to grind out the next words. "Don't act as if you didn't hear what Ned was saying. I married your father for one reason and one reason only."

"I am not exactly shocked." Wolf leaned forward, resting his chin on his crossed hands. "It never seemed a love match."

The cool, almost bored way he spoke was infuriating . . . or perhaps the news her brother brought was finally penetrating her brain. "I was penniless," she said her spine as stiff as a ramrod. "And your father didn't even live up to his end of the marriage contract." Caroline tried to ignore the little voice that reminded her that she hadn't, either. "He promised to take care of my brother and didn't."

Again he said nothing, only stared at her with those dark, intense eyes that seemed to draw her toward him. Stubbornly, Caroline held her ground. "What is it you want?"

She could swear something flashed behind his eyes, but his expression didn't change. "You would do better not to ask such open questions, Caroline. One of these days I may tell you exactly what I want from you. For now," he continued. "A simple explanation of just where the hell you think you are going, will suffice."

Caroline followed his gaze to the stuffed saddle-bag. She had bundled it off onto a chest in the corner when she set the table for Ned.

She refused to be cowed by him, no matter how low and threatening his tone. "I'm taking Mary and the baby . . . and now Ned to Seven Pines."

"Damnation woman. Don't you have any sense?"

"I have plenty of sense, and it all tells me we'd

be better off there than in this disease-infested fort." Caroline realized she was doing a poor job of keeping her voice down and whirled back to the dishpan, dismissing him. Or so she hoped.

"I will take you to Charles Town."

"What?" Of all the arguments she expected . . . of all the things he might say . . . this was not it. "I don't want to go to Charles Town.

"Damnit Caroline, you do not belong here."

"Then where do I belong?" She turned away, hoping he hadn't noticed the sheen of tears in her eyes. "You heard Ned. There's nothing for us in England." She took a deep breath and faced him again. "Seven Pines is all I have."

"Is that all you and your child have?"

It was the first he'd mentioned the baby since he showed up on her doorstep, and Caroline had almost forgotten their terrible parting before. Now everything crashed down on her. Wolf's anger. Robert's will that left her penniless if she didn't claim him as the father of her child.

"I think you should leave. Thank you again for bringing— Stop it. What are you doing?" She fought against him when he scrambled out of his chair and grabbed her upper arms.

"It is not your gratitude I want, and you damn well know it."

His presence was overwhelming . . . his scent, the feel of his strong hands, but Caroline steeled herself against him. " 'Tis all you shall get."

He didn't say, "We shall see about that," but the

words were there in his expression with his arched brow and flared nostrils. Then he kissed her and her resolve weakened. It was a hard, quick kiss. Possessive. Demanding. When he pulled away, Wolf stared down at her until her eyes slowly opened.

"I am expected at Estatoe tomorrow, actually today, but I did not think it a good idea to allow your brother to traipse about the countryside on his own. When I return, we will discuss this further."

And then he was gone.

She had to nudge him twice before he managed to open his eyes and then he moaned about the light. "Come on, Ned," she urged after placing the candleholder on the loft flooring. " 'Tis time to rise."

"Caro." The word was a drawn-out plea that reminded her of the boy he used to be. Laughing, she reached down to pull the quilt from where he'd thrown it over his face.

"You're on the frontier now, Neddy. We rise before the rooster."

"Mr. MacQuaid doesn't." Edward squinted one eye open.

"Well, Mr. MaQuiad isn't here, is he?"

Caroline didn't know if it was her tone that had her brother suddenly pushing to his elbows or not. She hadn't meant to sound so bitter, but there was no help for it now.

"I thought Mr. MacQuaid was your friend."

"What made you think that?" Caroline scooped up the candle and headed for the ladder.

"He said so," her brother responded in a way that reminded Caroline of how a clergyman might refer to the Gospel. Her lips thinned as she glanced over her shoulder.

"Hurry and get dressed, Ned. Breakfast is almost ready, and we need to get an early start."

She pretended not to hear the question he called after her as she hurried down the ladder. Mary was sitting, propped against her pillow, Colleen at her breast when Caroline entered the bedroom. She glanced up, bringing her finger to her lips. With a nod, she indicated Mistress Quinn lying beside her sound asleep. They both watched as the older woman took a breath, the air gurgling in her throat before she exhaled in a loud snore. The smile they shared lightened Caroline's step as she left the room to turn the bacon frying up in the skillet.

Mary seemed in good spirits. If only she didn't have those dark circles beneath her eyes that seemed to darken and grow daily. For the hundredth time Caroline prayed she was doing the right thing by taking them all back to Seven Pines.

Within minutes she was given the opportunity to review all her reasons for leaving.

"Where are we going?" Ned clambered down the ladder. "Didn't you hear me ask earlier?"

He looked sleepy and grouchy, and Caroline

wished she could throw her arms about his as she had last night. But something in his manner told her he wouldn't appreciate the gesture, so she simply turned back to stirring the cornmeal mush. "We're returning to Seven Pines today. You'll like it there, Ned. The house is much grander than this and there are—"

"Are you sure we should leave the fort? Mr. Mac Quaid said—"

"Mr. MacQuaid doesn't know everything."

"Perhaps." Ned slumped into a chair and stretched his silk-clad legs out in front of him. "But he is part Cherokee, and he thinks—"

"He said. He thinks. Ned," Caroline said dropping to her knees in front of him and grasping his hands. "Seven Pines is ours. The Cherokee just signed a treaty with the English. I saw them do it."

"But—"

"And there are other things to consider. The fort is full of smallpox. So far we've been able to avoid catching it, but the situation grows worse everyday. And it isn't just you and me to consider. There's another woman, Mary and her new baby. She was asleep when you came last night, but she lives at Seven Pines, too, and we're both counting on your help."

Edward stared at her a moment with eyes as blue as her own, then he nodded, and she gave in to her earlier desire and hugged him. She was right. He seemed embarrassed by the gesture, and Caroline noted again how much her younger brother had grown up in the months since she last saw him.

When Mary entered the room, Caroline made the introductions, then they sat down to eat as the eastern sky showed signs of paling. Mistress Quinn joined them, grumbling about the prospect of their leaving. But she refused Caroline's repeated offer to take her along.

"No, you young'uns be off with you. I'm not going trotting farther into the frontier."

Edward balked a bit when Caroline forced him to sort through the trunk he'd brought, discarding the finer silk breeches and coats. "Mistress Quinn will keep them for you, and later you can fetch them. For now 'tis no room to carry this with us."

"But I brought a pack horse."

"Which we shall need to help carry all our belongings. Believe me, Ned. 'Tis not fancy clothes you'll be needing, but something sturdy."

"Like Mr. MacQuaid wears?"

Caroline should have known she hadn't heard the last of his name from her brother's lips. "Yes, something like that," she agreed.

It was nearly two hours after dawn when they left the fort. Caroline waited till she was confident that Wolf was gone—unlike her brother, she was certain he would get an early start. And she assuredly didn't wish to run into him. She never promised him she'd stay at the fort, but she knew that was what he expected. Nay, demanded of her. As she led the way down the path toward Seven

Pines, Caroline wondered what he'd do when he discovered them gone.

Damn Caroline Simmons, nay, Caroline Mac-Quaid. He couldn't forget she was his father's widow. And damn himself for not being able to stop thinking of her.

Wolf leaned forward, bracing his arms upon his thighs and forced her from his mind as he concentrated on the words of hatred spewing from Tal-tsuska's mouth. The venom was aimed at the British, but Wolf wasn't sure most of it wasn't meant for him personally. Not that he didn't agree with much of what his cousin said. The treaty signed by several of the Headmen *was* an insult to the Cherokee.

"Wa'ya would have us believe that we are better off accepting this abomination than fighting it. I say he is acting like the frightened woman he is." With that personal affront Tal-tsuska crossed his arms and all eyes in the smoke-filled town house at Estatoe shifted to Wolf.

His first impulse was to leap across the smoldering fire and tear into his nemesis. What a relief it would be to rip him limb from limb, to pound his fist into that taunting face.

But he came to preach reason . . . caution . . . self-preservation for the Cherokee, and he had to keep that as his first priority. Yet his fists clenched and his blood boiled with impotent rage as he faced the Headman.

"Tal-tskuska speaks of the unfairness of the treaty and I agree," Wolf began in the language of his mother's people. "But to begin the slaughter of women and children as he suggests is to think with the brain of a dog." From the corner of his eye Wolf noticed the way Tal-tskuska jerked forward, and the hands of those beside him, holding him back. The town house was not for fighting, but for words, and Wolf tried to pick his carefully.

"The Cherokee are mighty warriors. No one, not even the English can dispute that. But they are also wise. Many of our Headmen are held within the English fort. If we begin killing, the soldiers will slay them. Is that wise? Is that the way of the Cherokee?"

"What would you have us do? Sit on our hands like an old woman?"

Wolf glared at his cousin, his eyes dark and burning with intensity. "I would have us think before we run off like screeching crows, starting a war we cannot win."

"Wa'ya speaks of the Cherokee's bravery, then talks of our defeat," Tal-tsuska said with scorn.

"The Cherokee will not fail because he lacks courage. He will fail because he is few compared to his enemy. Because the rifles he uses and the powder come from that enemy. And because he failed to plan."

"What would you have us do, son of Alkini?" the Headman asked.

Later, Wolf squatted by the side of the creek, staring into the rushing water. Had he convinced the council to be prudent? He didn't know. And the truth was, he didn't know what should be done. Killing all in their path wasn't the answer. He knew that as sure as he knew such actions would bring the wrath of the English down on his nation. Yet sitting by and doing nothing would not do, either. And negotiating? He dropped his head into the hollow made by his cupped palms.

For months he'd tried to bring the two nations . . . the two parts of himself together. To help formulate some plan that was fair to both sides. But it seemed hopeless. The white man may be rejoicing in the treaty they had made. But the Cherokee saw only the treachery of the English. The imprisonment of innocent men. Wolf knew it was only a matter of time before the Cherokee broke that treaty.

Before war raged through the land.

And he seemed powerless to stop it.

"There sits the old woman now."

Wolf sprang up when he heard the taunting voice of his cousin. There was no council that prohibited fighting now. Before Tal-tsuska could do more than blink, Wolf was upon him. The savage feel of his flesh beneath Wolf's fist was as satisfying as he'd imagined. As was the strangled cry that escaped his foe. The first punch was followed by another and another as they both rolled onto the rocky ground.

They were well-matched physically, though Wolf was the taller of the two and the struggle was vicious. First one was on top, then the other, but it wasn't until blood flowed into Wolf's eye that he even realized he'd been hit.

Wolf straddled his foe when he vaguely heard Tal-tsuska call out. But he paid no heed until his arms were yanked back and pinned behind him. Wolf struggled, but it was useless as two warriors dragged him to his feet. They held him while Tal-tsuska slowly stood. He wiped at his mouth, glaring at Wolf when his hand came away streaked with blood.

"You shall pay for this, Man who Cavorts with the English," he ordered. He gave an order to the two who held Wolf prisoner.

"The hell you say!"

"It is I who say." Tal-tsuska approached till he stood nose to nose with Wolf. "We listen to no more old women who preach caution. No longer will we allow the English to dominate us." He bared his teeth. "We shall eliminate them from our land." Though the air was cold, sweat glistened on his pockmarked face. "The wife of your father travels to Seven Pines. But do not worry, I shall not kill her . . . at least not at first."

Tal-tsuska jerked back, laughing when Wolf

broke free from the men holding him. He sprang toward his cousin, but before Wolf's hands were able to close around Tal-tsuska's neck, pain exploded in his head. Wolf struggled a step farther before crashing to the ground.

The journey to Seven Pines was easier than Caroline expected. Mary handled the trip well, speaking often of how glad she would be to get home and wondering if Logan might come soon. Colleen was still very small, even though she seemed to nurse frequently.

"She'll be better once we are back at Seven Pines," Mary would say.

The house was much as they'd left it, with only a few woodland creatures having sought shelter inside. Caroline and Edward made quick work of evicting them, then set about flushing the nearby forests for the farm animals left behind.

At least the chickens were still scratching in view of the house. The cow was a bit more difficult to find, but Edward finally located her calmly munching her cud near the river, several miles downstream.

In all this time, the forest seemed peaceful, the skeletal trees in the winter chill, hiding no hostile Indians. And Caroline began to breathe easier. There was no threat of smallpox here. Her bouts of morning illness were gone. She felt strong. And she tried to give some of that strength to Mary.

Ned seemed born to the frontier. He'd found a

cache of clothing that belonged to Logan; and after asking permission, set about wearing the hunting shirts and breeches, forgoing the silks he brought from England. Back home he'd learned to hunt for sport while visiting school chums at their lodges. Now he did it in earnest and kept them well supplied with rabbit and squirrel.

He was on a foray into the woods today. Caroline warned him not to venture far and every now and then she'd hear a gunshot echo through the forest. The scent of fresh-baked bread filled the kitchen. Mary sat by the fire, shortening another pair of breeches for Edward. Whenever Colleen fussed, she nudged the cradle with her foot rocking it gently.

"I don't know much about Logan's older brother," Mary responded to Caroline's question. "He left home when he was young to fight for Prince Charles. Apparently Robert was livid and never forgave him. Even after word reached the family that he was captured and to be hung, his father wouldn't allow his name to be spoken."

"Goodness. What a heartless thing to do." Caroline pulled a loaf of freshly baked bread from the oven. "Robert wasn't a very loving father."

"Hardly." Mary bit off her thread and looked up to meet Caroline's eye. "That's one reason I'm glad you're carrying Raff's child rather than his."

It was the first time the parentage of her baby was mentioned since Caroline confessed it to Mary. Caroline didn't know quite what to say. Mary acted almost as if the entire problem could be handled somehow, and Caroline didn't share that view. She opened her mouth to explain again why nobody must ever know Robert hadn't fathered her child, but a bloodcurdling whoop silenced her.

Before she could grab the musket leaning in the corner, the door burst open. Tomahawk raised, Tal-tsuska rushed into the kitchen.

Eighteen

For an instant it seemed as if no one moved. As if they were all caught, frozen in time by the brush of some diabolical artist. Mary was kneeling beside the cradle, her face contorted by terror, her arms reaching for her child . . . reaching yet unable to touch. Tal-tsuska stood, his entire body smeared with paint—red, black, horrifying colors that made him appear an escapee from hell looming, superimposed on the swarm of similar monsters who filled the doorway.

If there was sound, Caroline couldn't hear it. Fear overpowered everything. Except smell. All around her there was still the fragrance of fresh-baked bread, but now the scent was sharp, unpleasant.

Then like a sudden summer thunderstorm, upon her before she could seek shelter, reality crashed about her. Shrieks and screams sent shivers down her spine, overwhelmed her after the silence.

They were everywhere, exploding into the kitchen, despoiling it. How she heard her name above the din, Caroline didn't know, but she whirled to see a Cherokee grab Mary up to his chest. Caroline flung herself at the warrior. Her fingers dug into his skin. When he turned on her, his expression was a mask of disgust and annoyance. With a grunt he jerked his arm from her grasp. Then lifted his hand above her head.

It happened so quickly, there was no time to escape. Caroline saw the silvery glint of the tomahawk poised above her and sucked in her last breath, a vision of Wolf in her mind. But the final kiss of steel never came.

Something hard wrapped about her waist, forcing air from her body as she was hauled back. "No," her savior . . . her tormentor, yelled. "This one is mine."

She was dragged outside, her last glimpse of Mary one of despair as her friend collapsed onto the brick floor.

Struggling was useless but she did it anyway, kicking and scratching, biting as Tal-tsuska tried to subdue her. Somewhere in the back of her mind was the glimmer of truth that he could stop her vain attempts to hurt him with a single blow. But he didn't. Not that he was gentle with her by any means.

His hands were hard as he yanked her arms behind her. Tears streamed down Caroline's face when the rawhide strips wound around her wrists, not because of the pain, though there was that, but

374

because she was now truly helpless. To help herself, to help Mary and Colleen, to help her brother.

"Just do it," she yelled at her captor. "Just kill me, too."

As soon as the words, borne of desperation, escaped her, she was shoved down hard. Pain ripped through her hip as she went sprawling on the frozen ground. Tal-tsuska bent over her then, clutching her hair savagely. Wooden pins scattered on the frosty earth.

"You wish death," he said, his face contorted by his sneer. From his leggings he drew a knife and slid it against the edge of her scalp. "This is what you prefer, English woman?" His fingers tightened, the cold blade burned her flesh, and Caroline's breath tore from her in a frantic sob. His tone softened. "If that is the case, you are not the fighter I took you for."

"Besides," he said as he slipped the knife back into its sheath. "It is not my wish that you die now." With that he yanked her to her feet.

As she was dragged away from the house, Caroline twisted her head, searching frantically for some sign of the others. She could see neither Mary nor Ned, and then the thick smoke billowing from the house obscured her view.

Wolf saw the smoke from the ridge above the fork in the river. He wasted no time trying to convince himself that it was anything other than Seven Pines that burned. He was too late.

His pace didn't quicken with the knowledge, he already ran as fast as he could. He had been since early this morning. That's when he finally managed to untie his hands and overwhelm the man left to guard him. Wolf splashed through a stream, then crashed through the thicket of trees on the shore. He should be angry with her for leaving the fort. For placing herself in this danger, but he couldn't summon that emotion.

It was fear, true, uncontrollable fear that consumed him. Not since he was a boy and was dragged from his mother's arms did the bitter pill taste so foul. What would he do if she were dead? Could he live with himself then, without her? With the knowledge that he'd helped push her to her death.

He couldn't erase the expression on her face when he insisted upon knowing who fathered her child. She'd hated him then . . . and he'd hated himself. Branches tore at his clothing and flesh, but he paid them no heed as he climbed a hillock, then leaped across the gully at its foot.

He didn't care whose child it was she carried. She was his. Deep in his heart he'd known that from the moment he first saw her. But being the fool he was, he risked everything. Using her. Giving her to the one man whom he hated above all else.

His stupid hatred.

376

His foolish right to revenge.

Wolf vaulted over a fallen tree, his moccasined feet slamming into the leaf-covered soil with each long stride. She'd fled not only smallpox, but him. From his questions and scorn. And all the while, it was his fault. If she carried his father's baby, was she to blame? She who'd been willing to go with him, to live the life of a halfblood's woman, rather than forsake him. Whatever happened to her at his father's hands was his own blame to bear. And for the rest of his life, he would.

As Wolf neared the clearing, he broke stride only long enough to shift the rifle from his shoulder. The smell of smoke was stronger now, acrid, burning his eyes and filling him with despair. He thought he could go no faster, but now his pace quickened, covering the ground so quickly the leafless trees seemed to rush past him in a blur.

He burst through the last stand of birch trees into the clearing. And then he stopped, his energy spent as he viewed the scene before him. The house was no more than a smoldering shell, the chimneys standing starkly above the smoking rubble.

He should investigate, sift through the charred boards. Look for the remains. But he couldn't make himself move. An eerie quiet surrounded the place, and it briefly occurred to him that Taltsuska and his band might still be about. But even that possibility couldn't budge him. He just stood, his blood pounding in his ears, his life seemingly slipping away. Until he heard a whimper.

"Caroline?" He wasn't sure if he spoke her name until the word echoed back at him. Then he was running, pounding through the brush and brambles on the far side of the clearing.

Wolf paid no heed to the gun Edward swung up when he thundered into the small hole in the thicket they used as a hiding place. The boy cradled a woman. Her head was bloody and her body limp, and Wolf fell to his knees beside her. "Caroline." The word was torn from him on a sob.

"It's Mary," Edward said, and as Wolf gently brushed blood-encrusted hair from her face, he could see it was true. She had an open wound on the side of her head. She was still alive though each breath was shallow and hard-fought. "I can't find Caro anywhere."

Wolf forced his attention to the boy. "Are you all right?"

"Yes." He sniffed, and Wolf could see he was doing his best not to break down in front of him. Reaching out, Wolf grabbed his shoulder and squeezed. "I was hunting down by the river. I didn't know anything had happened till I saw the place burning. By the time I got back . . ." He did break down then, sucking in his breath and sobbing uncontrollably. "I should have been here. Maybe I could have stopped them." Giant tears streamed down his face.

Wolf's heart went out to him, but there was no time for sympathy, and he didn't think that's what Edward needed right now. "Do not be a fool. If

378

you had been here, you'd be dead now. When you live on the frontier, you have to learn to accept . . ." Wolf's voice trailed off. Accept what? Death? He looked down at the woman lying in Edward's arms and swallowed. She'd been kind to him from the moment he first met her, and he loved her like a sister. How could anyone ever accept this?

"Where's her baby?"

Edward shook his head. He was trying his best to regain control though this new question seemed as if it might break his resolve. But his voice was firm. "I buried her up on the hill. Mary had managed to crawl outside with Colleen, but she was . . . Caro told me Colleen was sickly," he added, glancing up at Wolf hopefully. "Do you think that might have been why she died? She had no marks on her."

Wolf nodded and squeezed the boy's shoulder again before pushing to his feet.

"Where are you going?" Edward's voice held a note of panic.

"Just to look around a bit. I'll be right back."

He couldn't get away fast enough, but Wolf forced himself to move slowly. He thought he was used to this . . . to death, but his knees felt weak, and his stomach churned. His heart ached.

Searching through the burned rubble of Seven Pines for Caroline's charred body was the hardest thing he ever did. But he moved slowly, methodically, and he forced himself not to think beyond what he might find. For if she wasn't here, then Tal-tsuska had taken her and he would go after them and find her . . . and kill Tal-tsuska.

"Mr. MacQuaid! Raff!"

Dropping a burnt timber, Wolf raced back to the bushes when he heard Edward's call.

"She's awake," he said, excitedly, still holding Mary in his arms.

When Wolf dropped to his knees and took her hand, Mary's gaze focused on him. She tried to smile, though her voice was raspy when she said his name. "Tell Logan . . ." she began, and Wolf touched her cheek.

"I will. I'll tell him."

"I love him."

"He knows. He loves you, too." Wolf wasn't sure he spoke the truth, but at this point he would lie to the devil himself to make Mary feel better.

Tears formed in her eyes and rolled down into her bloody hair. "I couldn't save my baby. I tried," she sobbed.

"Shhh." Wolf brushed away the tears with the back of his fingers. "Don't upset yourself. Just rest."

"No. I need to tell you." She took a breath and Wolf could hear the too-familiar death rattle. "They took Caroline. You have to find . . ." Her words trailed off.

"I will, Mary. I'll find her." Wolf's heart was pounding so hard, he almost missed her next words.

380

"She loves you, Raff. Loves you . . ."

"Mary? Mary."

Edward looked up at him, his expression anxious. "Do you think she went back to sleep?"

Wolf shook his head slowly, then pressed his hand over her chest to confirm what he already knew. Taking a deep breath, he pushed to his feet. His heart was sad, but his mind was racing ahead to Caroline. Where had Tal-tsuska taken her?

"Are you sure? Are you sure Mary's dead?"

Reaching down, Wolf pulled Edward to his feet. "You did all you could for her."

"But—"

"Edward." Wolf said the word sharply, gratified when the boy snapped his head up. "We have some things to take care of—quickly. Then we have to go. I'm taking you back to the fort, then—"

"No." Edward stood as tall as he could. "No, sir, you're not. Do you think I didn't hear what Mary said? They have my sister, and I'm going with you to find her."

Caroline wouldn't like it. When he found her, she'd probably chew his hide raw for allowing her brother to be put in more danger. But Wolf couldn't deny the fire in Edward's eyes. If he didn't take Edward with him, the damn kid would probably set out on his own.

"All right then. But you are going to have to keep up and do exactly as I say."

They buried Mary in the family plot beside her infant daughter. At Edward's prompting, Wolf said a few words over the grave. It took them all of a quarter of an hour, and Wolf felt guilty for be-grudging even those few moments. He chaffed to be underway. To find Caroline.

She forced herself to keep up. For as tired and uncomfortable as she was, the periods of rest were worse. That's when she had to listen to Tal-tsuska's taunts.

"Wa'ya will not come for you," he told her re-peatedly. "He is my prisoner. And if he tries to escape, he will die."

At least when she concentrated on walking, she could keep that and the rest of her fears at bay. Mary. Baby Colleen. Ned. What had happened to them? And were Tal-tsuska's words about Wolf true? Was he a prisoner, or dead as she feared the others were? Was she alone, the only survivor? And if that were the case, did she even care?

Caroline took a deep breath and realized her ploy to keep from thinking wasn't working any more. Exhausted as she was, forced to traverse the rough trail at a rapid pace, she still could think and worry.

"We rest here." Tal-tsuska grabbed her arm, and Caroline realized the others had stopped. She sank to her knees, then eased to sitting. Her hands were tied in front of her, the rawhide wrapped around -2her neck. Gratefully, she bent her legs then dropped her forehead to her knees, blotting out the scene about her.

"You should have said you were tired."

Caroline didn't look up, but she knew her captor was near. "Would it have mattered?" Caroline felt his hand on her and jerked away, but he grabbed her chin, forcing her to look at him.

"It will do no good to fight me."

Caroline said nothing, only glared at him.

"Do you hear me, white woman?"

"I hear the pounding of footsteps as the king's soldiers hunt you down." She anticipated the blow, but even though she'd steeled herself, the force still knocked her over. She lay on the hard ground, tasting her own blood and shut her eyes.

"I will break you, English woman. Then you will be mine."

They rested for only a short time. Caroline tried to sleep, to rid her mind of reality, but even that relief wasn't within her grasp. As soon as she began to drift off, she was jerked to her feet.

By nightfall the temperature had dropped. Where before the cold had kept her alert, now her feet and hands were numb, and she couldn't stop shivering. Still, when they stopped for the night, Caroline's heart sank when a campfire was built. Even as the flames licked over the wood, offering her some relief from the cold, her heart froze. Tal-tsuska wouldn't chance their smoke being spotted if there was any possibility someone might be following them.

Hopelessness washed over her when Tal-tsuska untied her hands. The thong remained about her neck.

"Sit," he commanded after spreading a blanket near the fire's warmth. When she hesitated, he settled his hand over her shoulder and pushed. "It will do no good to defy me, white woman. I have time. You are smart. You will see the wisdom of doing as you are told."

She wanted to scream at him that she would never, ever do anything but resist him. But she was so tired. When she finally spoke, her tone sounded no more than annoyed. "Why do you take this trouble with me, Tal-tsuska? Wouldn't it be easier to simply kill me?"

"Easier for who?" he said, dropping to the blanket beside her. "For you perhaps, but I find you worth the effort, white woman."

Trying to pull away only made him chuckle. And tighten his hold on the tether about her neck. "You did not turn from the touch of Wa'ya did you, white woman? Was it his English blood that made the difference?"

"No." Caroline stared at him and her eyes glittered in the flickering firelight. "It is the English blood that stains your hands."

He pushed her back on the blanket then, and Caroline tried to prepare herself for what was to come. But he left her alone, rising to his feet and seeming to melt into the woods that surrounded them. Another Cherokee, whom she didn't know, took his place beside her, wrapping the end of the rawhide thong around his wrist. But he neither spoke to nor touched her, and eventually she drifted into a troubled sleep.

When she woke a blanket covered her and light snow swirled through the morning air. She chewed on the dried deer meat she was given, grateful for something to eat. Sometime during the night, she realized her survival depended upon her. And it wasn't just her survival. She must think of her child . . . Wolf's child. It was up to her to protect them both.

So she ate what Tal-tsuska gave her, forcing her stomach to stop rebelling against the unfamiliar taste. She accepted the blanket he threw about her shoulders, resisting the urge to toss it to the ground in a show of contempt. She would escape. Caroline knew that. It was only a question of when. Until then she would pretend compliance.

They traveled north and west over terrain that gradually grew more mountainous. There were seven Indians, but no one spoke to her except Tal-tsuska. It seemed as if she were his personal responsibility . . . his personal property. He fed her, walked beside her, tugged on her bindings if she slowed her pace. Slept beside her. This last was the most unnerving, though as yet he had done nothing but share her blanket.

And he talked to her. Of the mighty defeat the Cherokee would inflict upon the English. Of the departure of the hated white man from his land.

Of his dislike of Wa'ya, the son of the treacherous trader.

"If you despise us so, I don't see why you insist upon dragging me with you," Caroline said as they trudged through a mountain pass.

"You are still of a mind that I should kill you?" When Caroline didn't answer, he continued. "You, I shall keep as a reminder of all we have overcome. I will look at you and remember that you were the lying one's wife, that you were his son's woman. That I have you now, long after they have gone to the 'darkening land.'"

After two days, they reached a Cherokee town, smaller than Keowee. Catherine didn't know for sure where she was, for Tal-tsuska refused to tell her their destination. However, by piecing together the things Wolf had told her, she imagined they had traveled to one of the Middle Towns.

Even though she could understand little of what was said, it was obvious Tal-tsuska was treated as a returning hero. And that she was looked upon with scorn. If she hoped for any help from this quarter, she soon realized it would not be forthcoming. The women yelled at her, some of them leaping forward and shaking their fists in her face as Tal-tsuska lead her into the town.

The cabin he put her in was small and illkept. The mats on the packed earth floor were dirty. Caroline shook them out, then looked around. Even though it was only late afternoon, the interior was dark. The only light came from rays of weak winter sun that slanted through the chinks between the logs and the smoke hole in the center of the roof.

There were no windows. The only way out was the way she came in, and it opened onto the center of the town. When an old woman brought her evening meal, nearly tossing it at her, Caroline ate it eagerly, then lay down to rest. If she was to escape, and she was determined to, she would need all her strength.

But as the drums began beating, their rhythm pounding through the earth beneath her ear, Caroline's resolve faltered. The Cherokee were chanting, their sing-song words growing ever louder and more frantic. She lay in the dark, her eyes open, wondering how she would ever get away from them.

She must have drifted off to sleep, for when the door opened, she jerked awake. For an instant a large figure loomed in the doorway, a grotesque silhouette against the light of the giant bonfire in the background.

Fear shot through her, and Caroline scooted back across the dirt floor, clutching the only weapon she'd been able to find, a potato-sized rock. The door closed and darkness fell around her like a heavy wool blanket. She could hear him moving toward her, and she drew back her arm. She would wound him at best, and then he would hurt her more. Caroline knew that. But now that the moment was upon her, she knew she couldn't simply submit to him.

Her heart pounded as he took one step, then another. Closer.

"Caroline?"

At first, she thought her ears must be deceiving her. "Raff. Oh, God, Raff." She was up and into his arms before she even caught her breath. He held her tightly, nearly crushing her in his embrace. "How did you find me? Tal-tsuska said you were his prisoner or . . . or dead."

"It is a long story. And we have to get out of here."

"But how? There's no way but the front door, and there's a guard." Caroline pulled away enough to look up at him even though she could only discern a vague outline. "If they let you in, it's a trap. Tal-tsuska hates you."

"He did not *let* me in." Wolf grabbed up a blanket and wrapped it around her shoulders. "Are you ready?"

"Yes, but—"

"Pull this over your hair and keep your head down." He tucked the gathers under her chin, his hand lingering a moment on hers when she reached up to hold the blanket in place. "No matter what happens, you are to run south toward the river. Edward is there and—"

"Ned? Ned is alive?"

"Yes and he is waiting with a canoe. Run there as quickly as you can." He grabbed her arm, propelling her toward the door, not realizing at first that she pulled back.

"What about you?" The drums and chanting rose and fell in waves.

"What about me?"

"What are you going to do while I run toward the river?"

"I will be right behind you." He said it with as much conviction as he could, though he knew if need be, he would sacrifice himself to insure her escape. She apparently knew it, too, for she threw her arms around his neck and held on with all her might. He could feel her heart pounding against his chest and knew his own beat just as frantically.

Her voice vibrated against his skin. "The baby," she began, but he found her mouth with his fingers, silencing her.

"I do not need to know."

"But I want to tell you. I should have from the very beginning." Now with their very lives at stake, her concerns about Seven Pines seemed ridiculous. Nothing was important besides the love she felt for him—and hoped he felt for her. "Your father never . . . It's—"

The silence, so sudden and overwhelming was deafening. No noise would have silenced her as effectively. Caroline sucked in her breath as Wolf shoved her behind him. Cautiously he moved toward the door.

He inched it open just as the drums began again

and the villagers erupted into a loud war cry that reverberated through the cabin. Without looking back, he reached for her hand and pulled her through the door. Caroline managed to keep the blanket over her head as she was yanked forward, out into the open.

The fires and burning brands made the square of land in front of the council house nearly as light as day. Caroline could plainly see the Cherokee milling about. There was no guard in front of the cabin, and she idly wondered what had become of him.

But there were more important things to worry about as she silently followed Wolf. They skirted the cabins, trying to stay in their shadows. Could the Cherokee see Wolf and her as clearly as she could see them?

When Wolf ducked beside one of the log buildings, Caroline breathed a sigh of relief until she heard a grunt of recognition. She glanced up in time to see a warrior blocking their path. They'd obviously surprised him as he returned from tending his bodily functions, or he would have shouted for help. And even though the drums were loud, there was a chance he would be heard.

As it was, he raised his war club over his head, arching it down toward Wolf's head. Pushing her out of the way, Wolf yelled, "Run," before propelling himself toward the man.

She couldn't. She simply couldn't run away and leave him even when both men ended up on the ground by her feet. Caroline looked around frantically for something to use against the Cherokee. Wolf hadn't had time to draw his knife, and she noticed he hadn't brought his rifle.

There was nothing. She did run then—into the woods, searching for a branch, anything to bash over the warrior's head. Seconds seemed like hours as she dropped to her knees, grabbing for a thick branch fallen from a hickory tree. She would bring it down over the Cherokee's skull. She could see the scene in her mind's eye, almost feel the crush of bone beneath her hands.

But when she raced back to where she left Wolf, neither man was there. If not for the rustle of fallen leaves, she wouldn't have known where to look. Without care for herself, she rushed toward the sound, gasping when something grabbed her from behind.

"Damnit, Caroline." The familiar voice hissed in her ear. "Is this what you call running toward the river?"

Caroline ignored his question as he let her go. "What happened to him?"

"Back there." Wolf nodded toward a dark shape huddled on the ground. She was tempted to ask if he was dead, but thought better of it when Wolf clutched her arm. "Let's go," he began, only to stop when he saw the branch. "What in the hell is this for?"

"I was going to hit—"

"Never mind. Come on." He turned, and Caroline dropped the branch and followed.

They crept back into the woods then circled around toward the south. They said nothing to each other, and Caroline tried to keep her step as quiet as his as they slipped between trees and sloshed into a stream. Her feet were numb with cold within seconds, but she did her best to keep up.

Wolf climbed up over a rocky outcropping and leaned down to help her up. Then they hurried on.

Caroline heard the river before she saw it. She was wet and cold, miserable, but she didn't care as she did her best to keep up with her rescuer.

She nearly screamed when Edward stepped out of the shadows, but Wolf pulled her toward him, covering her mouth till she broke free and enveloped her brother in a tight hug. "I was so worried about you," she said before Wolf hustled her toward the shore.

"There is a canoe down here." Wolf hesitated, his hand on her back. "Where is the blanket? The blanket?" he repeated when she didn't answer immediately.

"I—I must have dropped it."

"Where? Think, Caroline." He grabbed her shoulders and spun her around to face him, ignoring Ned's noise of protest.

"Stop it, Ned." Caroline pushed at her brother's hand where it rested on Wolf's arm. Caroline swallowed. "It was when the warrior surprised us as we left the village. I remember now, it slipped from my shoulders and I . . . I let it go. Does it matter?" Now it was she clutching Wolf.

"Before I came for you, I tried to buy us some time by making a false trail east through the forest. But if they find the blanket—"

"They'll know we escaped by the river," Caroline finished for him.

"I am going back for it."

"No, Wolf," Caroline cried, but he paid her no heed as he handed her over to Ned.

"Take care, boy. If I have not returned by the time the moon rises over those trees, go. Paddle as hard as you can till you come to a fork in the river. Take the southern branch and follow it till you get to Fort Prince George. It should take you two days and a bit. Then as soon as you can get an escort to Charles Town, go. Drag her kicking and screaming if you must, but get her back to civilization."

"Raff." Caroline reached out toward him, and he paused. In the dim light she couldn't see his expression, but she felt his eyes on her. There was so much she needed to say, so much she wished she'd told him before. But now it was too late.

"Take care of her, Edward," was all Wolf said before he disappeared into the woods.

Nineteen

"I won't leave!"

"Don't be stubborn, Caro. You heard what Mr MacQuaid said." The moon now hung just above the tree tops, limning the stark branches with its soft glow. "Caroline, where are you going?" Edward abandoned his spot near the canoe and raced after his sister.

Ignoring Ned's chatter, Caroline scrambled up the bank, staring into the shadows. It was difficult to hear anything above the rhythmic pounding of drums. Taking a deep breath, Caroline clasped her hands together. Despite the cold, her body fell damp with perspiration.

Where was he? Her silent litany seemed to pulse with the timbre of the Cherokee's chant. It couldn't have taken him this long to find the stupid blanket. Again and again, Caroline chided herself for her carelessness in leaving it. If she'd only thought to reach down and pick it up when it slipped from her shoulders. If she could only live that moment again.

But she hadn't realized. She just hadn't thought. And because of that, the man she loved was . . . was what? Her fingers twisted together. Why didn't he come?

"Caro." Ned's voice was breathless from the climb to her side. It also had a pleading quality that grated on Caroline's already taut nerves.

"I'm not leaving him here alone, Ned," she said facing him, her hands akimbo. "If you wish to go, then do so. But stop pestering me."

"For God's sake Caroline, I promised him I'd take you to safety ."

"I said no!" Caroline realized she'd raised her voice; and even though she doubted anyone could hear over the noise from the village, she lowered it. "He's the father of my child, and I love him." She hadn't planned to say that. The words simply spilled out.

Covering the hand that clutched her arm with her own, Caroline stepped closer to Ned. "I'm sorry," she whispered, before turning back to scan the expanse of endless forest.

"I . . . I don't understand."

"I know you don't." Caroline took a deep breath. "And I really can't explain it. Not now, at least." She was vaguely aware that her brother's fingers slipped off her sleeve, and she heard his footfalls as he slid back down the bank. She hoped he would climb into the canoe and paddle to the fort. She wanted him safe. She just couldn't sacrifice Wolf . . . not any more.

She watched and she prayed, but it was Ned who first heard the rustling upstream from them. He rushed to her side, pulling her down to the ground when she would have run toward the sound. "We don't know it's him," he breathed.

But moments later Caroline was struggling to her feet, surging forward and leaning against Wolf's chest. His arm tightened about her, and he lifted her up, only to set her down quickly.

"What are you still doing here?" It took him longer than he expected to find the blanket, then he'd run into a sentry who'd taken exception to him being there. Hiding the body was also time consuming. Considering how late he was, he assumed Caroline and Ned were already gone. But he'd planned to follow the river, hoping to catch up with them if they encountered any trouble.

"She wouldn't leave," Ned said as he pushed the canoe into the current. Wolf was on the shore brushing away their tracks with a pine branch. "And after she explained things to me, I thought it best to stay, too."

Wolf waded out into the water, then climbed into the back of the canoe. He resisted asking Edward, who sat in front of him, what exactly Caroline had explained. For right now, they needed all their energy for paddling.

The river above the fall line was shallow, filled with rocks that kept the current bubbling and the passage difficult. White water splashed over the sides, making all three occupants wet and cold. But they kept going. Through the long night.

Near dawn, Caroline heard a great thundering sound that reminded her of the Cherokee drums. For an instant she thought they were upon them again, and she twisted, looking back at Raff.

"We're coming to some falls," he answered her unspoken question. "We must paddle to shore soon and portage the canoe across land for a mile or so."

The current was already strong, pulling them closer to the precipice, but they managed to make it to the side. As Caroline dragged her wet skirts from the canoe, she looked around. Mist rose off the water and filtered through the bare-branched trees. "Do you think we're safe here?"

"I imagine they know by now that you are missing." Wolf shrugged as he pulled the canoe higher onto the shore. He turned, and his eyes met Caroline's. "It depends on how important you are to Tal-tsuska whether he chooses to come after you." He paused. "My bet is that he is already on our trail."

Caroline held his gaze a moment longer before taking a deep breath and turning away. "I've done nothing to—" Caroline's lashes lowered as she felt Wolf's hand on her arm.

"He knows it is I who came for you. I am certain of it. He also knows what you mean to me."

He stood very close to her; and when Caroline looked up, she could see the dark fire in his eyes.

His words were no declaration of undying love, yet she sensed he cared for her. She wanted to lean into him. To have him hold her forever. To take away the pain of loneliness. The reality that kept pounding in her brain as sure as the Indian drums.

But there was no help for the question that had haunted her since the morning of the attack. She'd waited this long to ask for she feared the answer . . . feared she already knew the answer.

"What of Mary?"

He reached out then, drawing her toward him with strong, steady hands. She held onto him, her fingers clutching the supple deer hide of his shirt as he said the words she dreaded to hear.

Caroline's face was tearstained as she lifted her head. "And Colleen? What of her baby?"

"She died before I arrived." Wolf rubbed his hands across her narrow back, wishing he could absorb her pain. "Edward and I buried them at Seven Pines."

Caroline nodded. "Mary would have wanted that. To be there when Logan comes home."

Wolf hadn't allowed himself to think of his brother's reaction to Mary's death, his child's. Logan had entrusted their safety to Wolf when he left, and now they were both buried beneath the sandy soil of Seven Pines. And now there were others who needed his protection.

Wolf held Caroline at arm's length. "We need to be on our way." His voice gentled, and he lifted one hand to skim away a crystalline tear poised on the fringe of her lashes. "Are you going to be all right?"

"Someone told me once that the frontier is unforgiving." She straightened her shoulders. "I shall be fine."

The trek over the rocks was not easy, and she wasn't even carrying the canoe. They rested near the summit of the falls, Edward sinking quickly to his knees after he and Wolf lowered the boat. After a quick admonition to stay where they were, Wolf slipped back the way they came.

"Does he think they're following us?"

Caroline turned and faced her brother. It was the first time they'd been alone together since she'd made her revelation, and she wasn't sure what to expect. He stared up at her, his innocent blue eyes seemingly out of place in a face hardened by the lessons of this wild land.

He was streaked with dirt and obviously exhausted, but he was managing, both the hardships of the wilderness and the knowledge of his sister's fall from grace. Perhaps he was stronger, more resilient than she expected. She'd tried to protect him for so long, it seemed strange not to continue. But in that instant, Caroline decided he was man enough to know the truth.

"Raff feels they'll follow. He only hopes we can reach Fort Prince George before they catch up with us."

He seemed to accept this, nodding and drawing his knees up beneath his chin. "Things have been difficult for you here, Caro." It wasn't a question, and Caroline saw no reason to respond. "Why did you write, telling me those fanciful stories?"

"I don't know." Caroline sank down on the sandy ground near him. " 'Tis an untruth," she admitted with a sigh. "I wished for you to believe 'twas no sacrifice I made, coming here. You were so happy in school and 'twas so obvious that's where you belonged."

"Do you know how that makes me feel, that you gave up so much for me?" His guileless face was creased with lines of consternation.

"Nay." Caroline reached out for his hands. "Do not think so. I have some regrets but—"

"Some?" He stood. "How can you say that when you are stuck in the wilderness, surrounded by savages, and carrying—" He stopped and suddenly grew very attentive of the rushing torrent to his right.

"When I spoke of regrets, Ned, it was the death of Mary and her baby . . . the death of my husband that I meant. And, of course, I would rather be somewhere warm, and dry, and safe. But I do *not* regret this child, nor do I repent the circumstances of his conception."

"Caro . . ."

"No, Ned, listen to me. I won't have—"

"I thought you two were tired." Wolf stepped into the small clearing and slipped the rifle from his shoulder. "If there was a Cherokee within a mile of here, he'd have heard you."

Caroline's hands slipped from her hips. Heat from her flushed face burned her cheeks as she tried to remember everything she'd said, and how loud she'd been. "Did you see any Cherokee?" She knew that should be her first concern.

Wolf finished drinking from his cupped hands and stood. "No. But I think we should get moving." He turned toward Edward, who stood, his hands hanging by his side, his expression closed. "You want to give me a hand with this?"

Together they hefted the canoe over their heads and started down toward the calmer water beneath the falls. By early afternoon, they were back on the river. Edward was asleep, his chore of paddling taken over by Caroline.

"Trouble with little brother?"

Caroline glanced over her shoulder. She lost the rhythm with the paddle, but Wolf simply arched his brows. His hair was loose and whipped about his face, making him look wild, part of the land around them.

"I suppose you and your brother are never annoyed with one another." As soon as she spoke, Caroline wished the words back. Thoughts of Wolf's brother only reminded her of Mary. Of the woman's desire to see her husband again.

"Logan and I never had much good for one another until right before he decided to leave. But I can not recall us ever yelling at each other."

"We weren't yelling." Perhaps she had raised her

voice in explanation but . . . Caroline slapped her paddle into the water. "What did you hear?"

"Not much." Wolf guided them around a rock jutting from the middle of the stream. "Just enough to know you—Get down!"

"What? I—" Before she could do more than look around, a powerful arm dragged her from her seat, knocking her to the bottom of the canoe. Caroline was vaguely aware of Ned sputtering a question, then dropping down beside her, landing on her leg. She shifted, trying to see what was going on, and then she heard savage screams that made her blood freeze. Above her, she could feel the unleashed energy as Wolf paddled feverishly, first one side of the canoe, and then the other. The canoe was moving quickly, jerkily through the water, but still the noise didn't cease. If anything, it seemed to grow closer.

Pushing up, Caroline could see Wolf huddled forward, the muscles in his neck standing out in bold relief as he pulled the canoe through the water. His eyes met hers for an instant, and his expression more than anything else told her how close their pursuers were.

"Let me help."

"No. I do not want them to see you. After we round the next bend, I will head for shore. As soon as we are close enough, jump out of the canoe . . . both of you. Hide in the woods."

"What about you?" Water splashed over the sides, and Caroline swiped at her wet hair.

"I will lead them on down stream for a while. After dark, follow the river to the fort." His eyes met hers before jerking back to focus on the river. "I will meet you there."

"No." Caroline clutched the birch bark sides of the canoe and pushed forward. "I won't let you sacrifice yourself."

"Damnit. Caroline, get down." He leaned to the right, maneuvering the canoe around the spit of pine-covered land that jutted into the winding current. "Do not argue with me. Ned! In about three minutes, when I give the word, I want you to drag your sister out of this boat and into the woods. Do you hear me, boy?"

"Yes, sir."

"Can I count on you to do it?"

"Yes, sir."

"No, he won't," Caroline said at the same time, drowning out her brother's affirmative response. "I'm not leaving you." She wouldn't have, either, if he hadn't chosen that moment to look at her, his dark eyes passionate.

"Do not make this harder than it is. Please."

In that same instant, the canoe jolted to a stop, and Caroline lost her hold and fell forward. He grabbed her, his mouth grinding against hers in a quick, hard kiss. When he pulled away, he murmured something in Cherokee, then scooped up the paddle again. "Take her now, Edward."

It happened so quickly, Caroline couldn't even remember climbing from the canoe. One moment she was reaching out to Wolf, the next she was pushed down, flattened behind a bramble-covered rock, and he was gone.

"Keep still," she heard her brother say, but it didn't stop her from rising enough to see the canoes that followed Wolf down the river. They seemed to have fallen for his deception, for no one even glanced toward the thicket where Caroline and Edward hid. Both of the canoes followed Wolf.

"Where are you going?" Edward's grip manacled her wrist, and he yanked her back when she tried to rise. "Raff said to stay here till nightfall."

With a jerk she pulled her arm away. "I'm not sitting here while they catch him. They're closer than ever thanks to his letting us off."

"But he said—"

"I don't care what he said. I'm going after him." Caroline stood. "You may stay if you wish. I believe you can find the fort from here." Without waiting for a response, Caroline picked up her skirts and raced down the shoreline. It wasn't until she heard noise behind her that she realized her brother was following her.

"I'm not going back," she said without even bothering to stop.

"I'm not asking you to." With a surge, Edward caught up with his sister. "Just tell me this. What in the devil are we going to do even if we do find him?"

"I don't know, Neddy." Caroline wiped hair from her face. "I don't know."

Just before nightfall she noticed the smoke filtering above the trees. Without a word, she motioned to Ned, who had stayed up with her despite his earlier reluctance.

"What do you suppose it means?" Edward bent over from the waist, his hands resting on his knees when Caroline stopped to catch her breath.

"I know it isn't Raff. He'd never give his whereabouts away like that."

"Then you think it's the Cherokee?" Edward straightened enough to peer at his sister from under his shelf of nearly white brows.

"We're going to find out."

"Lord help us. Caro." Edward scurried to catch up with her. "What good is it going to do Raff . . . any of us . . . for you to go marching into the Cherokee camp? We've no weapons." He threw up his hands in despair. "No nothing."

"I didn't say we were going into their camp. But I can't believe they'd chance having a fire unless they've captured Raff. And as for no weapons." She paused, not exactly sure what to say to that argument. "We'll think of something," she finally mumbled as they made their way toward the spot where she saw the smoke.

"This is insane."

"Shhh." Caroline glanced over at Edward, finger

pressed to her lips, as they hunkered down behind an outcrop of rocks near the Indian camp. They were far enough away to be in the shadows . . . she hoped. She also hoped the Cherokee wouldn't be expecting her to come sneaking up on them. She and Edward hadn't encountered any sentries except the ones she could see guarding their prisoner.

They'd tied Wolf to a birch tree. In the flickering light from the campfire, Caroline could see that they'd stripped the bark from the trunk and splashed the wood with black and red paint. It made an eerie background for their captive. Wolf stood, his hands tied behind the tree, his feet bound. He was naked to the waist, wearing only his loincloth.

"He's wounded."

"I know," Caroline whispered. She noticed that immediately and the pain in his bleeding arm seemed to shoot straight through her.

"So what are we going to do?"

Caroline took a deep breath. "Let me think for a minute."

"How does it feel now, Wa'ya?" You are alone. Stripped of your protectors, the English dogs. And waiting to die."

Wolf met Tal-tsuska's taunting stare, but made no comment. If he was going to die, he would do it with his pride intact.

"Nothing to say for yourself? You, who were always too ready to speak in the council house. So ready to work out a compromise between the two people who war for your soul." Tal-tsuska puffed out his chest and strode back and forth in front of Wolf. Despite the cold, he too was garbed only in his loincloth. The same ochre and black they smeared on the sapling were painted in designs of war across his chest and pockmarked face.

"This war will not help the Cherokee," Wolf finally said. "You may win at first, but in the end, they will destroy us."

"As you have prophesied . . . even hoped for all along." Tal-tsuska stepped closer, thrusting his face near Wolf's.

"In your heart you know better than that," Wolf said and returned the angry glare till Tal-tsuska finally looked away.

"I know the English are vermin who come to our shores to destroy us with their greed and diseases."

"There is no denying there has been greed—"

"And disease! You have only to remember the loss of my wife, my children . . ." He paused as he pulled a knife from the sheath at his waist. "To look at my face." He held the blade up threateningly close to Wolf's cheek, then smiled savagely as he slid the blade along his own thumb. There was no change in his expression as a thin line of crimson appeared.

"Tell me, Wa'ya, where she is."

"Drowned in the river." The change of subject had come quickly, but Wolf expected it. He gave the same answer he had from the beginning. Ever since his capture near the head of a second falls, Tal-tsuska badgered him about Caroline's whereabouts.

Wolf began to realize his cousin's interest in her was not merely a means to settle an old feud between the two of them. It made Wolf hope with all his heart that she and her brother were well on there way to Fort Prince George. Knowing she was safe would almost make what he was about to endure bearable.

Tal-tsuska's rough touch snapped Wolf's attention back to his captor. With eyelids lowered and lips drawn back tightly from his teeth Tal-tsuska smeared the blood from his thumb down the center of Wolf's chest. "Soon, Wa'ya. Soon your blood will stain this ground." Then with a flourish, he sank the blade into the soft, sandy, soil several feet in front of the tree where Wolf was tied. Firelight flickered off the polished steel and carved bone handle.

"Look at it, Wa'ya. study it, until you can feel the sting of its bite. Feel your lifeblood leave you as I cut away your white half . . ." He paused, his stare meeting Wolf's. "You may pretend you have no fear, but I know better. Too much cowardly English blood runs through your veins."

With those words Tal-tsuska turned away. He walked to the fire and hunkered down.

* * *

"Have you gone insane? Perhaps we should return to England . . . to Bedlam."

She wasn't returning to England, and she most certainly wasn't going to Bedlam, but Caroline didn't have time to argue *those* points with her brother. " 'Tis the only way, Ned. We can't overpower seven warriors. Raff has a chance to, but not if he's bound."

"And I'm supposed to race into their camp, grab the knife and slit his knots before several savages slit my throat?"

She knew it sounded foolish, and dangerous, but she could think of nothing else. "I told you," Caroline said, hoping she was right. "They will pay you no heed for I shall create a diversion."

"By walking into their midst." He took a deep breath. "I won't let you do that, Caro."

Caroline shifted to peek over the boulder they hid behind. " 'Twill work," she insisted as the plan played itself out in her mind. She was fairly certain the Cherokee didn't know her brother was involved in any of this.

"Let us pretend I do free him," her brother whispered. "What is to stop him from taking off into the woods and leaving us at the mercy of those heathens?"

"He won't."

He turned to face her. "Are you certain of that?"

Caroline raised her chin. "I am willing to bet my life on it."

"And mine, too, Caro."

She knew what she asked of him. Knew how much courage it would take for her brother to do as she bid. He was so young. And she loved him so much. And she was so proud when he sidled closer to her.

"Tell me again what I'm to do."

Caroline gave him a quick hug. "Now don't forget after you cut Raff loose and give him the knife, I want you to disappear into the forest. Then for Fort Prince George."

"I won't leave you here alone, Caro. What kind of brother do you think I am?"

"A devoted one." Caroline reached out to touch his smooth cheek. "I haven't thanked you for coming with me. And what you are going to do now—" She smiled. " 'Tis a very brave thing. But I need you to send help. Try to reach the fort as quickly as you can and tell them what happened."

"And they will send soldiers?"

"Yes." Caroline hoped he believed her lie so he would leave. But she knew there would be no one sent out from the fort to rescue them. If her plan didn't work. If Wolf couldn't defeat the warriors guarding him, they would both die.

What the hell!

Wolf heard the commotion, the excited shrieks and cries, on the other side of the camp. He glanced around to see a glimpse of moon-kissed

410

hair before it was obscured by Tal-tsuska's raised arm. Yanking on his ties did no good. But as his heart sank, Wolf did it anyway, so savagely his hands grew slippery from his own blood. Why was she here? What had possessed her to just walk into the midst of a Cherokee war party?

You. She did it for you. The nagging truth made him strain all the harder.

Then off to the side, another movement caught his eye as someone darted from the tangle of underbrush. "Edward, for God's sake help her!"

Sliding to his knees in the dirt, Edward fumbled for the knife. His hands were so sweaty he had to try twice to pull it out of the ground. He didn't even bother to stand, only crawled into the shadows behind Wolf and started sawing at the leather around his legs.

"Not me." The hooping and hollering near Caroline grew louder, and Wolf had to yell so Edward could hear him. "Help her."

"I am," is all Edward said as he pushed to his feet and sliced through the bloody thongs binding Wolf's wrists. Then he slapped the knife handle against Wolf's palm and disappeared into the darkness.

Twenty

He didn't miss a beat. With a savage roar, Wolf exploded toward the warriors . . . toward Caroline. His eyes and mind were active during his capture. He knew exactly where every weapon in camp was located and by the time he reached the the Indians . . . by the time they even knew he was loose, he'd scooped up a war club that he used to bash one warrior's head. The knife pierced the ribs of another as he turned toward the unexpected threat.

"Get out of here!" Wolf screamed as he swung out again with the club. One more Cherokee fell to the ground, his expression still registering shock.

But the element of surprise was gone. Three of the remaining men faced Wolf, their weapons poised. Only Tal-tsuska stood apart, behind them. And he held Caroline.

Without considering the odds, Wolf hurled himself forward. He slashed with both hands, catching one of the men on the temple with the club, slicing the other across the chest. But his attack was not without penalty. Though he dodged and ducked, the third Indian drew blood as he swung his tomahawk. The blow glanced off Wolf's shoulder, knocking him to his knees.

Dropping his weapons, Wolf lunged for his adversary's legs, yanking him down with enough force that he hit the packed dirt with a thud.

Caroline fought Tal-tsuska's attempts to drag her across the campsite, but he hardly seemed to notice. His one arm bound her to his side; and though she strained to see how Wolf fared, she could not. But she feared it mattered naught. With an awful sense of defeat, Caroline watched Tal-tsuska snatch up his rifle.

She wriggled and squirmed, trying her best to keep him off balance . . . unable to aim his gun.

"Stop it, you foolish woman," Tal-tsuska hissed when she managed to sink her teeth into his arm.

But she did not stop. Instead Caroline fought with all her strength. Fought till he tired of the battle and shoved her to the ground. Pain shot through her, and her eyes closed momentarily as breath escaped her. When they opened, she saw Raff struggling to his knees, his flesh bloodied and she cried for him to watch out.

But it was too late. She pushed up and jerked her head around in time to see Tal-tsuska lift the rifle's stock to his shoulder.

"No!" She saw Tal-tsuska glance down at her, then away. Gunpowder exploded, filling the air with its acrid scent, filling her heart with despair. She couldn't take her eyes off Tal-tsuska, who still stood, his head tilted toward the rifle sight. It wasn't until he crumpled to his knees that she noticed the tomahawk imbedded in his chest. Tal—1tsuska fell face down onto the ground, an outstretched hand catching in her skirts.

Caroline hardly had time to absorb what had happened before strong arms wrapped around her, lifting her to her feet. She turned her face into Wolf's chest, knowing, caring, only that he was alive.

Wolf held her, reveling in the feel of her heart beating against his. She wept softly and clutched him and he wanted them to go on like this forever, forgetting the outside world even existed. Except he knew better.

"Caroline." When she looked up at him, her blue eyes prismed by tears, he gently brushed a tangle of pale hair from her face. "We need to leave this place. Where is your brother?"

"I sent him off to the fort. It seemed the safest at the time, but now . . . Do you think he'll be all right?"

Wolf shrugged. "He knows to follow the river. We will probably overtake him soon."

They quickly gathered what they could use, guns, powder, blankets, and food. By the light of the moon, Wolf led them to the river. One of the two canoes that had pursued him was gone when they reached the shore.

"It looks as if Edward was here. He should be all right."

"Do you think more Cherokee will follow?" Caroline settled the blankets into the canoe, then reached under her overskirt and untied her petticoat tabs. After tearing the linen into strips she dipped some of the fabric into the frigid water.

"They will follow." Wolf took a deep breath. "These deaths will not go unavenged. But, hopefully, you'll be far away by then."

Caroline stepped close to him, so close she could smell his musky scent, the blood she gently wiped away. "What of you?"

Tucking his chin, Wolf watched her hands as she cleaned the wounds on his shoulder and arm. Delicate hands . . . strong hands. Hands whose touch could send him spiraling with desire. His eyelids lowered. "I belong on the frontier."

Then that is where she belonged, Caroline decided. But she said nothing else as she tied off the bandages she'd wrapped around his wounded flesh. He pulled on his shirt, slung a rifle over his other shoulder and helped her into the canoe.

Moonlight shimmered on the water, made the bubbling foam appear iridescent. But still navigating in the dark, especially at a fast pace, was difficult. By dawn, a biting wind swooped down from the mountains, bringing with it a smattering of snowflakes. But they pressed on.

Except for an occasional called remark, Caroline and Wolf did not talk. She paddled, trying to give him a rest, but the current was strong, and soon he was at it again.

The countryside changed, flattened, and Caroline knew they neared the fort. The winter night descended, Wolf maneuvered the canoe toward shore, and Caroline sighed with relief. She was more tired than she ever remembered being.

"There is a cabin over that rise," he said as he pulled the canoe onto the shore. "I imagine the Morgans are either at the fort or gone back to Charles Town, but it is a place to rest for a bit."

Wolf was right about the cabin. It didn't look as if anyone had lived there for a while. The front door hung from one leather hinge, and the room was full of leaves and debris. Caroline used a pine branch to sweep it out as best she could while Wolf fixed the door. He didn't gather wood, for though it grew colder by the hour, Wolf didn't think they should chance smoke from their fire being spotted. So they sat across from each other on a blanket and shivered while they ate the remaining food-stuffs they brought from the Cherokee camp.

"We should make Fort Prince George by midmorning."

Caroline lifted her lashes, but she didn't quite meet his gaze. "I'm glad."

"I realize this has been very hard on you." Wolf hesitated, wanting to bring up the subject of her baby . . . not knowing how to do it. She was look-

ing at her folded hands again, acting shy and with-
drawn; and after all they'd been through together,
he didn't know why she should. Except for the way
he'd acted when he discovered she was with child.

"Are you cold?" A stupid question considering
the circumstances. Of course she was cold, but she
only pulled her blanket higher about her shoulders
and smiled at him fleetingly.

"How about you? Are your wounds hurting?"

That and every other place on his body, but Wolf
shook his head no and took another bite of dried
venison. After he chewed and swallowed, Wolf took
a deep breath. "Caroline." She looked up then,
and her beauty nearly made him forget what he
was going to say. Even here in this rough, deserted
cabin on the frontier, after the hardships she'd endured, she still reminded him of a perfect cameo.

Her features delicate in her oval face, her hair
pale and flowing about her shoulders. Her eyes
large enough for a man to lose himself in their
depths. He leaned forward. "I do not care who
fathered your child."

Her lips thinned, and she suddenly found the
woven end of her blanket worth careful scrutiny.
"I see." What had been in her mind to think that
he cared for her?

"No. No, you do not." Wolf reached out and
grabbed her hands, tugging when she resisted. "I
mean it makes no difference in the way I feel about
you." Now it was Wolf who couldn't meet her gaze.
"I have no right to ask for your forgiveness. I have

417

been a bastard to you from the beginning." He paused, a ghost of a smile curving his sensual lips.

"It is funny. I thought the worst thing was being a bastard. Now I know it is much worse to act like one." His hands tightened around hers, and he searched her face. "I am sorry for the hurt I have caused you, and I would not blame you if—"

"It's yours." Caroline wet her suddenly dry lips. "You are the father of my child."

"Caroline, I—"

"No, listen." She pushed up on her knees. "You may say it matters naught, but it does to me. Anger and pride kept me from telling you." Her complexion darkened. "I never even . . . I mean your father didn't—" She squared her shoulders and faced him. "You are the only man I've been with," she finally said, almost daring him to contradict her.

At first he said nothing, only sat there, his eyes dark, his expression unreadable. Then he pushed to his knees, reaching out for her shoulders. "I am glad," he said before pulling her against him.

The wind still whistled through the pines and bare-branched oaks, the chill still seeped through the unchinked logs that formed the cabin. But Caroline and Wolf were no longer cold.

Their arms wrapped about each other, their hearts pounding as one, they settled down on the blanket. Wolf leaned on his free hand spreading her hair about her face. "Like moonlight," he said, and they both smiled.

But Caroline's faded as he traced the winged arch of her brow with his fingertip. "They will come after you, won't they?"

He stilled for only a moment before resuming his caress. "Let us not talk of this tonight." His lips brushed hers, then returned to press hungrily against hers. When he lifted his head, she was breathing heavily, but it didn't stop her from questioning him further.

"You've told me the ways of the Cherokee. They avenge their slain warriors." Her voice lowered. "And it was because of me that you killed them. That you were forced to choose between the Cherokee and me."

"No." He kissed her lightly again. "No, *Nakwisi' usidi'*, Little Star. It was no one's fault. Not yours, not mine. Not even Tal-tsuska's. And I'm not concerned that I will be sought for revenge. Believe me, Caroline." And he spoke the truth. For Wolf feared in his heart that war would come and bring so much death there would be no time for revenge.

But tonight he would force such thoughts from his mind and think only of the woman he loved. The woman he must give up.

She sighed when his mouth traced a path across her delicate jaw. Her neck was as soft as a butterfly's wing and tasted of the nectar they drank. He could not get enough of her.

Caroline moaned and arched toward his hand as he covered her breast. "Please," she cried as she dug her fingers into the blanket beneath her.

In answer to her plea Wolf lowered his mouth to the top of her breast while his hand fumbled with the boned bodice.

"I shall do it," she said, pushing up and unlacing the front of her gown. The light was dim, only what moonlight sifted through the chinks between the logs, but Caroline felt his eyes on her as she shrugged out of the bodice. She took a deep breath and untied the drawstring of her shift. Slowly the neckline yawned open, catching momentarily on the distended tips of her breasts before slipping to her waist.

She sat thus, naked from collarbone to hips, waiting for his reaction, letting her head fall back when his hand cupped one of her breasts.

"You are larger now," he said, bending down to nuzzle one full globe. "Readying yourself to nurse my son."

"Or daughter," she teased as he took her nipple deep into his mouth, mimicking the future movements of his unborn child.

He left her ruched flesh glistening wet as he lifted his head. "Or daughter," he agreed before sucking gently on her other breast.

Caroline tried to support herself, but all her bones felt as soft as hot tallow. He followed her down, feasting on her body, driving all thoughts but him from her mind.

Her fingers trembled as they wove through the thick black mane of hair. The locks were longer, as if he hadn't taken the time to trim them. As if he hadn't *had* the time to trim them. The why was obvious and painful, and she forced herself not to think of it, not to think of the horrors they'd faced . . . the horrors yet to come.

She pulled him closer, arching up to meet his hungry mouth. When he lifted his dark head to look at her, passion flared his nostrils and tightened the bronzed skin across his cheekbones. But another emotion vied with desire, and not long after he rested his forehead lightly on hers, Caroline knew what it was.

"I am sorry," he whispered, his breath hot across her face. "I am so sorry."

"Raff . . . Wolf." Her hands inched forward to cup the sides of his head. It took only light pressure for him to rise up so that their gazes met. In the grainy half-light his eyes shone dark as onyx, deep as a bottomless well, and her heart swelled with love for him. "I forgave you long ago. If not, I wouldn't be with you like this now . . . I wouldn't love you so much."

Her admission brought his lips to hers in a kiss of such intensity that it didn't occur to her until much later that he hadn't responded in kind. But for now Caroline could only luxuriate in his mouth pressed to hers, the long sleek feel of his tongue as it invaded her mouth again and again, and the magic of his hands.

He untied the tabs of her overskirt, then her one remaining petticoat and pulled them off her body. The shift and stockings followed and then she was beautiful and naked. Her skin pale in the dim light, her stomach mounded by her child . . . his child.

Wolf touched her, his fingers fanning out reverently, cradling the baby he would never hold . . . would never claim. A pain so real he almost cried out tightened about his heart, but he ruthlessly shoved it aside. For tonight she was his. They both were. For tonight.

He tore himself away only long enough to rid himself of his clothes, then Wolf was back beside her, loving her, showing her, even if he couldn't say the words, how he cherished her . . . loved her.

Tonight was theirs and he took his time, bringing her to climax again and again, with his hands, with his mouth, glorying in her pleasure and the sensual way she called him his Cherokee name.

His own body screamed for release, longed to be buried deep inside her, but he forced himself to resist until she touched him.

"Oh, Wolf." He straddled her then, careful of his weight and thrust deep into her womanly sheath. When she arched up to meet him, his hands clasped beneath her hips, and his seed exploded into her.

Wolf rolled to her side, gathering her close and pulling the blanket around them, cocooning them in the warmth of their love.

"Wolf."

"Hmmm?" He rested his hand on the curve of her stomach.

"What does that mean, what you said just now?"

His fingers stopped tracing the gentle slope of her body. "Beloved," he said, realizing that's what he had called her in the throes of passion. Beloved. He shut his eyes and wondered if he should tell her how very much he did love her. But then the vision of her leaving, sailing away from him for good, came to him and he faltered. It was better if they didn't speak of such things.

He thought her asleep, her breathing was so even, her supple body was so relaxed, until she spoke again. "What should we name our child?"

Wolf swallowed. He should tell her neither of them should consider the child his. And he would . . . tomorrow. For now he simply shook his head, rolling over to face her. "It depends upon whether it is a boy or girl, I should think."

"Mmmm." Caroline yawned. "I thought we might name her after your mother if the babe is a girl."

"Alkini? That is rather difficult for the English to pronounce."

"Is it?" Caroline cuddled up to his side. "But I want our child to be raised Cherokee, too." She propped onto her elbow. "I mean I know there is fighting now, but it will end someday, won't it?"

"Yes, *Nakwisi'usidi*, someday." Cupping her cheek, Wolf brought her head back to rest on his shoulder. "But for now, let us sleep."

Except that he could not.

All through the night as she snuggled in his arms, Wolf thought of the future. Of his woman and child living across the wide ocean. Of them safe. She would have money from Robert's estate. By dawn he had convinced himself it was for the best.

"Thank God, you were able to get through." Lieutenant Coytmore pushed away from the desk and advanced on Wolf and Caroline. "And both safe, I see." He grabbed Caroline's hands. "Your brother has been relentless in his demands that I send a patrol out to find you. I tried to explain—'

"Where is Edward?" Caroline asked.

"I don't know for certain. Perhaps Mistress Quinn's cabin. I could send someone to fetch him for you."

"That won't be necessary. I'll find him." Her eyes met Wolf's, and he nodded, then walked her to the door.

"See that you don't leave the fort," he said before she left the room.

When she was gone, the lieutenant sank into the closest chair, all presence of congeniality gone. And apparently most remnants of his good sense with it. "The blasted Cherokee have gone mad. Word's come through that about thirty of them attacked Elliott's trading house," he said referring to a trader's compound up river. "They killed nearly everyone, then set about looting and drinking rum." He rubbed both hands down his face, then looked up, seemingly unaware of Wolf's hard expression.

424

"Seroweh led the warriors, and he's supposedly sent runners with bloody tomahawks through the nations proclaiming war. Supposedly the pass between here and Fort Loudoun is filled with blood-crazed heathens, and I feel more a prisoner here than a soldier."

"And what of your Cherokee prisoners?"

The lieutenant let out a loud sigh. "Those savages are more a ball and chain about my neck than prisoners. Not a day goes by that I'm not petitioned by one or another of them for their release." His head fell back against the chairback, knocking his powdered wig askew. "They are such a bother."

"I imagine they find their captivity troublesome as well."

"What?" The lieutenant looked up, then dismissed Wolf's remark with a wave of his hand. "I want to know what you saw out there. Not one of my scouts is worth a damn. Wait a moment. Where in the hell are you going?"

Wolf paused, his hand on the latch. "I'm taking Mrs. MacQuaid and her brother to Charles Town."

"But . . . but what about the Cherokee?"

Wolf's brow arched. "You seem to forget, I *am* Cherokee." He left on silent, moccasined feet.

Caroline met him at the door to Mistress Quinn's cabin. But before he could tell her that they needed to leave immediately—a statement that was bound to shock since he hadn't mentioned the trip to Charles Town to her at all—she surprised him Grabbing his arms, she pulled him out the door and around the side of the log cabin.

"Caroline, we don't have time for this." Wolf expected her to throw herself into his arms, but she didn't. Her expression was grave.

"Logan is here."

"Logan?"

"Yes. But he's asleep right now," she said holding onto his arm when he would have rushed back inside. "Edward brought him over. It appears your brother arrived at the fort last night, on his way to Seven Pines. He'd gotten word Mary was to have a baby."

"I wrote him." Wolf felt as if someone had kicked him in the stomach. "Does he know . . what happened?"

Tears filled Caroline's eyes as she slowly nodded her head. "Edward told him." She reached for Wolf's hand. "He was trying to solicit volunteers to go after us, and he didn't know Logan was Mary's husband."

Taking a deep breath, Wolf tilted his head up toward the heavens, then back down to Caroline "I will talk to him."

"He's very . . ." Caroline paused searching for a word strong enough to describe the emotion she saw in Logan. Rage didn't come close to describing to Wolf his brother's reaction to the news of his wife and child's death. But she settled on the word

"Angry." She hurried on. "And he blames the Cherokee." Did he blame his mixed-blood brother, too? Caroline didn't know, but she felt she must warn Wolf of the possibility.

He only nodded. "I will talk to him," he repeated.

"He's drunk. He had a jug of something with him, and he drank almost all of it before he . . . fell asleep."

"Passed out, more likely." Wolf started toward the door, turning before he reached it. "You should try to get some rest. We are leaving in the morning."

"Leaving?" Caroline rushed toward him as he lifted the door latch. "Where are we going?"

"To Charles Town."

"But—"

Taking her shoulders, Wolf turned her into the cabin. He wanted to pull her back into his arms, and knew he shouldn't. Still, he couldn't stop his hands from lingering, from gathering warmth from just touching her.

"Please, Caroline," he whispered into her silken hair. "Just do as I ask."

Logan was flopped facedown, his feet and legs hanging over the edge of the rope-spring bedstead in the back room. Wolf wondered how Caroline managed to get him that far when he got a whiff of the rum odor permeating the room.

"Logan." Wolf laid a hand on his arm. "Logan, wake up, it's Wolf."

"Get the hell away from me," came the drink-deepened voice. "Just get the hell away from me."

"I need to talk to you."

The jug handle slipped from Logan's finger and crashed to the floor. Rum poured out, seeping into the packed earth. Slowly Logan twisted around, raising himself on his elbows. His green eyes were bloodshot, but fierce in their stare. "Well, I sure as hell don't want to talk to you." His mouth twisted with hatred. "Damn Indian lover. Hell, you're not just an Indian lover, you're one of those murdering savages."

Wolf said nothing, just continued to hold his brother's gaze.

"Well, what the hell you looking at?" His words were slurred. "Haven't you ever seen someone in mourning before?" He pushed to his feet, standing eye to eye with Wolf. "Your heathen people killed my wife and baby! Killed them, damn you." His voice trailed off as tears filled his eyes and spilled over his dark lashes. Like a man unable to support himself any longer, he collapsed back onto the bed, his head falling into his hands.

"Got me crying like a damn baby." He scrubbed at his face with the back of his hands.

"Logan, I know how you feel. Mary was—"

"Shit, you don't know anything." Logan was back on his feet again. "She loved me. The woman who lives here told me that. Hell, they were some of her last words. Mary loved Logan." He glanced toward the cracked jug with an expression of longing. "She loved me, and I left her to die."

"For God's sake, Logan, this was not your fault."

"Wasn't it?" Logan stumbled a step closer. "We both know why I left. I couldn't stomach the old man. But did I stay around and try to right the wrongs he did?" He leaned toward Wolf. "Well, did I? Did I do what you did?" He stuck his index finger at Wolf's chest.

"Hell no. I ran off to fight the Indians, and I left my pregnant wife to be slaughtered." He sank back on the bed. "She loved me, and I didn't love her." His head shot up. "Does that shock you, little brother? Everybody loved Mary. You even did, if you're honest with yourself. Everybody but her goddamn no good husband, who couldn't even save her from being hacked up by a band of savages." He reached for the jug, shaking it so that more rum sprayed from the crack, but smiling when he heard the swish of liquid. With a satisfied nod he brought it to his lips.

"I think you've had enough of that." Wolf's hand stilled the jug's upward tilt. "I want you to come to Charles Town with me."

Logan shrugged the support away. "On the contrary, brother. I haven't had nearly enough." He took a deep swallow. "But when I have, I'll let you know." He took another swig, backhanding the rum from his lips and glaring at Wolf from his sad, red-rimmed eyes. "And I'm not going running off with my tail tucked between my legs to Charles

Town. I'm going looking for Cherokee. Then I'm going to do to them what they did to Mary and the baby." His chiseled features grew hard. "Maybe if I kill enough of them, I'll be able to live with myself."

"More likely you will get yourself killed." Wolf grabbed Logan's arm, hauling him up to his feet. "You are feeling sorry for yourself but—"

"You're damned right I am." Swinging out, his actions slowed by drink, Logan missed landing a punch on Wolf's nose by a good foot. He did accomplish breaking free of his brother, and he used the opportunity to rush toward the door.

"Just leave me the hell alone," he yelled over his shoulder before bursting through to the other room.

Caroline looked up from her sewing, her eyes wide, when Wolf's brother exploded through the door. He staggered, grabbing hold of the door-jamb to steady himself before lurching toward her. Then he swerved and reached for the door latch, pulling it open, allowing a gust of frosty air to blow into the cabin, before he stumbled out into the darkness.

Wolf followed in his path, closing the door and turning to face Caroline. "You heard?"

"How could I not?" Setting her needle aside, Caroline stood and moved toward Wolf. "What are you going to do?"

His expression was unreadable. "I'm going to

try and get you and your brother to Charles Town before war parties block the trail east."

"But . . . but what of your brother?"

His eyes met hers then, and Caroline realized Wolf's were nearly as sad as his brother's. "There is nothing I can do, except hope and pray I don't end up like him."

Twenty-one

The citizens of Charles Town reveled in their ignorance. Confident that Governor Lyttleton had solved the Cherokee problem, they steadfastly ignored any word to the contrary. Caroline, Wolf, and Edward arrived in the capital city in mid-February, after a journey that left Caroline exhausted. They had traveled hard, finding evidence of Cherokee raids at Ninety-Six, but no farther east.

"He won't even listen," Wolf told Caroline as he settled into the chair beside Edward. They were in the room at the inn that Wolf and her brother shared.

Caroline stayed down the hall, by herself. But she was visiting Ned when Wolf returned from his audience with the governor. Actually, she purposely stayed here so she could hear what had occurred. Since leaving Fort Prince George, she couldn't count on Wolf coming to tell her himself. He treated her like the widowed wife of his father, not the lover she was. The change left her bewildered. And determined to find out the reason.

"Did you tell him of the attack at Seven Pines?" Caroline sank down on the stool by Wolf's feet. When he glanced her way, she thought there was a spark in his dark eyes, a spark of the passion they'd shared. But it was quickly extinguished as he turned toward Edward.

"He called that an isolated incident."

"What of Ninety-Six?" Caroline was determined that he look at her.

"Lyttleton refuses to believe the Cherokee will do anything substantial. He talks as if they are children too frightened of the king to go to war." Wolf leaned back and took a deep breath. He was not eager to relate this next information. He'd enlisted Edward's reluctant cooperation. But in truth he didn't think that would make things much easier.

Wolf focused on the flames dancing in the grate. "I was able to book passage for you both. Your ship leaves—

"You did what?" Caroline stood, knocking the stool to the side and faced Wolf, hands on hips.

He kept his voice firm. "Arranged for you to return to England."

"For me to—" Caroline was incensed. She'd come with him to Charles Town because Wolf had convinced her it was too dangerous on the frontier. But she'd never agreed to leave South Carolina, nor had he so much as mentioned it. "I don't wish to return to England," she said as simply as she could.

"Now Caro it might be for the best. Raff assures me that with the money from your husband's estate, you will be well provided for."

Caroline turned on her brother. "You two plotted this up together, didn't you?"

"Caro—"

"Answer me, damnit!" Pale curls swung over her shoulder as she turned herself to face Wolf squarely.

He didn't flinch at her tone. "Do not blame your brother. It was my decision. Made with your well being in mind."

"My well being." Caroline's snort was unladylike. "If you were so concerned about *my* well being, why wasn't I consulted?" Caroline grabbed her brother's arm. With more strength than she knew she had, she propelled him toward the door. "Please leave! Wolf and I have some things to discuss . . . about our child."

Edward looked toward Raff and shrugged as Caroline opened the door. She slammed it, twisted the brass key and dropped it in her pocket.

"That wasn't a good idea."

Caroline turned slowly, trying to control her anger. "If you mean telling him about the baby, he's known for some time. If you mean forcing him from the room, I think it high time we have a talk." Head held erect and knees shaking, she walked across the room and sat on the edge of the winged chair facing his. He watched her step over his long legging-clad legs, but he didn't pull them back.

When she could stand the silence no longer, Caroline cleared her throat. "When did you decide to send me back to England? And don't tell me 'twas a recent arrangement because I won't believe you."

Wolf took a slow breath. "I have thought it best since you arrived in the New World."

"So that's when you came to the conclusion that some day you would buy me passage to England?"

"You were not my responsibility then."

"But I am now?"

"Caroline, you don't understand."

"Then explain it to me." She leaned forward. "I thought—I thought we—" Caroline tried to summon back her anger but it was fast giving way to tears.

"That we what? Would marry, raise our child?" I can see from your expression that you did." Wolf let air out through his mouth. "Do you not understand that it would never work? That you are better off returning to England where you belong."

"And who made this decision that I belong there?"

"It is obvious."

"Not to me." Caroline stood and paced to the window, lifting the linen curtain and looking out over the harbor. "I thought I adapted to the frontier fairly well."

"You did, but for God's sake there is a war."

"And you're Cherokee." She turned back, her gaze locking with his.

"Yes, and I am Cherokee." After a moment, Wolf stood as well, but he knew better than to go near her. He'd held himself apart from her for a fortnight. It had been difficult, nearly impossible at times, but he'd done it because he knew it was what he had to do. "You are a widow, a beautiful widow. I have spoken with my father's factor, and his estate is yours. You will not want for money. If you return to England, I am sure your life will—"

"I'll marry again, is that what you mean? Some respected Englishman? Is that what *you* want, Wolf?"

"It would be best for *you*."

"I asked if 'twas what you wanted."

Time was measured by heartbeats as they each stood, their eyes locked. Wolf moved first, violently turning toward the mantle and pounding it with his fist. "It does not matter what I want."

Caroline let out her breath. Then, as calmly as she could, she walked toward him. "Answer me one question, truthfully if you would please. Do you love me?"

His head shot around, and he skewered her with his dark stare, but said nothing.

Caroline advanced a step closer. "When I came to the New World, I was afraid of nearly everything. You helped show me the strength and courage that lay within me. But now Wa'ya MacQuaid,

I believe 'tis you who are afraid . . . afraid to say three little words."

Caroline watched his jaw clench and dared to move a little closer. And waited.

"My feelings for you should be apparent, but they are not the issue."

When Caroline took another step, her body grazed his. She felt him stiffen and smiled to herself. "Say it Wolf."

"Caroline . . ."

"Say it."

His chest expanded, brushing against her breasts. He closed his eyes, the long dark lashes fanning against his skin. When he opened them, his hand reached out to caress her cheek. "I do love you."

Her smile was slow and sweet. "Was that so difficult?" His arms folded around her, and Caroline leaned into his hard body.

"What would be difficult," his arms tightened, "probably more difficult than I could bear is if something happened to you. If I took you back to the frontier and . . ."

"And the same fate befell me as did Mary?" she finished for him. Caroline felt his shattered breath and wove her arms about his narrow waist.

" 'Tis sad Wolf. But sadder still is the life they led. Mary loving her husband, knowing he didn't love her. Your brother guilt-ridden because he couldn't return her love."

Wolf lifted her chin with his thumb. "I will not take you back to Seven Pines."

"And I'd be foolish to go, wouldn't I? At least right now."

"But I must go back."

"I know that." Some of the joy drained from Caroline, but she took a deep breath and smiled, listening to his next words. He wouldn't be the man he was, the man she loved and do any differently.

"My people cannot win this war." Wolf shook his head, his expression pained. "I cannot fight for either side. I can only try to help bring peace."

Standing on tiptoe, Caroline pressed a kiss to his mouth. Their bodies molded, cradling their child between them. "Then know this Wolf," Caroline said against his lips. "I shall wait here for you . . . your son and I shall wait for the time when we can be together forever."

Epilogue

May, 1762
The South Carolina Frontier

"It has been a long time."

Taking a deep breath of pine-scented air, Caroline tore her gaze from the sweep of greening valley below and focused on her husband. They had stopped where the river forked above Seven Pines to rest the horses. "I often wondered if we'd ever return."

Wolf's arm draped about her shoulders, and he pulled her close. "I always hoped we could." He smiled down at her. "But more than that, I longed for the day when we could live as one." He rested his hand atop the curve of her stomach where another of their children grew, and he bent his lips to hers.

But a tug on his leggings interrupted the kiss, and laughing, Wolf scooped up his precocious son. "Do you see down there, Kalanu?"

Two-year-old Kalanu MacQuaid blinked up at his father with large, dark eyes and nodded.

"We shall build a house for your mother and the new baby there. And a barn for the animals."

"Domino?" Kalanu pointed a chubby finger toward the black and white dog whose front paws dug frantically in the rich earth. The spaniel had been a gift from Edward when he returned to South Carolina from England. Edward had finished his schooling only to decide he wished to live in the colonies.

"Yes, Domino can live in the barn." Wolf slanted a look toward Caroline. "Though perhaps your mother will allow her to sleep in the house."

Caroline just shook her head and laughed. It was no secret she might fuss at the energetic puppy, but she cuddled Domino into her bed when Wolf was away.

And he'd been away a lot over the last few years. As Wolf predicted, relations between the English and Cherokee deteriorated into all-out war. Hundreds on both sides were killed before a treaty was signed last September.

The Cherokee suffered terribly. Most of the Lower Towns and many of the Middle Towns were destroyed. Many of the Indians who weren't killed outright died of hunger and disease.

And Wolf had worked tirelessly to help bring understanding to both sides. Unfortunately, it wasn't until the Cherokee nation was on the brink of starvation that the war finally ended.

440

Caroline had feared the destruction and killing would make Wolf a bitter man. But it hadn't, and he credited Caroline's love and understanding with keeping him sane during those trying times. When they were apart, just the memory of her passionate kiss, the gentle way she cared for their son, healed his heart.

Last autumn was not the first time Wolf managed to visit Charles Town during the years of bloodshed—he rode for days to see her whenever he had the chance. But when he accompanied Attakullakulla, The Little Carpenter, to the colony's capital, it was finally the visit he and Caroline had longed for.

For it heralded the end of the war that kept them apart.

Now they were on their way home. To Seven Pines, to start anew. Lyttleton's replacement, Governor Bull had appointed Wolf a Commissioner of Indian Affairs for the Cherokee. He planned to take the position seriously, and in Caroline he knew there could be no better helpmate, lover, wife . . . no better woman for him.

Wolf lifted Caroline carefully onto the saddle. she still wasn't too fond of horses, though she wouldn't admit it to anyone . . . not even her husband. But he knew anyway and always found a gentle mount for her. "Are you all right to continue?" he asked as she settled into the leather.

"Yes, baby and I are fine."

Wolf patted her knee and mounted, then

reached down for Kalanu. He settled his son in front of him, took up the reins of the packhorses and glanced over at Caroline.

The afternoon sun caught the gold of her hair, and he marveled again that such a beautiful, delicate creature could be so strong. "Are you ready?" he asked, cocking his brow.

"Oh, yes."

Kalanu squealed, Domino barked, and Wolf and Caroline started down into the valley and their life together.

To My Readers

I hope you enjoyed *My Savage Heart*. The story of Wolf MacQuaid and Lady Caroline Simmons has haunted me for years, and I was thrilled to give their love a "happy ending." In telling this tale, I tried to stay as historically accurate as possible and to show both sides of the conflict between the English and Cherokee. But, as always, the characters and their love are the main thrust of my books.

My Savage Heart is the first of my trilogy about the heroic MacQuaid brothers. In my next book, *My Seaswept Heart,* due out from Zebra this November, we meet James MacQuaid. Yes, I know, you thought Robert's oldest son was dead—hanged after he fought with Prince Charles, The Young Pretender, in his unsuccessful attempt to capture the English crown. But the devilishly handsome Jamie escaped the noose in Scotland. Now he's a swashbuckling pirate, the scourge of the Caribbean. And he *thinks* he's given up on lost causes.

In 1995, look for Logan MacQuaid's story. I just

couldn't deny such a tortured man the redemption of a good woman's love.

For those of you who enjoy reading about brides and weddings, and who doesn't, look for my novella, "A Proper Victorian Wedding," in the June 1994, Zebra Historical Romance June Bride Collection, *A Bride's Desire*.

Thanks to all of you who helped make my Charleston Series, Blackstone Men of the Sea, so successful. I loved writing *Sea Fires*, *Sea of Desire*, and *Sea of Temptation*. A special thanks to you readers who wrote to let me know how much you enjoyed these and my other books. You'll never know how much your letters mean to me.

For a bookmark and newsletter write to me care of:

> Zebra Books
> 475 Park Avenue South
> New York, NY 10016
>
> SASE appreciated
>
> To Happy Endings,
> Christine Dorsey

WHAT'S LOVE GOT TO DO WITH IT?

Everything . . . Just ask Kathleen Drymon . . . and Zebra Books

CASTAWAY ANGEL	*(3569-1, $4.50/$5.50)*
GENTLE SAVAGE	*(3888-7, $4.50/$5.50)*
MIDNIGHT BRIDE	*(3265-X, $4.50/$5.50)*
VELVET SAVAGE	*(3886-0, $4.50/$5.50)*
TEXAS BLOSSOM	*(3887-9, $4.50/$5.50)*
WARRIOR OF THE SUN	*(3924-7, $4.99/$5.99)*